STOLEN THINGS

STOLEN THINGS

A Novel

R. H. HERRON

RANDOM HOUSE
LARGE PRINT

Copyright © 2019 by Rachael Herron

Published in the United States of America by Random House Large Print in association with DUTTON, an imprint of Penguin Random House LLC, New York.

Cover design by Alex Merto
Cover photograph by Gabriela Herman / Getty Images

The Library of Congress has established a Cataloging-in-Publication record for this title.

ISBN: 978-0-593-10439-2

www.penguinrandomhouse.com/large-print-format-books

FIRST LARGE PRINT EDITION

Printed in the United States of America

10   9   8   7   6   5   4   3   2   1

This Large Print edition published in accord with the standards of the N.A.V.H.

For Sophie Littlefield and Juliet Blackwell, my constant partners in crime and, now, in crime fiction. I could do this job without you, but I wouldn't want to.

STOLEN THINGS

ONE

NO ONE EVER called 911 because they were having a great day.

Well, sometimes Jocko Smith did, but he was a local drunk who didn't get along with his therapist, and 911 was free. When Laurie was on the beat, she used to arrest him so regularly for being drunk and disorderly that she still knew his birthday by heart. Once, years after she'd moved off the street and into dispatch, she'd seen him in Berkeley. She'd been taking nine-year-old Jojo to get her ears pierced for the first time, but Laurie's car had swerved automatically—violently—when she saw Jocko stumbling in front of the library. Within the time it took her heart to beat twice, she had wrested the wheel back rather than launching herself out of her vehicle and going after him.

What's wrong, Mama?
Nothing. I just forgot I wasn't a cop anymore.
Jojo was sixteen now, with multiple piercings, and she was angling for a tattoo.

The emergency line shrilled. Laurie's finger was fastest, beating Dina by a split second. Dina glared at her, and Laurie grinned.

"911, what's the address of the emergency?"

"My daughter." The man's words were a garbled gasp. "She's gone."

Dead or lost, it didn't matter till Laurie knew where **he** was. "Confirm your address?" He was calling from a landline, so Laurie had it on the automated number screen, but by law she had to get it verbally, too.

"I'm at 72 Dorset. **I can't find her.**"

Laurie tapped the keyboard. "How old is she?"

"Two."

Shit. This wasn't a teenager, then. Laurie's ear got different—she could almost feel herself leaning into the sounds coming over the line. "When did you last see her?"

"God, I don't know." A muffled noise. "God."

Was he drunk? He wasn't slurring, but he sounded out of it. On something, maybe? Teenagers went missing all day every day, in every town. That kind of call would hold for hours until they found someone who could take the report. But a two-year-old? Sylvia had already put it out on the air, and Laurie could see on the screen that two officers and the shift sergeant were on the way.

"What's her name?"

"Della. Della Sanchez. She's two. Did I say that?"

"What color clothing was she wearing?"

"God. I don't know—I just woke up. I'm so confused."

Laurie's breathing slowed. She had to ask the right questions and listen harder to the answers. "Okay." It was almost nine at night in early summer, not a normal time to wake up from sleep. "You've checked the house?"

"Everywhere," he choked. "Under her bed, and in the kitchen where she hides in the soda cupboard, and even outside. Then I ran back inside. . . . Wait. My wife . . ."

"Where's your wife?"

"My ex-wife. We're divorced."

Could be a custody problem, then. "Does she have keys to your place?"

"Hang on. I have to think. I work nights now—and I went to sleep, and before that Della was with me, and we had mac 'n' cheese, and then . . ."

"Could she be with your ex-wife?"

As if she'd given him the answer to an impossible test, he yelled, "She's with my ex-wife! That's it! Oh, fuck, she came over and got Della right before I fell asleep. I'm so sorry. Oh, my God. I'm so embarrassed. I just woke up, and I was so confused—it's a new job, and I'm not used to working nights." He sounded as if he might cry. His relief was palpable, and Laurie had no doubt he was telling the truth. She typed in the info, then ran her finger along her throat as Sylvia caught her eye.

Sylvia cut the units to code two, canceling the second unit and the sergeant. Bragg would continue without lights or siren and make contact. He'd call the mother and make sure it was all legit. And it was—Laurie would lay a paycheck on it. "Okay, sir, I'll have my officer contact you just to make sure you're all right."

"You don't have to—"

"Have a good night, sir."

"Oh, shit, thank you!"

It was nice. She almost never got thanked, for anything. "You're wel—" But the caller had already hung up.

"Coffee. I need coffee." Laurie stood and went into the break room. Back in the day, the coffee scent of the room had been as bitter as the dispatchers waiting to retire. Nowadays only the people remained that way; the coffee was Keurig. Laurie punched the button and waited for it to spit at her. She made a second cup and added vanilla creamer to it—Dina always had a hard time getting the Keurig machine to work for her. She carried both coffees back into dispatch and slid one across Dina's desk. Dina, who was talking to a citizen about why he couldn't get a fireworks permit, smiled at her gratefully.

Laurie sat at her station and plugged in. "I still don't like these K-cups," she announced to the room at large, as if for the first time.

Sylvia flipped through something on her cell phone and said nothing. Only Bettina rose to conversation.

"They're handy, though." It was what Bettina always said.

"The coffee tastes like plastic."

"So does 7-Eleven coffee, and you bring that in all the time."

At home Laurie drank her coffee black, but that was because Omid bought the good stuff, the locally-roasted-in-small-batches kind. He was a coffee snob, and now that he was chief and had an office big enough for a personal espresso machine, it had only gotten worse. He'd been talking about getting a home roaster lately. Laurie glanced at the dispatch screen—he still showed as being in the station. He was probably in his office, as usual, doing the paperwork he was too busy with meetings to do during regular hours. Where he **should** be was home, waiting for Jojo, since Laurie was stuck on shift.

Whatever. They could argue about it later. "I hope we get a good pursuit tonight." She said it at least once a shift. It was part of her routine.

"You're sick." Bettina shook her head. "If I get one, you can have it."

"Promise?"

"Especially if it's a foot bail." Bettina hated the stress that came with officers pursuing suspects over fences and through back alleys, the radio exchanges garbled, the primary officer panting too hard to be understood.

"First Friday night of summer. It's going to be busy." Laurie took the first plasticky sip.

Her seat was next to the only window. She set the terrible coffee down and stood, opening the slats of the blinds. Her headset was on, she was plugged in and logged on, but the phones were quiet. So far. Being a dispatcher was two parts boredom to one part adrenaline.

Dina, done with the fireworks caller, groaned and covered her eyes. She was the whiner of tonight's shift, and it was best just to ignore her.

Laurie touched the glass. "The sky is pink out there." The dispatch center was sunk into a half basement, and the window looked into the parking lot where the extra patrol cars sat. It was an excellent view if you liked looking at gravel and car tires and cigarette butts (Jimmy's litter—no one else at the department smoked anymore).

And the sky. If Laurie craned her neck— and she always did—she could look up into the San Bernal sky as twilight settled on the city. Tonight the sunset was a muddy streak of rose with a backwash of pale lavender. It was colder than it should be for June. A wisp of fog crept over the top of the library.

Dina gave another small groan. "Are you going to shut the blinds?"

"Come on. It's almost dark." The spotlight Dina was shining on her crossword puzzle was ten times as bright as the tired sun filtering in through the window.

"It's a different light. It hurts my head."

Laurie shut the blinds. "Better?"

Dina nodded, wincing, taking a sip of her coffee.

The cubicle walls that separated the stations were only four feet high, and they could talk over them without standing, but Sylvia stood anyway. "If you two are done, it's time for **Jeopardy!**" She raised the remote.

The phones stayed quiet enough that they got through the first six minutes of the show without pausing it once. Other shifts watched different shows, but the touchstone for Laurie's team was **Jeopardy!**, every night. They watched DVR'd episodes from their days off. Any of them could have cheated and watched at home, bringing all the answers in, but none of the four of them would have done that. Bettina was selfish, Dina was needy, Sylvia was depressed, and Laurie herself was a control freak, but they came together over the half-hour show that, on a busy twelve-hour shift, could last them all night, watched in fifteen-second bursts when all of them were off the phones and the radios weren't squawking.

Alex Trebek asked one of the players about her pet rat. The player answered in a cloying voice.

Dina harrumphed.

Laurie said, "Jojo wanted a pet rat when she was seven."

Her co-workers already knew that. Sitting in a room for so long with the same people, a person ran out of tales. Responding to the same stories over and over was part of the job, too. So boring. So rote. So life.

"Gross," said Dina, predictably.

Sylvia blew a disgusted puff of air out of her mouth.

Bettina said, "I like rats. I had one when I was a kid."

Its name had been Juliet, and it had liked dandelions.

"Her name was Juliet." Bettina's face softened. "She liked dandelions. I'd go out and pick as many as I could in the morning, and she'd nibble them from my hand."

Laurie said, "We got Jojo a guinea pig instead, and she's still not over that disappointment." Sixteen years old, but that rat argument seemed like last week rather than nine years ago.

They got four more minutes of **Jeopardy!** before the eager-beaver new hires hit the street and started pulling over everything with an expired tag. "Rookies," muttered Sylvia, running warrant checks on all five people in a car who apparently looked suspicious to the new officer. "They're exhausting."

"Run two more," said Knotcliffe over the radio.

The only time Laurie ever saw Sylvia get flustered was when she had too many people in a queue to check. Once, years ago, she'd missed a felony warrant for murder, and she'd never gotten over it. Sylvia's checks took twice as long as anyone else's, even though she could enter a full seventeen-character VIN with her eyes closed.

Laurie started on the first one. "Let me get those for you."

Sylvia shot her a grateful look. "Rookies," she said again, as if the word were a curse. "Too much fucking energy."

Laurie flipped through the pages quickly. "They're all clear, Sylvia."

"That last one, too?"

"Yeah."

911 rang. Laurie grabbed it, beating Dina yet again. She would **always** be the fastest on the phones, a small, silly point of pride. Still nodding emphatically at Sylvia, she said, "911, what's the address of the emergency?"

A long pause. "Hello?" The girl sounded far away and muffled.

But Laurie would know that voice even if it came from miles underwater, even if it came from the moon. Her response was frozen in her throat for a split, unforgivable second.

"Jojo?"

"Mama? Help me."

TWO

JOJO WAS ON a bed in darkness.

She'd walked her fingers to the side of the narrow mattress, but she still couldn't get her legs to move so that she could stand up and find the light switch. She'd managed to dig her cell phone out of her back pocket to dial 911.

The sound of her mother's voice in the darkness was a complete surprise, as if she'd totally forgotten what her mother did for a living. At least Jojo knew what city she was in now.

"Baby? Where are you?"

Her mother, always annoyingly calm in a crisis, wasn't calm now, and that was almost as scary as the fact that Jojo had no fucking idea where she was. "I don't know."

"How did you get there?"

"I don't know." Jojo's throat hurt, as if she'd been yelling.

She didn't remember yelling.

She couldn't really remember anything right now. Her thoughts were heavy and sluggish, towels dropped in a tub. She could barely move them around in her mind.

"Jojo?" The edge in her mother's voice was turning sharper.

Move your legs, she told herself. Why wouldn't they work? Had she been in an accident? Was she paralyzed? "Help."

"Baby, you have to tell me where you are." Her mother gasped a breath, and the sound of it sent a tremor through Jojo's stomach.

"Can't you see where I am?"

"You know I can't. You're going to have to help me, baby."

Shit. Technology was good and getting better, her mom always said, but cell phone locations were still approximations rather than accurate pinpoints. "I must be in San Bernal, right? If you answered?"

Her mother said, "Yeah. I've got you roughly in the Old Coast part of town. Do you know where you might be? I have to get your location."

In case they were disconnected. Jojo had been around the PD her whole life. Location was the most important thing. You couldn't get to a scene if you didn't know where the victim was, no matter how much you wanted to.

Oh, God, what if they got disconnected? "Mama, find me." The words came out of her mouth like she was five years old and lost in the Exploratorium. "Can you see me on **your** cell phone?" Her mother had made her turn Location Services on and share it with her. Jojo usually hated it.

"I'm trying." There was a fumbling noise. "Okay, I can see you on the map. Are you near Grand? And Seventh? Do you know what the house looks like?"

She had no idea. "I don't **know.**"

"Are you inside or outside?"

"Inside."

"Can you get to the door?"

"My legs won't move."

Jojo's mother made that sharp gasping-fish sound again. Jojo had never heard her mother make it before, and she hated it. That was a good feeling, the hating of it, so she stuck with it.

Annoyed at her mother. That was normal. That was real life.

Whatever **this** was, wherever she was in space, this wasn't real. This had to be a bad dream. How did you make yourself wake up from a dream? Jojo felt like she'd read the answer or seen it in a horror movie, but she couldn't remember how, so maybe this was real life, and if so, she was fucked.

"Do you know why your legs won't work?" Her mother had her calm voice on now, as if she'd pulled smoothness into her throat like a blanket, but Jojo could hear through it, to the raggedness of panic underneath it.

"Don't you think I would have told you if I did?" Jojo tried again, and her left leg jerked electrically, as if it had been asleep for hours. "Ow, shit. I have no idea what's going on. I woke up this way." She woke up. Which meant she'd been asleep. Why had she been asleep in a bed she didn't know?

"What can you see?"

"Not much. It's really dark in here. I'm on a bed."

"Can you hear anything?"

She listened. Silence. "No."

"Oh, baby. Okay." Jojo heard her mother suck in breath. "Okay. Look at your cell phone. What's your battery at?"

Jojo glanced. "Half full."

"Turn on the phone's flashlight for me, okay? While you're doing that, I'm sending a bunch of the guys in your direction, and they're driving as fast they can. You tell me when you hear a siren, all right? Listen for me, baby."

God, Jojo was stupid. She should have thought of the flashlight. She turned it on, expecting to find a creepy space filled with old chairs or baby-doll heads or something else from **American Horror Story.**

Instead it was just a generic room.

The bed she was on had a dark blue bedspread. The curtains were green. A low bookcase ran under the windows, filled with books on weightlifting. A treadmill was in one corner of the room, and in the other was a comfy-looking blue sofa that faced a large-screen TV. The en suite bathroom's door was open, and she could see the front of the sink.

She didn't recognize the room at all. "It's a bedroom. A normal bedroom. Kind of big. With a sofa."

"Personal items? A magazine or a piece of mail, with the address?"

She saw nothing that looked like it hadn't come out of the home-furnishing catalogs her mom liked to read in the bathtub. "No."

"Do you hear anything? A siren?"

A tiny wail. "Maybe, but it's really far away."

"What about anything else? Do you hear running water, or voices, or—"

Her mother broke off. Pieces of realization were dropping into Jojo's mind like the jewels in that Facebook game, clicking into place.

If her mother was asking about voices—that meant that people could be near.

People who had brought her here?

"No," Jojo whispered, trying to draw her breath into herself so that she could be as quiet as possible. "Is Daddy coming?"

"Yes, sweetheart. Daddy's coming." Jojo heard her mother tapping on the keys, so fast that the noise could have been a million popcorn kernels, all popping at once. "What were you doing earlier tonight?"

Muzzy. Everything in her head felt stuffed, as if her brain had been lifted out and replaced with a Styrofoam model. "I don't remember."

"Try. You have to try. We can get close, but I need an exact location. You can do this."

Harper. Something about Harper's laughter floated through Jojo's mind.

"I was . . . at a party." It wasn't a party, it was a . . . God, why couldn't she grab this? Why couldn't she pull it out of her stupid brain?

"Where?"

"I don't know." Something about making signs. It had been a community meeting. Hadn't it?

Kevin. Kevin, smiling down at her.

"Oh." Holy shit, she'd **kissed** him. Why had she kissed Kevin? She remembered the feel of his lips and nothing more. What about Zach? What had she done?

"What, baby? What is it?"

"Kevin Leeds."

A pause the space of a breath. "The pro football player? The one on the news?"

Jojo's heart skittered against her lungs. "He lives in Old Coast, I think."

"Hold on. Don't hang up, baby, no matter what, okay? If I lose you, turn off your ringer and watch the screen for me to call back. Stay with me." More frantic tapping. "Okay, I've got his address, and it's really close to where your signal is coming from. Tell me when you hear a siren getting closer."

As if her mother had pushed a police car on a game board closer to her with her finger, the sound outside filled Jojo's ears. "It's outside. There's a siren right here. But Kevin wouldn't—"

"I can hear it. Stay on the phone, baby."

"Is it Daddy?"

Another pause, a muffled shush of the phone as mother covered the microphone and said something to someone else that Jojo couldn't understand. "Daddy and everyone else, sugar."

So many sirens now. Jojo, her right leg newly under her control, bent it and pulled her knee toward her chest. If bullets flew, the smaller a target she was the better, right?

How had she gotten here?

What happened to me?

Kevin was her friend. She'd been in his house a few times, but just in the front, in the living room and kitchen. Once they'd swum in the backyard pool and she'd tried tequila for the first time, which had been Harper's idea—of course—and it turned out that tequila made Jojo wobble and giggle like a brain-dead cheerleader.

A banging came from another room, followed by a shout. "Mama, I'm scared."

"Don't be, sugar. We're almost there."

"You, too?"

"I will be. So soon. I'll drive to you as soon as we hang up, but don't hang up yet. Don't hang up."

There was a roar, at least two men bellowing like animals. "Mom! Kevin's my friend."

"We'll figure all that out later. Are you hurting, baby girl? I've got an ambulance outside. Tell me if you're hurting."

How was she supposed to know? All Jojo felt was fear, fear that locked every cell in her body into a frozen, stiff, unyielding piece of stone.

"Take a breath, Jojo. A big one, right into your stomach."

Her mother had always told her to do that when she was crying too hard to breathe. Was she doing that now? She couldn't tell.

"One breath."

Jojo breathed in deep and listened to the thumps and shouts from somewhere far away.

"Are you injured?"

Jojo's head throbbed. Her eyes stung. She felt dizzy even though she was lying down, and she thought she might throw up. Her feet ached as they came back to life, and her knees burned.

And something else hurt, something in the middle of her, something she didn't want to—couldn't—name.

"I hurt."

"Where?"

She could only whisper. **"There."**

THREE

JOJO SAID IT, but she didn't let her mind touch the idea. Not yet.

Instead she gave it to her mother to hold.

"Oh, baby." A choked sound came over the phone. "Okay. It's okay. We're going to fix it all. Tell me when—"

The door of the room burst open, slamming into the far wall.

Jojo dropped the phone to the bed. Her father had her then, his arms all the way around her, and he was holding her so tight she could barely breathe.

"Jojo. Jesus **Christ.**" Her father pressed her head into his shoulder, rubbing her hair so frantically it was like he was trying to smooth out her curls. "Jesus Christ. It's okay, Jojo."

Jojo wanted to pull her head away and say

something that would make him feel better, but it turned out that all she could do was release the sobs that had wanted to come out while she was on the phone—her phone!

Jojo reached for it now. "Mom?"

She heard her mother's sucked-in breath again. "Daddy's got you, sugar?"

"Yeah." Her father was letting her talk, though she was still scooped into his lap, her butt on the bed, her legs draped over his, his arms around her. Like she was five. And she didn't mind. "Are you really coming? Here?"

"I've got my coat on. I'm dropping my headset the second we hang up, and I'll be there in five minutes. No, three."

"You have the staffing?" Her mother never had the staffing to leave dispatch. Once Jojo had passed out in gym after attempting a three-day fast with a couple of friends trying to get skinny (she'd only made it to day two), and her mother hadn't been able to come get her because someone had called in sick. **I can't legally just leave 911 to ring unanswered, you know that.**

"No." A short laugh. "But they'll handle it. Let Daddy take care of you, and I'll be there in a flash, okay?"

"Okay." Jojo felt a tremor in her voice, a quake that ran through her whole body from the top of her head to the tips of her aching feet. She let the phone drop from her hands again.

Her father said, "I've got you. I've got you."

"I don't understand." Jojo wasn't even sure what she didn't understand, but it felt big and terrifying.

"Neither do I, babe, but we're going to figure it out, okay?" He smiled at her, a true, big smile, like there was nothing wrong at all. It was the smile he gave her when she used to be good at softball, the one he gave her when she slid into home. Like she'd done something to be proud of.

Instead of . . . instead of whatever it was she'd done.

Whatever it was, it was her fault. She knew that much. Guilt swamped her lungs, a hot, silty rush.

Her father looked up at someone in the hallway who'd said something in underwater-speak. "Yeah, send them in."

Jojo reclaimed her frozen legs and brought them up to her chest. She scooted so that her spine was against the headboard. "Who?"

He'd lost the total-father look and was back in partial-father/partial-police-chief mode, the mode she was most used to seeing him in. His eyebrows returned to their normal holding pattern at the top of his forehead, not squinched down like when he'd first come into the room. "The paramedics are going to take a quick look at you, okay? Then we're going to the hospital."

Jojo shook her head. "I don't want to." She didn't specify which part. She didn't want to do any of them.

"I'll be right here."

"I just want to go home."

"We will." He made a motion to someone in the hall she couldn't see. "We're going to take you home as soon as we can."

"Now."

But he wasn't listening. He'd gone into full-on-cop mode now. "Come on in, guys." He stood, like he was welcoming someone into his office for coffee. Jojo pressed herself farther into the headboard.

Her father craned his neck, as if waiting for someone else, but there were already three guys in the room. "No females on duty?"

"Not tonight, sir. But we'll take care of her, don't worry. Just like she was our own."

Clearly the whole contingent outside had been notified that she was the chief's daughter. Usually Jojo hated that. But right now it was okay.

The paramedic who had spoken to her father stretched out his hand. "Hi, there. I'm Mike. What's your name?" The man's eyes were tired blue, and he had a bare spot in his stubble the size of a quarter, as if the hair just wouldn't grow there. It looked smooth and shiny, and for a split second of craziness Jojo wanted to press her thumb into it and ask him why he was bald in such a tiny spot.

"Jojo."

"Jojo, I'm going to check you over, okay? Just a little bit, so that we can take you to the hospital. That okay by you?"

"I want to go with my dad."

Mike looked at her father, who shook his head the slightest bit.

"Dad!"

"I've got to stay here. Just for a few minutes. I'll be right behind you."

"Mom said she's coming. Let me go with her. I don't want to go anywhere in the ambulance." Funny, if anyone had asked her the week before if she'd like an ambulance trip, Jojo would have jumped at the chance. A moment to be special and to have an IV dripping into her arm like she had something terminal? A chance to ogle hot paramedics so she could tell Harper about them later?

Not now. Not like this.

"Maybe," Dad said. "If she gets here in time."

Mike held a clipboard with a pen poised over his form. "If you're able to, scoot to the edge of the bed for me, okay? Just some routine questions. What's your full name?"

She told him her age and her address while two other medics attached a blood pressure cuff to her and ran a thermometer wand across her forehead, like she had the flu or something.

"Do you have any pain?"

Jojo felt a pit in her stomach drop open. In a second she was going to fall right through. "My feet," she whispered.

"Do you mind if we take off your shoes and have a look?"

She shook her head.

"Where else?"

She shook her head harder.

I can't do this.

She couldn't say what she felt. Not with—she shot her father a glance under her lashes, and oh, fuck, it looked like he was either going to cry or hit a wall with his fist. "Can I . . . Is it okay if I wait till my mom gets here?"

"Jojo." Her father's voice cracked, and he swayed toward her on the balls of his feet. "You can say anything in front of me. Did anything—"

"I want to wait for Mom." Tears slid down her cheeks, tears she wished she could scrape up the sides of her cheeks and shove them forcibly back into her eyeballs.

"Jojo—"

"I want Mom."

FOUR

LAURIE'S THREE CO-WORKERS all reacted the same way. "Go."

"Get out of here."

"We're fine."

"We'll call you if we need you back."

They wouldn't, Laurie knew that. Once, years before, Sylvia's mother had stopped breathing at her care home. While Rita gave CPR instructions to the caller, Sylvia got up and left, a fireable offense. After her mother's funeral, Sylvia had come back to work as soon as her bereavement days were up. No one had said a word to her.

This felt like that, only Jojo wasn't dying.

Laurie would, though, if she didn't get there now. Right now.

It was a six-minute drive through the dark from

the station to the Old Coast. She'd told Jojo she could do it in three, and she almost made it in that time. She took the last corner at forty-five, blowing a stop sign. She almost hit an old man. He dove out of the crosswalk just in time. "Shit! I'm sorry!" She waved her hand uselessly and kept going. If she'd run over him, she might not have stopped—that was the full truth.

Kevin Leeds's house was normal for the neighborhood—huge and old. The upper floor was dark under the starless sky, but the lower floor poured light out every window. Four patrol cars, a fire engine, and an ambulance were in front, all their lights flashing.

Omid's unmarked car was there, the driver's door still wide open.

She jammed her car into park and hit the pavement so hard and fast that she stumbled. In another, bigger city, the uniform and badge she wore would have been what gained her entrance to a crime scene—here it was the fact that she knew every one of these men like family. Officer Dyer leaped forward and caught her arm. "Easy, easy. She's in there. She's okay."

Okay?

Officer Marks, posted at the door, took one look at Laurie's face and threw open the screen for her. "All the way back, third left."

Laurie ran.

The rear hallway was crowded with personnel and equipment. The medics had a fucking backboard blocking the way—surely Jojo wouldn't need that?

She tried to say something—anything—but no words came, so she pushed through them, one by one. If they hadn't moved, she would have pushed them all the way down.

She could see Jojo's knee through the forest of arms that reached for her, just her knee. Those jeans that Laurie had bought, that Laurie had looked at in the dressing room. **Really? Distressed this much is back? Because you'll be lucky if these last you a year**. Jojo had rolled her eyes.

Omid caught Laurie's hand and pulled her forward. "Here. She's here." His voice was rough.

Laurie still didn't have language back, but something eased as she saw Jojo. All in one piece. Somehow she'd expected limbs missing. Gaping wounds. Blood everywhere.

Most of the really bad calls went that way. And this was the worst call of her career.

But Jojo was there, intact, reaching for her. Roughly—almost violently—Laurie dug her fingers into Jojo's skin and pulled her close, as if she could pull her child back into the body she'd come from. Jojo did the same, her own fingers digging into the flesh around Laurie's middle.

"Laurie." Omid's voice.

What had she been thinking, just letting Jojo go out in the world, like she was a grown-up? She was sixteen!

"Laurie, we have to let them get the primary exam done."

Jojo made a terrified noise and buried herself farther into Laurie's side.

"No."

"We have to. We have to be sure she's fit to ride in the ambulance."

"No. Not here. I'll ride with her." She caught the expression the taller medic tossed at the younger one. "Do you have a problem with that?" The man looked startled. "I didn't think so." She scraped her fingers against the Velcro of the blood pressure band still around Jojo's arm. She pulled it off and tossed it to the floor. It didn't matter that medics didn't like parents riding in the ambulance. She wasn't going to give them a choice. "We don't do anything unless I'm with her and she's okay with it."

"Laurie!"

She shrugged. "So we can walk out to the ambulance now or I can take her myself in my car." The last part was an enormous falsehood. She wasn't calm enough to drive right now.

"I'll go in the ambulance with Mom." Jojo's voice was small but clear.

"Okay, then." Laurie stood, catching herself as her knees buckled the slightest bit. She felt Omid's hand on her elbow and was grateful for it. He extended his other hand to Jojo, and together they helped their daughter stand.

Jojo swayed, and the color drained from her face. Suddenly she looked green.

"Emesis bag," snapped one of the medics to another.

A blue bag appeared just in time, and Jojo vomited into it. God, later she would be so furious. She'd vomited once in public when she was eight, right into the school cafeteria's trash can, and she'd never gotten over it.

Laurie pushed the hair away from Jojo's face and rubbed her back. Her daughter swayed again. "How about we sit another minute."

Jojo spit into the bag, then took the Kleenex someone gave her and rubbed it over her face. She sat back down on the bed. "Oh, my God."

Her breath was foul—onion and rum and something meaty. Laurie took the bag and twisted it and put it on the floor. ID might need the contents later, which she tried not to think about. "I'll get you a wet washcloth."

Jojo's fingers gripped into Laurie's arm.

Laurie made an effort to soften her face. "Right there." She pointed at the open bathroom door that Omid and another officer were partially blocking. "I'll be back in one sec, I promise."

She moved past the men and into the bathroom.

What was the protocol on this? This was some kind of a crime scene. She shouldn't touch anything if she could help it. But goddamn it, a washcloth would help Jojo.

Of course there wasn't a washcloth. A scented candle yes, and an expensive bottle of pump soap. But there wasn't a single towel in the whole bathroom, not even a guest hand towel. "Just a second, Jojo. Omid."

Omid broke off in midsentence. "Yeah. What are you doing?"

Laurie just pointed at their daughter, whose face was still pale green.

He nodded and went to Jojo, putting his arms around her like a coat.

There had to be a washcloth somewhere.

Laurie yanked open the closet door.

It was dark inside, and deeper than she'd thought it would be, and it smelled strange, almost metallic.

Laurie took a step inside, the bathroom light behind her casting an odd shape on the floor.

She ran into something on the floor that felt soft and heavy.

Slowly the shape took form.

A leg, twisted the wrong way. An arm bent at the elbow, the hand resting against a low shelf, as if casually waving hello. The body was propped halfway up, the head leaning against a laundry basket.

A buzz started inside Laurie's head. She smashed her hand into the wall next to her, banging against it until she found the light switch, and the closet lit up.

A young man wearing a black sweatshirt and jeans lay at her feet. He was handsome—at least the right side of his face was good-looking: strong jaw, wide cheekbone, expressive eyebrow. The right side of his face was clean, bloodless. His one intact eye was open wide, the pupil startlingly matte instead of shiny.

But where the left side of his face should have been, there was just a bloody, lumpy mess—the top of the head caved in, the left eye scrambled, the cheek a mass of red viscera and raw tissue. Below that, the white bone of his jaw gleamed. Blood pooled to his chest and dripped down his side, soaking into the white carpet. His mouth hung open, the lower left lip split sideways, hanging below his jawline.

Laurie's right hand went to her own waist—it wasn't until she couldn't grab her gun that she realized she'd gone for it for the first time in seventeen years. She tried to yell, but her lungs were somehow empty.

She staggered backward, shutting off the light. **Don't let Jojo see.** She shut the closet door. "Omid," she managed, her voice strangled and too low for anyone to hear. She pushed past an officer and made it to the bed. Scooping her forearms under Jojo's armpits, she pulled her daughter to standing again.

"Mom?"

"We're going. Now."

"Laurie?" Omid stood, his arm going to Jojo's back, as if to steady her.

"Bathroom. Nobody cleared the closet." Laurie's brain stalled. Just the code came to her, nothing else. She whispered in Omid's ear, so that Jojo wouldn't hear. "187."

"Out." Omid helped them to the hallway. "Get her out of here."

"Mom, what's going on?"

"Follow me, baby."

Behind them, Omid roared, "Who the **FUCK** was supposed to clear this section?"

Laurie felt Jojo curling into herself again. "Come on. Can you walk?" They moved down the hall and toward the front of the house. "I've got you."

"Jojo!"

The shout came from the right, from the kitchen. Kevin Leeds, the football player, was seated at a round table, his shoulders twice as broad as the chair he sat in. Detective Nate Steiner sat across from him, a report sheet in front of him.

Laurie tried to drag Jojo along with her, but Jojo was quicker, lighter, suddenly not wobbly at all, surprisingly strong. She jerked out of her mother's grasp and dodged past Officer Jorge Rogers, heading for the table.

"Kevin! What's going on? What the hell happened to me? Why am I here?"

Leeds stood, but Steiner was fast, reaching to

press him back into the seat. "Don't even think about getting up."

Laurie yanked Jojo's arm. "Don't talk to him." She pulled again.

Jojo wrenched herself away. "What's going on? Did you do something?"

The football player, huge compared to Steiner, stood. "I didn't even know you were in the house. This shit is insane. Tell them."

"I don't know **what** to tell them! I don't remember—"

Laurie got hold of Jojo's arm again and dug in as hard as she could. "Don't talk to him. Don't say another word." She felt someone behind her shove her to the side, and she tugged Jojo along with her.

Omid.

He was a barrel of gunpowder lit with a dry match. He threw himself at Leeds, both arms around his waist, kicking the chair out of the way as they went. Leeds might have been used to being rushed on the field, but he hadn't seen this one coming, and Omid had the man rolled onto his stomach, his arm pinned high up behind him in less than four seconds. "Give me your cuffs," he panted at Steiner.

Laurie smashed Jojo against the counter, blocking her body so that she couldn't get closer to the men.

"Daddy!"

Omid's knee was in the middle of Leeds's back, and he was leaned forward, saying something urgently into the football player's ear. Laurie couldn't hear the words, but she had a good idea of what they were.

"He's okay, they're okay, we're getting out." Laurie jerked her chin at Rogers, who nodded. He and Laurie flanked Jojo, and together they pushed her from the kitchen, out through the expansive living room, and into the front yard.

The night sky was lit by the flashing lights. Neighbors gawked with wide-eyed stares. One called, "Everything all right?"

Jojo was sobbing. Laurie's face was wet, too, though she hadn't realized she was crying until she wiped her eyes with the back of her hand. Then the medics had the ambulance open, and Laurie was helping her daughter climb into it, and they were settling Jojo onto the gurney for the short, ten-block ride, strapping her in and motioning for Laurie to secure herself as well.

She'd been bored. An hour ago Laurie had been **bored,** complaining about coffee. And now life had spiraled onto a different plane, and she didn't recognize anything but the hand she held in hers, the hand that was alive and warm.

Jojo was alive. Someone else was dead—brutally so—but Jojo was alive.

That was all that mattered for now.

FIVE

THE PLASTIC, CHEMICAL scent of the hospital burned Jojo's nostrils, a sharp assault. How could anyone work with that shoved up their nose constantly?

She inhaled again and coughed.

Her mother turned abruptly, looking up from her phone. "You okay?"

Of course I'm not.

"Sorry," Mom said. "Texting Dad. He'll be here soon."

Fear filled the space between Jojo's shoulder blades. "Whatever."

"Baby, it's going to be okay." Mom leaned forward. "What you need to do now is just breathe. Like we learned in that stress class. In through the nose, out through the mouth. Do that now."

Less than an hour ago, all Jojo had wanted was her mother's arms around her. Now those grasping hands made her feel like she was going be trapped forever if Mom got hold of her. "Stop. I'm fine." She unlocked her phone for the hundredth time, looking for a message from Harper. Where **was** she? She would know what had happened.

"You're not."

"**You're** not." What a stupid thing to say. But Mom wasn't answering her about what had happened in the bathroom right before they left Kevin's house. Every time Jojo asked about it, Mom just shook her head, like she was angry.

On a normal day, that would have driven Jojo insane. She would have picked and poked until Mom gave in and told her whatever it was.

This wasn't a normal day.

Jojo flipped through Instagram on her phone, even though the pictures blurred into a dreary, wet mess.

"Can you tell me even a little bit about what happened?"

"If I could remember, I would." Would she? Jojo wasn't sure. And part of herself hated the fact that she was putting that look on Mom's face, that disappointed one, the one that said Jojo was a major fuckup.

Another part—a small, vicious kernel that she wished she didn't have—felt glad. Then that in itself sprouted guilt.

"You can't remember at all?"

Jojo shook her head so hard it set up an instant headache behind her eyes. "I told you. What are we still doing here, anyway? Let's just **go.**" She knew why they couldn't, though. The intake nurse had said it to them gently. **Rape test. We've called for an advocate, and she'll be here soon to walk you through the process.** All the **r**-words swirled in Jojo's brain. "Did I get roofied?"

Mom's lips pulled in at the corners, as if she hated the word, too. But her eyes were still soft. "They'll check for that in your blood work. How do you know Kevin Leeds?"

Jojo wasn't going to get out of it. Mom was annoying as shit, and as stubborn as Jojo was. And Mom was never dumb. She wouldn't let it go. "We're friends." She hated that her voice shook.

"Friends." Mom stared, her forehead channel getting deeper. "You and him."

Jojo bristled. "You have a problem with that?"

"With the fact that my daughter's hanging out with an adult pro football player? Yeah. I do."

"Because he's black."

Her mother's eyes narrowed. "Don't be stupid. Because he's probably thirty."

"Twenty-two." He'd graduated early and gotten drafted immediately.

"Jesus, Jojo."

"So he plays football. He's also really into baking bread. He goes to church. We're just friends.

Why do you have to make that sound disgusting?" What if Kevin **was** a bad man? Wouldn't she have known? Jojo remembered again that she'd kissed him. How—why—had she done that? Had she already been roofied then? How had she ended up at his house?

"H-he's . . ." Mom stuttered. "The flag-pin thing. He's the one who wears it upside down, right?"

Jojo writhed on the hospital bed, pulling the blanket over herself tighter, wishing she could tuck herself in. "Oh, my God. You say that like it's a bad thing. It's a pin. He's an activist, not a satanist." Six months before, when he'd first been drafted, he'd gone onto the field with an upside-down flag pin on his jersey. It was tiny, but it had been noticed. Not by Jojo, not right away. She didn't care about football, but guys she knew had talked about it. Kevin Leeds didn't sing along for the national anthem, and afterward he always touched the pin and then raised his fist.

Had she gone home with him?

Had she—Had he . . . ?

Holy shit.

Mom said, "He wears the logo of our nation upside down. Encouraging dissent in front of everyone."

Jojo stifled a groan. "He's encouraging **discussion,** drawing attention to the fact that black people are still mistreated in this country. People of color like me, Mom." She pointed at her own face. "Have you noticed?"

"You're half Persian. You call that being a person of color?"

"You're married to a brown man."

"Jojo!"

"And you have a half-brown daughter."

"Stop it. That's ridiculous."

Jojo stared. Even Dad joked about the cream in her coffee. They'd always laughed when people thought Mom had adopted her, when they wanted to give her credit for her passion for humanity. "What part of it is ridiculous? You think it's not on my mind every day?"

Mom ignored her. "How do you know him? Tell me now." It was inevitable. Mom was a pit bull with a piece of rawhide. It was going to come out.

"I know him through Harper."

Mom thunked back in her plastic chair with a small **oof.** "Harper Cunningham?"

Of course Harper Cunningham. What other Harper was there? "Yeah."

"You were with her tonight?"

"Yeah."

"Where is she now?"

Jojo had no idea. **Harper, where are you?** Sudden fear jolted her. "What was in the closet that upset you?"

Mom said sharply, "Nothing. Wait, you two

aren't friends. You haven't been friends for how long? Not since the arrest. What, two years ago?"

"We're friends."

"Jojo. I'm spinning here. You have to help me out with some of this. You have this whole secret life that I don't know about."

"It's not secret. You're just never around to see it." It was a low blow, and she meant it to be.

Mom went white. "You're right. Oh, baby, I'm so sorry." She reached out a hand.

The whole of Jojo's body recoiled, and she drew backward, hunching her spine into a ball. She couldn't take care of her mother right now. "Can we just go home?"

Mom shook her head. "I wish we could." Her cell phone pinged, and she grabbed it like it was on fire.

The curtain shook on its metal rod as a round-faced woman poked her head through. "Jojo Ahmadi? Can I come in?"

Mom said, "Of course."

The woman didn't even look at Mom, just at Jojo.

"I'm Gloria." She held out a hand, and Jojo shook it. She was wide at the hip and the bust, and her hair was a wild mess of gray-black curls. She wore some hippie-looking blue dress that looked as comfortable as pajamas and a purple jersey jacket with an ink stain at the pocket.

"I'm Jojo," she muttered, hating the hitch in her voice so much she wanted to punch herself in the face.

"I'm Laurie. I'm Jojo's mother." Mom stood up, making the space around the bed seem crowded. Jojo was caught on the bed. No way out.

"Hi, Mom," said Gloria comfortably. "Why don't you go ahead and stay seated. These teeny-tiny little cubbies, I just feel so claustrophobic in them sometimes."

Jojo's mother sat but strained forward. "What happens next?"

Gloria responded as if Jojo had asked, speaking directly to her. "What happens next is I go with you to do the sexual-assault forensic exam." She said it as if they were going to get a vanilla latte.

"We go, you mean," said Mom.

Gloria's smile looked real. "If that's what Jojo wants. Jojo, do you want to do this with me and your mother, or just with me?"

"I'm her **mother**. I go where she goes."

Gloria took a second to beam warmth at Jojo—she could feel it heating up her insides, which had been so cold ever since she woke up—and then turned to her mother. "And I'm her advocate. I'm here for Jojo."

"So am **I**."

Gloria crossed her arms. "I'm not your advocate, though. With respect, I'm going to let Jojo decide on her level of support."

Jojo shivered and pictured the room she might be going to. When she'd gotten her first Pap smear, Mom had held her hand, and it had been half comforting, half mortifying. "You can stay here, Mom. I'll go with Gloria."

Gloria nodded. "I'm just taking her down the hall to my office. We'll chat a little before we see the nurse. I'll keep you posted as we go. That okay, Mom?"

"**No—**" Mom broke off and took a breath. "You're right. I know you're right. That's why you're the advocate. I know. But I'm freaking out—"

"Of course you are," Gloria said in a friendly voice. "But Jojo's our focus right now. Now, Jojo, why don't you and I go for that walk down the hall? Put your shoes on. There's no telling what diseases they got on the loose in here. Mom, I swear to you, I will keep you posted."

It seemed childish to say aloud the mantra running through Jojo's head, **I want to go home I want to go home go home go home go home,** so instead she nodded. "Okay."

She slipped off the bed and stood. She glanced at her mother, who was blinking ferociously as if it could disguise the fact that the lower half of her face was tight in that almost-crying twist. Guilt swam up Jojo's spinal column. She had done all this. She was the reason all this shit was happening, and she couldn't even remember what she'd done.

Impulsively, she reached down to hug her mother's shoulders. It was awkward—she'd never hugged her mother from above. Mom's nose hit her clavicle, and Jojo banged her head lightly on the blood pressure machine. "Love you."

Her mother made a noise. Jojo couldn't hear exactly what she said, but it made her want to wail.

Gloria waited, still with that warmth in her eyes. "This way, Jojo. I'm going to be right here with you, the whole time."

Behind them Jojo heard her mother say softly, "Me too."

SIX

LAURIE HAD TO pee, which was ridiculous. It was a bodily betrayal. That goddamn coffee in dispatch. She couldn't go to the bathroom now, because she couldn't leave this chair in case Jojo looked for her.

Jojo had been twenty feet from a murdered man.

Omid had texted that they'd identified him as a friend of Leeds's, and that Leeds had lost his total shit when he'd been told he was being arrested. Omid had to help take him in, and then he'd get here. It should be soon.

Until then Laurie would stay right here in this chair. In case Jojo needed her.

Surely if Jojo insisted, Gloria would let Laurie be in the room for the kit, right?

The kit.

Laurie had said it a million times at work after rape calls.

Did they do the kit yet?

That question came right before the next, inevitable one:

You think it's a good rape?

It was just what they said. What cops had always said.

A good rape.

"Good" meant that it fulfilled the categories to fit the penal code for the crime. A good robbery wasn't a guy stealing a toolbox out of your truck while you were getting breakfast—it was when your toolbox got taken out of your hands, using force (strength) or fear (a threat or a weapon).

A good rape meant a forced rape by a stranger.

A good rape was one that hadn't been committed by a boyfriend after a few drinks. Sure, Laurie knew that one was still a rape. But it wasn't the kind the papers wrote about or the kind that got a whole department upset. A good rape was a grab-from-the-bushes horror show. The kind of rape all women feared, that almost never happened in this small, affluent, Bay Area city. A good rape was one that left evidence behind, as opposed to the kind that many women called in about days later, with no proof.

And Laurie was just like everyone else at the station.

Doubtful.

Callous.

Sure, we'll see what the rape kit says. Probably not a good one.

God. They were fucking awful. The air left her lungs in a whoosh, and she leaned forward, wrapping her arms around her knees. Blood rushed back to her head, and the urge to urinate increased.

Her baby girl, with her feet in stirrups. It was so invasive. And that wasn't the half of the invasion that had—no, make that might have—taken place.

God fucking **forbid** something like that had happened to her daughter. She gagged on the rage that twisted up her throat.

Her phone pinged.

Omid. **Almost there.**

Another text had come in at some point from Sarah Knight at work. **She okay?**

Sarah worked in the jail. That meant the news was all over the department. Laurie dragged her hand across her mouth. She typed, **I have no idea. She might have been raped by a football player or maybe by his dead friend.** She pushed SEND.

A second later her phone rang.

Sarah's voice was intense and tight. "You want me to come there?"

"You're working."

"You need someone."

"Omid's coming."

"He'll be busy, you know that. I can pull in a

rookie to help Bob, and I can be with you and our girl. Just sit with you."

A tight warmth wrapped around Laurie's heart. The department was her home, her safety. "No, stay there." The jail was running on even slimmer staffing than dispatch was. "I'll—we'll—take you up on it later, okay?"

"I'll help you kill him. If you need me to." Sarah cleared her throat. "Of course, let me state for the record that I'm joking."

Laurie knew she wasn't. "Thanks, friend."

"Hang in there. I'll call again later."

Laurie slipped her cell into her pocket and rubbed her forehead.

Her mind raced. There had to be **more** she could do. There had to be something to fix this entire situation. It wasn't too late.

The image of flames dancing up a white wall rose in her mind.

When Laurie was twelve, the dryer had caught on fire. **The lint.** She'd forgotten to take it out for a month, maybe more. She'd managed the rest of the house as her father drank himself to sleep by two every afternoon, as her mother—sober but just as absent as her father—painted late into the night. Laurie had learned early to write out the rent check and slide it to her father to sign before she stuck it in the mail. She bought groceries at the local convenience market. Her parents weren't terrible people, they were just neglectful. They loved her, but as soon as Laurie had proved herself trustworthy, they'd gratefully relied on her, bragging about her to their friends. **She handles it all—she wants to! Cutest thing.**

But everything had been a crisis to Laurie; any slip of focus could bring the house crashing down around her. Emergency: the sink, when it stopped up and flooded the kitchen. Emergency: when the bird smashed through the front window. Emergency: when the furnace went out. Laurie handled each, learning who to call, what to say, how to avoid further disaster.

That day, as she'd watched the flames lick up the wall behind the dryer, she knew she'd failed. Everything her family owned would turn to ash, and it would be her fault.

But her father had come to life behind her, shoving her outside onto the porch while with the other hand he sprayed the fire with the extinguisher Laurie had made her parents buy. Everything had turned out fine, but for that split second as the fire hissed and snapped and grew faster than anything should, Laurie had felt it all slip away.

Catastrophe was inevitable, how had she dared to think anything else?

Now, as she sat in the hospital chair, three more texts bounced across the screen. Steiner. Dyer. Rogers. The department was a better family than the one Laurie had grown up in. And Jojo was one of theirs. This was just the start of the onslaught of questions.

How is she?

What's happening?

Is she okay?

Laurie pressed her hand against her upper abdomen. Was she having a panic attack? She'd never had one before, but she'd heard them thousands of times on 911, and her breathing was sounding familiar to her—it was hitched, caught on the spines of terror in her throat. She had no **time** for it.

No. This was just normal panic, rising out of a good reason. Laurie shook her head. There was that idiotic word again: **good.**

Think about something else.

Harper.

Harper was back? What the hell was going on?

It was impossible. She would know if Jojo and Harper were hanging out. Wouldn't she?

Laurie scanned her phone again, ignoring the sweat that ran down the center of her spine and her increasingly desperate need to pee.

No new messages. Jojo hadn't texted saying she needed her yet.

The image of Kevin Leeds filled her mind, so huge and wide-shouldered. The dead man in the closet, his teeth gleaming white through the ripped lip, through the mouthful of blood.

How did her daughter know men like that?

And for the love of God, Jojo and Harper hadn't

spoken for the last two years. If this was truly happening, it had to be Harper's fault.

Everything had always been Harper's fault.

Jojo didn't have a spot in her body for hiding things. She was easy to read, open, generous with her thoughts and affection.

What the fuck, then, was happening?

Laurie crossed her legs tighter. And she waited.

SEVEN

THE EXAMINING ROOM Gloria took Jojo to looked like where she'd gotten her Pap smear last year, the only other time she'd had a pelvic exam. There was the horrible big bed thing with the splayed stirrups, and a rolling tray had silver devices all over it. Waiting for her.

Gloria opened a drawer and pulled out a pair of beige socks wrapped in plastic. She unwrapped them and put them over the stirrups. "That's a little better, anyway."

"Can I keep my shoes on?"

Gloria gave her a long, steady look. "It'll be head-to-toe. Remember we talked about that in my office?"

They'd gone together to a small blue office before coming here to the Pap smear room to do the rape kit. **Sexual-assault forensic exam** was what Gloria had said. But **rape kit** was what Mom and Dad called it when they were talking about work. Jojo was just doing it now because it was a good idea. That was all. Jojo didn't remember talking about its being head-to-toe. Was that the drug? "Even my shirt? My bra?"

"They're going to swab you all over, and then they'll use that comb I told you about. They're going to look at places that no one usually looks at, but I'll be right here with you the whole time, I promise. I'm not going anywhere. They'll probably keep your underwear—"

Jojo gave an involuntary squeak.

"—but I've got fresh ones in my bag. Clean and new. I've also got a brand-new sweatshirt and sweatpants, if you don't feel like getting back into those clothes."

"I don't." Suddenly the idea of sliding the jeans back on horrified Jojo. They should be burned.

"You've got this. Now. Here's a drape to lay over your lower half, and put this stupid-looking thing on like a shirt, opening in front, okay? I'll turn my back or leave the room while you change, whatever you prefer."

"Please stay?" Jojo's neck muscles felt tight, and her fingers clenched.

"You got it. Let me know if I can help with anything."

Jojo tried to ignore the voice that cried for her

mother, tried to drown it out with motion. She took off her boots, then her jeans and underwear. She stripped off her shirt and bra. Fear rippled through her as if someone were going to attack her here, in the hospital, under Gloria's watchful eye. She hopped up onto the bed, draped the blue paper apron over her lap, and said, "Okay."

"Now, if you're ready, I'll go get the nurse."

Jojo said the word quickly before she lost the ability to speak: "Yes."

"Want your mom?"

Yes, yes, yes, yes. "No, thank you."

"I'll be right back."

The nurse who brought in a white cardboard box wasn't anything like Gloria. She was short, with cropped dark hair. She moved with purpose, her shoes silent on the floor. She said hello to Jojo without smiling. She explained everything clinically, describing what each piece of equipment was for.

"I'll tell you what I'm doing before I do it. You might feel a little bit of a pinch, but we're not going into the cervix, like we do with a Pap smear, so it's less invasive."

Less invasive? Less invasive was a paper cut patched with a Kermit Band-Aid. "I think I'm fine," Jojo said to the nurse. "This is just in case."

The nurse nodded.

"I mean, I feel fine. Totally fine." But she didn't. The pain between her legs just seemed to be getting worse now that her flesh was exposed to air.

The nurse sat on the stool and rolled it between Jojo's legs.

Jojo's knees started to shake. Gloria had moved like magic to Jojo's side. "Want a hand to hold?"

Desperately, Jojo wanted to say no. And equally desperately she wanted to cry, and maybe that wouldn't happen if she were clutching Gloria's hand the way she already was without even realizing she'd grabbed it.

"This is the visual inspection." The nurse moved a lamp that screeched on the floor. "First the pelvic check, to get it over with, then the head-to-toe."

Gloria winked at her. "Can you feel the heat from the light?"

Jojo wouldn't have noticed if it hadn't been pointed out. It would have been kind of nice if she hadn't been in hell. "Yeah."

"How about your toes? Are they cold?"

It was a trick, Jojo knew, a trick to get her thinking about any other part of her body besides her vagina, and she was grateful. "No, they're okay."

"Now you'll feel the speculum. Might be a little cold."

A little cold? Jojo jerked backward. When she'd gotten the Pap smear, the speculum had been terrifying, but at least it had been small and pink and prewarmed. This one was huge and silver and made of ice.

And it hurt, stinging in a place she shouldn't sting. She wasn't a virgin (mostly not one, anyway), but she'd never hurt like this there: like lemon juice poured on a million tiny paper cuts.

"Stay still." The nurse's voice was curt.

Jojo coughed and felt herself tighten around the speculum, which scared her so much she choked on her next breath. Coughing again made the fear and the pain worse.

Gloria still held Jojo's hand and used her other hand to smooth back Jojo's hair, just like Mom used to do when she had a fever.

"Do you have kids?" Jojo's voice came out too loud, but Gloria didn't even flinch, keeping her eyes firmly on Jojo's.

"I do. I have three. You want me to tell you about them?"

"Yes, please," gasped Jojo. "Tell me everything."

EIGHT

"WHERE IS SHE?" Omid yanked back the curtain.

Laurie jumped to her feet. "She's with the advocate. I have to pee."

In the minute and a half it took her to find the restroom, pee, and wash her hands, Omid had vanished from the ER cubicle.

"Omid?" Shit, what if he'd gone looking for Jojo? No, that wasn't a what-if, that was a for-certain. "Omid!"

He hadn't gotten far—he stood at the nurses' station. His uniform shirt was tight across his back, pulling against his chest and bulletproof vest.

"Omid, she's fine."

He whirled on her, his cop face in place. His lips were drawn back, his eyes strained. Gray stubble broke along his jaw, even though he shaved twice a day. Rigid cords of muscle stood out in his neck. When she'd worked the street with him, that was the face he got before they had to thump someone down or after an unfruitful foot pursuit, except he looked a little green, too. "She's **not** fine. Jesus Christ, someone tell me where my daughter is."

Laurie tugged him away from the desk, pulling on the edge of his sleeve. "She's getting the kit done."

He straightened. "And you're not with her?"

Laurie's stomach churned. She should be there. "No."

"We'll find her. You need to be with her for that."

"No."

"Then me." Omid had already turned back to the nurse. "Where—"

"No. She doesn't want us. Tell me about the man in the closet."

"What?" He spun again, a rigid top wobbling to and fro. "She doesn't get to make that decision."

"That's **exactly** the decision she gets to make. It's her body, and she's the one in charge of it." Saying it out loud made the words true to Laurie, and the fact that she'd almost tried to force her way into the exam room made her feel ashamed.

"She's sixteen. **We're** in charge of her body." Omid scrubbed his hand over his face. "So we wait? That's all we do?"

Laurie nodded. She took his hand and led him

back to the cubicle they'd been in, where she'd left her jacket and purse.

She sat. Omid was pacing, and she knew he wouldn't stop. The man was made of action, muscle, and grit. Even now that he was chief, he sometimes worked all night on major cases, staying up with the detectives, bouncing ideas around. He pulled ID shifts to make sure he understood the new tech. He knew how to dispatch and pitched in when they were shorthanded. Paper pushing wasn't enough for him. He felt great pride in taking care of the people he loved at the department.

And that was nothing compared to how he loved his daughter.

Right now, somewhere so close to them, Jojo was probably scared out of her damn mind. Laurie tasted bile at the back of her throat but managed to say, "She'll be okay." Jesus, had she made a mistake not going with her?

Omid glared. "Of course she will be. She'll be fine."

Laurie dragged her thoughts back to Kevin Leeds. "Did you take him in?"

He nodded shortly.

"How did it go?" She could imagine, but she wanted to hear it. Desperately, Laurie needed to know that the man hurt.

"Not so smoothly. For him."

"Good."

"Yeah." Omid didn't meet her eyes.

"What?"

He shook his head. The greenish pallor under his cheekbones grew a deeper yellow.

"Omid, tell me what the fuck happened there."

"The guy in the closet was an assistant athletic trainer on the team. Zachary Gordon. Tight with Leeds. Blunt-force trauma to the head, unknown weapon."

"Did Leeds kill him?" Of course he had.

Omid rubbed his hands together as if he were cold. "I don't know. When we asked him about Gordon, he crumpled like a paper bag. Broke down, tear factory, the works. Said he'd been sleeping for two hours."

"Good actor, that's all."

"We found more blood. Near the kitchen door. It didn't match the spatter that was in the closet—could have been tracked there or . . ."

Laurie's heart rate spiked, and nausea flooded her throat. "Whose blood?" **Please make it Leeds's blood. Let it be Zachary Gordon's blood. Let Jojo have hurt them first.**

"ID took samples. Maybe Gordon's, but honestly, I think he went down in that bathroom. Too much blood in the closet for him to have been moved much."

Maybe Jojo's blood. "She didn't . . . I didn't . . . Jesus, what **happened** there?"

Omid snapped, "How should I know? You think I know everything somehow, because I was there forty minutes longer than you were, while you were with our daughter and I was there with him?"

Laurie raised her hands and then let them drop heavily into her lap. "Take a breath."

Sweat stood out on his forehead and dripped down his jaw. "Don't tell me to breathe. Why wasn't Jojo home?"

"Oh, no. You are **not** going to blame me for this one."

He pushed his toe against a metal cabinet. "I'm not."

"Because I was at work. **You** were scheduled to be at home, but you were at work, too. What about that?"

"I thought she was out with friends this afternoon!"

"She was."

He narrowed his eyes. "Obviously. She was just out with **friends** into the night, then."

Omid's skin looked clammy. He was as scared as she was. She needed to remember that, or she'd stand up and start punching him. Fucking men.

"You don't look good. Sit down." Laurie gestured at the hospital bed, still heaped with the blankets Jojo had left behind.

"I'm fine." But he sat, wiping his face. He breathed heavily, air rasping in and out of his lungs like he'd just gotten back from a run. "I think . . . I feel kind of dizzy."

"Omid?" Alarmed, Laurie stood and lifted his

wrist to take his pulse. His skin was wet and cold, his heartbeat thready. Diaphoresis. Green pallor. Rapid breathing. "Don't move. Don't you dare fucking move."

She pushed her way through and under the curtain, not bothering to find the opening. There was no one visible in the hall, so she ran to the nurses' station.

So many words, all of them pushing out of her, and they got bottled up in her throat. Laurie banged on the top of the counter with her fists, and two nurses jumped.

"Yes?"

"My husband . . ." she finally managed. "I think he's having a heart attack. Bed D."

The taller nurse snapped her fingers at the shorter one. "Get the crash cart." She punched a button on her terminal that sent out a low tone.

In minutes Omid was hooked up to the 12-lead, then given thrombolytics and Plavix. Through all the ministrations of the medical staff, he became more and more furious. "I'm **fine**! It's my daughter you should be worrying about!"

"For the love of God!" Laurie shouted over the doctor's head. "Shut up and breathe!"

"I'm giving you some nitro now," said the doctor. "It might cause a headache, which is a sign it's working."

"But my daughter." Omid's voice was finally lower. "Jojo. I have to be with my daughter."

A doctor who looked too young to vote ran another strip on the 12-lead. "Mr. Ahmadi, you just had a mild myocardial infarction. You were in the right place at the right time, and I'd venture to guess that you'll be fine. But if you don't calm down, we'll give you something to **make** you calm down, you hear me?"

Laurie watched Omid blink.

He met her gaze. With his eyes still locked on hers, Laurie said, "She'll be fine, but she needs you to be okay. That's your only job right now."

They were the right words. Omid nodded at the doctor and rested his head back on the pillow tucked behind his head. He closed his eyes and sucked in a breath. His color was almost normal again.

Laurie sank into the metal chair again and pressed her own hand to her heart.

Jesus.

Her phone pinged with a text from Jojo. **Where are you?**

NINE

JOJO DIDN'T FUCKING get it.

Somehow, while she'd been listening to Gloria chatter, while she'd had that metal up in her junk, while she'd been so terrified she saw spots in front of her eyes, her dad had been almost dying.

The nurses had bustled around, setting him up in his room, and he just kept joking about things. But his voice sounded weak, and his face was in this weird bunched-up position, as if he could convince her it was a smile.

As soon as there was a space next to the bed, Jojo stood as close as she could to him. She took his hand carefully, making sure not to pull on the IV that went into the back of it. "I wish I could get in bed next to you."

"You can't do that." Mom shook her head. "All the IV lines."

God. Of course Jojo wouldn't fit. It was just something to say to Dad. "I know."

"Why are you wearing those sweats?" Her mother's voice was sharp. "Where are your clothes?"

Jojo ignored her and kept facing Dad. "Are you going to be okay?"

Her father pointed to his cheek. "With a kiss I bet I will be."

She kissed his stubble. A beeping started overhead, loud and obnoxious.

"Bed alarm!" said Dad. "You set off the bed alarm!"

"There's a **bed** alarm?"

"Well, it's a kissing alarm. It's when the bed goes sideways, like when you tilt a pinball machine." He had that tone he used with little kids, but Jojo didn't mind.

Mom said seriously, "It's to prevent falls from bed."

Jojo ignored her. "Tell me again you'll be okay."

Her father's face softened, and he squeezed her hand. "I'm going to be fine, peanut. Just fine. How about you?"

Jojo's blood froze. For a few minutes, while watching him get admitted, while trailing behind the gurney as he was moved to a real hospital room, she'd forgotten.

She'd completely **forgotten**—or just managed

to push away—for a few seconds why they were there, why her father had had a heart attack in the first place.

"I'm fine."

His dark eyes, the same ones she saw in the mirror at home, lit up. "Yeah? You're fine?"

"I mean . . ." Yeah. She was okay. Gloria had said she'd find her in a little while, once the ruckus died down. "I'm pretty sure I'm fine."

Her father looked triumphantly at her mother. "Good. See, Laurie? She's fine."

There was a knock at the door, and Gloria poked her head in. "How's it going in here? May I come in?"

Jojo's mother started flapping her hands, ushering her in, as if Gloria had come to the house for a glass of wine. "Of course, of course. Sit down. Do you want some water? I could go look for some, I could find some cups—"

"I'm here to talk to you about the results of the kit." Gloria's face was smooth. Calm. That was a good sign, Jojo knew it was. Everything was fine— in a minute they'd be able to go home and go back to normal. "Is this an okay time? I can come back later if you're still getting settled."

"Now is good," said Dad.

Mom nodded.

Furious birds tried to claw their way out of Jojo's chest.

"Jojo? You ready to talk about this?"

"Yeah. Sure."

"It came back positive for rape."

Jojo's stomach churned, and she wondered if she was going to be sick again.

Kevin wouldn't have. He was kind.

He'd always been so **kind.**

Mom fell. She literally fell down, so that she was suddenly sitting on the floor. Jojo would have felt embarrassed about her mother's reaction, but she was suddenly crying too hard to feel much of anything except this weird pain right in the center of her chest, just where she imagined her heart was. "Are you sure?"

Gloria nodded and held out her hand to Jojo, completely ignoring Mom, still gaping up from the floor like a fish flopped out of its bowl.

Jojo took Gloria's hand. She didn't look at her father. She couldn't. But she heard his breathing, heavy and fast behind her. He said, "Are you sure?"

"I'm afraid so. Jojo, you showed signs of abrading both externally and internally. There's bruising and one small tear quite far up inside your vaginal wall."

A tear? Like a rip in a tarp? She was perforated now?

"It'll heal quickly. In terms of traumatic injury, it's on the low side, though the emotional trauma will make it harder to process. We're going to talk about—"

"Semen?" Dad's voice was guttural.

Jojo wanted to die. Right then, right there.

"No," said Gloria. "No trace."

"Any other evidence?"

Gloria shook her head. "Nothing visible besides the trauma, though the lab will test everything. But Plan B anyway."

Mom used the chair to drag herself up. She said, "Yes! We want that now." She took Jojo's other hand, and Jojo didn't pull away.

"I have to take the abortion pill." It wasn't a question—Jojo stated it to see how the phrase hung in the air. The words were almost solid things, black and viscous.

"That's what some people call it, but all it actually does is prevent a fertilized egg from attaching."

Fertilized egg. Horror crept up Jojo's arms.

"She'll take it," Mom said.

Jojo yanked her hand away from her mother. Of course she would take the pill. But not because her mother told her to. "So what are the next steps?" She was proud of how her voice didn't shake, even though the queasiness was rising again.

Gloria gently released Jojo's other hand and reached for a blue folder and a brown paper bag. "It's all in here. We start with Plan B—take it within the next twenty-four hours. You'll have your next period on time or maybe just a little earlier, and you might bleed a little heavier. Some girls get worse cramps, but not all. Curl up with a heating pad and an Aleve."

Mom huffed a breath. "And then what happens?"

Gloria didn't even glance at her, just kept looking at Jojo. "Counseling. I have a list of therapists in your medical network, and you're also always free to go out of network if you don't mind paying out of pocket. I've put stars next to the ones I think you'll like." She flicked her gaze over Jojo's parents. "That goes for you, too, Mom and Dad. Jojo will benefit from one-on-one counseling on her own, but we also recommend that the whole family get counseling together as well. Jojo, if you're religious, churches can offer strong community, too. Are you . . . ?"

Jojo opened her mouth to say she wasn't religious, but Mom said, "I was raised Catholic, and Omid's Christian, but none of us practice—I guess we're all kind of agnostic, but—"

Gloria interrupted smoothly, "Well, any community you share as a family is great. Do you have any other questions before I leave?"

Jojo shook her head.

Her father said, "Laurie, you should take Jojo home now."

Mom nodded and shook hands with Gloria. "Thank you so much, Gloria. And I agree with Dad, Joshi. You need sleep. Sergeant Montgomery texted—I left my keys in the ignition, so they brought my car here. We can leave."

Jojo shook her head at the babyish endearment—Jojo from Joanna was enough of a nickname—and at the notion that she would just be able to lie down and close her eyes peacefully.

She cleared her throat. "I won't be able to sleep. Maybe . . . Can I have a sleeping pill?" She would need something to knock her out. Not like her mother would have any at home, though. She was the boss of the medicine cabinet and didn't even like using Advil.

But Mom nodded. "Is Ambien too strong for her, Gloria?"

Jojo stared at her mother.

"Not a great idea. The Rohypnol, if that's what it was in her system, has a long half-life. We're running tests to see what it was exactly, but since it could have been any number of drugs, a narcotic alkaloid or a GHB clone, we might not ever figure it out. Best just to try to sleep naturally." She gave a small wave and was gone.

A young cop with acne knocked on the door. "Excuse me, Chief. Ma'am. Jojo. Is this an okay time to get Jojo's statement?"

Dad blinked. "No."

"Okay. Um, then . . . when would be—"

"She needs to sleep first."

"Omid!" Mom looked horrified. So like her. Always wanting to do things just right.

"I'm exhausted, Mom."

Dad nodded. "It'll be fine to wait."

"No." Mom folded her arms. "It won't be. If she doesn't grab what she remembers right now, if she starts to forget . . ."

Anger lit the tops of Jojo's lungs. "I don't remember anything." It wasn't true. Snippets were coming back. The street-medic meeting. Had there been weed? A car ride, she remembered the feel of motion and of light poles flashing past.

Dad closed his eyes as if he were about to go to sleep. A sudden stillness froze all of them as they waited. Mom looked like she wasn't breathing, and even the new cop turned to stone.

Finally Dad said, "More will come back to her. We'll let her sleep on it."

Mom's lips folded tight.

The officer's voice shook. "Sir, with all due respect, it's a 187 case. She was there. We need her statement sooner rather than later."

Jojo's pulse quickened as her breath got tighter. A 187? Why would he say the code for murder? **"Where's Harper?"**

"Honey—"

The worst words in the world came to her then. Her tongue felt thick, and her head felt too light. "Is Harper **dead**? Was she in that closet? Mom? Tell me."

Dad glared at the officer. "She's not giving her

fucking statement tonight, and get the fuck out of my sight if you don't want to be fired this fucking second."

The acne-scarred cop ducked his head like he was bowing and left the room.

"Dad!" Jojo gasped a shallow breath.

Mom took her by the elbow, which was okay because she felt light-headed again. "No, sugar. I told you. It wasn't Harper."

"Harper Cunningham? Why are you talking about her?" Dad's voice was sharp.

"But it was a murder, Mom? He said 187."

Horrifyingly, Mom nodded. "A man. A friend of Kevin's."

"Not Zach." Fear traced its way down Jojo's gullet.

Mom blinked and then looked at Dad.

Dad pushed himself higher in bed. "You know Zachary Gordon?"

Tears started again, like she was a freaking faucet. "Tell me it wasn't him."

Mom's voice was soft. "I'm so sorry, love. It was."

"How?"

Grimacing, Mom said, "His skull was hit with something. We're not sure what yet."

Jojo just shook her head as the rest of the world turned into a blur, a tiny, high-pitched whine.

What had she done?

She had to remember. What had gone wrong?

She had to remember what had happened.

Mom bent so that Dad could whisper in her ear.

Jojo didn't even strain to try to eavesdrop. She didn't want to know anything else.

Nothing else.

TEN

THE FRONT LIGHT at home had burned out last week, and as they drove home to a totally dark house, Laurie cursed herself for not getting around to screwing in a new bulb. It was a cool night for summer, the coastal air pushing inward over the hills, and the house would have cold in its bones when they entered. Laurie wanted desperately to warm Jojo, who was still giving the occasional deep shiver. "Sorry about the porch light—"

"Yeah, I actually know my way around the house where I **live**." Jojo's voice pulsed anger, and she slammed the car door so hard that the frame of the vehicle rattled.

Laurie could take the anger.

She followed behind Jojo, listening to her daughter's thumps as she made her way upstairs. They hadn't talked about her taking a shower, but Laurie heard the water running almost immediately.

By the time she brought a mug of hot cocoa into the bathroom, the room was full of steam.

And her daughter was crying.

"Baby?"

"Go away." The growl came from low down, knee level.

Laurie drew back the shower curtain.

Jojo was in a ball, her knees pulled to her chest, her long dark hair hanging forward. She shivered violently, even though the heat of the water stung Laurie's skin from two feet away.

Laurie got into the tub. Fully dressed, she sat on the floor of the tub next to her daughter and wrapped her arms around her.

"I don't want you!"

Laurie ignored her and slid closer to Jojo under the pounding water.

Jojo said something too muffled to understand and curled, sobbing, into her mother's side.

Laurie split into two pieces.

One piece was with Jojo. All her love went into the meaningless whispers she poured over Jojo as heavily and persistently as the water that beat down on them. **It's okay. It's all okay. It's going to be fine. You're okay. I love you. You're safe.**

The other piece was bright white with blind rage. It was probably just the steam, but she literally couldn't see. Fury spiked icicles up the back of her neck, over her head, and down into her heart.

She'd kill that motherfucker. She'd shred him with her teeth and nails.

Her lips streamed love over Jojo's head while the back part of her brain imagined Leeds's bruised face, his battered body, as he begged for mercy she would never give. Or had it been Zach? That couldn't be—she wouldn't be able to hurt him someday, then.

Jojo pressed farther into her.

Laurie had to call Harper's parents, see if they knew anything. But first Jojo.

A long time later, her daughter's shaking slowed, and then so did her tears.

The water started to cool.

Laurie's anger didn't. It felt like it was just getting started.

She hated to say it, but she didn't want Jojo to get chilled. "We should get out before the hot-water tank is empty."

Jojo nodded. She stood and toweled off. Instead of seeming unself-conscious, which was normal for her, Jojo wrapped the towel tightly around her body. She didn't meet Laurie's eyes, but as she saw the water pouring from Laurie's uniform, she said, "Guess you don't need to do laundry."

"Guess not."

"Harper hasn't texted me back."

"Where do you think she is?"

Her daughter's narrow shoulders shrugged, and her voice was tense. "I don't know. I'm freaking out."

"I'll call her parents in a minute."

Jojo's eyes went wide, then shuttered.

"What?" Laurie thought Jojo was about to speak, but instead she just opened the medicine cabinet.

Jojo rooted around idly—Laurie guessed she might be looking for Aleve—and then she held up the bottle.

"Is ten milligrams a lot?"

"You can't have an Ambien." It had been so stupid to leave it in the medicine cabinet.

"Why do you have sleeping pills, anyway?"

Laurie shrugged. "It's no big deal."

Jojo opened the bottle and fished out a tiny pill. "I could break one in half. Or even in quarters?"

"No."

"You just said it's no big deal."

"No way."

Jojo blinked.

Then she popped it into her mouth and swallowed it whole.

"Jojo! No!" Stubborn. Jojo had always been so **stubborn.**

"Am I going to die from it?"

"No."

"Okay, then. I just want to sleep."

There was a raw despair in her daughter's words

that made Laurie want to howl. "Go to bed. I'll be right there."

In her bedroom she dug Gloria's card out of her purse and sent a text, her fingers shaking.

She took an Ambien. I told her not to but she did it anyway.

The response was almost instant. **She'll be fine.**

But you said with the Rohypnol—

She's going to sleep her face off. Put her on her side just in case she vomits, but she'll be okay.

You're sure?

Sure. Maybe you should take one, too.

No way. She had to be awake, alert.

"Mama?" her daughter called.

"I'll be right there." Laurie didn't want Jojo to be alone for even a minute until she fell asleep, but she'd do her no favors by sitting on her bed like this and soaking it through.

She stripped, dried, and changed into her flannel pajamas, the ones with blue frogs.

Jojo had changed into her matching pair, but Laurie didn't point that out. She was under the covers, only her shoulders sticking out. Her old teddy bear, Randall, who usually lived on the shelf above the bed, was next to her, lying sideways, casually, as if he'd just fallen there.

Laurie sat on the edge of the bed. "How are you doing?"

Jojo's hands were in fists. "I. Don't. Want. To. Talk."

Laurie should ask where Harper was, how she was involved, she should ask how Jojo knew Zachary Gordon, but thirty seconds later Jojo's face was finally relaxing. From experience Laurie knew that an Ambien on an empty stomach took hold in mere minutes. "Okay."

And sure enough Jojo's breathing slowed. Her phone slipped from her hand. Just as Laurie thought she was finally asleep, Jojo lifted heavy eyelids. "Kevin will be so sad."

Laurie could only manage, "Mmm."

"Not sure how I feel . . ."

"That's totally all right."

"Maybe I feel okay."

Laurie pressed her hands to her thighs to keep from moving into the bed with Jojo, from crawling in and wrapping herself around her. Jojo didn't want her right now. She just needed sleep. "Good."

"Maybe I did something wrong." Her words were starting to slur.

"You didn't."

"The ring."

The shoplifted one, the one that had broken apart Jojo and Harper's closeness? "That was a long time ago, sweet pea. Don't you worry about a thing."

"Randall." Jojo poked the teddy bear with lazy fingers. "Randall?"

"What?" When Laurie first got the sleeping pill prescription, she would sometimes hallucinate images and voices right before falling asleep. "I love

you, Joshi. So much. You know that, right, snug-
glebug?"

Jojo slurred, "Aw, stop." Then she turned to her
side, put her hands under her cheek like a child
in an old-fashioned illustration, and gave a sweet,
contented snore.

Laurie held her breath.

She counted to ten. Then a hundred.

Then she reached for Jojo's phone.

ELEVEN

LAURIE SWIPED THE code, and the phone unlocked with a **snick.**

Harper: **He's going to be there tonight.**

Jojo: **Omg.**

Harper: **I know. I can't wait for you to meet him.**

Jojo: **U been hiding him too long.**

Harper: **Because he's delish.**

Jojo: **UR so bad.**

Laurie's breath got caught somewhere in her upper abdomen and stayed there.

Jojo: **What do I need to bring?**

Harper: **They r bringing the stuff.**

Jojo: **Ok. little nervous. We're learning how 2 pack wounds, right?**

Harper: **Don't be a baby, street medics r hotttt.**

Fake wounds. Don't forget your banana. We're going to stab the SHIT outta them.

Jojo: **That 1 street medic w/ the tattoo arms who always has all the answers—I'm going to get him to help me pack my stabbed banana.**

Harper: **No, that one's mine. Hot ass. He can pack MY stabbed banana. ;)**

Jojo: **I will CUT a bitch.**

Harper: **At least I'll know how to pack my own wound after you do.**

Jojo: **xoxoxoxoxbye**

Laurie looked at Jojo, suddenly sure she'd wake and demand her phone back.

Her daughter's breath was even, slow, and deep.

Laurie exited the room, leaving the door slightly ajar. She carried the phone into her bedroom, taking the cooled cocoa with her. The taste of it was too sweet, and it made one of her back molars ache sharply. She welcomed the pain, stretching her jaw into it.

In bed she turned out the lights and went on reading the texts. **Wounds.** Jojo used to say she wanted to be a cop or a paramedic, even though she and Omid had done their best to talk her out of it. Jojo could be **anything,** but emergency services were too hard—too soul-cracking.

So what the fuck were the girls playing at?

She scrolled backward in time on Jojo's phone.

Harper: **R says Kevin is into you.**

Jojo: **No he's not.**

Harper: **How do you know?**

Jojo: **Because I don't like him like that.**

Harper: **But how do u KNOW? U should at least try him out.**

Jojo: **Ew.**

Harper: **Test ride.**

Jojo: **Stop.**

Harper: **U might end up liking it.**

Jojo: **You're the worst.**

Harper: **I like it.**

Jojo: **Whore.**

Harper: **Super slut.**

Jojo: **<3 <3 super slutty whore of a hobag ho <3**

Jojo said she didn't like Kevin like that.

And then he'd . . . God.

He'd fucking raped her little girl and murdered his friend. Or had Zachary Gordon raped Jojo? Was it the last thing he'd done in his life? If so, Laurie was glad he was dead. If so, she hoped he'd died in unbearable pain.

Laurie's chest was so tight that air rasped in her lungs. She took another sip of the cocoa, hoping it would ease. She wanted desperately to take an Ambien herself, but she couldn't. She'd weaned herself off them with difficulty, and if she took one now, she wouldn't trust herself to wake up if Jojo needed her.

Her own phone pinged.

Omid.

She okay?

There was no good answer to that. She shot him a thumbs-up emoji, feeling ridiculous and juvenile as she did so. A fucking thumbs-up.

She's as okay as she can be. How about you? Why aren't you asleep? It's so late.

They keep poking me.

Don't die.

The words left her fingertips and flew to him before she even registered what she'd sent.

Okay, then. Since you put it that way.

I need you.

God, what would she do right now to be able to curl herself into his chest? To be able to hook her leg over his waist, her arms around his back, and hold on?

I need you, too, babe.

Laurie wanted to type, **I'll kill him.**

But she curled her right hand into a ball so tight her wrist got a cramp and then shook it out.

Sleep now, my love. We're fine here. We're safe. Xox

Laurie took a deep breath.

Then she opened Jojo's texts again.

Jojo must have been deleting messages recently, because the earliest string of messages was just eleven days ago. It was obvious that she and Harper had been talking a lot more than people would who had just become friends again.

Harper: **#resist**

Jojo: **#hellsya**

Harper: **R says we have to go to the Mission, there's a march from there to city hall.**

Jojo: **Burritos!**

Harper: **Is that what a resistance fighter says?**

Jojo: **This res. fighter says there's no social activism that can't be improved by burritos.**

Harper: **U have a point. W Oakland BART?**

Jojo: **K. Eta 1 hr.**

Laurie scrolled back in her own phone to see what had been happening that day. It was a Sunday morning. She'd gotten off work at 3:00, and at 10:00 Jojo had brought in the paper and woken her and Omid up. They'd read some of it together—Jojo liked the news section, Omid liked the book-review section, and Laurie liked opinions. Omid had attempted to make lattes, but the milk had turned. Jojo had said she was going into the city to see a movie at the Metreon with Olivia and her mother. She'd even asked if Laurie had wanted to come. Laurie had said no quickly—she actively disliked Olivia's mother and the way she pushed holistic vials upon her every time they were in the same vicinity. No, she didn't want any pulsatilla windflower crap, thank you. Laurie thought maybe she and Omid would stay longer in bed, together (they had, and they'd both napped instead of having sex). Omid had told Jojo, "Don't go to Civic Center, some big protest there today. CapB, I think."

Jojo wasn't stupid.

She hadn't been going to the movies with a woman her mother disliked and would automatically say no to going along with.

She'd been going to the Citizens Against Police Brutality protest.

Goddamn it. They'd talked about this, to death. No matter how much of a bleeding-heart liberal they'd raised—and they had, as both Omid and Laurie leaned further left than many of their co-workers—it wasn't safe. More than that, it wasn't **right,** the daughter of a police chief protesting the policing community. **But, Dad, you're brown, in case you hadn't noticed. That makes me half brown, and** that **counts as full brown. Police are killing black and brown people. Not** you **guys, San Bernal PD is fine. But I want to go stand up for what's right.**

No.

They'd told her no. They let her donate some money to an online CapB fund-raiser, and even that had made Omid sweat a little. **Antifa bullshit,** he'd muttered to Laurie, and she'd shushed him. It was one thing for Jojo to march and protest, but a whole other thing for her to be attracted to the anarchists' left-wing militia. Not that Laurie was totally against antifascists. Someone had to fight the Nazis. Just not her fucking daughter.

What the **hell** was Jojo up to?

And where was Harper?

Laurie pushed the covers back and stood, all tiredness gone. She thrust her feet into her leather-soled slippers. One more check on Jojo—who was still breathing deeply and evenly—and then she went downstairs to call Harper's parents.

TWELVE

THE PHONE RANG in Laurie's ear, unanswered. It was the Cunninghams' house line, and she knew that it rang in their bedroom as well as in the kitchen, both living rooms, and the great room. Even though it was just a few houses away, the Cunninghams' home was huge, almost three times larger than their own. Laurie and Omid's house was nice—nothing that special, but it had the same big lot, and they'd upgraded their kitchen and bathrooms four years before. Their new entryway tile was less than a year old. The Cunninghams' house, on the other hand, was always newly perfect, always being expanded and enhanced. Instead of adding new bathrooms, they added new wings. When they'd been so close, years before, Laurie had teased Pamela about her constant renovations and the smooth way she always pulled them off. The house could be full of workers making a bedroom closet into a new walk-in Finnish sauna, and Pamela would manage to hide the dirt and noise. If one area was under construction, they'd entertain in the other wing. The grandness of their lives and of their house had intimidated Laurie for years. Then she'd gotten used to it, asking Pamela to drive when they went for lunch so she could sink deep into the heated leather seats and smell the new-Mercedes scent.

Laurie gave up letting their house phone ring and dialed Pamela's cell phone as she poured herself a glass of wine she wasn't sure she wanted to drink.

Pamela mumbled, "Holy shit. Laurie? What's wrong?"

From the background she could hear Andy's surprised voice. "**Laurie?** What's going on?"

Leaving the glass behind, Laurie walked into the living room. She pushed the phone so hard against her head that it hurt. "It's me. Do you know where Harper is?"

"Is Jojo okay?"

Laurie couldn't answer that without getting dragged down into tears, a thing she would **not** do right now. "Can I talk to Harper? Can you get her for me?"

Pamela cleared her throat. "She's sleeping. What's up?" Her voice was cool.

The past didn't matter anymore. Nothing

mattered but Jojo. "Something happened to my daughter."

"What? What happened?"

"She's okay. But she was—" Laurie choked, unable to say the word. Not yet. "She was out with Harper, I guess, and she doesn't remember the whole night. I'm just wondering if Harper can fill in any of the blanks."

"Harper wasn't out with Jojo."

Laurie shook her head. "No, they're friends again. I know, I'm as surprised as you are. But I saw the texts. They've been hanging out for at least a few weeks, probably more."

"Oh, yeah. We knew **that.**"

"You did?" A spasm shot down Laurie's back, and she lowered herself slowly into the couch.

"Of course. She's been eating here at least once a week for a few months now." Pamela had her smiling voice on now. "I've been deep in a Thai cooking phase, and we've been working on getting her heat tolerance up."

Jojo hated spicy food, always had. "I didn't know." Betrayal hung thick in the back of her throat.

"But Harper wasn't out with her tonight. She's upstairs asleep."

Laurie's fingertips were icy, though the room felt warm enough. "Are you sure?"

"She was running a fever. Poor thing, she went to bed this afternoon and just passed out. I checked on her twice, and she hasn't moved all night."

"You're sure."

"Completely."

"Because Jojo says that they were together."

"Could she have just said the wrong name? Maybe she was with Jessie? Or Olivia?"

There was only one Harper Cunningham. "No."

A million times in her career, Laurie had called parents to come pick up their kids from whatever trouble they'd been caught getting into. **Can you come get Joey? We just caught him with a group of kids smoking weed by the railroad tracks.** A million times parents had sworn up and down that it couldn't be their kid—their kid was asleep upstairs. **Joey doesn't smoke marijuana. Joey's in bed.** They'd seen their children get into bed hours before—therefore they were still there.

They never were.

Laurie pushed harder. "Can you check?"

Pamela sighed loudly. "Andy, can you go check on Harper?"

Laurie heard Andy groan. "This is ridiculous. She's sick. She's in bed." Andy was Harper's stepfather, but he'd been around since she was four or five. CEO of a car-warranty company, he wasn't the warmest guy in the world, but Laurie had always thought Pamela made up for any lack. Harper and Pamela had a relationship that Laurie had been jealous of sometimes. Even at fourteen Harper had let Pamela hold her hand and braid her hair in public.

Jojo had stopped letting Laurie touch her in public by twelve. At the same time, Pamela had a more hands-off policy of mothering—she let Harper do her own thing, trusting her daughter to get stuff right on her own. Laurie, conversely, meddled too much, too often, according to both Jojo and Omid.

"So Jojo's okay now?" Pamela's voice was pitched low and soothing.

It was so irritating that her voice could make Laurie feel better, as if no time had passed. Laurie had missed her. Pamela had been a friend, and then she'd just been **gone.** "Jojo was raped."

"Fuck!" The exclamation was guttural.

It was small and sick, but Laurie took one half second of satisfaction from the sound. The feeling was gone almost instantly, replaced by shame. "Yeah."

"Is Omid with her now?"

"No, he's—"

Laurie heard a pounding and then heard Andy yell, "She's not there!" His voice was clear over the line. "She's gone! She bunched up the covers to make it look like she was in there. I thought you said you checked on her!"

"I did! I looked in twice!"

"You didn't think to look **under** the covers?"

"I didn't want to wake her!"

"Jesus, Pamela!"

"You could have checked on her, too. Don't

blame **me** for this." To Laurie she said, "I have to call her. Can you come over?"

"I can't leave Jojo. Come here if Harper doesn't answer." **Shit.** "Bring her here if you find her."

The sound of Pamela's voice was thin. "What . . . what if the same thing happened to her?"

Laurie dug her fingers into her thigh. "Where could she be? Her boyfriend's house?"

"She doesn't have a boyfriend!" roared Andy from the background—Pamela must have put her on speakerphone.

Pamela said, "She does."

"What? The fuck! What is going on in my house?"

Laurie said, "Call her. If she's not in the house, leave her a note and come over." Pamela disconnected without saying good-bye, and Laurie let the phone drop next to her on the sofa. She wanted the wine she'd left in the kitchen, but she felt too heavy to move. Tiredness wasn't an affordable luxury. She stared wide-eyed at the grandfather clock in the hallway until the front door shook with a thump. Then, belatedly, a knock.

She opened the door, and the couple tumbled in as if they'd been leaning against the wood. Andy's face was thinner than it had been two years ago. He wore black boxers and a deep blue T-shirt. His feet were bare, and his masses of black hair stood upright. His stubble was thick, some of it gray now. "You're the cop. How do we do this? Do we file a missing-persons report? Do we have to give it forty-eight hours, or is that just TV?"

"That's just TV, and we don't know she's missing yet." **And I'm not a cop.** "Pamela, she's not answering her phone?"

Pamela wore an open blue robe over a light red peignoir and didn't seem self-conscious at all that her nipples were visible through the sheer fabric. She shook her head, her frightened eyes meeting Laurie's. A mother's look, a terrified one. **Don't let what happened to your daughter happen to mine.**

"Can you call him? The boyfriend?"

Pamela bit her bottom lip and then said, "I don't have his phone number."

Andy rounded on her. "Our sixteen-year-old is dating a boy, and you don't know his number?" He towered over her—had he always done that? Laurie hadn't remembered him as being so tall.

"I don't even know his full name." Pamela's teeth were gritted. "And before you say one goddamned word about that, **you** try talking to her. She won't share a single fucking thing, you know that."

"What do you know about him?" Laurie's heart beat so hard in her chest that it seemed to shake her back and forth. "In the texts they sent to each other, Harper called him R."

"Ray." Pamela dropped into the couch, thumping her big red purse down next to her. "That's what she told me his name was. Ray."

That wasn't enough to help them find him. "No last name?"

Pamela shook her head.

Damn it. "What about her cell phone?"

Pamela held out her own, as if proving that she had one. "I'm trying! There's no answer!"

"Do you have tracking on it?" Laurie sat next to her.

"Shit. I **do**." Pamela dove into her bag and pulled out an iPad. Her negligee rose high on her thighs.

Pamela struck at the screen. "Hang on."

Andy sat on the side Laurie wasn't already occupying. Laurie could smell them both—the scent of their bed, Pamela's gardenia lotion.

"Okay." Pamela pointed at the map on the screen. "There's nothing showing now. No blue dot. Just a history. Oh, God, what does that mean?"

"Can you go back in time on it?"

Pamela nodded and clicked. "She was here at seven o'clock. What is that, downtown Oakland?"

"What the **hell** would she be doing in Oakland? We have to call 911—"

Laurie agreed, unless they could use the tracking to find her **now**. "We'll call them in a second if we can't figure this out. Keep rolling the time forward." Her fingers itched to wrest the tablet from Pamela's hands, to run away with it, to do the research herself: better, faster. "Where next?"

"At seven thirty, she's still there. Wait, here, at eight fifteen it moves. To . . . Wait. It looks like she was coming home." Pamela's gaze rose to her husband's. "Are you **sure** she wasn't in the bed?"

Andy glared and jabbed at the screen. "Keep looking."

Pamela did, apparently trusting Andy enough not to check the bed. Laurie wouldn't have been able to do the same thing with Omid. If their roles were reversed, Laurie would have raced upstairs and torn Jojo's bedroom apart, just in case she was hiding under the bed the way she used to do during thunderstorms.

"But then she doesn't come home. Look." Pamela touched the screen, rubbing the dot as if she could conjure her daughter from a lamp. "The signal stops here. In town. It's showing that it died, or she turned it off. Old Coast, right? Who do we know there?"

Even before she leaned in, Laurie knew where the dot had stopped. "Do you know Kevin Leeds?"

Pamela looked blank, shaking her head. "It sounds familiar. But I can't—"

"The **football** player?" Andy was up again, dancing on the balls of his feet as if he were getting ready to box someone.

Pamela shook her head. "She's not on cheer this year."

Andy stared at Pamela. "He's **pro.** Oakland. Jesus, do you not listen to me at all when I talk about sports?"

"Of course not," snapped Pamela. "What the

hell would our daughter be doing at a pro football player's house?"

"He's the un-American one. With the upside-down flag," Andy said.

"But—"

Laurie said, "We found Jojo at his house."

Andy's neck went red, followed by his face. "Fuck. Where is he now?"

"He's at the PD—"

"Then we go there." Andy pivoted and punched the back of an armchair with his closed fist. The chair skidded on the rug. "And we **make** him tell us where she is."

Pamela stood and strode toward the door as if she were ready to leave now, barefoot and in her nightclothes. "Let's go."

"You won't be able to talk to him."

Pamela stopped, rounding on Laurie as she stood up from the couch. "But you can. We'll go with you there."

Then a siren sounded, a shriek so loud that Laurie felt like she should recognize it, but it took her a moment—the fire alarm.

The acrid scent of something burning rolled into the room.

"Jojo."

Laurie raced for the stairs, taking them two at a time.

THIRTEEN

JOJO HAD NO freaking idea what was going on.

A banshee had crawled into her brain and dug its claws into her ears. The noise wailed and yowled and crawled up and down her spine.

She didn't even know how she'd gotten onto the floor of her bedroom—one minute she'd been blessedly unconscious, and the next she was using a glass of water to put out a small fire on her desk. She'd been dreaming of lighting incense. . . . Shit, the fire alarm set off strobes and Dad's ire every time he cooked burgers on the stove top. He was going to be pissed.

But the fire on her desk was out. A lighter sat next to a box of incense and a Kleenex box. One soggy and blackened tissue seemed to be the only damage. With a blurt of sharpened noise, the fire alarm finally shut up. Good, she could go back to bed. . . .

Then, from behind, someone grabbed her. Jojo folded forward with a scream and came up fighting, the way her father had taught her to do. Fight like a cat in a bag. **Fight.**

Or at least she tried, but her movements were sloppy and slow, as if she were moving through pudding.

Mom shouted as Jojo's fist got close to connecting with her cheek. "It's me! Jojo, it's me. Jojo!"

Jojo fell sideways on her rug, the smell of char still thick in her nose. "Mom. Mommy." Her words weren't working right, either. God, she was dizzy. Behind her mother stood the Cunninghams. Andy rushed at the desk and tried to slap away the smoke. He opened a window and waved his arms.

Jojo struggled to disguise her laugh but failed. It came out like a cough-snort. She pointed at Pamela. "Oh, my God, Mom, I would **die** if you ever wore something like that out of the house." Embarrassment filled her a second too late, just after the words had left her mouth. "Sorry, Pamela. Your tits look **really** good in that, though." It was getting worse. She rolled herself up into a ball on the floor, letting her mother pull her sideways into an awkward embrace.

"She's on drugs! She's fucking high as a kite!"

Jojo peeked, and Andy's face was a grimace of fury. "Where's our daughter?"

"Kite," she mumbled up at her mother. Her mouth still felt like it was on crooked. She smashed her hand against her lips, trying to push them back into place.

"Where's our **daughter**?" Harper's father leaned so far over into her face that Jojo could have booped him on the nose.

So she did. One finger to the tip of his snoot. "Boop." She giggled. "Andy boop."

Why did she feel so cheerful? Jojo knew there was something she was supposed to be remembering, something terrible and awful, but mostly she was just amused at the fact that now she knew what Pamela slept in, and it was like something from a nineties sitcom except sleazy. Harper had worn something like it to school recently, with a black bra underneath. Oh, dang, was it the same piece of clothing?

Harper had looked like candy in it. Mouth-watering.

"Did you start a **fire**?" Her mother's voice was hoarse.

Shit! Had Jojo started it, as well as putting it out? What did that mean for her firefighting skills? She'd basically given up the dream of being a detective—too much corruption—but if she could put out a fire in her sleep, did it matter if she was the one who'd started it? Her thoughts got woozy again.

It had felt like a dream.

She'd been raped.

Was that a dream, too?

Of course it was. Please.

Please let that be a dream.

Jojo sucked in a breath and felt the bottoms of her feet tingle. "Oh, no. Mom." Images rushed back in. She and Mom on the floor of the shower. Dad holding her in Kevin's house.

Kevin's face.

Zach Gordon. Was he really dead?

Harper—

"Where is my daughter?" Pamela's voice was a metallic screech.

"Hang on!" Mom whisper-shouted, even though Jojo was obviously awake. Why was she using that voice?

Mom tucked her up in bed under the blanket Gramma had made her right before she died. Andy whispered fiercely to Pamela in Jojo's doorway.

Mom's face looked like she'd worked an eighteen-hour shift, that sunk-down, eyes-shuttered look. "Honey, I know your memory is rough at the edges, but do you have any idea where Harper might be now? She was at that house with you, right?"

"How do you know?" Jojo's eyelids were so heavy. Words didn't feel right, not strong enough. **She** wasn't strong enough. "I don't remember."

"Harper's phone." Mom pointed at Pamela, who approached the bed on the other side from Mom. "We looked at the history."

"Dunno." She giggled at the sliding slur in her voice. "Dunno!"

"What is she **on**?" Andy's shout made Jojo jump. She looked down and then back up. "Bed."

Mom hissed, "She was **roofied**. Rohypnol? You may have heard about it on the news, you asshole."

Jojo suddenly remembered. Oh, it felt good to remember something! "And Ambien! Dude, this shit is better than weed!"

"Jojo?" Pamela stroked the back of Jojo's hand too rapidly, the strokes turning into pats. "Where's our daughter?"

Her stomach twisted. **Harper.** "I'm tired."

Mom smiled, finally, her eyes crinkling at the edges. "I bet you are, sweet Joshi."

Jojo suddenly felt very small, as if she'd been plucked out of her grown-up body and shoved back into a toddler one. She touched the crease between her mother's eyebrows. "Really tired . . ." She wasn't sure if she'd finished the sentence, but Mom seemed to know what she was getting at and tipped her onto her side, tucking the blanket higher at her neck.

"Sleep, sweet girl."

"Okay." It sounded like a good idea. Her mother's face looked funny, as if it were carved from something soft and rich. "You're the ice cream. I'm the cone."

Mom always said, **I'm the vanilla ice cream.**

Daddy's the caramel. You're the cone. When she was little, Jojo had liked it, but when she was older, she'd hated it. **Don't compare people's skin tones to food. It's racist and clichéd.** Mom had looked shocked the first time she'd said it. But now the analogy seemed right, except she kind of felt more like Dad's caramel. Mom's skin **was** ice cream, but Jojo's insides felt soft and sweet, rich and thick, not cone-brittle. Maybe she could explain that to Mom. . . .

Then Jojo closed her eyes, and the world went beautifully dark again.

FOURTEEN

"Is she okay?" Pamela leaned forward, touching Jojo's cheek.

Laurie wanted to slap away her hand.

"She's fine. She shouldn't have taken the sleeping pill, but the advocate said it was fine. She'll just sleep." And maybe wake up and eat. Twice after taking Ambien, Laurie had awakened to find herself on the couch, an empty box of unremembered Oreos next to her. "She probably won't even remember this. Come downstairs. We can talk there."

In the living room, Andy bobbed on his bare feet. "Why haven't we called 911 yet?"

Pamela pointed at Laurie. "She **is** 911. Where the hell is my daughter?" Her voice broke.

Andy was right—Laurie should already have called work. "We'll find her. Jesus, we have to tell the department, though. ID techs are at Kevin Leeds's house right now. They'll be gathering evidence, but they don't know to look for Harper yet."

Andy's hands fumbled at his phone. "I'll call. I'll call." He looked up at them. "What do I say?"

Pamela's eyes were platter-size. "Tell them to **find** her!" She whirled on Laurie. "You knew? You knew she might be missing, but you didn't call them first? You let us walk all the way over to your house—what is **wrong** with you? You're supposed to be the expert!"

Laurie stepped toward Andy, her hand out. "Give me your phone."

Bettina answered on the second ring. "Bettina, it's Laurie. Look, we have another situation. Jojo was with a friend tonight, and we can't find the other girl." She gave the Cunninghams' address and then said, "But they're at my house now. Meet us here first. We haven't fully checked their whole house, and we'll need a couple of guys to help with that. Name, Harper Cunningham. White female, sixteen years old. About five foot six. Blond hair, green eyes. Last seen wearing—" She looked at Pamela.

Pamela's voice shook. "I don't know. She was wearing a black tank and black shorts when she went to bed, but I don't know that she would have gone out in them."

"Maybe black tank and shorts, unconfirmed."

Pressing her hands together as if she could stop them from shaking, Pamela stepped forward. "Take me to the station. I have to tell all of them. What to look for." She gasped. "How to find—"

Laurie said, "Hang on a sec, Bettina. Pamela, they'll come to us."

"No. **Take me there.**" Pamela looked as if she were about to freak the fuck out and not be able to bring it back in. "Take me there **now,** goddamn it."

"I told Jojo I wouldn't go anywhere." But it struck her—if Laurie were in the station, she could go to dispatch and run Kevin Leeds through the system. She could comb through his known contacts, if he had any. She could start to push the buttons she knew how to push and dig the way she did best.

In her ear Bettina said, "Laurie? Are you coming in with her? Does she know about the 187?"

God, she had to tell them. "Send them to my house, and we'll go from there." She disconnected and handed the phone back to Andy, who was nodding hard, as if in silent agreement, as if she'd done it right.

"Look," Laurie said. "Both of you, sit down for a minute, okay?"

"I will **not** sit. Are you fucking kidding me?" Pamela's voice was on the far side of a shriek.

"I have to tell you something." Laurie stuck her hands in the pockets of her pajama top. It would be better coming from her, rather than a uniform. "A man was killed in the house where Jojo was found. A friend of Leeds."

"Jesus **Christ.**" A vein throbbed in Andy's forehead.

Pamela said, "But Harper wasn't there. Right? You didn't find her there. Has she been taken? Kidnapped? Is that what you're trying to tell me?"

Laurie didn't know **what** to tell her. "Maybe she's just gone away with her boyfriend?"

Andy shouted, "Every single damn minute we stand here **talking** is another minute we're not looking for her!"

"She wouldn't go away without telling us," Pamela insisted. "We **talked.** After that last time she ran away, we really **talked.**" She lurched forward. "We need to make the report. Now."

"Yes, but—"

"We go, then. We go now."

"I have to stay with Jojo." She'd promised.

"No." Pamela shook her head desperately. "We go. We tell them about Harper so they can look. You're slowing that **down.** We go. Together. You can make them work harder. You know them. You can get into the system, right? Do something with the computers? Whatever it is you do?"

It almost hurt, the feeling in Laurie's fingertips. She was the best at digging things up in RMS, the in-house records management system. Everyone knew it. The new cops came to her with questions about how she made the connections she did in the back end of the computer, and old cops just relied on her to help them as she always had.

Andy moved to the couch and sat at the end of it. He put his palms firmly on top of his thighs. "You two go. I'll stay here. No one comes in or out. I'll stay right **here.**"

"I'm not leaving her." Not alone with Andy. She trusted him—she did—but she couldn't leave Jojo with a man who wasn't her father, not so soon after what had just happened. "But if you stayed, too, Pamela, then I could go do some investigation." She could go to work and dig deep. She could find Harper.

Pamela shook her head. "It'll be faster for me to go with you."

"The officers assigned to the case are already on the way over here. If you come with me, then they'll have to get the info from you both separately. It'll take longer." This was true. "They'll take your statements from you here and get all the info they need. I'll be back as soon as I can." Was this fair? To leave Jojo with them after she'd said she wouldn't leave her? But if she was at work, she could **do** something instead of simply sitting here doing nothing but waiting for Jojo to wake up.

"**Your** daughter is safe," Pamela spat accusingly, as if Laurie were the reason Harper wasn't safe. "Your daughter's here. **Go find Harper.**"

"I'll be back as soon as I can." **I promised her. She's too small.** But Jojo was sixteen. Old enough to understand a broken promise.

LAURIE drove fast, her grip painful on the wheel. The streets were mostly empty, and she could auto-pilot her way to the station, her other home.

Goddamn Harper Cunningham.

The arrest. The ring.

Jojo and Harper had been best friends since they'd met at age four. Friday nights they slept at the Ahmadis' house, giving the Cunninghams a date night, and they reversed it for Saturday nights. Sometimes the girls had pretended to be twins, insisting on wearing matching clothes. The parents had laughed together. One light girl, one darker girl, both wearing matching Lululemon shirts and tights.

Harper got whatever she wanted from her parents, whereas Laurie, the one who did the budget, had to be more careful about their spending on Jojo. Together she and Omid brought in a good living. She routinely broke six figures with over-time, and Omid had made more than a hundred and seventy thousand a year as soon as he hit lieu-tenant rank. That didn't compare, though, to the money the Cunninghams made.

Somehow it hadn't seemed to matter in the girls' friendship. Harper shared her Pinkberry card with Jojo, and they split huge frozen yogurts every day after school. Jojo taught Harper how to make pot holders with yarn. They were always laughing, in a pitch that sometimes made Laurie's head ache.

Then, at fourteen, Harper and Jojo had stolen a diamond ring from a jewelry shop.

Of all things.

Most girls stole stuff like barrettes. Laurie herself had made a habit of stealing stickers at their age. Pens. Gum. SweeTarts.

Petty theft.

Grand theft was anything over nine hundred and fifty dollars in California, and it was a felony. The ring had been priced at five thousand two hundred dollars. They'd gone in together, talking to the store owner about buying a friendship ring that they'd share, one girl one day, the other girl the next. To be honest, it was the kind of thing they **would** do. Harper once talked her father into buying them a helicopter ride on the Fourth of July, just because she wanted it. She was the kind of girl who would easily have been able to convince her parents to buy her best friend a shared diamond ring.

But they'd stolen it. They'd tried on many rings, admiring them in the mirrors and on each other. It never would have worked in Oakland, or in San Francisco. The owner wouldn't have let them try anything on without parental supervision. But San Bernal was the kind of place two girls could walk into the jewelry store and expect good service. Rich parents were implied in San Bernal, parents who could make or break a store's reputation on Yelp if their children were disrespected.

So the owner, the moron, had let the girls try on all the rings. When they left, a ring was gone.

The owner called the cops.

The cop who showed up looked at the security footage and recognized Jojo. He called Omid, who had the school resource officer, Darren Dixon, yank both girls out of class. Then Omid himself had driven to the school, siren blaring, lights blazing.

There, in the hallway surrounded by bright pink-and-blue posters for the spring dance, Omid himself arrested both girls. He told Laurie it was one of the worst moments of his life, watching his daughter cry in front of the principal. Harper hadn't cried at all, he'd said. She just stood there, her chin tilted up, the ring held tightly in her palm. She hadn't given it up until Jojo told her to, and then she'd thrown it on the floor. It skittered across the tiles and under a locker, Omid said. He'd been furious and embarrassed and had made Darren Dixon reach under the locker to pull it out.

The girls were put in jail. Really, truly in jail. Laurie had been so angry at her daughter that she'd just stood in front of the cell door and stared through the glass. Jojo's head was bowed, but her foot had tapped impatiently, as if she were just waiting for it to be over.

The Cunninghams had been equally livid when they came to get Harper out, but not at the girls.

Pamela, her face red, had stuck a perfectly manicured finger in Omid's chest. "You should have just written them a ticket. We would have paid the fine, whatever it was. You shouldn't have put her in there. With actual criminals! What about germs? Bugs? How do we know she's coming out of there clean?"

Clean? Harper was the one who'd stolen the ring. It had been found on her person, not Jojo's. It was all Harper's idea—Laurie knew it.

The girls had been cited, fingerprinted, then released to their parents after less than three hours inside the PD. Harper had told Jojo to fuck off. Jojo had said it back, and then she cried the whole way home. She'd blamed the tears on being upset that she wouldn't be able to be a police detective with something like this on her record, but they all knew a juvenile record didn't matter. (Not that Laurie wouldn't have jumped at the chance of preventing her daughter from going into emergency services. Since Jojo was little, she'd wanted to be first a cop, then an EMT, then a DA, then a cop again.) No, the tears were because Jojo was completely brokenhearted over losing Harper, plain and simple.

The friendship between the families was over, even though the store ended up dropping the charges. Harper's parents were furious at Omid, and Jojo had tearfully told Laurie that Harper turned away from her at school when they saw each other in the halls. Jojo hadn't gotten over it easily, crying herself to sleep at night for weeks.

And as far as Laurie and Omid knew, the girls had stayed apart for the last two years. How stupid they'd been. How long had the girls **actually** been mad at each other? A year? A few months? Less?

Laurie swung into Omid's parking spot. She didn't have her badge on her, so she used the code— 5150—to open the glass front door. It wouldn't unlock automatically to the public until eight, and it was only six now. Light was just starting to show over the sycamores on the east side of the parking lot, and no one was behind the front desk. She punched in the code at the interior door, and then she was through and into the station itself.

The rookie, Dyer, was at the sergeant's desk writing paper, even though he was approximately a million years and forty IQ points from making sergeant. He sprang to his feet. "Laurie!"

"Where's Colson?" Lieutenant Mark Colson was the midnight watch commander, and a close friend. He'd been at the scene, but Laurie hadn't spoken to him.

"I . . . I think he's in the break room."

Hurry. "Who's lead officer on this?"

Dyer blinked. "Um . . ."

"Do you not **know**?"

Dyer's face fell, and Laurie felt a pang of remorse that lasted less than a heartbeat. He was going to have to toughen up. "I think it's Steiner?"

"And where's—Never mind. I'll find them."

Colson and Steiner were both in the break room, which was a room more for working and drinking coffee than it was for eating. The refrigerator always smelled sour, and the overhead fluorescent lights pulsed, out of sync.

Colson stood. "Laurie! What an awful night. How is she? How's Omid?" He hugged her, his body rigid under the vest. His clothes smelled like Omid's, like dry-cleaning fluid and deodorant. He was a good cop, one of the best on the force. He and Laurie had started at about the same time, and they'd worked beat four together for a few months. They'd dated for a short time, before Laurie fell for Omid. He was leaner now than he had been then—he'd lost the heavy ropes of muscle in his arms and legs that he'd worked so hard to build up for the first ten years of his career. Now he cared more about bicycling and energy smoothies.

She didn't answer his question about Omid. "Mark, we have a new problem. There's a girl missing, Jojo's best friend."

Colson nodded. "Dispatch told me. But wait, Bettina sent Jones to take a statement from the parents at **your** house, right?"

"I want to do some digging."

"Wait, so who's at your house? You left the parents of the other girl with Jojo?"

Laurie nodded.

"And you trust them?"

Her stomach jumped. Of course she did. "My gut says they're not involved in any of this." What if her gut was wrong, though? What if she'd just left her daughter with . . . ? No. "I trust them."

"Good enough for me. You'll be downstairs?"

Laurie nodded with a firmness that was forced. He could shut her down right now and send her home. That's what Omid would do. No part of this was her investigation. She was just a dispatcher, for God's sake.

But Colson said, "Okay. I'll keep you posted, and you do the same."

So she moved fast.

She took the short staircase two steps at a time, racing around the trash can that the janitor always left right in the middle of the hallway. She slammed into the dispatch center.

Yes, she needed to dig through the database. But there was something even more important to do in dispatch.

Her co-workers said words to her, but she didn't hear them.

The cameras—she needed to look at the cameras, the ones in the jail.

Laurie needed to see the man who might have hurt her child.

FIFTEEN

"I'VE BEEN WATCHING him," said Shonda. The computers were above her terminal, and she scooted left so Laurie could lean in closer. "He doesn't move much."

It was hard to see much from the small black-and-white image—Leeds was just a blanketed hump on the cot. Laurie sucked in a breath and closed her eyes. She backed up and turned around.

Then she spun again, examining his form. She tried to memorize his position. If by some method she could be spirited into his cell, she'd know where to punch, to stab.

Fuck. She'd thought seeing him would help her deal, but it didn't.

So she sat at the spare terminal and logged in.

"What are you doing here?" Dina was the kind

of person who liked rules and who liked sharing with admin when someone else didn't.

"Nothing."

"Laurie?"

So she looked up. "I'm just pulling RMS on him. Okay?" Their records management system was open. There was nothing **strictly** confidential about checking the database. Unlike running state and federal checks on people without a good reason, which was prohibited by law, anyone who worked at the police department could poke around inside the local system.

Dina blinked. "Should you?"

Laurie didn't break her gaze. "My daughter was raped." The word sent a small shock wave through the room. They already knew, of course, but Laurie would lay a million dollars that the word hadn't been said out loud yet. Not in here. They would have walked around it, softening the phrase into an acceptable euphemism. **Sexually assaulted. A 261. Gathering evidence.**

No one better have **dared** to ask whether it was a good one. (She knew they had. Goddamn them.)

The 6:00 A.M. changing of the night-to-morning crew had already begun. Maury had taken Rita's seat, and Dina was packing up her things—she always took the longest to leave in the morning. Charity was in the tiny break room, sticking her food into the fridge.

Maury flapped a hand in her direction. "Don't

be idiots, you guys. Let her look." That was his way of telling her he cared.

Laurie pulled up the system. **Kevin Leeds.** There were six listed, but only one with the right address.

Black male, twenty-two years old. Six foot two. Two hundred forty-six pounds. He'd been contacted a year before as a witness in a car accident.

Laurie's breathing was tight in her lungs, and the room was almost silent. The phones didn't ring. The new crew would usually be chattering the usual daily inanities: how tired they were, how they couldn't wait for their weekend, where they'd order lunch from. Instead they were silent. Creepily so.

But it was better than watching them try to act like nothing was wrong, like the sky hadn't fallen in and the earth collapsed.

She scrolled further down. Three years before, when he was nineteen, Kevin had been cited for public intoxication. He hadn't been arrested. She checked the names of the people he was with that night and didn't find anything interesting.

Where the **hell** was Harper Cunningham?

There were still avenues to go down, lines to throw out and pull in, but instead of going deeper into the system, Laurie shut down her terminal.

She didn't look into Shonda's pod, didn't let her eyes stray back to the box that held the creature who'd hurt her daughter.

Maury stood. "Whatcha doing now?" He looked

nervous, as if he knew she was up to something but didn't quite want to know what that was.

"Leaving."

"How's Omid doing?"

"Also fine." He'd better be. She couldn't do this without him.

"Laurie, for fuck's sake. This is awful. Sit down. Let us get you some breakfast. We'll have Ruby go for us."

She tried to smile at him, but it felt crooked. "Ruby hates running for food."

"Yeah, well, parking enforcement has wheels and they get to see the sun. We don't."

Small talk. They were trying to fit her back in, and Laurie wanted to give in to the tidal pull of complaints that didn't matter and stories that were old news. She wanted to complain about the K-cups and be bored by what her co-workers said to her for the bazillionth time. She wanted to bore them right back. She wanted to sit and tell a Jojo story that they'd heard so often they could probably tell it as well as she did (the night Jojo fell down the stairs and lost a tooth, the time Jojo head-butted a boy in preschool for calling her skin color poop brown). The eternal co-worker small talk was familiar and comfortable.

She couldn't stay, though. Just like when Laurie was a kid, there was safety nowhere—unless she held her finger in the hole in the dike, the sea would sweep them all away. So she had to **make** it safe.

But there was still one more thing to do before she raced home to Jojo.

She waved a half-assed good-bye and went upstairs. She walked down the hall and turned right.

Then she let herself into the jail.

"No," said Sarah Knight. "No fucking way."

SIXTEEN

"COME ON." THE video screens were bigger in the jail, in color, and higher resolution. Laurie strained to look at them over Sarah's shoulder.

The shape of Leeds was a dark shadow against the pale wall. He was still under the thin blanket that was obviously too short for a man his size. His bare feet were off the end of the bed. His back was to the camera, and she couldn't see his face.

Laurie had thought she'd felt anger before.

She hadn't, though, not like this. Her forehead ached with the heat of it, and her fingers trembled.

"I love you. You know that. But get out." Sarah narrowed her eyes.

"No," said Laurie.

"Omid will fire me." Sarah had been in charge

of the small San Bernal jail for more than ten years now. She ran a tight ship. Before she'd started, there'd been a jail scandal in which a local drunken wiseass was locked up without being arrested as a kind of joke, and then he'd been forgotten. That was before they had cameras in the cells, before they cleared them every night no matter **who** they thought they were holding. The man had stayed almost four days in the soundproof cell with nothing more than tap water to sustain him. The lawsuit was enormous and deserved, and now whenever that guy saw an officer in town, he flicked a balled-up dollar bill toward the cop. Sarah had lateraled from the Oakland jail, and she always said there was nothing more soothing than San Bernal wannabe assholes. She had a wife named Georgia and a dog named Shackle that Jojo loved. Sarah was blond and small and pretty and constantly underestimated.

And even though she was Laurie's closest friend at the department, for a minute Laurie thought about knocking her down and steamrolling right over her. Instead she shook her head vehemently. "He won't fire you. Omid adores you."

"You can't go in."

Laurie held her arms out. "I'm already in." She did a quick twirl. "I'm in the jail because I let myself in. Not your fault. Now, pay no attention to me. Pretend I'm not here."

"You're not getting to his cell." Sarah crossed her arms over her chest. Bob Ringon eased himself out from behind his desk. Sarah shook her head at him.

"I just want to look through his cell window."

"No."

"Please?"

"No way."

"I'm not asking to **talk** to him. Just to look at him."

"I know." Sarah leaned her hip against the watercooler. She seemed relaxed. And from hundreds of hours of idly watching the jail cameras, Laurie knew she could go from relaxed to sprung in a split second. If Laurie ran for the door that separated intake from the cells, Sarah would have her on the floor before she took two full steps.

"You can see him fine from here, my friend. On this big ol' camera right here."

"He hurt my daughter."

Again Sarah said, "Honey, you don't know that yet for sure. None of us do."

Laurie put her hands together in front of her chest, prayer position. "I promise I won't kill him."

"Out of respect to you as a close friend, I'll prevent you from having to make that decision."

"He raped my baby." The words were agony, raw flames in her throat.

The whites of Sarah's eyes widened. "Technically he's still just a suspect—"

"While she was unconscious."

"**Laurie.** It's my **job** to protect him."

He was there, he was less than twenty feet away, just through that door. Laurie couldn't physically get to him, but she wanted so desperately to see him through nothing more than thin glass, to hurl her body at his cell door over and over again until he was terrified of her.

One more try. "Please." He probably knew exactly where Harper was. He had the information, and he was right **there.** What was worse—what she barely wanted to think about—was the fact that she didn't care where Harper was half as much as she cared about who had hurt her own girl.

"If you see him, you're contaminating whatever case we have against him."

Mutely, Laurie shook her head.

"You know that. It's all on camera. All of it. Anything you say to him or, God forbid, do to him in here would destroy the entire case."

"So turn off the cameras."

Sarah bit her lip, and for one hopeful second Laurie dared to dream. She could still control this. Somehow. If she could just get to him and figure this all out—she could understand what the fuck was going on, and then she could fix it.

But Sarah said, "No fucking way. I'm so sorry, Laurie, but you've **got** to get out of here."

Laurie waited one more long, quiet second.

She wasn't going to be allowed to control this.

So she lost what little control she had.

Laurie ran at the door that led to the corridor where Leeds's cell was. She didn't even get to the keypad. It was enough to throw herself at the door, enough to feel Sarah behind her, grabbing her arm and twisting it behind her. The pain felt good. Bob Ringon tried to help Sarah, but Laurie lashed out with her foot and kicked him sharply in the shin.

"Fuck, Laurie!" Bob bent forward to rub his leg.

Sarah frog-marched Laurie to the jail's front door. Laurie's elbow banged against the jamb, shooting sparks into her shoulder.

Unceremoniously, Sarah shoved Laurie into the hallway. "You know you're my girl. But don't you dare try that again."

Laurie looked up at the camera trained on the jail door. She knew—she **knew**—that Maury, Shonda, and Charity were all watching, riveted. She stuck the hand that wanted to flip them off into her pocket and banged her way out the heavy door into the lobby. **Home to Jojo.** To Pamela, to Andy.

Will Yarwood stood at the reception desk making notes on a report. "Hey. Nice pajamas."

No, no. **Not** Yarwood. He was a bantam rooster, all voice and fighting legs. He'd had three on-duty shootings, all ruled good ones, but one more and the department wouldn't be able to afford the liability insurance and they'd have to bring him inside. Laurie dreaded that—if Yarwood was confined to a desk job, he'd spend half his time in dispatch, talking up the good old days and sucking audibly on his too-large teeth.

"Hey yourself." Laurie didn't slow.

But he caught her arm as she passed him on the way to the front door. His hand was hard on her elbow, almost painful, and for one split second Laurie thought she was going to lose it, like that other time, so long ago now. She was going to come around with her left fist and pound him in the right temple. She'd follow up with a groin strike and then one to the head as he went down. She'd leave him gasping and retching in the department lobby, and then she'd go home to her girl and a bag of ice for her hand.

"Whoa!" He laughed and backed away, holding up mock-surrender hands. "I just wanted to say I heard what happened and that it sucks."

Laurie drew in a quick breath and tried to swallow the chemical flood of adrenaline in her mouth. "Yeah. Thanks."

"How is she?"

She'd bet it was the first time in a month he'd talked about anyone other than himself. "Fine."

"How's Omid doing? Can we bring him anything?"

By "we" he meant he'd sign his name to the card that dispatch would send from the department. He'd been a piece of shit when they'd started on the force together, and this many years later he was still a piece of shit, except with a bigger gut. Single, he lived alone and worked his way through the badge bunnies who fell for his alpha-male routine at an astonishing rate.

"He's fine. I gotta go."

Yarwood lurched forward, his arms moving into shapes that looked like he wanted a hug, and she'd be damned if she would waste a single second making **him** feel better. She spun sideways, out of his reach, and gave a short wave.

"Take care, Laurie," he said. "See you later."

The large glass doors of the lobby were on a weight that closed them gently, which was a pity, because Laurie wouldn't have minded slamming them so hard they shattered.

SEVENTEEN

JOJO WOKE TO find light streaming through her bedroom windows. The police scanner in her parents' room babbled softly down the hall. There was always radio traffic in the Ahmadi house, but Jojo never heard it as anything more than white noise unless someone yelled on the air, usually a foot or a traffic pursuit. Now she wondered what it had sounded like last night, when they'd been looking for her. When she was little, her father used to let her say good night on his radio on her birthday. It had been more exciting than cake, the chance to click the big button and speak the words clearly so that everyone in the whole city could hear her. It wasn't till she was older that she realized that not everyone in the world kept one ear on the police radio, that some families didn't even use police code at the dinner table, that not all kids had a police-code nickname (she'd been Car 143, chosen because her parents said the number was old pager code for "I love you").

Now, for the first time, she realized that all the noise on the channel was bad news. Except for her birthday good night and the occasional (frowned-upon) light banter on the airwaves, everything that was said on air was because of something bad that had happened. Always.

She felt unbearably naïve.

Jojo was in pajamas as if she'd gone to bed, but she didn't remember doing so. Carefully, she untangled her legs and pulled them out. She stood slowly.

She wobbled her way to the bathroom to pee.

Snippets of the night before floated back to her— Andy and Pamela in her bedroom. The hilarity she'd felt at seeing Pamela wearing that sheer nightgown. The feeling of being sucked down into sleep as if she were light and sleep was a black hole. No wonder people freaking loved sleeping pills. They were magic. She should scoop up a couple more of Mom's before they disappeared forever, which was bound to happen soon.

The thought of the pill brought it back: **Plan B. Raped.**

What the hell, was she a #MeToo? She was a freaking hashtag now?

And it wasn't even the worst thought.

Zach, poor sweet Zach, Zach who seemed to know everyone's name, Zach who always got queasy when they did anything in the street-medic trainings that involved theoretical blood. They had to be prepared to help anyone who got hurt in protests, and that included knowing what to do in case of stabbings, teargassings, shootings. **He's just here for me,** Kevin would say with a smile. **That's what friends are for,** Zach would respond, his face sweaty. Jojo herself felt queasy, sick with the thought that she'd never see him again. How was that possible?

And where was Harper? Her stomach dropped another ten feet, right through the floor. She sent another text and prayed to whatever gods there might be that she'd feel a return buzz in her hands: **Chill, jeez, I'm fine.**

She sat on the toilet and waited.

But no text came back. Frantic flutters beat in her chest. **Harper. Come on. Jesus, Harper.** Jojo **needed** her. She'd lost her once for a little while—the worst thing that had ever happened in her life. She couldn't—wouldn't—lose her again.

Jojo was done peeing, and soon she'd go take the pill. She knew that it was in the brown paper bag on the kitchen counter. She was supposed to take it with food, but her stomach hurt and she didn't want to make it worse. What if it backfired somehow—what if it made her bleed forever? She knew that wasn't the way it worked. Mathematically, if she remembered her human-sexuality shit, the chance of her being pregnant was so small that—

No. She would take that fucking pill. She'd take ten of them.

What did Kevin do to her?

It couldn't be him. He was her friend. It could **not** be him. There was something she was missing, something she would remember. . . .

Jojo wadded up a piece of toilet tissue and wiped. It stung.

Somehow the feeling of it, that slight sting as if she had a rash down there, made everything in her whole body contract into a tiny ball. When Jojo was a kid, she and Harper liked to make those roly-poly bugs roll up and then flick them at each other. The goal was always to shoot it back and forth, but the bug was always too good a roller and it had always disappeared. She would do that. She'd drop to the bathroom floor and roll into the hall, then find a crack in the wood. She'd just go back to sleep, dry up, and die alone.

Jojo blinked. She was folded so far forward over her thighs that her lower back hurt. No, hell no. This wasn't how the world **worked.** Yeah, shit was fucked up everywhere—she knew that. But girls like her—girls who were feminists and worked for social justice and believed the victims—they weren't supposed to **be** victims.

Fuck, this was stupid. She had to **do** something, even if she had no idea what that might be.

She pulled up her pajamas, washed her hands, and went back into her bedroom.

Jojo pawed through her closet. A conviction grew in the recesses of her mind that if she just kept doing all the normal things she did on a daily basis, she wouldn't have to think of what had happened.

Not until she had to give her statement.

But until that moment, maybe she could fill her brain with other things. She propped up her iPad on her desk and turned on Spotify. Stupid pop music, as loud as her Bluetooth speakers could handle.

She pulled out clothes. Jeans, the baggy ones that looked terrible on her but that she couldn't give up because she and Harper had inked hearts and skulls all around the cuffs in Sharpie. The blue shirt that Harper had borrowed once and hadn't given back for three months. Jojo'd had to go into Harper's closet and pull it out herself. She'd waved it at her. "Once a thief, always a thief, huh?"

Harper had blushed, and the way her face had gotten pinker had made Jojo feel so weird inside that she regretted teasing her, something that normally didn't ever happen. Their whole friendship had been about teasing, about mocking, about making each other harder on the outside so nothing could hurt them. Mom was a big gardener, and she always started plants growing inside right about this time of year. When spring came, she'd put them on the porch during the day, bringing them back in at night or making Jojo do it if she was at work.

Once Jojo had completely spaced, and the baby to-matoes had all died in an unexpected freeze. Mom had looked so sad in the morning when she got home. "I was hardening them off, but they weren't ready for that kind of cold."

That's what Harper and Jojo did for each other.

And it turned out that Jojo wasn't ready for the cold, either. Fuck, if they didn't find her, what the hell would that—No. It was impossible to think of, a great black rush of frigid air that would kill her. Harper was somewhere. She was fine. She had to be.

"Hey." Mom pushed open her door slowly. "How's my girl?"

A tug of salt at the back of Jojo's throat made her wild with sudden anger. She jabbed at the volume of the music, turning it down so that her mother would be able to hear the anger in her voice. "How do **you** think I am?"

Mom didn't even give her the satisfaction of wincing. "I think you're probably terrible."

Jojo would not cry.

She would **not** cry. Not again, like she had in the fucking shower.

And then she stupidly—childishly—did. The tears came in this dumb flood, and she was mak-ing noises like a dying cow, and Mom had her arms around her. Jojo was freezing, even though her chest felt like it was on fire. Somehow Mom wasn't crying, and thank God for that—it allowed Jojo to cling to her for a moment, to pretend she was seven and nothing worse in the whole world could happen than her guinea pig dying.

"Shhhh," Mom said into her hair. "Shhhh."

Mom didn't mean for her to be quiet. Mom had never meant that when Jojo cried. It was her way of sounding like the ocean, she'd once told Jojo. **Like the conch shell you raise to your ear. That's me. The big ocean, holding you. Shhhh.**

No, now Jojo was the big ocean, full of salt and scary slimy-ass shit that she didn't even know how to **begin** to get out of her system. **Harper . . .**

Finally, a million unbearable years later, Jojo wiped her snotty nose on the back of her hand. "Stupid," she muttered.

"Shhhh." Mom stroked her hair, and Jojo wished she could just stay here for another month or two.

"I didn't take that pill yet."

"You want me to be with you when you do?"

Jojo did want that. But she said, "It's not a big deal."

"I'll just get it for you, then." Mom was up and out of the room before Jojo could tell her not to.

She came back with the paper bag and a glass of water. She pulled out the paperwork and started reading it, holding it far from her face in that way that always made Jojo irritated, like she was showing off the crappiness of her eyesight.

"Just give it to me." Jojo grabbed the bottle. A whole bottle for a single pill—what a tragedy for the environment. She'd make sure to recycle it.

"No, wait. Let me read. Are you supposed to take this with food or anything?"

Since Jojo didn't feel as if she'd be hungry ever again in her whole life, she wasn't too worried about it. She popped the pill and swallowed. Mom stared, just as she'd done when she'd scarfed the Ambien.

Jojo shrugged. "What can I say? I like drugs."

Mom's eyes widened. Her mouth opened slightly.

"Oh, my God, Mom." A true laugh climbed out of Jojo's lungs. "You look horrified. I don't like drugs."

Mom gave a pant of relief.

"I **love** drugs."

Mom flashed her a fake frown, the same one as when Jojo was stealing bacon from her plate. "Good to know."

"Can Dad get me some from evidence? Like that officer who got fired? What was his name?"

"Jason Stern."

The guy had been using crack out of the evidence locker for like nine months, and no one had noticed, even though he'd been getting skinnier and skinnier. Dad still felt bad about that one, which didn't actually make sense, since it wasn't as if Vice and the chief of police worked together every day. "Yeah, him. I think crack would be fun."

"Crack is fine," said Mom. "Just stay away from sugar. That's the real killer."

Good, they were back to talking but not talking. That was better. Jojo was used to that.

Mom stood up. She crumpled up the papers and the bag and tossed them and the recyclable pill bottle into the wastebasket next to Jojo's desk. "Okay, sweet girl. Let's get going."

"Where? To see Dad?"

She looked almost startled. "I meant the station. We've got to get your statement. But yeah, we can see Dad, too."

That snake of irritation that lay coiled in Jojo's belly rattled. Did Mom even give a shit about him? "'We'? It's my statement."

"You know what I mean."

"You're just a **dispatcher,** Mom. You're not going to take my **statement.**" She checked her phone for the billionth time, hoping Harper had sent her a text. Nothing.

Her mother took a deep breath in through her nose, noisy and whistling. "We can get Starbucks on the way."

Jojo wanted to say something cutting—**I don't like anything they have there,** but it wasn't true, and Mom knew it. Jojo would just about kill for a Venti Caramel Macchiato right now.

But it was her statement. Hers. No one else's, especially not Mom's.

"Fine. But I'm getting Dad something at Star-bucks, and you can't stop me." Not that Mom would stop her. It was just something for Jojo to say, to push Mom back those few inches, getting herself some goddamn space while she waited for Harper to come back and fill it.

EIGHTEEN

OMID WILL KNOW what to do next. Laurie waved a hand at the nurses' station and moved faster toward Omid's room.

Jojo darted in front of her, shoving the door open. "Daddy! We brought you presents!" She held up the bag and shook it.

Omid looked tired, his eyelids heavy, but he smiled at their daughter. He always did. "And here I was thinking you'd forgotten all about me."

"Never." Jojo darted forward with a kiss for his cheek.

"What about you?" He looked at Laurie.

"Never," she echoed, kissing his other stubbled cheek.

Honestly, he'd been the first person she'd thought of when her eyes had opened on the couch. She'd assumed she'd fallen asleep there after watching TV. Sometimes Omid woke her to come to bed, but sometimes he said she looked too peaceful and just draped the afghan over her. She'd thought Omid must be upstairs, twisted in the sheet—he slept like a hurricane—his CPAP mask whistling because he'd pushed it off his head again. Laurie had thought that she would start the coffee. She'd take him a cup, the way he did for her.

Then she'd seen Jojo's empty red hoodie on the other end of the couch, and it all came back.

Her daughter had been roofied by an assailant and then by her own mother's pills. Those fucking Ambien were going down the toilet today, the water supply be damned.

"Here." Jojo opened the white plastic bag and shook the contents out on top of Omid's legs. "Your favorite, sunflower seeds. And a **People** magazine. I know you don't normally read it, but I'm telling you, it's good. You can skip past the celebrity stuff and go right to the heartstring articles. I flipped through it, and there's an article on a dog stuck in a well for three days."

"Wow!" Omid opened it in the middle.

Harper's missing. Laurie had told Jojo not to tell her dad, not right when they got there. Of course Omid knew that Harper had been with their daughter and hadn't been located yet. But he didn't know she was officially missing. Laurie could almost see the words bubbling up from her daughter's head, a cartoon balloon of fear. **Harper's missing.**

But Jojo held it in. "And Red Vines. And look, you love these." She held up the sealed glass of cold-brewed coffee. "Snobby, hipster coffee, not even Starbucks. We bought it in the lobby."

Laurie took half a step forward, rethinking their purchase. Wasn't his heart supposed to be calm? "Wait, are you allowed to have coffee? Maybe it's something you should cut back on?"

Omid barely glanced at her. He reached for the drink and snapped it open. "Coffee's fine."

"Did the doctor say that?" Although it was nice of him to want to please Jojo, he shouldn't take it too far.

But Jojo shot her a look of fury so heated that Laurie felt sweat start under her armpits. "Way to go, Mom. Ruin my present. Thanks."

Omid, though, waved a hand. "The doctor said coffee's fine. I have to get some more levels checked, and it's possible my ability to eat a pound of bacon on Sunday mornings might be suspended for a while, but coffee's fine. Just nothing too high-stress for a little while as the meds kick in."

Their daughter's rapist was sitting in Omid's jail, two and a half miles away. A man had been murdered just feet from her. Jojo's childhood friend was missing. No stress, though.

Jojo dove into the plastic bag. "And gum! I

got you so much gum! Look, honeydew flavor. That's gonna be **so** disgusting. You have to chew it right now."

Obligingly, Omid popped a piece in his mouth. He chewed and made a face. "Horrible. You gonna have some?"

"Gross!" Jojo squealed, sounding closer to twelve than sixteen. "I'll have some sunflower seeds, though."

And that squeal that Jojo made—that was maybe the hardest part of all to hear. That girly, innocent sound. Laurie wanted to roll time backward until she was kissing Jojo's baby soft spot. She caught Omid's gaze. He gave her a half smile, that slight lift to the corner of his mouth. Something calmed inside her.

Then he turned back to Jojo. "Honey." Omid caught her hand. "How are you?"

Jojo glanced up at the ceiling, exactly like an adult would who didn't want to answer a question. "Fine."

"Did you sleep?"

Jojo looked at Laurie, the fury gone somehow. She snorted. Relief flooded Laurie's brain like sunshine.

"What?" said Omid.

"She slept." Laurie winked at Jojo. "She slept her face off."

Omid looked at her. "Statement?"

"We're going there next."

"Nate Steiner's lead." Steiner was good—they both knew that. "But make sure you're in there, too."

"Dad!"

Omid shook his head. "Honey, I'd be there if I could be. Goddamn it, I should be." He jerked his IV line.

"I don't need either of you."

Was Jojo hiding something? Laurie hated that her mind went there, but she couldn't help it. Jojo must know that both her parents would read the report, no matter what. Nothing would be a secret from them.

Omid reached to squeeze Jojo's hand. "You know I love you more than anything in the whole world, right?"

Instead of rolling her eyes, Jojo nodded solemnly, and that by itself brought a lump to Laurie's throat.

"Good. Now, get out of here. Wait in the hall, okay, kiddo?"

"Hey!"

"I have to talk to your mom."

Jojo crossed her arms, but Omid's face didn't budge from its firm look. Eventually she broke the stare first and muttered, "Fine. But I'm taking the magazine." She snatched it from the top sheet and stomped into the hall.

Laurie closed the door behind her gently.

"How is she really?"

Laurie perched on the edge of his bed. Omid

shifted his weight so she could sit closer to him. "She's okay. She's cried twice, big time." Just saying the words out loud made tears spring to Laurie's eyes, as though they'd been waiting right behind her lids.

And it pissed her off. She didn't have the luxury of crying, not right now. Omid was here, out of commission. **She** had to be the tough one, the one who fixed this whole thing.

Omid gripped her hand, hard. "How about you?"

Laurie shook her head. "Don't worry about me. I'm here to worry about **you.**"

"I bet a million dollars that Jojo had to remind you to come here. You were probably headed straight for the station as soon as you woke up."

Sheepishly she said, "I was already there. Early this morning."

Omid scooted upward in the bed, tugging impatiently at a cord that got stuck beneath him. "Did Jojo go?"

"No, the Cunninghams stayed with her."

"Back up. I still don't understand the Harper connection. Has she been located yet?"

Laurie shook her head.

"Shit. You're kidding."

"She's in the wind."

"Like, run off?"

Laurie winced. "Maybe? Her parents are freaking out."

"But—the girls are friends again?"

"Apparently."

"And we didn't know?"

Jojo wasn't their baby anymore. She had things, maybe lots of them, that she didn't share with them anymore. "Nope."

"Fuck, Laurie." Omid's face went red, and he pulled at the neckline of his hospital gown. "Harper's **always** been bad news. Always. I gotta get out of here."

"Chill." She pressed her hand against his chest, right over his heart. With more confidence than she felt, she said, "Harper's a tough cookie—we'll find her."

"But she's—" He jerked sideways again. "The blood . . . in his house . . ."

"ID thinks it's Zach's."

Omid wiped his hand across his stubble, a dry, papery sound. "They'll do the fast DNA kit."

"They're swamped with the scene and making sure they've gotten everything there, but Vero said they've already got it working. Should be done by this afternoon." DNA tests used to take weeks, if not months. They had to be sent away to the state, and the backlog was always impossible. There was inevitably someone's more important case ahead of yours. Now the ID techs did it in-house, with their own level of urgency, which in this case was going to be pretty sky-fucking-high.

"We have to make him talk. He has to tell us where she is." Omid was the one who handled things, who got shit done. It would make him insane to be left out of the investigation.

"They'll get it out of him." Steiner was the best detective on the force when it came to getting suspects to admit to things. If anyone could do it, it would be him.

Omid said, "I can AMA out of here. I'll go home and shower and get back to—"

"Over my dead body you'll leave here against medical advice." Laurie pressed down on his chest harder. She pushed until she could feel his heart pumping under her hand, the thump steady and fast. "You will stay in this bed if I have to use your own handcuffs to get you to stay."

Omid shook his head. "I'm sure about this. I'm fine."

"If you die, Jojo will think it's her fault. Forever." She kept her voice light, but she was serious.

Omid went pale, and sweat stood out at his hairline. "Shit."

"And I'll have to kill you if you die. Don't make me do that."

He tried to smile, but his face didn't look right.

"Are you okay?" Laurie looked up at the heart monitor. His pulse was faster, at ninety now, but it was steady, still thumping strongly under her hand.

"A man hurt my girl, a man who might be the one sitting in my jail, and Laurie—" His voice broke. "I really think I'd kill him if I saw him right now."

"I know."

His voice dropped to a whisper. "I honestly think I would." His eyes flickered open wider. "And you—you stay away from him. For that reason."

It hurt. Of course it did. But he was right— Laurie had proved long ago she wasn't reliable in terms of high-stress incidents. That time with the taser was why she got off the street and went to dispatch, where there was always someone else in the room, always someone to back her up, to stop her from making bad decisions.

"Whatever. That was a long time ago. And that's why you stay here." Laurie's shoulder ached from where Sarah had pulled her arm back, keeping her out of the locked cell area. She shifted so that she could put her other hand over the one already on his chest. She pushed harder, as if she could weld him to the bed. The thumps slowed. Eighty-six, said the monitor. Then seventy-two. "That's better. You just lie there and breathe, goddamn it. I'll tell you everything I learn, every single thing we do."

Omid closed his eyes. "Everything."

I love you. She said the words in her head, the way they always did. They told Jojo they loved her all the time. But for her and Omid, I-love-you's were saved for going to war, for the apocalypse, for the very last moment.

NINETEEN

DAD HAD ALWAYS called Jojo and Mom his station girls. Growing up, Jojo had had free run of the department. This interview room—the blue one—was where she'd always preferred to hold her doll interrogations. Once Barbie had confessed to stabbing Sheriff Woody to death, and she'd been sentenced to die. Jojo had stolen a ladder out of the janitorial closet and fashioned a noose out of her hair ribbon. She'd attached the noose to the light fixture over the table, but just as Barbie had swung for her sins, Darren Dixon kicked Jojo out because he needed to interview someone. He hadn't noticed the doll's corpse dangling overhead, but the suspect had and raised bloody murder, thinking the cops were threatening his wife, whom he apparently called Barbie.

Jojo got into big trouble for that one.

Now she was alone in the room. Mom was getting them both Cokes, and Nate Steiner was getting some paperwork together.

She finally had a moment to think.

It was coming back. In the car ride on the way here, a whole chunk of the night before had dropped into Jojo's brain all in one piece, as if driving over a bump had dislodged something and opened a ZIP file of memories.

They'd been in the backyard of a squat in Oakland. Some guy named Squid, who was a wannabe crusty punk but actually liked showers, had invited them over after the meeting.

Harper was across the yard, laughing with like five guys that Jojo didn't know. Jojo sat on an ancient swing. It creaked so much she wasn't sure it wouldn't break if she swung high, so she kept it mellow, her feet in the dirt, just swaying. She drank her beer and felt the small hit of weed she'd inhaled move in her blood. She liked the way it relaxed the skin around her bones. She didn't worry as much when she was high.

Kevin gave a laugh at the back door, and honest to God, all the people around him laughed, too, even the ones who hadn't been talking to him. He was charismatic as fuck. And he liked her.

She **really** wished she liked him back. That way. It would make everything easier.

He headed across the yard to her, gesturing to the

beer bottle she held. "Don't go crazy with that. Last thing we need is your parents finding out you're drinking underage. You'll never be invited to street-medic training again." Kevin was the only CapB who knew what her parents did for a living. Harper had told her not to tell anyone, ever. **They'll think you're a mole. A narc. A squealer.**

Are you done spouting sixties television?

Screw you, I watch The Americans.

But Kevin had been different. When he'd asked what her parents did, she'd told him. And he'd thought she was brave, doing something they might not be proud of. ("Might not." Ha! They'd kill her!)

Now she said, "They wouldn't care if I had a beer."

"They so would."

She laughed. "Oh, my God, they **so** would."

"How are you getting home?"

Jojo aimed the neck of her beer bottle at her best friend, who was slow dancing by herself on the overgrown lawn. "Harper."

"Where do your parents think you are?"

She grinned. "Hanging out with a friend they like."

"You'd think that parents would realize at some point that kids lie their asses off."

Something about the way he said "kids" smarted. She wasn't a kid. She was **so** not a kid. How else could she explain what she felt about Harper?

Kevin sat in the swing next to her, settling in slowly. The chains protested with metallic shrieks. "This gonna hold me? I'm big." He laughed that infectious laugh again, and Jojo felt her heart lighten.

"Look at her," Jojo said, gesturing again to Harper. "She's up to her old tricks."

She watched Harper with a greediness she hoped didn't show on her face. Harper was doing the cigarette dance with a bummed smoke, the way she always did to whatever music happened to be on. Right now it was some lame trip-hop, all beat and no groove, but Harper made it seem like the sexiest music in the world. She held the cigarette up in the dark, and someone on the porch shut off the single bare bulb that had been burning. Now all they could see of Harper was her shape, moving in the dark, and the low red glow of her cigarette. She wound it above her head and spun, slowly, the red gleam tracing her motion. She inhaled, and the tip glowed so bright that her face looked feral. Needy. Gorgeous. Jojo's stomach twisted as Harper spun the other way. She tore her eyes from Harper's outline and glanced at the other people in the yard. Everyone was watching, the girls with thinly veiled looks of envy and the guys with obvious lust.

Only Kevin's face was unreadable.

The dance ended. Harper tossed the cigarette to the dirt and ground it out with a flourish. The weak porch light came back on. People went back to talking, flirting, planning.

"So," said Kevin, rubbing his palms against his jeans. "You in love with her?"

It was like he'd set a bomb off inside Jojo's chest. The detonation left her ears ringing, her head hollow. "What? Who?"

"Nah, don't be like that. It's cool."

"You have the wrong idea. We're best friends."

"Mmmm," was all he said.

Jojo's legs were numb from the small plastic seat, and Harper was busy making out with some guy who'd come to his first meeting just tonight. The guy was going to think social activism always meant getting laid. "I mean it. She's my best friend."

There was a long pause before Kevin spoke. She felt him looking at her, taking her in, but she didn't turn to face him.

Finally he said, "Yeah, well. I feel like that about my best friend, too."

She must have heard him wrong. Zachary Gordon, the assistant athletic trainer on the team, was his best friend. They were both CapB activists. And they were both straight. "Huh?"

"Yep."

"Holy shit," she breathed.

He turned his head fast then, facing her. "I'm not gay, though."

"Me neither!" Was it a lie? She wasn't exactly sure.

"I just like him. Love him."

"I just love **her**!"

Kevin's chin jutted out as if he'd forgotten to

retract it. "That's cool. Like, besides that, though, I'm totally straight."

"Me too."

"I like you, for instance."

Pleasure curled in Jojo's belly. "I like you, too." The weed in her bloodstream unwound, and she let her arm trail to his. They linked hands and swayed on the swings.

"Want to come over here?" he asked.

"Where?" She knew.

He patted his lap.

She got off her swing with some trouble, one leg still asleep, and then straddled his lap, fitting her legs somewhat painfully between the chains and his upper thighs. Kevin grinned. She grinned back at him. Would she feel a boner if he had one? She assumed she would. She waited for it.

She knew that Harper, who was always conscious of the people around her, would be watching. So Kevin was twenty-two and she was sixteen. Why should that matter? And so what if she didn't feel anything for him but fondness and the notion that she **should** be more attracted to him than she was? They were playing parts in a play she hadn't auditioned for but didn't hate being cast in. Words she didn't see coming tumbled out of her weed-loosened mouth. "What do you like about me?" God, she sounded like any other sixteen-year-old girl trying to get a boy's attention. Stupid.

But Kevin spoke without even appearing

surprised by the question. "I like how you think. You listen, and you process, and then you speak your mind. You're careful, like me. You act like you're not scared of anything—like when we almost got kettled at that march in the Mission—and you're an overachieving stubborn fucker like me, too."

"Come on." He was right, though. She liked that he'd seen the things she tried to hide, even though his accuracy made her feel exposed. He looked past her appearance to the person she really was.

He went on, "But I think that you're terrified by the way **she** makes you feel."

"Um, okay." She pushed at his chest, feeling a little trapped by the way her thighs were locked between his and the swing's chains. "You're crazy."

"Nope," he said.

"You don't know everything. Sometimes I'm scared of stuff." She readjusted on his lap a little, hoping Harper would see, and then leaned forward, arching her back so that her breasts were high. "For example, I'm scared to kiss you." She inserted that breathiness that Harper used when she was talking to a guy, the airy sound that seemed to make their brains come unglued at the edges.

"No you're not."

He was right. She wasn't scared. She was just kind of curious.

So she did.

His lips were softer than she'd expected, and

the sandpaper stubble on his upper lip surprised her. Her own lips suddenly seemed inadequate to the task. His tongue was stronger than hers, surer. He tasted like beer and weed and barbecue potato chips, which was a surprisingly delicious combination. She realized, with his tongue in her mouth, that the flavor of him was making her want potato chips, and maybe that wasn't the right thing to be thinking about.

So she wiggled a little more. If he was going to get hard underneath her, maybe that would shoot a thrill up her spine.

But he didn't get hard.

She didn't get a thrill.

Eventually, her lips just got . . . bored.

He pulled back. Did he look amused? His gaze made it seem like he was laughing at her, maybe. Was she a bad kisser? Oh, shit, maybe she was.

She sat farther back, closer to his knees. "What?"

"That didn't work."

Jojo narrowed her eyes and tensed her muscles, ready to leap off him and get the hell out, no matter who she had to pull Harper off of to do so. "Yeah."

"Born this way?"

What was he actually saying? Jojo grabbed a breath and held it.

She waited.

He watched her face.

Finally she nodded. "Maybe. I'm not totally sure."

Kevin exhaled, and she felt his thighs tense and then relax. "Me neither." A beat. "But I'm pretty sure."

Surprise coursed through her. "Why not come out?"

"Shhh," he hissed. **"Dude."**

"Sorry." She had said it too loudly—dick move. "But why not? Literally half the nation hates you already. How much worse could it get?"

He rewrapped his hands around the swing's chains. "I could be a social activist till I bleed Che Guevara's own tears on the field, and in the long run it's good for the team. Gets people talking. Gets eyes on our games. Love me or hate me, they watch me. But if my team knew that I was . . . It's just not the way we do."

"What about . . ." She searched for the name in her head. "Michael Sam."

"Played four preseason games after he came out. Then he was cut. I'd last another whole season, maybe. For show. Then they'd find a reason to not renew my contract. No one would trust me."

"But you could change things. Make a difference."

Kevin's eyes got hooded, and even though he didn't move, Jojo felt him get further from her. His thighs tensed again. "I **do** change things. That's my whole mission in life, to change things. Don't tell me I don't."

"You can be yourself, you know." Her tone was

too strident, she knew, but she was suddenly angry at him. "You're, like, a role model."

"I'm just a kid from a shithole Alabama town who's trying to build a retirement plan because my body'll be toast in less than six years, and I'm already pissing enough people off. No matter what I **want** to do, I have to keep providing for my family back home. And that family prays every week in church that God will sweep the nation of sinners, including the fags."

"Fuck." And here **she** didn't want to admit to her parents what she might be. In her liberal state, in her liberal town. Her mother's best friend, Sarah from the jail, was gay. Jojo had nothing to worry about, while Kevin had everything to lose. "I'm sorry."

Kevin raised a shoulder. "Is what it is. I just have to take my future seriously."

"But . . ." She didn't know what to say or how to say it. It was still important, though—she knew that. "But you're not telling the truth."

He clicked his tongue. "You want to talk about truth? How about you decide on your own and I'll decide on mine. Bonus: How about you get up off me." He walked his feet back so that she had to scramble to pull her legs from around him. He ended up standing, the swing at his back, and Jojo was suddenly on the ground, feeling drunker and more stoned than she had ten minutes before.

"Hey!" She clawed her fingers into the dirt,

hoping she didn't hit something gross: cat shit or an old needle.

He kept his gaze up, level, his feet planted firmly, as if he were surveying the playing field, waiting for the ball to come his way.

She stood. "Kevin!"

From behind Jojo came a wicked laugh that got louder and more insistent the closer and faster it came at her. She turned, and then Harper was there, her pale hair a tangled whirl of light, her tight pink sweater glowing in the streetlamp. "I found you! I was looking **everywhere** for you, Joshi." Harper jumped up and into Jojo's arms, wrapping her legs around Jojo's waist. Jojo staggered a little but managed to stay standing.

"You found me," she grunted.

"Oh, **good.** You're my **favorite.**"

Great. Harper was super fucked up. "You have your party pants on, I see." Jojo couldn't hold her for long. Harper was already slipping down her body, but the truth was, Jojo didn't hate it.

Of course she didn't.

A cell phone pinged. "Oh! That's Ray!" Harper slid her feet to the ground and dug her phone out of her pocket. Jojo's arms felt strangely empty.

"He's here! You're finally going to meet him, the love of my life! Let's go!" Then Harper kissed her—out of the blue, a long, wet, very drunk kiss.

A kiss that set everything inside Jojo's body ringing in the exact opposite way as kissing Kevin had—or hadn't. As if her body were a bell and Harper the only clapper that could set her vibrating.

Behind her she heard Kevin laugh. Fucker.

Harper grabbed one hand and pulled her toward the gate that led to the street. With her other hand, Jojo flipped Kevin off, but there wasn't much heat in the motion. She darted one last glance at him, and he shot her a peace sign.

Good. They were still friends, then.

Harper flagged down a black Range Rover. It screeched to a halt, and the passenger door was shoved open.

"Hey, little girls. Want some candy?"

Jojo couldn't see around Harper, who was launching herself inside, but the man's voice was weirdly familiar. A trickle of fear stroked her cheek.

She didn't want to get in.

The memory shut down there. No matter how hard Jojo tried to unzip the rest of the recollection file, she got no further.

Fuck.

TWENTY

THE DOOR TO the interview room opened, and Steiner and Mom both came back in. Mom had overruled Jojo's objections—steamrolled, really—and gave her the choice between having either a lawyer or her in the room while giving the statement.

A lawyer.

That **had** made Jojo want Mom, which had probably been her mother's plan all along. Still, Mom was better than Dad, if they had to talk about sex stuff.

And they would have to.

Jojo felt the urge to curl up again to make herself into the roly-poly bug and disappear under the door into the hallway.

Nate Steiner sat across from them. "Hey, Jojo," he said.

"Hi." At least it was him. Last summer she'd been at the lake with some friends smoking weed, and he'd just told her to get home quick and text him when she was there. He'd never said anything—as far as she knew—to either of her parents.

Or, God, maybe he had, and her parents just decided it wasn't a big enough deal to punish her. Jojo had no idea what really went on in this building. She felt her cheeks color, and a wave of heat spread up her spine.

Steiner pointed at a small digital recorder. "This is just for the record. You mind if I use it to help me take your statement?"

Jojo shrugged. "It's fine."

Steiner sat back in his chair. He wore a blue button-down shirt and a darker blue tie. He'd taken off his suit jacket when he'd sat down, and he radiated ease, like he'd sucked up all of hers. But then his eyes suddenly filled with tears.

Holy shit. He was going to **cry**? Mom was staring at her lap, no help at all.

He rubbed the back of his neck. "Oh, my God, I'm sorry. I just remembered Car 143."

Oh, how fucking embarrassing.

"On your birthday," Steiner said.

Car 143, 908D. Her call sign, logging off for the night, using Dad's radio.

Mom's voice sounded thick as she spoke to Steiner. "She'd be all tucked in bed, with Omid's radio in her hands. Remember how everyone on duty would click?"

Clicking was laughter, usually mocking, but on those nights she'd known they were laughing with her.

"Car 143," said Steiner again.

Jojo thumped backward in her chair, her ears hot. "Come **on**."

Steiner shook his head as if to clear it. "Okay. Yeah. This is going to be hard to get through, and I just want to acknowledge that up front. I'm going to be asking you some really personal questions. Are you sure you don't want a female officer in here to ask these?"

They'd asked her that already, like three times. The only female officer on duty was Maria Bagley, and Jojo had always secretly thought Maria was dumb as a stick. If only Sarah Knight from the jail could do it. Sarah was awesome and fun, one of Mom's best friends, practically an aunt to Jojo. "I'm fine." Maybe she could just answer that to every single question she was asked. **I'm fine, fine, fine.**

"Okay, then." Steiner clicked his pen. "Let's go back to yesterday. What did you do in the morning?"

Friday. She'd slept late—that's what summers were for. In the afternoon Harper had come over, and they'd made root beer floats. Harper tried to get her to throw hers up, but Jojo had laughed.

I like my tooth enamel. Harper had turned sideways in front of the mirror and said, **But am I getting fat?** Jojo said, **You look prettier than ever, Cordelia.** She'd tried to keep her voice light and used the pet name they called each other, the one they'd been using since they were eleven when Jojo had fallen madly in love with Anne of Green Gables and tried to force Harper to read it. (Harper hadn't given in, thinking nonrequired reading a waste of time, but they'd watched the miniseries over and over, swearing to be each other's Cordelia.) Then she and Harper went to Sephora.

"Slept late. Harper came over around three, I think. Went to Sephora for a lip stain." Which Harper had taken and not paid for. Where was Harper? Did they understand the **magnitude** of this? "You know she's missing, right? That's the most important thing here. **Right?**" Jojo ignored the way Mom was staring at her and just spoke to Steiner, who kept his eyes on hers encouragingly. He didn't answer her question.

"Then where did you go?"

"We went to Justin Sands's house. We hung out." Justin was boring, but he was a good driver and had a sweet Mustang. He'd do anything Harper wanted him to, which was handy.

"And you were with Harper Cunningham this whole time?"

Jojo nodded.

"Then where did you go?"

Now they were getting to the part she hadn't told her mother. "To the city."

Next to her, Mom sucked in a breath.

"What was in San Francisco?"

"A meeting."

"How did you get there?"

"Justin drove us to West Oakland, and then we took BART."

"What kind of meeting?"

"CapB."

That stopped Steiner's pen moving. He looked up, honest surprise in his eyes. "Citizens Against Police Brutality?"

Jojo resisted the urge to slide onto the floor in a display of passive resistance. "It was put on by them. Street-medic training."

Mom's voice was cold. "You should have **told** us."

Steiner saved her. "Laurie, it's fine that you're in here. But you have to stay quiet. No interjections, no interruptions, okay?"

"She doesn't **have** to be here," said Jojo, hoping all over again.

"You're sixteen. I'm here. I'm not leaving." Mom folded her arms like some tough guy, but her eyes looked scared, which in itself freaked Jojo the fuck out. "But I'll be quiet."

Steiner nodded. "Okay. So. CapB. Was this the first time you met with them?"

Jojo shook her head. "Uh-uh. I guess I've been to a bunch of meetings."

"How many?"

"Maybe . . . a dozen?" She could practically feel Mom coming unglued. And what about when Dad found out? He'd think she was part of the black bloc, taunting cops on the front lines.

Holy shit.

And where the **fuck** was Harper?

"Okay. Tell me who was at the meeting."

Calling it a meeting made it sound as if they sat lined up in folding metal chairs like they were in a business club at school or something. Instead they met at a café on Valencia, an old place with a big back room. Most of the people who came drank beer. Harper and Jojo never pushed their luck, sticking with vanilla lattes, though once Zach had bought them each a glass of wine. When they did street-medic training, they huddled at one big table, keeping their voices low so they didn't scare anyone with talk of how much Maalox to mix in your water bottle if tear gas started to spray. "Um, I don't know last names." Except for Kevin and Zach.

"Give me what you can remember, that's totally fine."

"Greg, Dionne, Leandre, Nikki, Barclay, Mack. Maybe some others." Jesus, did she just turn into a **narc**? The names had simply tumbled right out. Thank God she didn't know much else, or she'd probably have given it all up like some baby weasel. "Zach, of course. And Kevin Leeds."

She felt, rather than saw, Mom straighten. She expected Steiner to jump on it, to start questioning her about Kevin, but he didn't. Instead he wanted to know what they'd all talked about—congressional appointments, an upcoming march, handcuff injuries—and who talked to her specifically about what. Jojo gave him what she could remember—it couldn't hurt that much, right? The night started to fragment in her memory right about the time they were leaving. The afterparty memory was clear, when she was on Kevin's lap on the swing, but the time connections were fractured.

"You're doing great. Do you remember who Harper talked to in the café?"

Jojo had a clear image of Harper giving her sideways sex smile to the barista, a guy with like twenty holes in each ear and a huge septum barbell. "The barista, I don't know his name. Mack and Dionne. Zach and Kevin."

Steiner flipped a page in his notebook. "Harper's mother said in her statement that she has a boyfriend named Ray. Do you know his last name?"

Jojo shook her head.

"Was he there?"

"No." Harper had kept him such a secret. Jojo knew he was an older guy (as usual—she had some daddy issues) and that he did something with computers. Single. Big house over the hill in Danville. Big Range Rover. Big cock. "I've never met him.

I was supposed to meet him that night. After this party."

"Where was the party?"

There was just a gray mist where the memory of the location should be. "I don't know. A squat in Oakland."

"Did you meet this guy Ray?"

"I think so, but I don't remember his face." There was a scene in **X-Men II** where Jean Grey feels something coming—she knows it's going to be bad, but she doesn't know what it is. That's what this felt like. The skin on Jojo's arms prickled. Goose bumps rippled through her, and she pushed her hands deeper into her sweatshirt pockets. **Zach's death. Harper's disappearance.** "I don't remember," she repeated.

Steiner looked up at her, and then, more irritatingly, he looked at her mother. "You're doing great, Jojo. Okay, what else do you remember about last night? Take me through, step by step."

Jojo closed her eyes, more to block out the peripheral view of her mother than for any other reason. "We left the café. We were . . . we got high on the street, I think."

"Weed or something else?"

He said it so matter-of-factly. Like he thought she actually might smoke crack or something. "**Weed.** Obviously. Like that time you caught me at the lake," she said slowly and deliberately.

Mom stiffened. He hadn't ever told them, then. Huh. Well, hell, it was technically legal now. Okay, it would be if she were twenty-one. Which she wasn't.

Steiner didn't flinch, though. "Whose weed?"

"Harper's."

"How did you smoke it?"

"What?"

"Joint? Vape? Bong?"

Yeah, they just carried bongs around in their purses. "Vape."

"Okay. Then where did you go?"

"We got some chips at a liquor store." It sounded stupid when she said it out loud. **Got high, bought some snacks.** So teenaged. So predictable.

"Then?"

"We went to the party at the squat." Kevin's mouth, Harper dancing as everyone watched. "I don't remember."

"Okay."

Jojo's throat was tight. "But—"

"It's really okay, Jojo. Let's try a different angle. Have you checked your cell phone for messages you might have forgotten sending or receiving?"

"Yeah. Nothing." Just a lot of texts to Harper, unanswered.

"Did you go through your pockets?"

Jojo stared at him. "I didn't even think about that. They kept my clothes at the hospital."

Mom leaned forward and said quietly, "I asked ID. There was nothing in your pockets."

Steiner said, "What about your bag? What were you carrying last night?"

Jojo lifted her black shoulder bag. "Just this."

"And you've gone through it?"

Dumbly, Jojo shook her head. Her bag, like her pockets, hadn't even occurred to her. She scooted forward in her chair so she could set the bag on top of the desk. She scrabbled inside it, pulling items out at random. Her phone. Empty water bottle. Two packs of Doublemint gum, both opened. Seven pens. Her notebook. Four tampons, which she did **not** put on the table. Two chargers, one that went to her phone, the other one Harper's, because Harper never remembered to bring an iPhone charger anywhere she went and her phone was constantly dead. A bruised apple that was damp and soft on one side.

And a white phone.

"Holy shit."

"Whose is that?" Mom's voice was reedy.

"Harper's."

Steiner reached for it.

"No." Mom lunged forward and grabbed the phone, dumping it into her purse. "Sorry, Nate. We're going to look at it first."

"It has to go to evidence."

"It will."

"Come on, Laurie. You know this. You might lose fingerprints."

"Break time." Mom stood. "Come on, Jojo."

"**Wait.** Laurie, I'm doing your daughter a favor here. Just chatting. No lawyer. Don't push it, okay?"

Mom whirled on him then, one finger pointed directly at him, her eyes blazing. "Are you threatening us that you'll start treating her like a suspect?"

Steiner went rigid. "There was a murder not ten feet from her."

"And she was **unconscious.**"

He gave a hangdog look but said, "Still have to clear every possible angle."

What did that mean? Jojo's heart did a backflip into her stomach.

"So she **is** a suspect." Mom slammed her hands against the tabletop. "Are you arresting my daughter, Nate?"

TWENTY-ONE

LAURIE WAS READY to get Jojo out so fast that Steiner wouldn't even have a chance to grab his flex-cuffs. She'd pull Jojo's arm, kick open the door with her foot, and in twenty seconds they could be through the lobby and out the front door.

But Steiner said, "Of course not. She's not a suspect, but she has to keep her nose clean. Just in case. Don't be like this. Give me the phone, and I'll get a forensic dump and grab the prints on it."

Laurie stayed still.

Steiner said, "Damn it, don't compromise this case. You're a dispatcher, remember? Not a cop."

Laurie shoved it at him. "Fine. Take it."

"I'm happy to return it after I pull the data. Then I'll put you in charge of getting it back to her parents, okay? In case anyone else tries to get hold of her."

Laurie tried not to huff as Steiner left the room. Jojo said nothing.

They sat in silence for fifteen minutes. Jojo didn't even try to talk. Laurie sat as still as she could, clasping her hands so tightly her knuckles hurt.

When Steiner came back and handed the phone to her, Laurie said, "We're taking a **break.**" She didn't give Jojo a chance to say no.

It was Saturday, so there was no one staffing Omid's admin's desk, no one to stop them. Laurie fumbled with the key ring. There, the big heavy one. Other rooms in the department had coded entry pads. The chief's office, though, only had two official keys, Omid's and his admin Marge's. When Omid had taken the promotion, though, he'd paid a hardware-store buddy to make a copy for Laurie, giving him a hundred-dollar tip to ignore the "Do Not Duplicate" instruction. **Just in case,** Omid had said, giving it to her.

In case of what?

In case of whatever.

In case of now.

Laurie closed the door behind them. The blinds that looked out into the meeting area and at Marge's desk were already shut, as were the blinds over the exterior windows. It was dim, the fluorescent lights taking long seconds to warm up. The room smelled like Omid, like his Old Spice deodorant and Proraso shaving cream. His desk was uncharacteristically messy—papers strewn over the surface and an empty coffee cup resting on its side.

He'd run out of the office to save Jojo, and he hadn't come back yet. Laurie's heart twisted with a sharp pain she didn't see coming—Omid was in the hospital. He could have died. How close had she come to losing him?

To losing both of them?

"Mom, do they think I'm a **suspect**?"

Her breath still traitorously shallow, Laurie said, "No."

"But he said—"

"They don't." If any of her cops spent even a half second wondering if Jojo had killed Zachary Gordon, Laurie would personally detach their nuts from their bodies. "You were there, so they have to say that. But you're not a suspect."

"But you said—"

"Enough. Don't worry." Laurie dropped onto the dark orange couch she'd helped Omid pick out. She waved Jojo next to her.

Her daughter thumped down, her purse clutched tightly between her hands.

"Can I have that charger, please?" Laurie pressed the ON button again and again, but the phone was obviously long dead.

Jojo handed it over wordlessly, and Laurie plugged it in.

The phone gave a jolt, vibrating to life.

"Mom."

Laurie looked up. "Yeah, baby?"

Jojo shook her head. Her cheeks were pale. "Nothing."

A lock screen came up, a picture of Harper making a duck face. Who made their own photo a lock screen? "Do you know the code?"

"Here." Jojo took the phone out of her hand. "I have thumbprint access."

Laurie felt a thud in the middle of her belly. The girls were so close again, and she'd never known. What else didn't she know about her daughter?

Jojo held the phone so that both of them could look at the face of it. Text after text rocketed past, coming to life.

From Jojo: **Where are you?**

What's going on?

I don't know what happened.

You have to answer me.

ANSWER ME.

From the boyfriend, Ray:

Where you at? Call me.

Come on. Why don't you call me back?

Laurie reached to click on his contact info, but there was nothing else in it—no last name, no address, no other social media accounts. She shot a look at Jojo, who just shook her head.

From Pamela: **For the love of God, call us back.**

We're out of our minds.

Harper, I'm losing it. Call me.

Nothing from Kevin Leeds.

"What was the last text **she** sent?"

Jojo clicked. "Looks like . . . to Ray." She held out the phone.

Meet us at the side of the house—in the yard.

Laurie felt her breath catch in her chest. "'Us.' That's you and her?"

"I guess."

"Did you meet up with Ray?"

"We were supposed to, yeah."

"But you don't remember."

Jojo shook her head. She squinted as if she had a headache. "I got in his car with her. But I can't remember what he looks like or—" She made a frustrated noise in the back of her throat. "God, I'm so **stupid.**"

"Okay," said Laurie. "It's okay. Let's keep looking. Can you see who she called last night?"

Jojo's fingers flew over the screen. "No one."

Well, teens didn't call anyone, ever. "What about her e-mail? Facebook? Snapchat?"

"Hang on." Jojo pulled up app after app. "Nothing in e-mail but some school stuff. Last Snap was to me, but it's gone. Doesn't look like she downloaded it." Her daughter's cheeks colored.

"What about Facebook?"

"Mom." In Jojo's voice was what she wasn't saying: **Facebook is for the olds.** But she pulled it up. There were dozens of messages, but only eight unread ones.

"Okay." Jojo flicked them open. "These two are just some jewelry company she was messaging about some earrings."

Harper and jewelry. "What about the others?"

"One from her dad from two days ago." Jojo grimaced. "A cat GIF."

"And?"

"Five from . . . Wait, Jack Ramsay? Like, Captain Ramsay?"

Laurie tugged the phone from Jojo's fingers. "Huh?"

There he was. Jack Ramsay's wide-jawed face looked at her from the tiny avatar. Confusion made Laurie's thoughts sludgy. Jack Ramsay had retired the year before, on his fiftieth birthday. He lived on the east end and had broken up with his third wife a few months ago. She and Omid had had him over for dinner twice since his retirement. He'd been excited about his new speedboat. "What the hell?"

I need to see you.

Harper, this isn't a joke.

I'm getting desperate.

Don't do this.

You need to come to my house ASAP. I'm not kidding around. We could be in a lot of trouble.

Jojo wriggled and reached for the phone. "I don't get it. Why is **he** messaging her?"

Laurie kept her grip tight as she scrolled backward. "I have no idea." There were dozens of messages, going back six months or more.

You're like a flower. A perfect flower.

Laurie's stomach tightened painfully.

From Harper: **Well, you're like a gray-haired sugar daddy, and I like sugar and daddies and gray if it's like fifty shades of it.**

TWENTY-TWO

LAURIE TURNED THE phone so Jojo couldn't read it.

"Mom, let me have it."

"No." She could outstubborn her daughter any day.

"I **have** to see it, too. You know that, right?"

Her daughter's voice was stern. She was right, damn it.

"Jesus, okay." She leaned against Jojo's small shoulder. "Did you know about this? About him?"

Jojo shook her head. "Scroll back some more."

Laurie turned a gasp into a cough. A picture of Harper in a cheesy red negligee, the kind Frederick's of Hollywood sold, the kind that was scratchy and uncomfortable. The image showed only Harper's upper half, nipples clear through the red mesh.

"She **sent** this to him? To Captain Ramsay?" Jojo's eyes were huge.

"You really didn't know?"

She shook her head harder. "Uh-uh."

Laurie believed her. She stood, putting the phone in her pocket.

"What are you doing?" Jojo sounded scared.

"Taking you home."

"But my statement. I wasn't done, was I?"

"That can wait." Though Laurie hated like hell to admit it to herself, Harper was more important right now. Jojo was physically okay. She was safe. Harper wasn't.

She should tell Steiner; she **should** divulge this. But this couldn't be what it sounded like. Ramsay was an old friend. He'd saved Omid's ass one time when a suspect went sideways on him on Webster Street. Maybe he'd talk to her.

Jojo began, "Steiner said that—"

"I don't care what he said. You're not a criminal, nor are you a real suspect. He can't keep you here. You did nothing wrong. He can come to the house if he needs more." Laurie knew exactly what their rights were. "After I drop you off, I'll go to Ramsay's house. I'll sort this out." Yeah, right.

Jojo narrowed her eyes. "Take me with you."

"No effing way."

"Do you think he has her? Do you think Harper is there with him?"

If she were, Ramsay wouldn't be sending such

frantic messages. The last had come in just an hour ago. "No."

"Then it's safe, right? Take me. Maybe he'll tell me something he wouldn't tell you."

Laurie balled her hands into fists. This wasn't happening. "Honey . . ."

"Please don't leave me alone. **I can't be alone.**" Jojo's voice cracked.

Laurie lost her breath. "Oh, honey."

"Take me. I'll stay in the car. Just don't **leave** me."

"Of course. Of course." She wanted to pull Jojo into her arms, but if she did, Jojo would melt down—she could feel it—and then Jojo would be furious at losing it. So instead Laurie dug out her own cell phone and pulled up Steiner's number.

Cops lied all the time. Dispatchers did, too. They were trained to. **Of course your husband won't be arrested if he comes to the station to see if he has a warrant.**

No, we're not sending the police, just an ambulance.

If you open the door to talk to the cop, he'll just take a statement and let you go on your way.

She texted Steiner, **Jojo just got her period, probably stress, running out to drugstore, back in a few minutes.**

JACK Ramsay's house was an older bungalow on the east end, the cheaper side of the city. He couldn't afford the monster houses he'd had with any of his three wives—he'd lost one house per divorce—but this place had seemed warm when Laurie visited him a few months before. Even though the garage was leaning and the backyard an overgrown wasteland, the house's exterior had a rigidity that disguised a soft kindness, like Jack himself.

"Stay here." Laurie unstrapped her belt.

Jojo said, "Hang on."

Laurie waited. One beat, then two. "Yeah?"

"What if . . . I mean, I know it's him, and I grew up with him and everything. But what if he does have her? Do you think, like, Steiner should be here or something? Or someone higher?"

Or Dad? The words her daughter didn't say rang clearly inside the safe shell of the car. Yeah. Laurie wanted Omid, too.

But she said, "It's Jack. I've known him for twenty years. I'll be safe with him."

"Do you think she really, like, slept with him?"

Laurie would lay a million dollars that Harper had. Girls didn't send those kinds of pictures, nor did they flirt that hard with someone they didn't want to bag. "I don't know, sweetheart. But I really want to find out."

"Can I just come to the door?"

"Don't you dare move from that seat. You got me?" Laurie used her strongest don't-fuck-with-Mom voice, and it seemed to work. Jojo melted back into the seat.

"Yeah."

Saturday afternoon in this kind of neighborhood meant outdoor action. It meant lawn mowers and weed whackers. Two kids across the street shot hoops, and another kid Rollerbladed by. Laurie avoided the eye of the guy next door who was trimming a camellia. No time for small talk.

She rang the doorbell. A dog two houses down seemed to hear it, barking its head off.

Nothing.

She rang it again.

This time the door was yanked open forcefully. Ramsay's eyes were bright until they registered who she was. "Oh. Hey, Laurie. What's up?"

Had he been expecting Harper? "Can I come in?"

"Of course." He brought her through the living room and into the kitchen. On the large table was a huge puzzle, halfway done. It had to be a two-thousand-piece one, **Star Wars**–themed.

"Wow," she said.

Ramsay shrugged. "What can I say? I'm working the Coliseum for A's games, but I gotta pass the time when I'm not there."

"How's retirement treating you?" The words came out of her mouth without her thinking. As if she'd honestly dropped by for a social visit.

"Good, good. Want something to drink? I can make coffee, or I think I've got some Coke in the garage fridge." He waved at the door to the garage.

"I'm good. Listen, Jack, I can't get into everything

that's going on, but I'm looking for Harper Cunningham."

Ramsay's face flickered.

She knew this man. You didn't work with someone for so long without knowing him better than any short-term wife ever could.

He was scared. That split-second flicker had given him away.

"Who?" he said.

Laurie didn't have to repeat it. "She's missing. We're worried about her."

He gave up the pretense. "What do you mean, 'missing'? Where is she?"

"I was hoping you could help me with that." It was a cop phrase, and it came out of her mouth like she'd never gotten off the street and into dispatch.

"How did you find out I know her?"

"Facebook."

He blanched. "Oh, God."

"Jack—" She reached toward him, but he pulled back.

"I'm going to get you that Coke."

"I don't need anything. Let's just talk. I'm hoping you know more about her relationship with Kevin Leeds."

"The football player?" He looked honestly surprised.

"Yeah."

He glanced down at his hands and brushed them

on his pants, as if wiping something off. "I guess I'm the one who needs a soda. Fuck it, I need something stronger."

Laurie nodded. Jack had always been a drinker.

"I'll be right back." He let himself out the kitchen door into the garage.

Laurie blew a tight breath from her lungs. He was freaked out. Of course he was. Yeah, it was going to be a big deal that he'd been sleeping with a minor, but it was an even bigger deal that she was missing, and Laurie found that she didn't really care how freaked out he was. He just needed to help them find her. He didn't seem like he had any info on Leeds, but she wouldn't know for sure until—

A bang sounded through the kitchen. It could have been interpreted as a car backfire or an M-80 firecracker going off.

But Laurie knew without a doubt the sound of a gunshot.

TWENTY-THREE

RAMSAY WAS ON the other side of the Lexus in the garage. He'd fallen sideways from the force of the bullet, landing on his back, his left arm trapped below his body at an unnatural angle. There was a small entry wound at his right temple, and the left side of his head was gone, leaving brain matter and clots of blood all over the tools on the bench. The blood pooled into a puddle—soon it would be a lake. Hollow-point bullet, of course, to deliver maximum damage to internal organs, making death more certain. Cops never fucked around when it came to suicide.

"Fuck, fuck, **fuck.**" Her breath came in small, tight bursts. She pulled her phone from her pocket with clammy hands, but it wasn't her phone, it was Harper's, and she could barely figure out how to get to the emergency option, and why the **hell** had she left her own phone in the car? She couldn't go out there, not yet. And what about Jojo? Had she heard the noise? **Fuck.**

She scanned the walls and found an old-fashioned corded phone hanging next to the garage-door opener. She punched 911.

"911, what's the address of your emergency?"

"Maury, it's me. I'm at Jack Ramsay's house. This is a landline—you got the address?" She couldn't have pulled it out of her brain if a gun had been pressed to her—Oh, God. "He's dead. Ramsay's dead."

Rapid keystrokes clicked over the line. "What the fuck, Laurie?" He'd get in trouble for that later when the tapes were pulled—which they would be—but she would have said the same thing.

"Gunshot wound to the temple. Suicide."

"Where's the gun?"

She stretched the cord till she could see Ramsay again. The blood was still moving like a sluggish red river on the floor, the scent of copper rising from it. "The gun's next to him."

"Don't touch it, okay? You want EMD?"

Like she didn't know all the instructions by heart, like emergency medical dispatch instructions would help him now. "Too late."

From behind her came a high-pitched female scream, a whine that wound its way up into the rafters and ricocheted back down. Laurie dropped the phone, knowing that the line would be left open, that Maury would keep listening. She didn't care.

She turned and opened her arms, planting her feet wide. She made herself as big as possible, as if she could block Jojo's view. "Out!"

"Mama!"

Laurie stabbed the air with her pointer finger. "Get **out.** Back. Come on. Come with me. Into the kitchen."

Jojo stumbled up the two steps that led back into the house. "Is he dead? Did he shoot himself? Is he really **dead**?"

"It's okay," Laurie lied ridiculously. In the kitchen she shut the garage door and leaned against it with all her weight. "It's okay."

Jojo had already sunk to her knees, her hand clamped firmly against her mouth. Laurie sank down, too, keeping the door shut with her shoulders. She wrapped her arms around Jojo and continued to hold her until the sirens outside drowned out the sound of her daughter's sobs.

JOJO sat in the hard blue plastic chair in the front lobby of the police department. She unlocked her phone for the fifty-millionth time in the last ten minutes, as if there would be something waiting for her, a message that had sneaked in silently. She pulled up a Tumblr she liked, where puppies regularly cavorted with baby hippos, that kind of thing, but all she could see was blood.

So much blood.

All of it pouring out of his body, and her mother hadn't done anything to stop it. It hadn't seemed right. Logically, Jojo knew that Ramsay was big-time dead, but shouldn't they have tried **something**? CPR? But then she saw an image of her mother pressing her face to the half of a face that Ramsay had left to blow air into—of course Mom couldn't have tried.

Jojo shook her head hard. She stared at a small bird singing "The Lion Sleeps Tonight." It was supposed to be funny.

She closed her eyes and saw the image of the blood again, flowing like thin lava across the garage floor.

Nate Steiner had told her to wait in the lobby for her mother. There'd been something in his voice like he was mad at her, but she didn't know why. They'd finished Jojo's interview fast, like he didn't care anymore. Maybe he was just angry about everything. If so, that was good. Harper was the one who mattered now, not her.

Harper was the **only** one who mattered. The only one in the whole world. Jojo held her breath for a beat to see if she could slow her racing heart.

When Mom and she had gotten back to the station—after the ambulance and the fire engine and like seven thousand cop cars had shown up, after they'd shoved them out and told them to get back to the station—they'd practically carried

Mom into the interview room with them. Mom had been sagging, her shoulders terrifyingly slack. She'd looked as if she'd needed propping up. She had to give a statement to Lieutenant Colson and Officer Frank Shepherd about Ramsay.

While she did that, Jojo had finished giving her statement about the rape to Steiner. The word echoed in her head every time it bounced in. **Rape, rape, rape.**

Other words started bonging in her head, as if words had become clappers and her brain a bell. She saw Zach's face, could almost hear his laugh. **Murder, murder, murder.**

Harper was still missing.

Missing, missing, missing. The terrible but true thing was that the word **missing,** when attached to Harper, was more important than even **murder.** No one could help Zach. But someone **had** to help Harper.

Jojo's heart clenched. How many investigations were happening? Four—her attack, Zach's murder, Harper missing, Ramsay dead?

They couldn't all be related, she tried to tell herself.

But no, they had to be. Dad always said there was no such thing as coincidence, that there was always something that connected things.

Harper.

They had to **find** her.

Ramsay—the blood—

What if Harper . . . ?

Jojo thought about praying, but she wasn't sure what god to pray to, and she didn't think she had anything to offer. **I'll give up Raisinets in my popcorn at the movies. I won't let Harper copy my math homework senior year. I'll be nice to Mom every day.**

Stupid. God wouldn't give a shit about such trivial things.

Jojo flicked her phone on again, not trusting that she'd hear the notification sounds, not with the blood pounding in her ears. She hoped for something—anything—from Harper, or Kevin. . . . No, that was impossible, he was **here.** In this very same building, right now. So close. She hated him.

But he couldn't have raped me. He's gay. **Was it like his test kiss? Would he do it to see if he felt anything?** Did **he rape me? Zach was the one who was killed. . . . Whatever happened had happened in Kevin's house. Kevin wasn't roofied. Or was he? Do we know that? So what did he do to me?**

She'd liked Kevin so much.

Now . . .

Rape. Murder.

So much blood, a lake of it.

Yeah, this feeling in her chest felt like hate, all right. It felt like something sitting on her spleen, smashing her internal organs so that they wouldn't work anymore.

Had she ever hated a person before? She'd despised some, sure. That girl in third grade who stole her lunch every day for a month. The kid in gym in seventh grade who'd told everyone he'd seen her staring at Harper's breasts. (He wasn't wrong—that's why she'd despised him.)

But hate? This felt new. And painful. Her blood had been replaced by gasoline, and her arteries ached with it. One match and she'd blow.

A homeless man shouted something about needing the bathroom key. Jojo knew that it didn't take a key, that if it was locked, someone was in there, but **she** wasn't going to talk to him. She hoped the desk sergeant would hear and come out and rescue her soon.

Although why was she waiting? She knew the code to get in. She could wait for Mom in the break room as easily as out here.

"I'ma shit my pants!" roared the man.

Jojo punched the code in so fast she got it wrong twice, the red light goading her.

"You know how to get in there, little girl? You spend too much time here, huh? Can I use the bathroom in there?"

The light finally buzzed green. She slipped inside and shoved the heavy door shut behind her.

Usually there were at least a couple of people in

records, chatting or getting coffee from the fancy auto-espresso machine, but it was silent, as if everyone were hiding from her.

Just across the hall from records, Jojo's feet slowed. Her feet **made** her stop. Just like that.

Right in front of the door to the jail.

She put her hand on the metal door. It was freezing to the touch, almost as cold as her own bones.

Kevin's gay. He couldn't have raped me. He was my friend.

Couldn't have.

What the fuck?

No one was visible in the corridor. In the distance she heard a man laugh, maybe from the traffic office, but otherwise there was only the hum of forced air and the low buzz of the lights overhead.

Her fingers punched the code into the jail keypad. They should really change the codes so that they were different for every door.

The green light glowed at her. An invitation.

She pushed the door open. Sarah would kick her out in five seconds. Maybe less. Or someone in dispatch would see it on their cameras and do an overhead announcement to get her out. Jojo would blame it on the Ambien still being in her system, and she started rehearsing the apology in her head.

But no building announcement came. Sarah wasn't there. None of the jailers were. Dimly she heard, "Get the mask!" from the sally port. They must be dealing with a spitter.

Which left the way clear to the door that led to the cells.

Jojo's fingers danced the same pattern, entering the code into the second keypad. Another green light grinned at her.

There was a solid thunk as the door lock released.

She shoved through and into the hallway.

Fuck.

What was she doing? Jojo's neck was tight, and her fingers trembled. She stuck her hands into her pockets. She peeked into the small window of the first cell.

No one, just a folded gray blanket resting on the cot.

Second cell, also empty.

Third cell.

There.

Kevin lay with his back to the door, face to the wall. He looked enormous on the small cot, a lion resting on a house cat's bed.

Jojo's heart beat so hard in her chest she thought it might beat right out and whap its way down the corridor. She sucked in a breath and then rapped on the glass. She felt the hair rise on her arms and raised her chin.

He didn't turn.

So she spoke through the small speaking hole in the window. "Kevin. It's me."

He turned then, flipped over and stood so fast that the cot scooted sideways with a screech. "Jojo?"

Kevin was at the glass then, and Jojo felt her back press against the wall before she was aware that she'd moved.

"Jojo, what the fuck is happening?"

Fear held Jojo's throat shut. She raised a hand and rubbed at her neck and then forced out air in the shape of the only words she could find. "Did you drug me?"

"What?"

"Did you . . . **rape** . . . me?"

"No." His eyes seemed sunken, the skin underneath them a deep, dark olive. "Of **course** not. You know I didn't."

Did she know that?

"Jojo. I wouldn't ever do something like that."

He was telling the truth.

She knew it. Jojo never trusted her mother when she talked about her famous gut intuition, but she almost understood it now—sometimes you just knew you were right.

He'd chosen to trust her, to tell her about him and Zach. He'd had the same serious look on his face then.

"So you **didn't** do it?" She needed just one more clarification.

He shook his head as his eyes went glassy with tears. "I have no clue what the fuck is happening. Help me."

Relief sagged through her, and she had to lock her knees to keep herself from sinking to the tile. "I don't know what to do."

He shook his head. His voice was thin through the glass and metal, but still audible. "They said Zach is dead."

Nausea flooded Jojo, sending a sour-salt pang to the back of her throat. "Kevin . . ."

He shook his head again, harder. "But that's not right. Right? Zach is fine."

Jojo forgot every word she knew. Her mouth opened, but nothing came out.

"No." Kevin shook his head. "This isn't happening. This is a dream."

"Did you hear anything?"

"I was **asleep.** I always sleep hard—like, I mean a brass band could come through my room and I wouldn't wake up." He paused. "Nah. This is just a bad dream, the worst fucking dream in the world, and I have got to wake the fuck up. I was asleep in my own house when those cops jumped on top of me, and while I was sleeping—what the fuck. You said you were drugged? Was I drugged? I don't feel like it. But I must be asleep." He rubbed his cheeks and then his neck. "I have to figure out how to wake **up.**"

"I'm so sorry." Stupid words, meaningless words.

"I have to get out of here." He scrubbed at his eyes. "Jojo, get me out of here. I have to tell his family. It has to be me."

He was probably the last person who should talk to Zach's family. Jojo moved closer to the door. "Harper's missing."

"Harper? What?"

"Do you know where she is?"

His eyes were huge, the whites wide. "I saw you leave the party together. We went home. I woke up to cops jumping on me. Some asshole clubbed me with a stick and almost broke my arm putting me in handcuffs. They said I raped you, and that my . . . my best friend is dead, and that they think I did it." He put his hand over his mouth, as if stopping the words could change the facts.

Some asshole. Dad. "I know."

"They dragged me out of **my** house and threw me in this cell. They gave me a phone call, and I called the team lawyer, but he hasn't gotten back to me. They haven't even questioned me yet. I've just been in here. Jojo." Kevin put his palm against the glass. "You know I didn't do any of this."

Three minutes ago she'd been hating him with her whole body.

But he didn't do this.

She was sure.

Okay, she was ninety percent sure.

Maybe eighty-five. Dad always said to take odds that were more than eighty percent.

"Kevin—"

From behind Jojo came a woman's shout. "What the **shitting** fuck are you doing, Jojo?"

Kevin's eyes were panicked.

That was the thing that got Jojo, that struck her to the heart. Kevin was scared.

The look on his face made her ten times more terrified than she'd already been.

Sarah's hand was like steel around her upper arm. "Your dad is going to **kill** me."

Apparently this was how it felt to be her prisoner. "Ow! You're pulling too hard! Ouch!"

"I can't **believe** you just did that." Sarah continued to drag Jojo until they were through the door and in the main intake area. "Do you even know how you just compromised this investigation?"

It wasn't compromised. It was aided. Now Jojo knew that Kevin hadn't done it.

But Sarah didn't need that information. Once in the main part of the jail, Jojo said, "Sorry."

"Seriously? That's all you've got? Letting yourself in here? Jesus. You and your goddamn mother."

Mom? "Huh?"

Sarah opened the main door and pointed. "You'd better tell your dad, because I'm sure as **hell** not going down for this."

In the hallway Jojo spoke as the door was falling shut. "Don't worry. I'll tell him."

Then panic settled again into her belly, claws scuttling inside her.

If Kevin hadn't done this—hadn't raped her and hadn't killed Zach—then someone else had.

That someone else wasn't locked up.

That someone else had Harper.

TWENTY-FOUR

LAURIE PUT HER head on her folded arms on the table. "It's all related."

Mark Colson wasn't listening to her. He was a good lieutenant, just like he'd been a good street cop, but he was known for his bluster, and his bluster got louder the more uncertain he was. When they'd stopped dating because Laurie had been interested in Omid, he'd blustered so hard he'd broken a blood vessel in his eye. Now his voice was raised. "We can't **know** that, Laurie! Not yet."

Laurie stole a peek at Frank Shepherd. "Frank, you see this, right? It's obvious."

Frank—the scaredy-cat—shrugged.

She sat up straight. The sooner this was over, the sooner she could get back to Jojo.

Fuck Ramsay. He'd killed himself like a coward,

but what if he knew something—what if he knew everything?

At the same time, her head throbbed, her throat full of salt. Ramsay had been her friend. Once, long ago, they'd gotten bombed in La Precia at eight in the morning after Laurie's first suicide-by-hanging call. He'd just sat there with her, letting her cry, buying her more margaritas, and then driving her home.

"Laurie?"

When she was done giving her statement, she and Jojo could go right home and stay there. Preferably forever. "Harper Cunningham was sleeping with Ramsay. Harper Cunningham is missing, and Ramsay is dead. Harper was with my daughter before she was 261'd at a house in which a man was killed. Jesus, you guys. These four things are related." She hated herself for not being able to say "raped." But she just couldn't, not again.

"I know this is hard, Laurie. Especially with Omid in the hospital. It's emotional." Colson patted her hand.

She wanted to slap him with it. Colson wasn't stupid, so why this stupid routine? Was it some cop-protecting-cop bullshit? If only Omid **were** here—wheels would be moving so much faster. "Are we done?"

Shepherd flipped the pages of his notebook. "Yeah. That's about it." He leaned back as if he were getting ready to chat about baseball. "So tell us how

Omid is. Someone said he's got to stay in there another couple of days? And how's Jojo holding up? It's been a hell of a twenty-four hours, hasn't it?"

Laurie didn't answer. She stood and left the room, slamming the door behind her. They'd talk shit about her in T-minus three seconds, and she didn't care.

"Hey," she said to Maria Bagley, who was at the traffic desk. "You seen Jojo?"

"Today?"

Genius. "Never mind."

The break room held only a couple of uniforms eating burritos. It smelled like carne asada, and Laurie felt her stomach rumble. "Have you seen Jojo?"

Connors nodded. "She was headed down to dispatch, I think."

"Thanks."

"Hey, Laurie!" Will Yarwood again, strutting his short chicken walk as he came out of the firing range door. "How's she doing?"

Laurie ignored him completely. She took the steps down two at a time, so fast her feet were blurred when she looked down. It was comforting, that every cop in town knew Jojo. It was nice knowing that Jojo couldn't get up to much in San Bernal without Laurie and Omid hearing about it. (Though they hadn't heard about Steiner catching her smoking weed—Laurie would talk to him about that.)

Laurie had seriously thought their biggest problem would be helping Jojo decide where to go to college.

And now? She went around the corner, dodging Captain Marbella's ficus plant. Now her daughter's accused rapist, a man who might be a murderer, was sitting upstairs in the exact cell the girls had been in.

And where the hell was Harper?

She punched in the code to enter dispatch.

Inside the ComCen, Jojo was sitting at an empty terminal, pecking at her cell. Shonda was on the phone, Maury was talking on the police radio, so only Charity was free to gawk at Laurie's entrance.

Jojo was who mattered. "Hey, cookie." God, she hadn't called her daughter that for ten years. She'd almost forgotten the endearment entirely. "Want to go home?"

Jojo nodded without looking up.

Laurie felt tears start at the back of her throat as the eyes of her co-workers fixed on her, looking at her like she was someone else, someone they didn't recognize or know how to handle. That was rich. Dispatchers always knew how to handle everything.

But they didn't know how to handle **this.**

Maury moved first. He rose. "Laurie."

She put her hands out. "Don't hug me." If he did, she'd crack. "Thanks for watching her."

Jojo stalked out, no doubt offended by the idea

that anyone at all had been watching her like a kid. The door shut behind her.

"Did she say anything to you? About Harper or anything?"

Maury shook his head. "We told her she didn't have to talk. You okay?"

I can't do this by myself. I need Omid.

Laurie folded her lips tight and shook her head.

TWENTY-FIVE

IN THE HOSPITAL Jojo felt nauseated. The smell of bleach and something acrid, almost burned, wasn't making it better. She felt deep-down sick, like she was going to throw up again.

At least Dad wasn't giving her those big sad eyes anymore. Now he was working. Being Dad, dealing with death and murder.

And his daughter's rape.

The thought made her feel sicker—was this something that was going to hit the media at some point? Even if they didn't officially name her, it would get out. God, why hadn't she thought of that? She'd be the one that got raped, right? Everyone at school would think about her, unconscious and—Jesus.

Jojo wanted her father to stop it. To put a halt to all of it.

But he couldn't. He was out of commission, and Mom was just a dispatcher, and Jojo was shit out of luck. She balanced on her toes while holding lightly on to the bar at the foot of the bed. No one noticed when she wobbled and whacked her hip on the blood pressure machine.

Dad had both his cell phones out and was typing furiously with his thumbs, all the while asking Mom questions. "Who's doing the ID at Ramsay's?"

"Veronica and Rattan."

"Veronica's not ready for that. She's done one homicide in her whole career."

"Two now. She's doing Zachary Gordon's, too. And Rattan is good. You know that."

Dad shook his head. "If she fucks it up—I've got to get Thompson over there, too." He stabbed at his phone some more.

"Don't forget," said Mom. "You're not the chief right now."

Dad's eyes tightened. "Don't tell me."

"Brent Stanley."

"Seriously? That's who's on rotation?"

Mom nodded. "But can you imagine if Darren Dixon was still around? He'd have been next on the list."

"Screw that guy," Dad said cheerfully. Dixon had

posted anti-Muslim shit on the department's Facebook page when Dad had been promoted to chief. One of Dad's first responsibilities in his new position as chief three years ago had been to fire him. Dad wasn't even Muslim, just a first-generation Iranian American raised nominally Christian, but the press didn't care—it had been a good scandal. Jojo had forgotten all about that until now. How many other people hated Dad because they thought he was Muslim?

How many people hated her for the same reason?

Mom's cell rang, and she held up a finger. "Yeah? Go ahead." Then she shot Jojo a look. "Hang on." She pressed the phone to her chest. "I'll be right back." She went into the hall.

Jojo folded her arms over her stomach, slightly relieved it was just her and Dad now, even though he was pecking at his phone.

What would Veronica do? Cut Zach open? Like they did in the movies? Was that for Identification or the coroner? Did they work together? What about Ramsay? Would they need to do that to him, even though his cause of death was obvious? Well, presumably Zach's was obvious, too.

All that blood inside the bodies of everyone she knew, ready to spill out at any time.

She shook her head. **Think of anything else.** "You call Veronica by her first name but Rattan by his last. Why do you do that?"

"What?" Dad looked startled, his wide, dark eyebrows lifting.

"It's, like, totally a respect thing. You do it all the time. Like Maria Bagley. You call her Maria. You only call women by their first names. That's sexist."

Dad barely looked up. "It's not sexist. We call her Bagley, too. Veronica's ID, not a sworn officer, so it's different."

"But Rattan isn't sworn, and you use his last name." It was only a matter of time before he found out she'd broken into the jail and had seen Kevin. "I just think it's messed up. Yet another act of diminishment within the patriarchy."

Dad actually snorted.

"Really?" She wasn't a baby. She'd seen a dead friend—okay, it might be a stretch to call Ramsay a friend, but she'd known him her whole life—today. He gave her a tea set when she was like five, and she'd loved it. She'd seen his blood still **flowing.** Presumably still hot from his veins. And then there was the pale image in her mind of Harper, moving against Ramsay. . . . Bile rose in the back of her throat again. It wasn't Dad's fault, but she could glare at him like it was.

"I was just clearing my throat. Honey, how are you?" His voice was weirdly hoarse, and his eyes, now that they were on her, were too intense. His gaze made her feel prickly, like he was searching for something that she didn't know how to give.

"Fine."

"You've had to deal with so much." He dropped his cell to the bed. "So much. It breaks my fucking heart, you know that?"

Dad tried never to swear in front of her. His casual f-bomb made Jojo's stomach tighten. "I'm fine, really. We just have to find Harper."

"Do you think she could be off with someone? Her boyfriend? Like she did in the past? You know, stoned and sleeping it off somewhere?"

"**You're** the one who says there's no such thing as coincidence. I was with Harper, shit happens to me, and Harper turns up missing?"

"They're **looking**." His voice was louder than necessary.

"**How?** I just saw people in the station doing their everyday things. Like it didn't matter. Like **she** doesn't matter."

Dad's hands were shaking on top of the sheet. "She matters. You have no idea what's going on, honey. You know how much I love you, right?" He rubbed at the bridge of his nose, closing his eyes. "If you were missing . . ."

Jojo was the only one he ever got emotional about, and she usually loved it. Not today. "What's your main priority right now?"

He answered without appearing to think. "To fuck up the animal who hurt you. But I can't. Instead"—he shook the bed rail so hard it clattered and jumped—"I'm trapped in **here**."

It was the wrong answer. "Harper is **missing.** I'm here. She's not."

Dad cleared his throat. "It's not like we can organize a grid search or something. They're doing the best they can with what they have."

"Why not?" Jojo swallowed hard, pushing down the queasiness. "Why can't you do one?"

"I'd love to do one, but we can't. She's not a little kid or an Alzheimer patient who wandered off. Sending out all our officers to sweep the streets for her without a clue where to look is a misuse of the few resources we have right now. I don't think she just got lost, do you?"

What else did lost look like? "Yeah. She's lost."

"If she wandered off and lost her way, even if she was roofied like you were, she would have come to her senses by now."

"She doesn't have her phone."

"She has abilities, though. She'd be able to flag someone down. To ask to borrow a phone. She would have called her parents. She's not disoriented in the woods somewhere, Jojo." Dad's eyes were all work now, and Jojo didn't like it one bit.

And the fact being drilled home that Harper wasn't simply lost was crushing, even though Jojo'd already kind of known it. "Oh." She took a breath. Dad was staring at her like she was something breakable, which was crap. She might not feel great—it was that morning-after pill, or maybe the Ambien—but she wasn't going to shatter. "What about the dogs? You can get the dogs in, right?"

Dad nodded. "K9's been in already."

"And?"

"And nothing."

Jojo narrowed her eyes. "They didn't have anything to track. I have a sweatshirt of hers at home. I can go get it." She held up her phone. "Look, Harper's mom is blowing me up. She can bring a piece of clothing to the station." As if on cue, her phone pinged with another message from Pamela. **Anything? What's going on? Can you ask your father to call me? Or your mom?**

Dad shook his head. "They had a shirt her mother gave them to track."

Mom barreled back in. Her mouth was open to speak, and then she looked at Jojo. She stopped.

Dad spoke instead. "Did you get the e-mail about what they found in the kitchen at Leeds's?"

Mom blinked. "The white stuff in the kitchen?"

Jojo stuck out her chin. "I bet it's flour."

Dad's head swiveled to her. "How did you know that?"

She gave a groan. "Because he likes to bake when he's not running balls for millions of dollars or actively working to help oppressed people rise up. Is that against the law or something? He's **not** the killer rapist you think he is." She wouldn't be able to prove it to them. There was no way they'd ever believe her.

Jojo caught the look that flew between her mother and father. "What?"

Dad put his glasses on and tapped his phone faster. He read something. Then he made a low noise in the back of his throat that raised goose bumps on Jojo's arms.

"What?"

"Jojo, leave the room. I need to talk to Mom."

"No, tell me."

Mom took a step toward her, but Jojo backed up to keep the space between them the same width.

"There was blood at the scene."

Jojo's stomach lurched. "Zach's." Jojo hadn't been bleeding. Not as far as she could tell, anyway.

Her parents stayed silent.

"Tell me."

"Sugar, they ran a DNA test on it." Mom looked at her own phone.

"And?" Jojo couldn't breathe.

"They took a sample of Pamela's when she made the report. ID just matched it to Pamela's blood sample by DNA. It was Harper's blood."

TWENTY-SIX

JOJO SHOOK HER head. "No." She felt her legs start to shake again.

Harper was her person.

Harper saw her.

Harper **loved** her.

Jojo's parents extolled her virtues, telling her she was good at math, at science, at English. She'd make a good scientist, they said. Or she liked animals—why didn't she want to be a veterinarian? Never a cop, or a firefighter, or a paramedic. They didn't listen when she said that she wanted to help people—that kids who wanted to be accountants and journalists baffled her. Where was the fun in just making a paycheck when you could run toward emergencies and prevent some of the fallout? Maybe save a life? Her parents, though, wanted her to be boring and safe, never thinking about what Jojo actually wanted.

Harper saw into Jojo's heart and didn't give a shit what Jojo was good or bad at. She didn't care what she became in the future, what she would eventually turn into. She could give a crap if Jojo ended up a police detective or an arsonist. She just loved her. Harper was her **person.**

Jojo felt herself start to sway.

Dad said, "You see, Laurie? **This** is why we weren't going to tell her. Goddamn it."

"No! Don't hide things from me! This is **my** life. Harper's life!" Jojo lurched at the side of the bed and gripped her father's wrist, the way he used to when pulling back her arm from things that might hurt her—a hot stove, a growling dog. "Tell me. When you know things, **tell** me."

Dad's face was perfectly still. His work face again. This was the face he used in morning lineup, when telling his officers how to do their job. This was the face he used when he was pissed off with the world, or with Mom, or with her. But he said, "Okay."

"Okay?"

He nodded. "Okay. You tell me everything, and I'll tell you everything."

Jojo didn't want to tell him every single thing, though. Not yet. "What about Ramsay? I was thinking about that movie **Room,** and what if he has, like, a shed or something, and she's in there? She **was** seeing him after all, right?" **How had Harper**

not told her? "What if something happened to her at Kevin's house, and she called Ramsay, and he came and got her, and he was keeping her hidden? And Ray is kind of close to the name Ramsay, right?"

Dad shook his head and held up his cell phone, as if it were proof he was telling her the truth. "Full search. Nothing."

"What if he has a secret room? Like in the walls?"

"Thermal-imaging camera says no one else is there."

Jojo took a moment to breathe and think. Thermal. Looking for Harper's body heat.

But if she was dead, there'd be no thermal image.

Dad had for sure thought about that.

As if reading her mind, he said, "K9 was there, remember? No match, no hit."

Mom gave a small, high-pitched sigh that hurt to hear. Then she said, "Jojo, everything keeps pointing back to Kevin Leeds as the best suspect."

"Then **where** is she? If you think he did it, wouldn't he have her somewhere?" Jojo shook her head so hard the top of her brain hurt. "It wasn't him."

"Honey—" Mom did that reaching thing again, and Jojo shrank back farther, so that her shoulder jostled a vase of red carnations someone had sent Dad. It didn't quite fall, but Mom pulled back.

"Mom. Stop."

Mom's fists clenched at her sides. "Joshi, I know

that Harper's our number one concern right now, but, honey, please hear me when I say this: Your first time is still coming. That didn't count. It doesn't **count**."

Nausea swelled again, and Jojo's stomach tightened. Her mother was bringing this up **now,** when she could have said it at the house, or in the car, but **now**? In front of Dad, too? "What makes you think that was my first time?"

"It wasn't?" Mom's words were crystal clear and slowly enunciated.

"Maybe it was. Maybe it wasn't." She actually had no fucking clue, not really. **Why** the hell had she said that to her mother? Why make it even worse?

"Okay." Mom raised her hands and then let them fall in that take-a-deep-breath thing she did. "That's okay. Sixteen-year-olds have sex. We know that. No big deal."

"I wasn't asking for permission. The only thing I need from you is to accept that Kevin Leeds didn't do anything wrong. That he's my friend and he wouldn't hurt me."

Dad spoke then, his voice dark and terrible. "Are you **sleeping** with him?"

"No! Dad!"

His caterpillar eyebrows were having seizures. "Then why do you think he's innocent?"

"I just do."

Dad's face was tinged yellow. "How?"

"Because he told me."

Dad blinked. Sweat beaded at his hairline. "Excuse me?"

Jojo's words tumbled out quickly so she wouldn't be tempted to reel them back in. "Sarah Knight caught me in the jail. I snuck in. She said I had to tell you before she did, but I only went in to talk to him for a minute."

Dad roared, "What?" He fell backward with a cough. "How do you **sneak** into a jail? Into **my** jail?"

She lifted her shoulders. "I know the code. There was no one in intake. They didn't see. It was totally my fault, but listen—"

"**Jojo!**" It was a roar.

"Listen. I asked him. He said he didn't do anything. And I believe him."

Mom stepped around the end of the bed. She came between them, as if Dad were going to rise up and hit Jojo or something.

Dad had never hit her. Neither of them ever had. Not yet.

Mom's voice shook. "You can't talk to that man. No one in CapB, either. Ever again. You hear me?"

"You can't just—"

Her mother leaned forward. "Never talk to him again. Do you hear me, Joanna Mercer Ahmadi?"

Dad made a muffled sound behind her, but Jojo's mother held up a hand as if to tell him to wait.

"But I'm trying to tell you, he—"

Dad stuck his hand out between the rails of his bed. He yanked Jojo's mother's shirt.

"What?" Mom turned. "Oh, Jesus."

Jojo looked around her mother's torso. Dad was paler now, his lips a dark blue. Sweat streamed down his face. His eyes fluttered like he was going to pass out, and he was trying to say something, but no words left his mouth. His lips twisted to the side. He looked like a stranger.

Jojo froze. Nothing worked, not her heart, not her lungs, not her voice.

Mom ran out of the room, knocking Jojo with her shoulder as if she couldn't see her. **"Nurse!"** The sound of her voice got smaller and lower-pitched as she went, Doppler-like.

"Dad." Finally able to move, Jojo lunged toward the bed. She touched his cheek, cold and wet. She grabbed the hand that didn't grip hers back, his fingers limp and heavy. "Daddy!"

Nurses ran in and started thumping his chest. They hooked him to a machine. His whole body leaped in the bed like a fish on the dock, the fish that she used to catch when she was six. Dad was always proud of those tiny smelts she caught, and he'd laugh as they flopped around, dying, in exactly the same way his body was doing now.

Mom gripped her shoulders and tried to force Jojo into the hallway. She resisted. Then she puked on the floor under his bed. Her vision narrowed, her head spun. Her mother forced her into the hallway and made her put her head between her knees.

Behind her eyelids she could only see those smelts. Leaping, flashing in the sun, dying on their way down.

TWENTY-SEVEN

LAURIE STOOD IN Omid's room, her spine pressing against the doorjamb. She swayed slightly to the right and the left, feeling vertebrae skip over the corner, back and forth. It hurt. It felt good.

Jojo sat in the chair next to Omid's empty bed. She hadn't raised her eyes in the last hour. Nothing was in her hands. She just sat there. Staring.

It was breaking Laurie's heart, and she didn't know what to do next. She'd thought—up until yesterday—that she was doing a good job of being an adult. She was forty-five years old. She had a Platinum Amex. Their mortgage was halfway paid off. Her daughter wasn't on drugs, or at least not on the ones that wound you up in the gutter. She and Omid still had good sex.

She'd thought she'd kind of figured some shit

out along the way, and now she realized she knew next to nothing. A woman in Syria, lugging four children through gunfire across a border into a refugee camp, that woman was a grown-up. She probably knew a thing or two.

Not Laurie.

She didn't know shit.

But she had to keep pretending she did. "He'll be okay."

He'd been dead. For a few seconds, her husband had been all the way dead.

Jojo didn't respond.

"They're putting the stent in. He'll be totally fine. People get them all the time."

Her daughter kept her gaze down, on her empty hands. The only sign of life in her was the way her right heel jiggled, so fast it reminded Laurie of the way a stereo speaker vibrated, lightly, almost too fast to see.

"Did I ever tell you about the guy I talked to on 911 once? He was ninety-two years old. He'd had four massive heart attacks at forty-nine, Dad's exact age. Triple bypass. And there he was, fit as a fiddle, forty-three years later. He was as surprised as anyone. Just think about it. He'd probably thought he was on death's door, you know? And then he goes and lives almost double that. When he called me, he'd slipped on his stairs and turned his ankle. No heart trouble." **Death's door, death's door.** Why had she said it in those words?

Jojo didn't move, but her phone pinged next to her.

She checked it seemingly automatically, but it didn't seem like her eyes even took in whatever was on the screen.

"Honey, you want some coffee? We're both exhausted." It was only 6:00 P.M., still less than twenty-four hours since their lives had been upended. Neither of them had gotten more than a couple of hours' sleep. "A latte? Sound good? Let's take a walk."

Nothing.

"We'll only be gone ten minutes. We'll be here when he gets back from surgery. It could be hours, anyway."

"I don't want to be here." Jojo's voice was scratchy.

"What?"

Jojo picked up her phone and stared at it. "I asked Pamela to come get me. She says she's in the lobby."

"What?"

"I'm going to sleep at their house tonight." Jojo blinked. "If that's okay with you. I figure you're going to stay with Dad."

Of course she was. Somehow, in Laurie's mind, they both were, even though he'd be in the ICU for hours, maybe a whole day, before he came back to the tiny room that would barely even hold one cot, let alone two. Laurie had thought she and Jojo would be with him in the ICU as much as the nurses would let them.

But Jojo deserved to get the hell out of here. "Okay. Yeah. Um. I'll come down with you."

The brightness of the lights in the hospital lobby felt like an assault, as did the laughter at the table surrounded by six or seven children arguing over a board game. One kid threw a handful of pieces up into the air, and a mother shushed him cheerfully and ruffled another boy's hair.

Normality.

Why had Laurie taken it for granted, even for a single minute? She was an idiot.

Jojo marched forward, allowing herself to be hugged by Pamela Cunningham.

Pamela kept Jojo in her embrace and held out one arm wide, urging Laurie to step into a three-person hug. There was no way to say no, so Laurie awkwardly swayed toward them, bumping hips with Pamela and elbows with Jojo. She stepped out again as soon as possible.

"Thanks, Pamela." This wasn't fair to her. How did the mother of a missing girl end up taking care of the friend? "But maybe I should go home with her. You're . . . you don't need anyone else to worry about."

"I want to." Pamela's voice cracked like fine china dropped on tile. Her eyes were sunk deep into her face. Laurie knew she was forty-two years old, but she'd never, not once, looked anywhere near it. Now she'd passed it, had hurtled right past her fifties and sixties, landing at old age, literally overnight.

"Please, Laurie, let me take care of her. I want to fuss over her until I can fuss over Harper. Have you heard anything? Anything they haven't told me?" Pamela's motherhood was all over her face right now. That terrified yearning. She was feeling something Laurie had felt when she got the 911 call from Jojo, something Laurie was so grateful she didn't feel now. There but for the grace of whatever was out there.

"I'm so sorry, no." Laurie didn't know what to say next. "How are you?"

She heard Jojo clear her throat. Yeah, it was a stupid question.

Thankfully, Pamela didn't answer it. She laced her hands together in front of her belly and said, "Andy is home now until I get there with Jojo. Then he'll go back to the police department. There's something . . ." She paused and closed those sunk-deep eyes for a second. When they opened again, they were almost back to normal, as if Pamela had dropped her dipper into the well inside herself and brought it up. "There's something about a cop. Who killed himself. They're asking us if she knew him. Jack Ramsay?"

Jojo coughed.

Laurie turned to her, "Honey, would you get me another coffee?"

Her daughter narrowed her eyes, as if to challenge the request.

Then Laurie saw the understanding filter through—she watched Jojo realize that Laurie was going to tell Pamela how her daughter knew Ramsay. Laurie was giving her busywork, so Jojo didn't have to listen. Jojo nodded and stomped away in the direction of the coffee cart.

"Did she know him?" Pamela plucked at the wrist of Laurie's sweatshirt. "Was she really sleeping with him?"

"We think so. According to some Facebook messages we saw."

"He must have hidden her. Somewhere." Pamela's pupils were tiny and constricted.

"They checked."

"They told us they did, but what if they missed something?"

Laurie explained the dogs and the thermal-imaging camera. She explained how every section of the department was working together to find Harper. Pamela couldn't seem to grasp more than a sentence at a time. Laurie didn't blame her.

Jojo came back with the coffee—the last thing Laurie's nerves actually needed—and Laurie said it one more time. "They're looking. They're doing everything they can, and they're using all the resources available to them."

Pamela knotted her fingers in front of her

stomach. "If he wasn't guilty, why would he kill himself, though?"

Laurie said, "We don't know." Was it actually safe to let Jojo go with Pamela? Would she be able to drive okay? Pamela hadn't slept, either, and sleep deprivation caused fatal crashes. "We're investigating." **Laurie** wasn't. It was the royal, departmental "we," but it was what Pamela needed to hear. "And we'll keep you posted every step of the way."

Pamela's shoulders lowered, and she sighed a breath. "Thank you." She reached to touch Jojo's shoulder. Jojo jumped. "Our girl needs sleep."

Our girl. Jojo was **Laurie's** girl. A huge wish rose inside Laurie's chest—to keep Jojo tucked under her arm, to not allow her to go with this woman who was careless enough to misplace a whole child. Even her own untalented parents hadn't ever managed to misplace Laurie completely.

But Pamela needed to be a mother right now.

So Laurie let Jojo go.

TWENTY-EIGHT

"Do you have everything you need?"

Jojo nodded. She sat up in Harper's bed, wearing Harper's pajamas. She felt like some bird taking over the wrong nest. "Yes. Thank you."

Pamela's face was all wrong, and it was freaking Jojo out. Normally when Jojo was there, she'd sit on the bed and gossip with them until Harper kicked her out. She'd stroke Jojo's hair as easily as she did Harper's. She never seemed to listen very closely to them—it seemed like she just wanted to be near them without thinking too hard about anything they said, as if their chatter were a favorite radio channel playing in the background. **MIA face,** Harper had called it. Jojo had always thought it was sweet, though. It was the opposite of the grilling her own mother gave her if she so much as looked sideways at something.

Now, however, Pamela's features were fevered. Her expression had a grasping neediness, as if Jojo had to give her something—and soon—but a glassy smile had been plastered over the top. Downstairs, Andy had looked similar—strung out on worry, shaking and exhausted with it. When they'd arrived, his eyes had been all wet and red.

Pamela clutched the doorframe. "Are you sure? Do you want some water? Or a cookie?"

"I'm good. Thank you for letting me stay over." It sounded so weird, the words slanting awkwardly. In the past, when she was smaller and when Mom's and Dad's shifts often overlapped, she'd stayed at Harper's house two or three times a week. Harper would yell good night down the stairs and then slam her bedroom door shut, and that was that. Pamela didn't check on them much, none of the doorway hovering she was doing now. And Jojo hadn't been formal like this, propped upright on Harper's pillows, thanking her host politely.

Pamela reached down to touch the moon nightlight that Harper still slept with as if to check whether it was warm. Then she straightened. "Wake me anytime if you need me. Anytime."

"I will." Would she have nightmares about Ramsay? About the sound of the shot that had echoed out of the house and into the car where she'd been sitting waiting for Mom to come back? She'd thought for a terrible second then that it had been Mom who'd been shot, that Ramsay had killed her. That's why she'd run inside so fast, so fucking scared, though what she would have done, she had no idea. "I promise."

Pamela looked angry for a split, terrifying second. "Good."

A pause. Jojo waited for the other shoe, whatever it was, to drop. **Get out. You're the wrong child. Go home.**

But all Pamela did was nod firmly and shut the door with a click.

Jojo's parent-polite face fell into the sheets as she slumped down.

Her whole body hurt, as if she'd started some new workout routine. And it just didn't feel **right** to be here in Harper's bed, not without Harper.

Jojo felt her face flush.

She rolled to her side to stare at Harper's bookcase. Harper wasn't the biggest reader, preferring TV and her phone to books, but she kept all the books that she'd loved the best growing up, saying she'd give them to her kids someday. **Black Beauty, Harry Potter, The Hunger Games.** Jojo thought it was a little silly for Harper to save the books that she'd never read again, on the off chance she had children someday.

It was also cute.

She turned her face to inhale the pillow. Harper's

scent, Victoria's Secret Bombshell, rose from it, and Jojo's heart clenched as hard as it had earlier in the hospital.

She'd thought she was dying.

While her father was doing the same.

She'd really, **truly** believed they were both going to die. And her life hadn't flashed before her eyes—instead her whole future had. No Dad dancing at the wedding she'd never have. No Dad at the college graduation she'd never achieve. They'd both be dead, and Mom would be devastated, and there was a small part of her that had rejoiced for like a millionth of a second that she wouldn't have to go through deciding between colleges.

She took another breath of Bombshell, then rolled to her back to look up at the ceiling.

Harper, though.

Maybe she **was** actually dead.

Jojo let the thought fill her mind for the first time. She didn't push it away as she'd been doing up until now. She let it swirl in her mind.

Dead.

Harper dead.

Cold. Buried. Gone.

For a moment sadness threatened, then retreated.

It was just impossible.

Jojo couldn't be sad about something that just flat-out wasn't true.

Harper was somewhere. Jojo would feel it if she were dead. She knew she would.

Her very first memory was meeting Harper at four years old in a local playground. It was a clear memory—she felt as if she could almost remember the whole day. It had been raining, but the sky had gone blue. Together they'd swung on the monkey bars and then gone down the slide twice. Harper refused to relinquish her Tickle Me Elmo Extreme, the one that Jojo was dying to own. So Jojo had grabbed it out of her arms. Harper, who'd been wearing a pink checked cowboy shirt and pink boots to match, had pulled her arm back and slapped Jojo across the face. The sting had been secondary to the noise that roared inside Jojo's head. She'd slapped Harper right back, and then this amazing girl with the bright green eyes broke into an inexplicable grin that was so contagious that Jojo, even while her cheek throbbed, laughed back.

That was it. They'd been glued to each other until the ring thing when they were fourteen, and then Jojo had suffered her first broken heart when she'd lost her best friend. She'd felt like she was dying. Life without Harper, who snubbed her in the halls and moved seats in English to be away from her, was in black and white. Existence felt pointless.

But they'd even gotten over **that.**

They'd run into each other at a resistance meeting at a café near school. Jojo had seen it advertised on a flyer with Nia Wilson's picture on it. Nia had been killed on BART, stabbed while taking the same train Jojo often took, just because of the color of her skin. Jojo had walked into the café with her heart racing, worried she'd get arrested immediately. (For what? She had no idea.)

There was Harper, sitting at a table laughing with a blond woman and a guy who'd turned out to be Kevin.

Jojo's breath caught in the back of her throat. Should she turn and leave? Sit at another table? Avoid eye contact even though it almost physically hurt to look away from her?

But then Harper winked at her.

Jojo, automatically, winked back.

And they were friends again, just like that. The relief was visceral—as they left the café, Harper laughing with her as if no time had passed, Jojo's bones felt like liquid gold. She'd floated all the way home. Harper had told her not to tell her parents. **They think I'm bad for you now, and maybe I am.** She'd dropped another wink that lit Jojo's chest as if fireflies danced inside her.

Friends again.

More than friends.

No, what did that even mean? Jojo's stomach flipped, and she was glad she'd rejected Pamela's offer to make her a quesadilla before she came to bed.

She'd spent the night at Harper's house just last

week. Jojo's parents thought she was at Emily's house, and it was true, she **had** been supposed to stay there, but Emily had some reaction to cashews, and Jojo had said yes so fast it almost wasn't even a word when Harper asked, "Want to stay at my house instead?"

They'd slept in this bed.

Together.

The way they had a million, bajillion times before. Jojo knew that when Harper dreamed, she made blowing-bubbles sounds with her mouth that were so funny that sometimes she'd wake Harper up by laughing. She knew that Harper slung her body carelessly around the bed, draping her arm or leg over Jojo's, and that had always been nice, growing up. Friendly. Sisterly.

What she'd felt last week, though, hadn't been sisterly.

"Want some lip gloss?" Harper'd been sitting at her vanity—of course she had one—holding up the wand.

Jojo didn't want any. They'd already rebinged season one of **The Office** for the umpteenth time, and her body felt heavy and ready for sleep. "Nah."

"Come on. It's sugary."

She sighed. "Fine. You have to bring it to me, though, I'm not getting up."

Harper smiled like a cat. She really did. Her green eyes straightened, and her lips curved, and she seemed to be almost purring. She sashayed away from the vanity toward Jojo, applying more lip gloss as she came. "You'll like it."

Something about her voice made Jojo's stomach lurch sideways. "Fine. Give it."

Harper turned and tossed the lip gloss onto her vanity, where it landed with a clatter. "I put on too much. Have some of mine."

Jojo blinked. That wasn't . . . Surely she didn't mean what it sounded like.

Harper's smile got even more catlike.

Jojo knew this face. She'd seen it—studied it—a thousand times before, when Harper was going after some boy. Harper got all velvety-voiced and kept that mild look of amusement on her face as whatever boy it was in question spun, twisting, in her gaze.

Jojo spun.

Then she called Harper's bluff. "Okay."

Harper wouldn't do it—she'd break, she'd laugh. **You should have seen your face,** she'd hoot, and then Jojo would spend the next year living it down.

But Harper didn't laugh.

She sat on the edge of the bed. "Have you ever kissed a girl before?"

Dumbly, Jojo shook her head.

"Do you want to kiss me?"

It was a trick question. Maybe Harper was filming her to tease her later. They'd always teased each other. Harper loved practical jokes.

So she answered, "Kind of."

Harper's eyes lit. "I knew it."

"But it's not kissing, not really. Not if you're just sharing your lip gloss."

"True," said Harper. "It's really just environmentally responsible."

Jojo, her stomach tied into knots, nodded. "There's petroleum jelly in there, right? That's just straight-up refined oil. You can't waste that."

Harper shook her head. "I can't. That would be bad."

Oh, God, the way she said the word "bad," like it was a mango or some other sticky, juicy fruit.

"Bad," breathed Jojo.

Then Harper leaned forward and kissed her.

They pretended for a second that it was about the lip gloss, moving their lips against each other's demurely.

Then—and Jojo wasn't sure how it happened, but it did—their mouths were open and they were kissing harder. Their tongues touched.

Holy shit.

Was this the way a kiss always felt? No wonder the kids in the hall at school were constantly locked at the mouth. Harper's tongue was soft and small. She tasted like the Junior Mints they'd just shared, and something else—something that was just her. Harper's hand came up to Jojo's breast, her fingers tentative over the cotton of the pajamas.

"Oh!" Jojo pulled back.

Harper blushed.

She blushed! Jojo had never, ever seen Harper seem embarrassed about anything. It made her feel like she was flying.

"Yeah," said Harper, recovering. "It's good gloss. I hate to waste anything, you know that." It wasn't true. Harper threw away clothes and shoes and boys like they didn't matter.

"Yeah." Jojo froze in place.

She hoped.

She hoped so goddamn hard, and she didn't even know for what.

Then Harper slid the flat of her hand under Jojo's pajama top, skimming it up her ribs and back down again. She came close to—but didn't touch—Jojo's nipple.

Jojo'd had no idea a nipple could need to be touched so bad. She would die if Harper didn't— and then she did.

And then they did more.

TWENTY-NINE

JOJO WOKE ALONE in Harper's bed, the previous two days coming to her in fast lightning bolts, like flashbulbs going off all around her. Kevin's face. Steiner as he remembered Car 143. Sarah's anger in the jail. Dad's blue lips. And Harper.

Harper might be **dead**.

Jojo rolled to her side, facing Harper's tidy desk. Light streamed through the sheer curtains. She should get up and go downstairs, ask Pamela to drive her to the hospital, but her legs felt too heavy to move.

No. Harper wasn't dead. They were connected—they always had been. Jojo would know if Harper was dead.

Especially now. Sex was a powerful connection, right?

Then again, she had no idea if what they'd done even counted as sex.

How were you supposed to know, when it came to girls? Like, she literally didn't know. She'd Googled, because she wasn't a moron, but entering the words "Are you a virgin if you're a girl who had sex with a girl?" she'd ended up in the ass end of the porn universe. She'd practically gotten an STD from the pop-up ads.

She and Harper hadn't really even talked about it. They'd gone to sleep after they'd done whatever-the-hell-it-had-been, and then they'd had cereal with Pamela, and then she'd dropped them at school. Harper had winked at her a few times and even kissed her hello on the quad, but Jojo knew that was more to freak out Jason and David than anything else. (And they **had** freaked out in the predictable way—they were probably beating their ugly meat to the memory right now.)

Harper still had Ray. She was **in love** with him, she said.

Whereas she and Jojo just plain loved each other.

Jojo spun in bed, unable to settle her limbs. She reached for her phone and then put it back on the nightstand.

It **wasn't** like she was gay or anything. She didn't lust after girls on TV (Ruby Rose didn't count—everybody lusted after her). Chris Hemsworth was one fine-ass piece of man.

It was just about Harper herself, about how damn

beautiful she was, with the way her skin glowed, and that cluster of freckles on her nose, and those predatory eyes that seemed to rattle everyone in her path. It was about the way she moved like a dancer, the way she stretched unself-consciously, her shirt rising up to show her waist and belly button as she reached her arms overhead.

She was objectively beautiful.

Proof: Jojo got catcalled on the street the normal amount. Once or twice a day, maybe. Dudes were gross, and every dude wanted to pork a young girl. Disgusting.

But Harper got it absolutely all the time. She walked into Starbucks and three different guys would try to buy her a frap and get her number. On the street guys walked with her until she broke and talked to them. They yelled out of cars. Sometimes they **stopped** their cars and got out, trying even harder.

Guys couldn't help it. They were wired that way when it came to drop-dead-gorgeous girls.

I'm wired that way, too.

Maybe. Maybe not. Was she bi? She didn't actually **have** to decide, after all. Her friend Alyssa was pan. Maybe Jojo was, too.

Maybe.

Jojo didn't want to open her cell phone—if she did, she'd be stuck. She'd have to check e-mail and Snapchat and every other list of things she did so habitually that it felt weird if she didn't.

So she reached for Harper's cell—charging next to hers—instead.

When Steiner gave the phone back to her, he'd asked her to give it to Harper's parents in case somehow she was okay—in case she decided to call her own phone. **It happens. No one knows anyone else's number now, but you always know your own.**

Pamela had nodded in the car when Jojo'd mentioned it. "Yeah. I guess . . . I should go through it. I should be desperate to, right? But I'm scared."

Harper's mother wasn't ever scared of anything. Jojo had croaked, "You want me to do it for you?"

"Yes. Is that bad?" Relief had been stark in Pamela's voice. "Go through it. Tell me everything I need to know."

I slept with your daughter.

The phone sprang to life under Jojo's thumbprint. More texts scrolled from people who obviously didn't know that Harper didn't have her phone. Two from the guy who ran the CapB meetings, telling her when the next meeting was. Another from a girl at school who wanted to go to Six Flags next weekend.

She swiped the texts away, heading straight for Instagram. Not for the photos she could have seen by looking at Harper's account on her own phone, but for the photos saved as drafts, the selfies that Harper hadn't gotten around to posting yet. Harper had a method to her social media—she used the weekends to get hella hot and posed in different locations looking amazing, and then she sprinkled those out through the next week. There were bound to be some Jojo hadn't obsessed over yet.

There were, and the funny thing was that Jojo had taken this photo series, so they weren't even selfies, though Harper was alone in every shot. They'd been in Emeryville, on the shoreline just down from IKEA. Harper had been fending off advances from dudes getting their parasails ready to fly, and Jojo had been trailing her with the phone, snapping shots as she turned, the wind lifting her hair. Those drafted posts, the ones where Harper was grinning her **real** smile, those were meant for Jojo.

Weren't they?

She longed to press SHARE on one, to make Harper **be** out there somewhere, if only popping up in other people's feeds, but that would freak the shit out of everyone who knew she was missing, so she didn't.

Harper's Instagram mailbox had messages in it.

Jojo clicked over.

And . . . **holy crap.**

The first one she opened was from a man who said he'd had a crazy-hot time with her and could he see her again, this time with two of his friends? **Same hotel, and I'll have the champagne on ice. Strawberries, too.**

Jojo swiped to the next message. Another old

man—at least forty by the looks of him—saying that he had what she wanted most. A picture of a freckled dick was attached. So gross.

Then there was another dick pic from someone else. This one was curved at the end and lit terribly by a flash so it looked almost blue.

Another dick pic. And another.

Jojo felt sick.

She knew that Harper got busy with a lot of people, but that was her thing. She always said, "I like everybody. I want to kiss everyone I meet. Who knows when the frog will turn into a prince?"

But holy shit, the next guy named a **price.**

A high price. A thousand bucks for an hour of letting him be her daddy.

There were more.

Frantically, Jojo leaned over and aimed for the wastebasket. But she only dry-heaved, miserably, for a moment or two. Her head pounded, and her eyes felt sticky.

Sitting back up, she closed Instagram.

She locked the phone and carefully placed it back next to her own.

Wriggling lower, she pulled the blanket up to her neck. She'd call her mother in a second, but for right now she just needed to think.

In the streaming morning light, she saw their faces. Their dicks.

Their names.

She knew so many of those names.

THIRTY

LAURIE ROUSED, UNCOMFORTABLE and stiff, in the hospital "lounge" chair. The room was still dark, the curtains closed, but sunlight filtered through the cracks. Her phone said it was almost ten in the morning. She'd missed two phone calls from Jojo—shit—but the only text said, **On my way to see Dad, c u soon.**

In the hall multiple alarms beeped, but in their small room there was only the sound of Omid's heartbeat, being tracked along the darkened screen.

Omid's eyes fluttered, the skin of his lids creased and thin. His face looked as if he'd aged ten years overnight, his crow's-feet deeper, his lips flattened somehow.

Still handsome, though. She could still see the man she'd fallen in love with. Maybe that was the best part of marriage—knowing what your partner had been like in his so-called prime and holding that as now, forever, automatically.

"Hi," she said as his brown eyes found hers.

"Hey." His voice was a hoarse croak, barely above a whisper.

"How are you feeling?"

Omid rocked his head from side to side, slowly. "I don't know."

"That's okay." Laurie took his hand. "You're okay."

It was true—the doctor said he came through with flying colors. **The stent is in place, and he did great in surgery. Think of his body as a car. Sometimes you blow small things, like a tire, and other times you need a new catalytic converter. This was more like the latter, but you'll get a lot more miles on this model with it in place.**

"Why . . ." His voice trailed off, and his eyes darted to peer behind her, next to her. He swiveled his head. ". . . am I here?"

"You had another heart attack." It sounded so simple said with so few words. It hadn't been simple—she'd almost lost him, right there in front of her.

"Another?"

"You had a little one Friday night and another, bigger one yesterday. Do you remember?" Fear was a cold, sharp stick poking into her ribs.

He shook his head.

Oh, God. "What **do** you remember?"

He shut his eyes. "I remember . . . going to work?"

"Lucky guess. You go to work a lot."

He smiled, his eyes still closed. "Am I going to be okay?"

"Yes," she hoped out loud.

"Are you and Jojo okay?"

His voice was normal. Not that concerned. Like he was checking in on their general welfare, asking if they'd had a good day.

He didn't remember.

Laurie didn't know how to tell him.

"Yes." They **were** okay, after all. Technically they were both in one piece.

"Where's Joshi?"

"She's at . . ." She almost said at the Cunninghams'. "She's at home."

He looked to the curtain. "It's morning?"

"Yeah."

"You stayed here all night?" He looked at the chair.

"You were in ICU after the surgery, so I waited there, mostly." She couldn't stay next to his bed for more than a few moments there, but she'd gotten to hold his hand and listen to his raspy breath. Then she'd slept a little, propped up in the ICU family room, ignoring the blaring of **Judge Judy.** If pressed, she'd guess she'd gotten four hours of sleep in the last two days, and she was feeling it now, heavy and stupid to her very bones.

"How long do I have to be here?"

"Probably a week, maybe less if you're lucky." A whole week without him, in this week when they needed him most.

"Work—"

"Is taken care of."

"Who's on rotation for me?"

"Brent Stanley is acting chief." He'd known that yesterday. "And he's ecstatic, you know that."

"Oh, crap. He'd be happy if I died. He's wanted my position for so long."

Yesterday you did die. She'd seen it. That machine had brought him back. A **machine.** If they lived fifty years ago, he'd be dead.

"I have to tell you—"

"Joshi!" His voice was as bright as his eyes.

Laurie spun. There Jojo was, looking beautiful as always, dressed in a black T-shirt with something about water protectors on it, and a pair of blue jeans for which Laurie had exchanged four hours of being in her chair at dispatch.

"Daddy!" Jojo hurried forward and kissed Omid's cheek. She wiped her mouth. "Jeez, you need to shave. This"—she pointed at his fast-growing beard—"is a nightmare. Handle that."

Omid smiled. "How is my girl?"

Jojo's face fell. "Okay."

"What? What's wrong?" Omid looked worried.

Jojo looked at Laurie.

Laurie shook her head. "He seems to be having a little memory loss."

Omid struggled to scoot up on the pillow and lost his breath, going pale. "Whatever it is you're not telling me, spit it out."

Jojo's eyes were huge. And scared. They looked the way they used to on the first day of school. "Mom, can I talk to you in the hall?"

Omid scowled, but he shut his eyes.

They watched him, waiting for him to protest more.

Instead he fell asleep, almost instantly, an unfamiliar snore rattling out his nose, and the fact that he just went out like that, like a man hit on the head, was terrifying.

Laurie followed her daughter into the hall. She shut the door quietly behind her and ducked out of the way of a nurse hurrying past. "I didn't tell him, not yet. He doesn't quite remember, but I'm sure it's going to come back to him." What if he remembered right now? What if he was alone when he did? "I should get back in there, so—How did you get here, anyway? Pamela? Has she heard anything else?"

"We have to find Harper."

"That's our top priority. What about Pamela, poor thing, has she—"

Jojo shoved Harper's white cell phone at her. "Harper was sleeping with more of them."

But the words didn't make sense to Laurie. "Huh?"

"Harper. She was sleeping with more cops." Jojo drew back the phone and unlocked it. She swiped at the screen. "Look."

Laurie looked.

Messages from men.

Men she knew.

Will Yarwood.

Ben Bradcoe.

Heinz Tollis.

Sherm Naumann.

She clicked on Yarwood's message. What the hell would that bantam rooster send to Harper? **You see anything you like?**

A picture of a cock, the balls spilling out of the side of the frame, hairy as a spider.

THIRTY-ONE

"DAMN IT, JOJO." Laurie thrust the phone at her daughter and then thought better of it, snatching it back. These were her guys. Hers. Omid's. What the hell was ID going to do with this info, if they managed to get past the password protection in the forensic files? What **else** didn't she know about the men she'd worked with for years? "What the fuck is this?"

"I don't know." Jojo crossed her arms. "But I'm freaking out."

"Come on." She led Jojo down the hall to the family waiting room. It was early enough for it to be empty. There was a candle burning under a cross-star object that was obviously trying to stand in for all religions, and there were Kleenex boxes next to every chair. The room felt soggy with other people's emotions.

They sat next to each other. The phone had locked as she carried it.

Laurie held it out for Jojo's thumbprint, feeling sick to her stomach as she did so. "Are they all like this?"

"Some worse than others."

"And they're all—"

Jojo rubbed her forehead. "Yeah."

Laurie flicked to the next message. "Dan Toomey. Shit, that motherfucker." Seeing Toomey's hand on his cock, his wedding ring gleaming in the foreground—God. "He's newly married. Like, less than six months. What is his goddamn problem?" She looked into Jojo's face, as if her child could provide an answer as to why men were such idiots. "I'm sorry. I shouldn't be—"

"Mom, what's going on? I don't get it. I mean, Harper has sex, but . . ."

A bright red headache bloomed behind Laurie's forehead. "I have no idea, honey."

"Does one of them have her?"

Laurie shook her head hard. Did they? As if she fucking knew. "No, of course not." They knew these men. They were **good** men.

"But they were paying to have sex with her."

Laurie caught an unexpected sob before it roiled up her throat, forcing it back into her superheated chest cavity. "It looks like that, but you know what we always say, innocent until proven guilty."

"Bullshit. Cops say guilty until proven innocent."

It was true. They joked about it. Even Omid said it sometimes with a laugh.

But they were all kidding.

"We don't mean it. You know that."

"You have an innocent man in jail right now. His best friend is dead. Harper's gone somewhere, maybe dead or something, and Dad has to **do** something about this. Dad has to **fix** this."

Laurie's patience cracked. At one point she would have been one of the people out there looking, being paid to investigate, being depended upon. "The only thing Dad can do right now is try not to die."

Jojo's face went white. She lurched backward as if Laurie had hit her.

"Jojo—I'm sorry."

"**Is** he going to die?" Jojo's upper lip went darker, the way it did before she burst into tears.

"No! I'm so sorry I said that. Dad's going to be fine."

Jojo stood and moved, sinking into a chair opposite Laurie. "Is it all my fault? If this hadn't happened to me . . ."

"This still would have happened. His heart was a time bomb, ready to go at any time. That's what the doctor said to me." It was a lie. It was what Laurie had hoped to hear, but all the doctor had said was that it was probably a long time coming and that stress had set it off.

Jojo's lip flare calmed. "Are you sure? That's what the doctor really said?"

She would slap anyone who challenged her lie. "On Gramma's grave."

Her daughter's eyes widened.

Jojo believed her.

Thank God.

Jojo slipped back to the chair next to Laurie. "We have to find her."

Of course they did. Laurie nodded, still scrolling.

"You and me, Mommy. We can find her. We don't need Dad or the department."

"**Excuse** me?"

"And don't tell Dad. About anything. About what happened to me."

"Honey, I have to." She couldn't handle this on her own. She'd fuck it up. She needed Omid.

"Remember when I did that project on Alzheimer's? You told me that if when you were a million years old and you got it and you didn't remember that Daddy was dead, you wanted me to tell you he was at work."

Laurie felt the bottom drop out of her stomach. Ironically, she didn't remember that at all. It was what she would want, so she could clearly believe she'd said it. But **why** had she said it to Jojo? She must have been shaken by a bad dementia call. "This is different. This is Dad's job."

"But he can't **do** his job right now. That's what you just told me. So don't tell him."

Jesus Christ. "But he'll see messages on his phone from work." Panic lit the edges of her thoughts. "I was with him when he woke up, but when he wakes again, it's the first thing he'll reach for."

Jojo's words were rapid-fire, bullets from a fully automatic. "Get in there. Take his phone. Tell him it died. Tell him you'll let him know if he's needed at work. Tell him nothing's going on. It's San Bernal, for God's sake. There's never anything going on."

"Jojo—"

"We can find her."

Laurie's head throbbed. "What?"

"You and me."

Never. "Honey. That's not my job anymore, and it's sure as hell not **your** job."

"Whose is it, then?" Jojo stuck out her chin. "The cops? All those detectives on her phone? How can we trust any of them?"

Laurie rubbed her temples.

Jojo went on. "Don't you think if it's one of them, it would be easier if Harper just stayed disappeared? No victim, no crime, that's what you and Dad always say."

These were men she **worked** with. Men she'd always trusted.

Men she now knew were fucking her daughter's best friend for money.

Was one of them hiding more than just dick pics? Omid couldn't help.

Who the fuck could she trust? "Joshi. We have to believe that—"

Jojo folded her arms, pulled up her legs, and swiveled in her chair so that she faced Laurie directly. "You know those meetings I go to?"

"You can't believe everything a group against police brutality tells you." **Brutality.** Right there—in the name of the group itself—was inflammatory language. "You know, better than anyone, that police officers aren't brutal." But the words felt thin in her mouth, a Communion wafer of a lie.

A couple were. A few.

"Mom." Jojo's face was rigid. "You were a cop. You know every system there is in the department, and you have as much access as any detective to the national databases."

More. Detectives had to run some queries through dispatch—they didn't understand the more difficult strings of commands it took to run warrant and gun and domestic violence checks on people from out of state or country.

But, stubbornly, she went back to her previous statement. "**Our** department isn't brutal." Linn had broken a suspect's arm with his asp, which he wasn't supposed to carry, but that was Linn. Connors withheld insulin from a sex registrant just to watch him freak out, the guy's brain going sideways as his glucose levels rose. Tollis and Maria had physically taken down a man they thought was psychotic but turned out was just deaf. That one had been expensive. And if Will Yarwood shot at one more person, he'd be permanently desked.

But they weren't brutal. That was the wrong word for it. An excitement ran through the blood every minute you were on the street, a high hum set right in the thick of your bloodstream. There was always tension when arresting someone, when bringing them in to be booked. You had to be on the highest alert. If they twitched, you brought your A game. If a prisoner went squirrelly, even for a moment, there was a certain pleasure in dropping the person. Cops just standing around piled on. It was fun. They were like puppies that way. After a good tussle, they'd head downstairs and laugh about it with dispatch.

Honestly, except for the time that she'd lost it herself, the time that had sent her off the street and into dispatch, Laurie had always thought it was funny, too—both when she was knocking elbows on the jail floor and when she was in her chair watching it like it was reality TV, which, in a way, it was.

Gallows humor. That's how you got through a job like that. You laughed about inappropriate things.

You shoulda seen how he squawked when Tollis persuaded **him into the car.**

No, really, he "fell." Wink.

His head ran into my knee!

It wasn't brutality. Good men and women **died** doing this job. They were doing their best and keeping their heads up while they did it.

"Mom? I know you can do this. We can figure it out. Together."

Jojo. Laurie brought her attention back to her daughter, who was now rolling up and unrolling a magazine, over and over.

What if Jojo were right? What if one of the cops looking for Harper didn't want her found? Worse, what if there were a group of them who wouldn't mind if ID "lost" the Instagram messages?

"Okay," said Laurie. "I'll do a little digging."

"**We** will. Not a little, a lot. It's an investigation, right? Dad always says there was no one better at digging up dirt than you. I totally believe that you can do it, and you'll do it faster than the detectives can. There's no one we can trust to help. No one but us."

The flattery was working. Jojo hadn't leaned on her in a long time, and it felt good. Laurie reined herself in. "You do **not** call the shots here, you hear me?" She could hear herself—her voice pitched high and sharp—but she goddamn meant it. "You step one toe out of line and you'll be not only grounded for the rest of your life, but you won't get your phone back till you're thirty. I'm the boss."

Jojo nodded. "You're the boss."

"Who are you, and what have you done with my daughter?"

Her stupid attempt at levity failed. Jojo didn't so much as blink. "We have to find Harper, and we have to be **fast.** What if it's getting worse for her? I'm here to help. You tell me what I can do."

Laurie took a breath. "Let's go check on Dad. Hopefully he's still sleeping. I'll get his phone."

"Then what?"

She looked at her watch. "Then we switch off hanging out with him."

"We fake it."

Tiredness made Laurie's bones heavy as lead pipes. "Yep. All day, we're going to fake it. I'll sneak out at lunch and go to work and run some more checks. You'll entertain him if he's awake."

Jojo practically looked chipper. The girl had always liked a challenge. "Okay. Then what?"

"You do more sleuthing in her social media. And I go to Ramsay's drink-up tonight." After every department death, there was, of course, a huge funeral with bagpipes and dozens of tear-wrenching heroic photos up on the screen, cycling over and over. Every funeral was followed by an enormous wake, with wives and families in attendance, all the officers spit-shined in Class A's, their spouses in formal black. But the unofficial drink-up was the real funeral, with just department folk in plain clothes. It was usually held in a parking lot on the west end where the lights were burned out, far enough from residences that no one would call the cops on the cops. It would be tonight, she knew. Probably down on Seventeenth in the currently favored parking lot of a defunct Chinese restaurant. "And I start asking questions."

THIRTY-TWO

RUNNING CHECKS WHILE Jojo sat with the still-sleeping Omid had brought up nothing. She didn't know where to start—how did she pull files on her own officers? She'd plugged away, inputting their names into the RMS, but nothing except their own reports chugged back at her, thousands of them.

The good guys.

They were the good guys.

On the lobby camera, she saw Pamela come in. She leaned on Andy. A minute later her cell pinged. Pamela: **We're in the department again, in case you are, too. They're not doing anything. Help us, please?**

She sent a quick message back: **I'm working on it right now, I promise. Keep you posted.** Then she kept punching in names. There was nothing she wanted more than to find Harper, but she couldn't handle talking to the Cunninghams. Not now. Not yet. But hopefully soon they'd know where Harper was. Laurie had to keep working.

Maury and Charity had peered over her shoulder a couple of times, and she'd minimized the screen. **Omid asked me to try to do more to find Harper's boyfriend.** They might have believed her. They might not have. The good thing was, they didn't ask.

Jojo texted that Omid had been cleared to drink broth, so at lunch Laurie brought him and Jojo pho. They let him sneak a few rice noodles. He acted like he was getting over the flu, except he was still sleeping most of the time. He hadn't challenged either of them for his cell phone, which was worrying in and of itself.

After visiting hours she drove Jojo home. She dodged the questions Jojo hurled at her. **I don't know. They're checking. I'll look into that, too.**

She triple-checked the alarm before leaving the house. "Get pizza or something? I want you to eat. Call me if you hear anything. Don't text me, call my phone so I hear it. Okay?"

Jojo sat on the couch in her red pajamas, flipping through the Roku, though she didn't look as if she were reading the words on-screen. "I will."

"I'll be home soon."

Her daughter shrugged, obviously trying to be

the girl she usually was, someone who didn't really need a mother to tell her when she'd be home. But when she waved at Laurie, her eyes looked over-wrought.

Laurie took a step back toward her. "I can stay."

"Mom, **go.**"

"Yeah. Okay. I love you."

Jojo nodded and turned on an **SNL** replay.

Laurie stopped at the All-American Liquor store near the west end—she'd never been in it except to respond to 911 hang-ups and one robbery, many years before. Scotch, but cheap. She didn't plan on getting drunk, though most of her friends would.

Friends.

"Yeah, that one." She pointed at a small bottle of Johnnie Walker. "Please."

The clerk turned to grab it.

Next to her a man said, "Laurie?"

She didn't recognize him at first. He was out of context and in the wrong uniform, but then it came to her. "Darren?"

Darren Dixon shrugged and looked down at his rent-a-cop uniform. It bagged on his long frame. "What can I say?"

She hadn't seen him since he'd been fired for posting the anti-Muslim crap when he hadn't been promoted and Omid had. He'd been such a dick about all of it.

What if **he** was on Harper's list?

He shifted his weight so that he leaned against

the bulletproof glass. "I heard about Omid. Is he okay?"

The clerk pointed at the credit card reader. "Chip in there."

Laurie fumbled with her card before slotting it in. "How?"

"The bottom," said the clerk.

"No," she snapped, and jerked her gaze to Dixon. "How did you know about Omid?" There was only one way, she knew that already. He still had friends at the department. Of course he did. He probably knew about—

"And your daughter. I'm really sorry. Is she okay?"

Why did people **ask** that? "So you heard about Ramsay, too?"

Dixon frowned. "What about him?"

The image of the moving blood rose in her mind, and she felt nauseated. She didn't cushion the blow. "Killed himself."

He stiffened. "What the fuck?"

"It's a shitshow, what can I say?"

"Seriously, Laurie, what's going **on** over there?"

God, who knew? She took the receipt and, with it, a deep breath. Dixon was still talking, but she couldn't hear him for the buzzing in her head.

She turned. Took a step toward him, so close that he stumbled backward. "Do you know Harper Cunningham?"

"Who?" He looked honestly confused.

"Do you have her?"

"What? Have who? What's going on?"

Laurie **knew** him. She'd worked with him for how many years? He didn't know or have Harper—she could see it from the bewilderment in his eyes. The link was Kevin Leeds. He was their only link. It had to be CapB. They'd done all of this.

But she didn't stop. She couldn't stop. The switch had flipped in her head, and heat filled her with a silty rush, a tide she couldn't hold back. Even if Dixon didn't know anything, **someone** did, maybe someone he knew. She poked her finger into his chest and felt the give of muscle. No bulletproof vest. He was turkey bacon, a fake pig. She lowered her voice to the growl she'd used on the street on bad days. "If you have her, or if you know where she is and you're not telling me, I'll kill you." She meant the words that came out thick and guttural.

He raised his palms and backed up farther. "What is **wrong** with you?"

"What's wrong with me? With **me**?"

In her peripheral vision, she saw the clerk reach for his phone.

Laurie panted a hot breath. She wanted to hit Dixon. She **needed** to. Her fingers curled into fists. She protected her thumbs.

And Dixon saw her do it. He'd always been a better cop than she had. He kept his hands up, the universal I-don't-want-trouble signal. "I swear, Laurie, I only want to help. Let me know how I can help you."

The switch in her head flipped back.

Laurie was physically and verbally threatening a security guard in an ill-fitting uniform in a liquor store that smelled like piss and spilled beer. The clerk had probably already dialed 911.

Fuck.

She grabbed the bottle and ran.

THIRTY-THREE

LAURIE HAD BEEN right about the parking lot—when she pulled up, there were already more than thirty other cars pulled onto the gravel. Someone had brought a long folding table, and it was covered with bottles, mostly tequila, Ramsay's favorite.

She parked and tried to calm her breathing. Her face still felt hot, and her limbs were weak.

She could do this. Someone here knew something.

A roar went up when she got out of her car. "All hail the chief's wife!" yelled Linus, a sergeant who'd been demoted for sleeping with a parking tech and lying about it.

She took a red Solo cup from Mark Colson. "Thanks." The sip of scotch burned, boiling its way down her throat.

Colson stepped nearer, his boots crunching against the gravel. "How's Omid?"

"Okay."

"I'm going by in the morning to check on him. Anything I can bring?"

Shit, Laurie hadn't even thought about the department visiting. They'd sent another bouquet of flowers, but no one had come by during the day, probably because they thought he was still in the ICU. They'd start coming by tomorrow for sure. "Mark, he's forgotten everything that happened leading up to the first heart attack."

Colson frowned. "Everything? You sure?"

"Jojo. Leeds. The murder. Harper Cunningham. And we want it to stay like that. For now, anyway. He can't be stressed out again. He has to heal." Knowing that his own department was full of pedophiles and possibly a killer/kidnapper wouldn't help.

"I'll pass it on to everyone. Should we wait on visits until we get the all-clear from you?"

"Can you? That would be great." That was what she should have done when she was in dispatch this afternoon, sent an all-department memo: **Don't talk to my husband, any of you, and this goes double for you pieces of shit who fucked Harper Cunningham.**

Pieces of shit.

She'd never thought of them like that before.

Heinz Tollis had crocheted a baby blanket for
Jojo when she was born. Laurie'd been astonished. He'd compared his crocheting to Rosey
Grier's needlepoint, saying that it kept him calm.
Sherm Naumann ran the model-airplane club of
San Bernal and spent most of his weekends teaching
low-income kids how to build and paint and fly the
planes. Yarwood, of course, was a pain in the ass,
but he coached Little League and had never missed
his team's games, trading time with other cops and
paying them back relatively uncomplainingly.

Laurie would have sworn they were men who
wouldn't sleep with a child, who would fight for
justice for the victimized.

"You okay?" Colson's face creased with concern.
"How's our girl?"

Their girl? The department's girl? Heat flashed
up Laurie's neck. What if those guys had looked at
Jojo the same way they'd looked at Harper? **Not
important right now. Take a breath.**

"You're lead on the Harper Cunningham case,
right? How's that going?" **Tell him what you
know. He should know.**

He gave a sigh and took a sip of his drink. "Not
good. Parents seem mostly legit, the mom is losing her shit and the stepdad seems honestly upset.
But he has a prior for underage sex, did you know
that?"

"No, what?" Andy Cunningham had a prior?
Fuck.

"Not too big a deal. He was twenty-five and she was seventeen—her parents pushed the charge, not the girl. Tracked her down, and she confirmed it was consensual."

Relief trickled through Laurie. "He's a good guy. We've known him for a long time. You should have seen him yesterday." She reached up and put her thumb against the deep ravine that ran between Colson's eyebrows. "You didn't have this years ago."

He smiled self-consciously. "Twenty pounds and twenty years later."

Laurie suddenly remembered the way his mouth had fit hers. Their bodies had never really worked out—the sex had been awkward, banging limbs and knees—but the kissing had always been nice. And he'd always been one of those good exes. They'd parted friends and stayed friends.

"You okay, L?" The crease on Mark's face grew even more pronounced. "Dumb question. I know you're not." He turned to the side and drew her into a one-armed hug. "Fucking fuck. Am I right?"

"Fucking fuck," she agreed.

"We'll find her. We're doing everything we can."

The words fell from her mouth. "No you're not."

"Laurie!"

She spread out her hands. "You're here. Drinking." And what if—what if he were another one of the guys who knew Harper?

"Dude. I just spent seventeen hours on shift."

"I once did twenty-six straight on a 261." It wasn't

a competition. She was being a dick—she knew it and couldn't stop.

Colson opened his mouth to speak. His brows drew in. Then he snapped his mouth closed and spun on his heel. He held out his cup toward the rookie who was pouring.

Laurie's shoulders slumped as she stood alone. He deserved a goddamned break—of course he did.

The smell of lighter fluid filled the air as Linus tried to start a small hibachi. Laurie inhaled sharply, the acidic tang stinging her lungs. Tall eucalyptus swayed on the edges of the lot, and the moon winked on and off through the fingers of fog rolling in.

Sarah Knight came up and hugged her. "Hey, you. How are you doing?"

Laurie's eyes burned. "Okay."

Sarah arched an eyebrow. She wore a black Raiders T-shirt and black sweats. "Really?"

It was the hand Sarah placed on Laurie's shoulder that let the words come. "I'm a wreck."

Sarah rubbed her back and clinked plastic cups with her. "Drink up, my friend."

"I'm sorry my daughter broke into your jail."

"Good. She told you."

"She said you were going to if she didn't."

Sarah shrugged. "Eh. I didn't actually know what to do, so it's nice she took care of that for me."

"How did she get through?"

"Dumb luck. We had a spitter in the sally port

the very second she chose to let herself in. Otherwise there's always one of us in the control room, you know that."

"That girl."

"She's something. How is she?"

Laurie took another taste of the fiery scotch. Not normally her drink of choice, but she could see how it grew on people. "Hanging in there." Her throat tightened again.

"Leeds has a lawyer fighting to get the bail amount."

The idea of the man being out, on the street again, in her town, made Laurie grind her teeth. If Leeds were with someone else at his house, if that person had killed Zach and still had Harper, then they had to hold Leeds until he talked. "I assumed he would." But what if Jojo was right, that Kevin Leeds didn't do anything, if the person that had Harper was a cop . . . ?

"Hell of a thing," said Sarah. "Anything on the missing girl? I mean, I know you haven't been at work, and if you don't want to talk about it . . ."

"Mark Colson's running lead on that one. I know that her parents are panicked. We all are."

"Media's on it, did you see?"

Laurie nodded. She'd seen the vans outside the station, but she'd exited by the side door. White girl hurt, another one missing, black guy dead, infamous black superstar athlete at the middle of all of it—it was on the front page of every local paper now, and by tomorrow it would hit the major media channels. Total strangers would know about the rape, and at some point, Jojo would be outed as the victim. It was only going to get worse. "Yeah. I've got to keep Jojo away from all that somehow."

Sarah touched her shoulder lightly. "I can't imagine."

"I don't think I can do this, Sarah." The words felt torn from her throat. Over Sarah's shoulder Laurie saw Ben Bradcoe pull up in his Lexus. He'd been on the list. Laurie'd seen his dick on a sixteen-year-old's phone. He'd be easier to talk to if she reached him before he got out of his car. She shuffled her feet, trying to get her legs to follow her commands.

Sarah grabbed her hand. "You **can** do this. You'll get through it. They'll figure it out. You're going to be okay. So are Omid and Jojo—"

"Yeah, well, what if they're not? What if I do something wrong and screw it all up and we don't get Harper back and never find out who—I wish I could tell what we—" Laurie swallowed the rest, shoving the words back down her throat along with the clog of emotion that threatened to rise. She wanted to show Sarah the photos, the texts. But that would put Sarah in the position of having to work with the men when not much was known, when they didn't know anything yet. . . . **Except that they're wrong. They're criminals.** "I have to talk to Bradcoe." She gestured with her chin to the Lexus.

"Honey, you've got us. You've got me."

Every fiber in Laurie's body was so tense that she thought strings might start to break, like on an overtightened guitar. "Thank you."

Sarah raised her chin in greeting to Will Yarwood. "What's up, Will?"

"Laurie!" Yarwood reached for a hug with his cocky chest thrust forward, but Laurie ducked away from his skinny arms. She wouldn't let this man touch her, ever.

"Be right back," she muttered.

She had to get to Bradcoe before he stepped into the light of the fire pit.

THIRTY-FOUR

THE GRAVEL CRUNCHED under her feet as she approached Bradcoe's car. Almost six foot five, he was in the process of unfolding himself from it. He was blond and sweet and had apparently been a Mormon before falling in love with his wife, a Catholic woman named Lee who loved her religion more than he loved his. "Oh, my God, Laurie. Come here." He wrapped her in a hug, Laurie's nose hitting the middle of his chest. For one second, Laurie forgot what she'd been going to say and let herself be embraced.

Then she yanked herself backward, her breath coming fast.

Bradcoe tugged at his Cal sweatshirt. "We're going to make it right. Somehow. That murderer can't get away with doing that to our Jojo."

Laurie had let him hug her. Jesus Christ. "Let's get in your car."

"What?"

"In your car. Before anyone comes over."

He frowned but opened the door for her. "Laurie, if you need to cry, you don't have to hide."

Fuck him.

Inside the car he turned to her with a concerned expression, his blond eyebrows pulled together. He flipped on the overhead light, and Laurie knew exactly why—in about thirty seconds, a whisper would run through the parking-lot crowd. If they were in his car together in the dark? Guaranteed they were sleeping together. With the light on, they were just having a friendly chat. Probably.

"You slept with Harper Cunningham."

Bradcoe's jaw dropped, and he didn't recover well. He stammered, "W-who?"

"What the fuck were you thinking?"

"I don't know what—"

Without thinking Laurie kicked her foot up into the glove box. It broke open with the force and swung down, displaying his off-duty weapon. For one second the idea of picking it up and pointing it at him crossed her mind. Just to see what he did.

But she didn't actually want to get arrested for brandishing, so she kicked it again to jam the glove box closed.

"Laurie . . ."

"There's no excuse. There is nothing you can say to make this right."

His face darkened. "What is it you think you know?"

"You sent her a dick pic."

"Someone else must have done that."

"From your phone?"

He shrugged. "I guess."

"Does your dick have a mess of ugly freckles on one side?"

He paled. "All I know is that she's a prostitute. That's literally all I know."

"She's a **child,** not a prostitute. If she's anything, she's a sexually exploited minor. Exploited by men like you."

He shook his head and folded his arms.

"You paid to fuck a child. You did, didn't you? You know you'll lose your job over this?" God, why was she pushing him, threatening him? What if he was the one who had Harper? What would he do to protect himself? She reached for the door handle.

He grabbed her elbow. "Laurie."

"Do **not** touch me." She shoved her body weight toward him and twisted so that she was free. She knew the same moves he did.

He held up his hands as if to say he wouldn't try it again. "If Chief told you this much, he must have told you why we're doing it this way."

Her bones turned to immovable steel. She was stuck in place. Chief—**What?** "Go on."

Bradcoe rubbed his palms together hard, back and forth. "It's just that we haven't gotten that far yet. With what she wants."

"Uh-huh."

"Chief said maybe her parents don't even know. I guess you guys know them? Her parents?"

Pamela and Andy. God, what was going on? Laurie's head felt like she'd hit it against something. Her thinking went fuzzy. "We know them."

"So if she's just threatening a lawsuit but hasn't even told her parents, then maybe it's something the department can handle quietly. You know? Without making it front-page news. He's supposed to get the parents involved this week."

Omid knew.

He **knew**?

"Uh-huh. What about the others?"

Bradcoe frowned. "Others? I swear to you, I don't think anyone else knows. I went to Chief directly."

He'd skipped all chain of command, then. Well, that's what she would have done if she were a fucking child predator on a police force. "Ramsay."

"Huh?"

"Ramsay was sleeping with her."

She watched him go pale as pieces clicked together. "Oh, shit."

"That's why he killed himself." Laurie would never be able to prove it. But she knew it was true.

"Does he . . . What if he took her?"

"They checked. Doesn't look like it. Unless he

had her someplace else, but his cell records showed he's been mostly at home or at A's games."

Bradcoe rubbed the lower half of his face. "I don't know what to do."

He didn't know where Harper was. She could feel it in her gut. She'd learned to pay attention to that instinct on the street, where listening to a lie was like trying to put the wrong piece into a puzzle. It seemed like it would fit, all the edges looked right, but it just didn't. She still used her intuition in dispatch—when she called back a 911 hang-up and heard the right words (**Oh, sorry, my three-year-old playing with the phone**) but still felt that gut kick, she'd announce to the room at large, "He sounded good, but there's something wrong there." Nine times out of ten, there was. Her gut was smarter than she was, and she knew by now to trust it.

Bradcoe didn't know shit except that he was screwed.

"How about you go home. Tell your wife."

He looked at Laurie blankly. "She'll leave me."

Bradcoe had been her friend. Years ago, when she and Jojo had both been incredibly sick with the flu and Omid had had to work a homicide, Bradcoe came over for the day. He held the five-year-old feverish Jojo while Laurie slept, and when he got the flu himself three days later, he just said he'd been looking forward to some time off work.

But she hardened herself against the face that

she'd trusted up till now. "You should have thought about that before you slept with a child for money. Better you break it to your wife than she see it on the news. Tell her if Harper doesn't show up soon, you're going to be a suspect, too."

She got out, her heart hurtling painfully inside her chest. He drove away, his lights still off. She headed for the fire.

"What was that about?" Frank Shepherd gave her another red cup, this one with at least three fingers of scotch in it. There were going to be some very drunk cops driving home tonight.

Laurie took a long sip and then gave the cup back. "I have to go check on Omid." Her vocal cords felt wobbly, and she wasn't sure if it was the liquor or the heat of her anger.

"Give him our best."

"Oh, I will," she said. Omid's heart had better be stronger now, because she didn't feel much like taking care of it.

THIRTY-FIVE

WHEN MOM LEFT her at home, Jojo got out her cell and ordered sushi.

She stayed curled up on the couch after the order came, cradling the plastic box of bay scallop rolls and two orders of salmon nigiri in her lap. Yesterday Ramsay had shot himself in the head. Would it make the news? She flipped from the Roku to the cable box to watch.

She'd smelled Ramsay's blood, the coppery, sour tang of it.

Damn it. She'd been so hungry, but now she put the box of sushi on the coffee table. She couldn't—the salmon was too fleshy, like the inside of skin.

She didn't know why she was so astonished when Harper's image filled the television screen, but there Harper was, in her living room, a place she hadn't been for a long time. For a brief moment, Jojo was just happy to see her. **Oh! There's my best friend!**

Then her brain snapped on again, and she heard the words that went with the on-screen photo. **Teen girl missing. High risk. Suspicious circumstances. The community is urged to call San Bernal PD with any information.** There was a picture of Pamela crying against Andy as they entered the department. The red coat Pamela wore in the photo was the one Jojo had borrowed from her last Christmas, when they were caroling at Union Square. She knew the smell of it, the weight. And there it was, going into her parents' police department, in search of Harper.

In the next shot, Pamela's tearstained face filled the screen. "We beg of the person who knows where our daughter is, please have pity on us. Have mercy. She's just a baby. Give her back." She swallowed audibly. "If anyone knows anything, **tell** us. The police won't tell us what's happening, and we don't understand what's going on. Please, someone, help us!" Andy rubbed her back as Pamela burst into tears. Oh, man. Jojo hoped Mom and Dad wouldn't see this segment. The shot cut away with an image of Harper, her last yearbook picture.

Then, while they didn't say anything about a possible link between the two stories, the story on Kevin's arrest and Zach's murder filled the screen next. **Did Harper know who killed Zach? Did she see?**

In the very back of her mind, Jojo let herself wonder—just for a second—if Harper could have hurt someone. Could have hurt them that badly. Harper **had** been a bit strange in the last few months, a little more manic when she talked, her motions more energetic than ever, but she'd seemed happy, too.

And they'd done . . . that.

No. Harper couldn't hurt anyone (anyone who wasn't a boy she was dumping, that is). Harper had stepped on a lizard sunning itself by her parents' pool when they were twelve, and she'd cried on and off for days. She **could** eviscerate a bully in the halls with six words and a disgusted look, but she couldn't go fishing, because she couldn't take the looks on their dying faces. She could barely eat sushi.

Who then?

A middle-aged black lawyer stood on the front steps of the police department, the red brick behind him as familiar to Jojo as the siding of her own house. "Besides being an outstanding athlete and beloved by a nation for sharing his belief that we can make this a better country, Kevin Leeds is an upstanding man. He believes in his community and is active in giving back. We believe this is a racially motivated charge—his involvement with Citizens Against Police Brutality has brought him both respect in some areas and ill will in others.

A man was slain in his house while he slept." The lawyer looked into the camera as if his very own life depended on it. "The truth will set him free. This intolerance and bigotry will not stand. Kevin is being released on bail tonight, because while these atrocities happened in his house, there is absolutely no evidence that implicates him in any way. While I'm sure you have questions about the investigation, please rest assured that my client is innocent, and this will be proved as we move forward. Now, excuse me."

Jojo held her breath. They wouldn't name her. They couldn't. That wasn't allowed. Was it?

But all the reporter said was, "Kevin Leeds has been held on counts of suspected homicide, suspected rape, and suspected forced imprisonment. We'll have all the up-to-date details as they're released. Stay with us."

She kept watching through stone-heavy eyelids, and thirty minutes later, on the eleven thirty recap, they showed the same lawyer leaving the PD, Kevin at his side.

Kevin didn't look at the cameras. He didn't answer a single question. He just kept his head up and moved slowly. If Jojo had just turned the TV on tonight to see her friend come out of the police department, she would have assumed that whatever charges being brought against him were false. She would have assumed someone was trying to frame him, and she would have considered a girl accusing him of whatever to be a big fat liar. Kevin had morals. He had standards. He believed that everyone had the responsibility to leave the world a better place than they'd found it. He believed that America had to be better, and even if it got him hated by old white guys, he believed that it was his job to point out the injustices done to people of color every day.

But Jojo wasn't just watching a news story unfold. She was part of it.

And she'd been raped by **someone.**

When she'd left the jail, Jojo had been pretty damn sure Kevin hadn't touched her.

Now she was only seventy percent sure, and the number was dropping just by virtue of time passing.

Jojo went upstairs to her room. She pulled back her covers and shoved herself under them.

She picked up Harper's cell phone again and opened Instagram. There wasn't anything new in messages, but she scrolled automatically down the hundreds of selfies. She scrolled far enough that she reached the one of the two of them on the quad. Harper had been sitting on the grass, and Jojo had lain down next to her, putting her head on Harper's thigh. Harper had handed her phone to Jaquil, and he'd snapped a few photos. The one Harper had posted was the one in which Jojo was yawning, and Harper's fingers were playing with Jojo's hair.

It was too painful to look at.

Fine, she could go through some of the older messages in Facebook.

She opened Messenger.

Oh, shit.

There were so many, most of them read, up until two days ago. She should have looked at them all before this, but something had held her back until now—she'd been so positive that Harper would find herself and come back. Jojo'd just **known** that she would turn up, furious and beautiful.

And there were so many names she knew in the in-box.

Jojo felt sick again, right to the bottom of her stomach. Who **was** Harper?

She scrolled.

The same names, guys from the department. And more of them. Peter Marberry. Frank Shepherd. Disgusting. She couldn't make herself click to open, couldn't imagine learning one more thing about any of them. They were all horrible. Sick.

But what did that make Harper? How could she do what she did with them?

Where did that leave Jojo?

Just another conquest?

She tried to breathe around the sudden excess saliva that filled her mouth with a sour tang.

Then she saw it.

Omid Ahmadi.

Don't do it. Don't click, don't open. Make Mom do it. Delete it all, unread.

Jojo pushed the computer away and threw herself out of bed.

She stood there in the darkness—she hadn't bothered to turn on any lights when she got home, and she regretted it now. Breathing heavily, she bashed at the light switch, and the room that had for a second felt so unwelcoming became just her room. Her posters on the walls. Her desk. The black bookcase her dad had gotten her at IKEA.

She panted, her face burning. It wasn't him, it wasn't her dad, he wasn't in that message box.

Yeah, right.

There were, no doubt, other Omid Ahmadis on Facebook. But Jojo would bet her life that her father was the only one Harper knew.

Carefully, as if the bed might buck her out, she crawled back under the covers.

Pulling the computer onto her belly, she tried to breathe.

Then she clicked.

THIRTY-SIX

THE NURSE ON duty was one Laurie hadn't met. "Hi," she said, wishing to everything that existed that greetings didn't exist, that she could wear a flashing BREAKABLE sign above her head that would cut through all the crap and she could just start talking. **I'm too fragile to fuck with right now, so just give me the answers.** "I'm Laurie Ahmadi, Omid's wife. Can I ask you a question?"

The woman dropped a red folder on top of a pile of identical ones. Her hair was messy, as if she'd forgotten to brush it that day, but her dark brown eyes were kind. "I'm Elmaz. Sure, what's up?"

Laurie pointed at Omid's room. The door was closed. "I know it's late, and it's after visiting hours—"

Elmaz waved her hand. "Oh, it's fine. Go on in.

If he's sleeping, I'd say just let him, but I think he'll know you're there no matter what."

That was crap. When you were asleep, you were asleep. You didn't **know** anything. It was like being dead. "No, not that. He's lost some of his memory."

"I'd heard, yes."

"What if I remind him?"

Elmaz tilted her head to the right, either stretching her neck or trying really, really hard to look like she was listening. "Go for it."

"It won't hurt him?"

"Not unless it was traumatic. I wouldn't remind him of anything that would get his blood pressure up, but other than that you should be fine. He might already be remembering things."

Laurie shifted her weight. "What **if** his BP goes up? Does that automatically mean another heart attack?"

"Nothing automatically means anything, and theoretically his heart is much stronger now that the stent is in." Elmaz grinned as if they were sharing a joke. "Don't get him too riled up, but I'd say that to about any patient recovering from surgery." She winked. "Keep your clothes on. That's all I ask."

Laurie knew she was supposed to smile but couldn't quite make her face respond to the nurse's command. "Gotcha."

Inside the room Omid slept on his back, something that Laurie had rarely seen him do in eighteen years of marriage. Even with his CPAP strapped on, he usually managed to mash his face mask and the hose sideways into a pillow and sleep on his stomach. In the dark at home, she liked the rhythmic whoosh of his machine. Here the sound of it was lost among the other mechanical sounds, and with the tube coming from the front of his face he looked like a pod person, outfitted to sleep through space travel.

Laurie sat in the chair at the side of his bed. Her limbs felt too heavy to lift again, ever.

Who was this man?

"I would have sworn I knew everything you did at work," she said.

His eyes fluttered. His head turned. His eyes smiled at her over the mask.

"But I guess I missed some crucial information." Impatiently, she hit the POWER button on the CPAP. "You want to take that off?"

Omid reached for the mask. He croaked, "What time is it?"

"Time for you to talk."

"Hoo. You aren't playing." He used the bed remote to lift his head higher. "Is Jojo okay?"

"No." It was cruel, and it was awful, but she let him sit with it for ten seconds. She watched the fear land in his eyes, and she waited as long as she could before she said, "She's as fine as she can be for someone who was raped."

"**What?**" It wasn't his normal roar—instead it came out as a pathetic yelp. He tried to twist himself upward.

Fuck. She shouldn't have—no, she had to. He had to be made to remember. She stood and pressed his shoulders back into the bed, keeping him down. "She was roofied and raped. She's fine now. Really. But you have to remember. I need you to remember."

He shook his head, tears filling his eyes. "Laurie, stop. Tell me you're lying."

Laurie said nothing.

"Who was it?"

"You were the first to get to her. You were there with her. Do you remember that?"

"Where?" His breath was strong, medicated, foul. He didn't smell like a man she could ever kiss. "That house. The football player. It's . . . What the fuck."

She stepped back. "You found her in his house, yeah. But Harper's still missing."

"Harper **Cunningham**?"

He said it as if he hadn't thought of her in ages. "Tell me what you do remember."

"Is she involved in this?" He twisted to look at the tray. "Where's my phone?"

"Why do you need your phone?" It was heavy in her pocket.

"I need to—"

"Check on what Harper's saying to you?"

"Laurie. What's going on?"

He winced, and Laurie's own chest went fluttery inside. Was she killing her husband? What kind of woman was she?

No, she would not feel sorry for him. "What were you hiding?"

"Honest to God, Laurie, I have no fucking idea—"

It was his lying voice. He might not remember rescuing Jojo, but she knew the voice he used when he was trying to convince someone to believe him. "Don't you dare bullshit me. Harper might be dead, and I need you to start talking **now.**"

He rubbed at his eyes. "What do you know?"

"I know she's been sleeping with our guys."

"Fuck."

"Are you one of the guys?" She hated that her voice wobbled. If Omid had slept with Harper, their marriage was over. The whole life they'd built together, torn apart. And if she didn't love him so goddamn much, she'd kill him for hurting a girl the same age as their daughter, their daughter who had also been violated—

"No."

"Swear to me."

He held up his hand, as if he were taking an oath. "I swear to you on my honor."

Honor.

What was she supposed to do with that? She had no idea if he was lying or not. "What do you remember about what's going on with Harper?"

Taking a deep breath in through his nose, Omid closed his eyes. "She's threatening the department with a lawsuit."

"For?"

"For being a sex-trafficked victim of multiple officers."

Laurie felt her lungs contract suddenly, as if she'd stepped outside into subfreezing air. "Omid," she said.

He nodded. "She says they've been paying her for sex. She knows it would be big if it got out."

"It **will** get out." And they should, too—could Omid lateral to another agency? Could she? How could they stay in a department where it wasn't safe for Jojo—

"It doesn't have to."

"It **always** gets out." How many stupid things had she and Omid seen people try to cover up in the years they'd been with the department? Samuels's drunk-driving crash. The racist comments made on the mobile data computers in the cars, which the media pulled with the Freedom of Information Act. The stolen property that Eric Dunham had been reselling. Goddamn Darren Dixon and his racist Facebook rant. The jail scandal with the forgotten drunk.

"She just wants money, that's all."

Laurie folded her arms tightly against her chest, hoping it would help her heart quit racing. She looked behind her to make sure the door was shut. "That's blackmail."

"It is."

"Why the hell would she want money? Pamela and Andy have never seemed short on cash."

Omid shook his head slowly, as if it hurt. "Maybe they're running low? Maybe it's just a power move? I don't know. I just know she wants money now."

"But those men really slept with her. They sent her **pictures**." Sweat ran between her breasts.

Omid flinched. Then he nodded.

"How did she contact you?"

"She Facebooked me."

Laurie felt a thud in the pit of her stomach. "Let me see."

Omid closed his eyes. His eyelids flickered, as if he were reading something in the dark of his mind. Omid was careful, always. Cautious. He thought things through, whereas Laurie had always been more impetuous. Then he said, "Okay. Get my phone."

"Here." She handed it to him. "But if you open Facebook and start deleting things . . ."

Omid gave her a look, and Laurie's heart dropped to the floor. She'd always trusted him. Until now.

"Here." He pulled up a string of messages and scrolled backward. He handed the phone back to her.

Laurie breathed through her mouth.

Your officers are very bad boys. We should meet to discuss it.

What are you talking about?

You want to meet me.

Whatever it is you want to tell me, you can tell me now.

I can make it worth your while, Daddy.

I will call your parents right now if you don't tell me what the fuck you're talking about.

The next message came almost instantly, less than a minute later. **Seven of your guys have fucked me for money. But I'm still broke. Let's talk about my needs.**

Why should I believe you?

Screenshots followed of Instagram conversations. There was goddamn Bradcoe's freckled penis again. And one—holy fuck—shot of Harper's face, seen from above, the blow-job angle. A cock was in her mouth, and she wore a police jacket around her naked shoulders. Laurie couldn't make out the name, but the embroidered badge number was 5236, Will Yarwood.

Laurie's hand cramped around the phone.

What do you want?

A million dollars.

What are you TALKING about? This is a police department, not a retail establishment. You think I have money in my desk?

All I know is that I'll make a shit-ton more if I go public and sue the department. If I sue, you all lose your jobs, and I want you to be able to take care of Jojo, so I'm doing this as a favor to you. There are seven of them. That's less than a hundred and fifty grand from each guy. They can each pull a second mortgage to shut me up, don't you think?

It's impossible.

Make it possible.

There were more—Omid saying he was working on it, saying he needed more time, saying he needed to meet with her.

You had your chance. Just work on making it rain for me, Daddy.

"How? How did she get like this? This is Harper!" She sank into the uncomfortable chair next to Omid's bed and flicked through the messages— more of the same. Omid saying he was working on it, Harper threatening to go public.

"I have no idea." Omid rubbed his temples. "Fuck, I have a headache."

"That's what you get for not telling me about this and then forgetting about it."

Omid closed his eyes. "I wish I hadn't remembered."

"Did you talk to all the guys? All seven?"

Omid nodded, his eyes still shut.

"And?"

"And they're trying to come up with the money. Toomey has it liquid, and the rest are pulling it from their houses or selling stocks."

"You're serious."

He blinked his eyes open and stared at her. "As a fucking heart attack."

This wasn't Omid.

Omid took the high road.

Omid cleared house, he took names, he righted wrongs, he flipped tables in the temple. It's what she loved about him. He was strong where she was weak. She'd crossed a line once, but he never would.

Omid was one of the good guys.

He didn't cave to blackmail.

"Oh, my God." He **had** to cave, and Harper was smart enough to know it. If he didn't, he'd lose his department. They'd—all the men involved—lose their jobs, the city manager would sweep in and take it over. Omid would be the top sacrificial lamb.

They didn't have enough in savings to get them through this kind of storm. No money for Jojo and college unless they sold the house. Their Golden Years Fund, the money they'd been planning on spending on a sailboat even though neither of them had taken sailing lessons yet, would be drained—and fast.

Not like she'd need golden years. Not with this man, the one she didn't know anymore.

She leaned forward. "Who has her?"

Omid shook his head and stayed silent.

"Do you **know**?"

"Of course I don't. But it's not one of ours—it's that fucking CapB. It has to be—everything is about that goddamn Kevin Leeds."

"Your memory is back now, huh?" The trust Laurie'd had in her husband for eighteen years was gone. She would leave Omid for this. She could forgive infidelity before she could forgive him for covering up this serious a crime. **She** was the one in the family who had fucked up, who couldn't be trusted. Not Omid. It had never been Omid. "Convenient."

"Who do you think I am, anyway?"

Laurie had thought she'd known. "We have to go public, give it to the detectives and to the media. One of our guys might have her, even though that sounds impossible—"

"Kevin Leeds. There are no coincidences. Jojo was found at a murder scene. We go after him, after them. It's a CapB thing, I know it."

Laurie dug her nails into her palms. "If there are no coincidences, then what the hell do you make of a teenager threatening to take down a police department and then disappearing?"

He didn't answer her.

Laurie gripped the rail on his bed. "What if this were Jojo? What if she were missing? You'd go to each of their houses and take them apart with your bare hands, just in case."

Over the sheets his hands flexed. "Laurie."

"You'd tear off the roofs and rip up their sub-floors. You wouldn't rest until you'd gotten her back." She paused. "Why protect **them**? What if it was Jojo?"

"Jojo wouldn't be having sex for money."

It was such a terrible response she could barely take it in. "You asshole." **I can't do this alone.**

"Don't tell her I knew." He reached for her.

Laurie lurched backward. She hadn't even considered telling Jojo. But Jojo knew everything else.

"Please, Laurie." His face was a rictus of pain. "I'm begging you like I've never begged for anything in my whole life. Don't tell her. She can't know. She'd never get over it."

Screw him. **He'd** never get over it.

But neither would Jojo. "What are we going to do?"

Finally he looked at her. Those black eyes, the ones she'd seen in every light, the ones she'd fallen in love with, were flat. There was no life behind them. "I don't know."

It was the last thing she expected him to say.

Laurie bent at the waist and tried to breathe.

THIRTY-SEVEN

IN HER BED Jojo read the Facebook messages—all of them—a dozen times.

The ones to the cops were gross. Super disgusting, actually. **I want you to lick my button again. I get so wet when I think of u, like, I'm dripping right now.** Who in the world would, number one, sleep with any of them and, number two, apparently get off on talking about it afterward?

And it seemed like Harper really got off on it. There was nothing she didn't seem happy to discuss, and now that Jojo had imagined her getting the shocker from Dan Toomey, she had to admit that sex had gone back to just sounding nasty.

And the messages to her father . . .

She looked around her bedroom.

Randall, Jojo's old teddy bear, was flopped

sideways, as if he, too, had lost the will to live. She pulled him into her lap.

She squeezed.

There it was.

The lump.

Time for surgery. Using her fingers, she ripped into the side seam of his belly—the same one she'd gone into years ago—and pulled out the paper-towel-wrapped cube.

She unwrapped it. The small diamond gleamed. It fit on her middle finger, though she knew she couldn't wear it there. The second ring they'd stolen that day, the one that hadn't been reported or apparently even noticed missing, the one only she and Harper knew about.

Jojo got out of bed, scattering Randall's innards as she did.

She pawed through her wooden jewelry box. There it was, the long silver chain Dad had given her last Christmas. She slipped it through the ring and clasped it around her neck.

Why, though? Why was she trying to get closer to Harper, a person it seemed like she barely knew?

What they'd done together in bed couldn't have mattered at all, could it? Sex was apparently a job for Harper. Either that or she was really sick in the head, or both.

Jojo didn't know which option made her want to cry more.

Downstairs, the front door gave its opening creak,

making her jump. **Mom.** Jojo ran down the steps, carrying the cell phone with its fatal messages.

Mom was hanging up her sweater. "Hey."

If Jojo didn't tell her now about Dad, she'd lose her nerve. "Mama, there's something . . . something you need to know."

Her mother froze. "Is Harper back? Did they find her?"

Jojo shook her head. "Uh-uh."

Her mother didn't say anything. She held up one finger and kicked off her shoes. She left them there, which was freakish in itself. Mom didn't usually ever leave shit lying around except in the trunk of her car, which always had enough junk in it for her to hold a garage sale. "Just give me one second."

"No—"

"**Seriously,** Jojo. One second."

She went into the kitchen, leaving Jojo's heart hammering in her throat.

And under her terror at telling her mother about what was on Harper's cell phone was a sicker, darker feeling.

Dad wasn't Dad. She'd read the messages he'd sent to Harper. He wasn't the man she thought she knew. Dad, covering shit up? Willing to talk about blackmail? With the girl Jojo loved so much it sometimes hurt her heart?

Mom came back carrying a glass full of wine. "Okay. Tell me. Is this about your father?"

Shock was a gut punch. "Yeah."

"I saw his Facebook messages to her. He showed me."

Tears rose in the back of Jojo's throat, but she was angry, and she didn't want them. She swallowed as hard as she could. "He's not doing it right." Childish playground words, but they were all she had. "He's doing it **wrong.**"

"I know." Mom sat next to her and held out her arm.

Jojo leaned in. "How could he?"

"He's doing the best he can, but he doesn't know how to—"

"He's a good cop," she interrupted, in case Mom had forgotten. "He's not a bad cop." But Dad was **covering up** a crime. Multiple crimes. Big ones. "He knows that she's underage. Like, technically, she's a child." God, it sounded sick that way. Jojo was a child by those standards, too. She tried to picture herself fucking any one of the officers and only felt a slick of nausea rise in her gullet.

"I know."

The words came then, the ones she wanted to hold back but couldn't. "Harper saw me." Oh, God, that was the wrong tense. "She sees me. No one ever sees me."

Mom frowned. "Huh?"

No one saw her. Not in her whole life. Harper, on the playground when they were four, had seen her. She'd never stopped. Harper made Jojo feel special, sparkly, like someone magical, not just a girl who got decent grades and didn't suck at soccer. Harper saw inside her—Mom and Dad never had. Her parents thought she was going to become someone impressive and smart and important someday, which was why they didn't want her going into emergency services.

Harper had **always** thought she was impressive and smart and important.

But what if that had all been a lie?

Like Dad had been lying. "What's he going to do? Does one of them have her? He has to go public with it, right? He **has** to."

"I don't know."

Jojo twisted and pulled her legs up, so that she sat cross-legged facing her mother. She folded her arms. "What part don't you know?"

"Any of it."

Panic streaked through Jojo's body, opening like a zipper from the top of her head to the bottom of her feet. If Dad didn't know, and if Mom didn't know, then what the **fuck** were they supposed to do? "Mom?"

"I'm sorry. I don't mean to scare you."

"Too late."

Mom looked surprised. Jojo guessed it was a long time since she'd admitted she was scared of anything, least of all to her mother. "Baby—"

"I wish you'd stop calling me that."

"Okay." Mom closed her eyes, as if by doing that she could shut Jojo up.

So Jojo said, "Also, I might be gay."

Mom choked on her wine.

The terror grew wider, opening into a chasm in her chest, the Grand Canyon of fear. She didn't know if she was more scared of Mom not accepting her or the fact that it might be true. "I mean, I might **not** be gay. I have no idea."

"Joshi."

Tears spilled down Jojo's cheeks, and she swiped them away angrily. "I don't want to talk about it." Why had she said it? She was such an idiot.

Mom reached out a hand to touch her cheek. Her palm was warm, and it smelled like the Jergens lotion she'd used forever. "I love you."

Jojo made a strangled noise. It was all she had.

"Listen to me, Jojo. I love you so hard that you could do anything, **be** anything, and I'd love you. You could murder six babies and eat them, and I'd be really upset, but I'd love you."

Jojo's spine went rigid. "So being gay—**possibly** being gay—is like being a baby-killing cannibal? Are you actually serious?"

"No! Shit. Sorry. I'm just—"

"Because that's **completely** offensive, you know that, right? I thought you were all for human rights."

"I am. Jesus, Jojo, it's just a lot."

Jojo unfolded and refolded her arms even tighter against her chest. "Sorry that you found out your daughter might be a dyke"—it was the first time

she'd said the word out loud, and it sounded dirty
and hollow in her mouth—"and that your husband
is a piece of shit all on the same night."

Mom looked wounded, as if Jojo had said something unfair, but she hadn't. Jojo might be a dyke.
Dad was a crooked cop, willing to cover up crimes
of his own staff to avoid a scandal.

Jojo's phone pinged with a text. She looked at
it automatically—it was from a number she didn't
recognize.

Cordelia, where's your ring?

Her heart pounded in her temples.

No one called her Cordelia but Harper.

No one.

No one else knew about the second ring she
still had.

**Harper's still alive, but she probably wishes
she wasn't. Love, CapB.**

She felt the blood drain from her hands and face,
and she went cold all over. The ring on its chain felt
heavy under her shirt.

"What?" Mom demanded. "Give it to me."

Jojo held out the phone.

Mom gasped. She stood and then sat right back
down. "Whose number is this?"

"I don't know."

"Who's Cordelia?"

"Me. I am. So is Harper." Literally **no one** knew
that. They'd kept it their secret code name for each
other.

The rings they'd stolen had been their Cordelia rings.

Harper's still alive, but she probably wishes she wasn't. Harper was wishing for death? What were they doing to her? Jojo's stomach heaved.

Now Mom said, "How are you both Cordelia? I don't understand!"

Was she ignoring the most important part on purpose? "She wishes she wasn't alive! Mom!"

"Honey, if it's CapB, it's him. It's Kevin. You know that."

They were missing something. She could feel it. As her mother finished talking, Jojo closed her eyes and thought as hard as she could. It felt like doing math in her head, the same kind of preliminary confusion, but if she just thought for a minute . . .

"I'll call dispatch," Mom said, her phone already in her hands. "They can run the number and see if it matches anything we have."

Jojo formed herself into a ball on the couch, bringing up her knees and hugging them against her chest as hard as she could. "You can't call them."

No answer from her mother.

"Mom? Mom! Hang up! It **has** to be a cop."

THIRTY-EIGHT

LAURIE WAS SO involved in trying to figure out what the next steps would be—no Omid to help her—that she didn't listen to her daughter's words at first.

She didn't hear her until Jojo was standing up, in her face, almost shouting, "It isn't CapB! And it isn't Kevin! **It's got to be a cop!**"

"But the text says—" She caught herself. She sounded like an average citizen, believing what was in front of her face instead of really thinking about it. "Okay, what?"

"Kevin. It wasn't him. He wouldn't set CapB up like that—he loves them. They love him." Jojo shook her head hard. "I think someone is trying really hard to make it look like it's CapB, except it's someone else, trying to throw us off the scent. But that message means it has to be someone who knows that Harper and I are involved with the group."

"You were assaulted in his house." She still couldn't stay the word **rape** to Jojo. "In **his** house."

"Kevin's gay."

The sudden pivot of topic made her head hurt. "No he's not." Kevin Leeds was dating some model, wasn't he? He was last year, anyway, when he first started hitting the news for being an activist.

"He told me. I didn't want to tell because it's not my secret, but I had to. Didn't I?"

Laurie crossed her arms hard across her chest. "So what?"

"So he didn't rape me. And that means that—"

"Believe it or not, a gay man can rape a woman. It's about power, not—"

"I know." Jojo cut her off. "I get that. I'm not stupid. But listen. Kevin is my friend. The people in CapB are my friends, too. I know you hate that, but it's true. I know I can trust them."

"How?"

"How do you know you can trust yours?"

Laurie winced. Most of her friends worked with her. And she had no idea how she could trust any of them anymore. "What are you saying, exactly?"

"It could be anyone on that list that she was chatting with. You know her, she'll tell anyone anything. Except Ramsay. It's probably not him because he's dead." Jojo covered her mouth for a moment.

Laurie's heart clenched in her chest. "I still don't . . . I can't accept that it's a cop. Not one of ours."

"Mom, use your head. Why would CapB, a group working for the good of humanity—"

Laurie resisted the urge to roll her eyes.

"—kidnap a girl, one who's been working with them? That would mean Kevin was in on it, right? And his lover is dead."

Laurie gaped. "Zachary Gordon was his . . ."

Jojo nodded shortly. "He wouldn't rape me and kill the man he loves. He wouldn't hide Harper, and he wouldn't try to implicate his group with a terrifying text. Unless he hated CapB or something, but he doesn't." Jojo's voice was raw. "He loves it. And the organization loves him. They idolize him. They wouldn't do this. There's nothing in it for them except the end of the group. On the other hand, Harper has been extorting money from these officers. From Dad." It hurt so bad to say it out loud. "To keep it out of the papers. The one thing that would make it go away is if **she** went away. It has to be one of the guys on the list."

There was no guarantee Jojo was **actually** right, but it sure made more sense, and if Laurie had learned anything in twenty years at the PD, it was that the likeliest answer was usually the correct one. "We need to get info on that phone number."

"Don't call dispatch," said Jojo.

Her daughter was right, so right that it ached. "Yeah. I'll go run it myself. Put on your shoes."

Jojo shook her head. "No. Just take the number with you. I'm staying here."

"You're going with me."

"I am **not**."

"I'm not leaving you here."

"You left me here all night. What's changed?"

"There are more of them now." Seven of the men Laurie worked with. And at least one . . .

Jojo folded her arms over her chest and crossed her legs. "That's why I'm not going. If I see one of them in the hall, I'll lose it."

That was fair. "Then you'll stay in the car."

"Do you think I'm safer in the police department parking lot in a metal box surrounded by glass, or here? With all of Daddy's dead bolts?"

Fuck. "Fine. I'll be back in an hour. Less."

"Mom." Jojo clasped her elbows, her shoulders hunched forward. "I'm scared."

Laurie was terrified. Her head dropped, heavy.

But she was the ex-cop. And the dispatcher. And most important of all, she was the mom. She lifted her head again. "It's all going to be fine, Joshi."

Sometimes mothers had to lie.

THIRTY-NINE

LAURIE PARKED IN front of the station and tried to take a deep breath. She had to get this right. She needed to steady herself before she went in.

Before she saw any of them.

If this all came out, if it hit the media . . .

All the men involved would lose their jobs. Including Omid. And the way this kind of thing went, she wouldn't keep her job, either. Wife of the ousted chief would be ousted. They wouldn't be able to get other jobs in the industry. They'd lose the house. Their savings.

But if Laurie found Harper first—then what? Harper was on the local news. She'd made national press on Fox, maybe other networks. Blond and white and pretty—she was the kind of story the press drooled over.

When Harper was found, all of it would definitely come out. There was no way it wouldn't. If Omid had just done the right thing in the first place, the very first time Harper had contacted him, then his position would still be secure. The cops all would have lost their jobs, but he could have stood up for his department—he would have been the decent face, the outraged one, the one who separated the wheat from the chaff.

On second thought, no matter what he'd done, he would have gone down, too. The person at the top was always a scandal away from being booted. That came with the job.

But he wouldn't have been disgraced, as he would be now. He would have gotten a golden handshake, a wad of money, and a good reference if he needed it to start over at some new department. Laurie could have kept working.

Now it would all go to hell.

Unless they could find Harper and somehow convince her not to talk about the men. If she and Omid sold the house, they'd make at least seven hundred thousand. Would that be enough? Would she accept that?

No, no, **no.** This—right here—**this** was how it started.

Laurie smacked her hand against the steering wheel. Pain shot up her wrist.

No. She wouldn't cover up a damn thing. What

was she even **thinking**? No matter what Harper had done, or how Omid was somehow complicit, someone else in her department was crazy enough to harm people. Laurie had to find Harper before whoever had her did anything worse, before he hurt or raped or killed again.

Then, when Harper was safe, Laurie would figure out what to do, and she'd do it right. Truly right. She had to, or Laurie wouldn't be the kind of mother that Jojo deserved.

Omid, how could you?

DISPATCH was busy—Dina and Rita were working what sounded like a failure-to-yield, and Maury was tied up talking to Jocko Smith.

"Jocko!" Maury yelled. "I'm glad you're okay, buddy, but my boss says I have to get off the phone! I don't want to get in trouble!" Maury was the boss. It was a line they all used when drunks were safe in their own houses and didn't want anything but to talk.

Laurie slipped into the open seat and logged in. She ran out the phone number even though she knew it was a cell phone, on the remote chance it was a VOIP cell with a physical address.

It wasn't.

She pulled up the records management system. Maybe they'd had contact with a person with this cell number—her heart beat faster. If it was one of their guys, then for sure his cell would be on file, and it would hit—

But nothing came back. UNKNOWN.

Futile. She'd have to turn the number and the verbiage of the text over to Investigations. She could call the wireless companies, of course—start the ball rolling to see who owned the phone. It was something they often did in dispatch, usually with suicidal callers who refused to say where they were.

But it took ages, and Maury would be off the phone soon enough with questions about what the hell she was doing.

She ran through the names on the list.

Ben Bradcoe. She'd seen his honest reaction when she sat with him in his car. He couldn't be behind it. He wasn't smart enough to dissemble that fast. Was he?

Heinz Tollis. He was married, with four kids and a tiny house and a wife he appeared to be in love with. He laughed all the time. He wouldn't kidnap someone. Would he?

He'd slept with Harper.

Sherm Naumann. He was too stupid to try to pull off something huge. He literally couldn't parallel park.

But he'd had paid sex with a minor.

Dan Toomey and Peter Marberry, both too young and too neurotic. They both got nervous in lineup when they had to distribute the hot sheets.

But they were grown men, abusing a child.

Frank Shepherd. She just couldn't see him being involved at all. He'd once painted bike lanes in his neighborhood with a paintbrush because he was worried about the local kids. It wasn't him.

But they'd all fucked Harper for money.

The only one left was Will Yarwood, the bantam rooster.

He was single. He dated a lot but kept no girlfriend more than a couple of weeks, though he professed that he couldn't wait to start a family. He'd been friends with the ex-cop Darren Dixon and had actually liked the racist Facebook post. (He'd unliked it before anyone thought to screenshot it, so he had deniability. Then he'd carefully commented favorably on the department's post, supporting Omid. Backstabber.) The women he brought as dates to department parties were always very short and very thin, with huge breasts. They never spoke.

Yarwood lived alone in a big, sterile house full of generic white furniture. She'd been there once for a pool party during a period in which Yarwood was briefly friendly to her and Omid. There'd been a huge old garage in the back, the kind with barn doors. Yarwood had said it was full of spiders and that he was going to get around to doing something with it someday.

Someday.

She glanced at the screen. Yarwood was in the station.

"Hey! Whatcha doing?" Maury slid his chair into her pod.

"I don't want to talk."

Maury adjusted the mic on his headset. "Sorry, kiddo. Too bad. Tell me what's going on. We're all going crazy here."

"You think **you** are?"

"Don't worry. With Colson working lead, they'll get to the bottom of this sooner rather than later. But, shit, I think he's on the way to your house right now."

Laurie shook her head. "No. I saw him at the drink-up. He's off duty."

Maury glanced at the terminal. "No, he came back in after that. Still working. He just left to go see you and Jojo a couple of minutes ago."

Fear was a jolt of ice water. "Why? Why would he do that?"

Maury shook his head. "To check on you both. Because we're worried. You know that."

No. What if he was in on it? "I'm sorry. I've got to go." Maybe she could beat Colson home. She and Jojo could show him the text info—Laurie could watch his face, see if any flicker gave him away.

Maury started to say something else, but she moved too fast for him to even finish the sentence. The door to dispatch slammed behind her, and she took the stairs upward two at a time. She came around the corner and ran full speed into Will Yarwood.

The rooster himself.

"Sorry," she mumbled, hating the fact that she'd felt his gun belt against her stomach. Now she needed a shower. And he needed to move out of her way.

Yarwood shifted back and forth on the balls of his feet so that he was blocking the entire hall. "How's Jojo?" His voice was too loud.

Too thick.

Laurie shook her head. "I've got to go." She took a step forward, but he blocked her again.

"We're all worried, you know." Yarwood's eyebrows rose. "We're learning things about her little friend. Seems like she was a liar, huh? Not the best person for Jojo to hang around."

Had Bradcoe already spilled the info that Laurie knew about what they'd been doing? Laurie screwed her hands into fists and leaned forward. "Yeah, so I've heard **you** know her pretty well."

Yarwood glanced over his shoulder. Montgomery was making his way out of the sergeant's office, lumbering toward them.

Then Yarwood leaned forward, too. Their faces were less than a foot apart. Laurie smelled his deodorant and caught a whiff of old sweat.

"I bet she's never found," he whispered in her ear. "You wait and see if I'm right."

The blast of white heat swamped Laurie's vision.

She punched him right in the jaw, a sharp blow that came out of nowhere, as if she were channeling lightning. One moment she was fine, the next she was cradling her hand as Yarwood bleated like a goat from down on the floor.

She swayed above him. "Where is she? Where do you have her?"

He scrambled to his feet. "Fuck! Sergeant! Sergeant, did you see that? She hit me!"

Sergeant Shane Montgomery sped up to a trot. "What in the ever-loving hell, Laurie?"

Some rookie whose name she couldn't even remember had jumped out of the woodwork and was pulling her back.

"You fucking piece of shit, Yarwood! Tell me where Harper is!"

"You crazy bitch! She hit me!" He sounded like a whining child. His jaw was already beginning to swell.

The sergeant rounded on her, his mouth open, but she didn't let him speak.

"Sarge, he's got her. I know he does. He practically just admitted it."

"I did **not**!"

She could barely breathe around the heat in her throat. "You need to send units to check his house. And his old garage."

The sergeant looked incredulous, his eyebrows sky-high. "Who the fuck are you talking about?"

Laurie went on, her breath hitching in her chest, "I'm pretty sure he's hiding Harper Cunningham at his house. You need to go! Go now!"

The color in Yarwood's face reached a deep plum. "You're insane!"

"Now!" screamed Laurie, pulling against the multiple arms that now held her back. And it was probably good they were—if she could get to him, she'd rip the information right out of his throat.

Montgomery, who was generally known for being the most relaxed of the lower brass, stomped his boot hard into the wooden floor. The hallway shook. Laurie jumped. So did the three other officers who'd gathered behind him.

"Laurie, do you have any idea what the hell you're suggesting right now? Are you actually saying that Officer Yarwood kidnapped a girl and is keeping her at his house? The girl who is missing from a **murder** scene? Are you out of your goddamned **mind**?"

Pain from the tension in her head bloomed red behind Laurie's eyes. "I know it doesn't make any sense, but you have to check!"

"No!"

Goddamn it, Laurie knew she looked deranged. And every minute they waited was a minute that could mean life or death.

Yarwood jabbed a finger toward her face. "I know you're just a dispatcher, and it's been a long time since you were on the street, thank God, but you **might** be aware that battery on a police officer with grave bodily injury is a felony, right?"

"Bodily injury, my ass!" It was just his jaw. "When they let me go, I swear to God I'll show you—"

Yarwood puffed out his chest. "I want her arrested."

Laurie squawked a laugh. As if he would.

But Montgomery said, "You sure?"

"Seriously?" Laurie jerked her head back. "Are you **kidding** me right now? You know he's fucking her, right? Yarwood has been fucking Harper Cunningham!"

Yarwood's face drained of color. "Sarge, she's crazy. Or she's cracked out on something. I swear to you—she's lying."

Montgomery said, "Come on now. Laurie?"

"Are **you** fucking her, too?"

Montgomery raised his arms and dropped them fast. "I want this bullshit **out of my hallway**! Yarwood, you actually serious about pressing charges?"

"More serious than I've ever been about anything."

She was right about this. Yarwood had Harper. He wanted her locked up. Out of the way.

And the fucker managed to look smug even while he was still breathing hard. He crossed his arms. "If you don't put her under arrest, I'll arrest her myself."

"I've got to get home to my **daughter.**" Jojo was alone. Colson was going over. There was no way she'd allow herself to be arrested by her own co-workers.

Sergeant Montgomery stared hard at Yarwood. "It's a dick move, Will. You **sure** you want to press charges against the chief's wife?"

Yarwood pressed a hand against his chest. "Currently **my** chief is Brent Stanley, not that useless sack she's married to who can't even take care of simple problems. And her sick fantasy is just that, something they cooked up together!"

Laurie lunged at him, almost reaching him before the rookie twisted her arm back behind her. "Fuck! Get **off**!" Her shoulder would hurt later, but she felt nothing now except rage and desperate fear. They were going to be too late. Why couldn't they see that?

"Get him out of here!" Montgomery yelled at two nearby lookie-loo officers who dragged Yarwood into the sergeant's office. The door slammed shut.

"Just look, Shane. Look in his house." Laurie spoke hurriedly, not sure how much time she had left. "Promise me you'll look."

The sergeant closed his eyes and rubbed his forehead. "You seem fucking insane right now, you know that. And I've got to take you into the jail."

"You **know** me, Shane. You know I'm not crazy. Just do me this favor. Look through his house. Promise me. Don't be like Antioch." Just a forty-five-minute drive from here, cops had missed the girl being held in a shed behind a house for eighteen years. **Antioch** was code in the department for "don't fuck it up like the Jaycee Dugard case."

Montgomery leveled his gaze at Laurie. "You'll promise to walk into the jail with me without losing it again?"

Laurie's knees shook. The most important thing was getting them onto Yarwood's property. She stopped trying to wrench out of the rookie's grab and met the sergeant's gaze. "If you screw this up and don't search those premises, when Harper Cunningham is found, I'll tell the media that it was you who refused to investigate."

"Goddamn it, Laurie."

"You can arrest me. But promise me you'll search."

Montgomery shot a look down the hallway. Yarwood was still yelling from behind the closed door. "We'll look. Come into the jail with me, though, okay? Won't take long."

"Fine." It wasn't fine, none of this was fine. But maybe Harper would be found, and then—Jesus, they were putting **Laurie** in a cell when any number of people who worked in this very building were the ones who deserved to be getting slung in there. Yarwood had committed a felony. **He** should be the one getting hooked up, not her. Anyone who'd hurt Harper deserved this, not Laurie, who was taking Harper's disappearance seriously when **no one else was.**

Oh, God, Jojo was going to be so scared when Laurie didn't come home.

When Colson showed up instead.

FORTY

Mom still wasn't home, and Jojo still hadn't eaten anything. She was starving. Cereal would be better than nothing.

As she grabbed a bowl out of the cupboard, she heard the number "406." The scanner was always on in the living room, but she couldn't remember the last time she'd paid any attention to it. Every once in a while, a traffic pursuit would happen and she'd try to figure out which officer was screaming bloody murder while he went seventy miles an hour in a residential zone, though most of the time she heard nothing. But dispatch had clearly said "Copy, 406 in custody." She turned the radio up and listened more intently.

Because 406 was Mom's dispatch badge.

What the hell did that mean? Would they actually

arrest one of their own? Wasn't that against all of the professional courtesy whatever they were supposed to have?

What would Mom have to do to get arrested?

Someone banged on the front door, and Jojo almost screamed.

Through the peephole she saw Lieutenant Mark Colson, someone Jojo had always liked. He and her mom had dated before she got with Dad, but it never seemed to be weird with them—when she was little, she'd called him Unca Mark.

But she didn't want to talk to anyone, not until she knew what was going on with Mom.

"Jojo! You home?"

She stayed still, hoping he couldn't tell she was at the peephole.

"Jojo, I can see your shadow on the curtain."

"Hey." She opened the door just wide enough for him to enter.

Colson hugged her. He always did. This time, though, Jojo remained stiff. Her own arms didn't move.

"How you doing?"

Jojo didn't answer.

"Your mom here? Because on the radio just now, I could swear—"

Silently, Jojo shook her head.

Mark cocked an eyebrow but seemed to take it at face value. "Where did she go?"

"To the station." Her voice was scratchy.

"Why?"

"I don't actually know." She was a bad liar. No matter how smooth Jojo had tried to be in the past, she had so many tells that even total strangers knew when she wasn't telling the truth. Now she felt her ears flame and her nose go hot.

A loud ping that Jojo didn't recognize rang from Colson's body. He pulled out his cell phone, and then he shot a glance at Jojo.

406 in custody echoed in her head.

Texts were the fastest way of disseminating information that needed to stay off the air. And cops were the biggest gossips in the world.

Mom had totally just gotten herself arrested somehow.

And it had to be one of them who'd made that happen.

Jojo's hands were clammy. "Well, I guess you should . . . I mean, we'll call you as soon as she's back."

Colson tilted his head, and for the first time Jojo realized how tall he was. Taller than Frank Shepherd, maybe even taller than Nate Steiner. His shoulders formed a box, a square of muscle. His shirt had to be three times larger than Dad's shirt.

Colson said, "What's your mom trying to do?"

"I don't know what you're talking about." Jojo felt the heat spread from her nose to her cheeks. Colson wasn't stupid.

"Jojo. Whatever she's doing, she has to stop."

"I . . . I don't know what you mean."

Colson moved an inch closer to her. He kind of smelled like spilled beer—was he drunk? Was that possible?

"Jojo, honey, this isn't a game."

Jojo felt flapping wings of panic in her chest. "I know."

"She's making trouble where there should be none. She's got to stop. Do you get me?"

No. Jojo didn't **get** him. Jojo had no freaking idea what this guy thought she should tell Mom to stop doing, but it certainly wasn't stopping the search for Harper. "You're kind of scaring me." The words weren't completely true until they came out of her mouth, but then she felt the swell of panic rise from her stomach into her chest and up into her head.

When he spoke, his voice rumbled in the deep way it always had, but he sounded funny. Not quite himself. "Your dad has it under control, even from the hospital. If your mom doesn't stop, I won't be able to protect her."

Jojo was frozen in place, her mind a blank.

But he stepped backward, nodding his head as if everything were normal. "Well, all right, then. You should probably get to bed. It's late." He gave a half salute and left the kitchen, the front door banging behind him as he left.

Jojo stood in the same spot, in the corner, her body still as rigid as an ice sculpture, except that she'd probably never melt.

She tried to breathe, panting through her mouth. **Move, do something. Anything.** She made a small squawking sound in the back of her throat, and somehow that freed her frozen limbs. She grabbed her phone and her house keys and headed for the front door. But when she put her hand on the doorknob, she realized she had no idea where she was going. Dad was in the hospital, and Mom was probably going to jail. **406 in custody.**

At the moment Jojo had no one. No Harper, no parents, no freaking clue what to do next. She couldn't put this on Pamela and Andy—it wouldn't be fair.

She opened her phone and texted. **I know it wasn't you. Can I come over?**

Kevin's answer was almost immediate. **Yes.**

FORTY-ONE

THE LYFT CAME in five minutes. Mom would receive an immediate notification as soon as Jojo got out of the car and hit the PAY button on her phone, but who knew what the hell Mom was doing, or when she'd be able to look at her phone again? As the driver pulled onto Kevin's street, he said, "You know, this is the neighborhood where that football player lives. The one who killed that guy. Did you hear there's a chick missing, too?" Jojo resolved not to tip and slammed the car door hard.

Kevin answered the door as if he'd been standing there waiting. His chest and hands were covered in flour, and white powder streaked his cheek.

"Hey," said Jojo. Now that she was here, she wasn't sure it had been the right thing to do. Maybe she should've just stayed home. Or gone to the hospital to see if Dad was awake, if he could possibly start to explain how everything had gone so wrong.

Instead she'd gone back to the place where she'd been raped. What was wrong with her?

But then Kevin wrapped her in a hug. He smelled like cinnamon, and her heart slowed just a beat.

"How are you?" She pulled away from him, regretting her words immediately. Kevin's face stiffened along with his shoulders. "I take it back. Don't answer that."

Kevin just shook his head and gestured for her to follow him. "My mom keeps calling, keeps asking me that, and there's nothing I can say. I don't have any kind of answer for her. She wants to fly out, but her doctor says her lungs aren't strong enough yet from that last pneumonia. I can't stop baking. I got out, what, six hours ago? I've made three dozen chocolate chip cookies and one loaf of zucchini bread." His voice broke. "Zach loved zucchini bread."

The kitchen was trashed. It looked as if someone had picked up the room and shaken it, a small, localized earthquake with the stove at the epicenter. Jojo had seen him bake before, but this wasn't normal cooking. Batter-covered spoons lay on the floor. A tumbler of milk had fallen over on the counter, and it dripped off in steady plonks.

"This is . . ."

"Yeah." Kevin held a sponge under the tap and

squeezed it out. For a moment he appeared to be about to start to clean, but then he crammed the sponge into the garbage disposal and turned it on. The noise was monstrous, and it got worse as he shoved a wooden spoon in after it.

"Kevin!" Jojo lunged for the button to turn it off. "Dude!"

He looked up at her as if in confusion. "Want a cookie?"

She didn't. Her stomach hurt. But she said, "I'd love one."

He handed her one, still warm and soft, and then said, "Can you help me with something?"

"Of course."

In his bedroom the sheets had been stripped off and were draped on the floor next to the bookcase that had been upended, its books strewn from the wall to the bathroom door.

He grabbed one end of the naked mattress. "Help me outside with this?"

"What are you doing?"

"I don't know. I don't know **anything.** But I know I need to change this room. This is where we slept. It's got to go." The mattress thumped its way down the hall. She tried not to look at the closed door, the door of the room she'd been in, where Zach had been found. Had there been crime scene tape up across it while ID had done their work? How many of her own fingerprints had been found there?

Tears streamed down Kevin's face. He turned right, and they dragged the mattress through the living room to the open slider door.

"Where are we taking it?"

"Just out." Kevin picked it up and heaved it into the middle of the backyard.

Jojo was startled by the motion, but she wasn't scared of Kevin. Not the way she'd been freaked out just twenty minutes before by Mark Colson.

Kevin didn't look at her, just walked past and back into the bedroom. She followed, and they grabbed the box spring, performing the same maneuver through the house. Again Kevin hurled it into the middle of the backyard. On any other day, there would've somehow been humor in this. One of them would have bounced on the mattress for sure, probably both of them. But there was no laughter, not anymore.

Once back in the living room, Jojo ventured, "When did you last eat? Besides cookies." God, it sounded like something her mother would say. But Kevin's skin looked ashen, and when he stood still, she could see that his fingers were shaking.

"I don't think I'll ever be hungry again."

Jojo wanted to touch him, wanted to reach out and press her fingers against his wrist, the way Mom did when Jojo was upset, but honestly, Kevin looked as if he were about to break in half.

"Want to help me paint the bedroom?" he asked.

"Paint? You have paint?"

"TaskRabbit to the rescue. Anything delivered, any time of the day. Not that I'll have money much longer. But yeah, I've got all the supplies. I just have to finish clearing out the room."

Suddenly it sounded like the best idea in the world. Throwing her body into something physical, something she'd have to think about, something distracting. She'd come over to talk, but this would put it off. Thank God.

Jojo had never painted anything before. She found she liked the rhythm of it, the way the dark purple paint sounded squishing off the roller and onto the walls. As she painted each wall, Kevin moved to the next, taping off the trim. She liked the sound of that, too. He had music playing in the kitchen, just a random Internet pop station, and as they worked, she heard him start to whistle unconsciously to the faraway tune, then catch himself. It was almost 4:00 A.M., and the night outside was quiet. Inside, it felt like time didn't exist. Mom hadn't texted her yet, so Jojo assumed she was still in a cell. If she was, there was nothing Jojo could do, not at the moment. Better to swing a paintbrush than go crazy.

Hundreds of times she felt the words bubble to the top of her tongue. **I'm so sorry about Zach. I'm so sorry.**

But that didn't feel fair. Saying she was sorry about Zach was perhaps the biggest understatement she could utter. She wasn't sorry about him. She was brokenhearted. She was knifed through with the knowledge that something had gone wrong, something she didn't understand, something that had left the man Kevin loved most dead.

Jojo didn't know that grief could feel so big.

Harper.

As if he could read her thoughts, Kevin said, "Any news on Harper?"

So much news. So much shit, and Jojo didn't know where to start. Or even if she should.

"Just tell me, Jojo."

"I got a text. Wherever she is, she's alive."

Kevin dropped the tape, and it rolled into the corner, bumping softly against the wet paint Jojo had just rolled on. "How do you know that?"

"The text called me a name that no one but Harper knows about, and she mentioned something I have that's a secret. And some other stuff."

"What else?" Kevin's frame was rigid, but she could feel the energy coming from it.

"We found out lots of other stuff. Um, bad stuff. She's been sleeping with a bunch of guys for money." Jojo dropped her chin and looked at her toes, newly decorated with purple paint droplets. "And some of them are cops. I mean, like, a lot of them are cops."

Kevin blinked, then shook his head. "I don't get it. What does that mean?"

"The text I got was from the person who has her, or at least that's what it implied."

"And?"

"The text was signed from CapB."

Kevin's eyes widened even further. He held up one finger and then walked out of the bedroom into the hallway. Jojo, frozen in place, heard him take a long, shaky breath. Then he turned on his heel and walked back in.

"What the **fuck**?"

"I know," Jojo said hurriedly. "It can't be—"

"CapB wouldn't do **anything** like that."

Jojo needed him to catch up, to be on the same page. "Of course they didn't. I know that."

"We struggle to get our shit together to hold protests. At the last one, no one even remembered the megaphone. We couldn't kidnap someone if we wanted to, which we never fucking would, because we're not fucking animals."

"Obviously," said Jojo. "That's kind of why I came over here, I guess. I wanted to run my ideas past you." Dang it, it wasn't like she really **had** ideas. All she had was a need for comfort and some floating terrified feelings, and those weren't helping her much. "I think it's a cop who's behind all this. I think it's someone Harper was sleeping with, and I don't know who it is or what to do."

With a paint-smudged finger, Kevin gestured for her to follow him into the kitchen. "I need a drink," he said. He poured himself a shot of something brown and clear. He looked at her, then shook his head as he shot the liquid back, immediately pouring another one. Then he placed both palms on the tile of the kitchen island and leaned forward. He kept both his eyes and his voice low. "So someone somehow hurt you, dumped you in my house, killed my best friend"—his voice crackled as if static had interfered with his speaking—"and kidnapped Harper, and they're saying **CapB** did this? In order to . . . what? That's what I don't get."

"To discredit CapB. It has to be someone else. One of those police officers, someone angry enough to—"

"But what's the **connection**? None of this makes sense, Jojo. Help me out here."

She wished she could. She wished she knew. "I don't know how."

They were the wrong words.

The sides of Kevin's hands slid along the tile, gathering into fists. "What about you?" He turned to face her.

Jojo felt a shiver shoot down the backs of her legs. "What?"

"I'm going to have to clean up Zach's blood, did you know that? They said I could hire a company to do it, but they can't come out for a week. I can't wait that long. It's in there right now, all that blood, still soaking through the carpet and blasted up the closet wall. I didn't kill Zach. And I know **you** were in my house. Why isn't anyone looking at you?"

Jojo's heart skittered into overdrive. She could run. But Kevin was fast—his salary was dependent on it.

"Remember when you told me that you didn't rape me? And I believed you? You didn't have to do anything or say anything to prove it to me. I just believed you, because I knew you were right. Because we're friends."

Kevin's eyes were still narrowed, his fists still clenched. He said nothing.

"I didn't hurt Zach, Kevin. And I'm not the one who has Harper. There's someone out to get both of us, and the only chance we have of finding her is to work together. This all happened Friday, and it's already Sunday night—No, wait, it's Monday morning now—"

"How is that **our** job? Oh, yeah, right. It can't be the police department's job, because they're all fucking the girl who's missing, am I getting that right?"

Jojo nodded silently.

"What's her father like?"

"What?"

"Her stepfather. Could he be pimping her out for some reason?"

The thought wasn't as shocking as it should be. Jojo swallowed uncomfortably around a lump in her throat. "I asked her once. If Andy had ever hurt her. She was fine around him our whole lives, and then, right before we got in trouble together, she started to act really weird around him."

"Weird how?"

"Like she hated him but also like she loved him

more than anyone else, even her mom." Harper would leap at Andy when he picked them up at school, kissing his cheek frantically, but then being as rude as humanly possible, which for Harper was pretty damn rude. **Fuck off, Andy. Love you, Andy. You're an idiot, Andy. What does my mother see in you? You're the best, I mean it.** "He's never felt creepy, not like some Chester the Molester. It was more like . . . like **she** was creepy around him."

"What did she say when you asked her if he'd hurt her?"

"She said no, that he loved her."

"Did you believe her?"

Jojo didn't know. She had then. "I have no clue about anything. I know that he and Pamela just look like parents who're losing their minds. Pamela's always been kind of absent but super loving when she's present. She's not absent now, that's for sure. Andy's just acting like somebody kidnapped his daughter. Someone evil would give you the creeps, right? Andy just seems freaked out and normal. And my mom said that they really thought Harper was home that night. She's good at knowing when someone's telling the truth."

Kevin lifted an eyebrow. "Uh-huh."

"She **is**."

"Do you know how it feels to grieve the person you love the most in the whole world?"

Jojo shook her head. She wasn't grieving Harper, not yet. Harper was out there. She would find her. "Kevin—"

"You know I don't even feel sad?" Kevin grabbed at the front of his own sweatshirt, yanking it, pulling at the spot roughly over his heart. "I can't feel anything. It's like someone came and ripped away every feeling I have. I can't figure out how to find one single emotion. All I want to do is cry, but that would require me to own some pain. I'm just numb, from the top of my head all the way down. You know we had kids' names picked out? For someday, for that future we constantly talked about. I lost them, too. Jayden and Jihra. **Fuck.**" He shot her another glare, as if challenging her to refute him.

"I can't even imagine what you're going through." Jojo bobbed on the balls of her feet, unable to decide whether to get closer or farther away from him. "But it seems to me like maybe you're in shock. My dad says that when a body is in shock, they can't feel anything, they just go numb. Maybe grief is like that."

"You **really** want to bring up your dad right now?"

"Yeah, I do." Kevin could be numb, or sad, or angry as shit, but she needed his help to find the person who mattered more than anyone else. "My dad's in the hospital, and I think my mom just got arrested for breaking into a cop's house, looking for

Harper. No matter what, we know that Harper has to be found, and then we'll get whoever did this to Zach."

Kevin mumbled, "And to you."

Right now her assault didn't seem to matter very much at all. "Dude, I wasn't even awake. It fucking sucks, but a man was killed in your house, the man you loved. What I went through is nothing compared to that."

Kevin finished the second shot he'd poured. He coughed and gave a short nod. Then he banged his fist against the counter. "So. How do we find Harper?"

Jojo reached for the blank grocery list stuck to the refrigerator door with a magnet. "First we make a list."

FORTY-TWO

"HOURS." LAURIE STARED at Sarah. "You left me in there for **hours.**"

Sarah dodged her gaze, keeping her eyes on her paperwork. She mumbled, "You know there's nothing I could do about that."

"In **that** cell." She'd thought Sarah had been kidding when she first led her to the same cell Kevin had been held in. But it hadn't been a joke—there'd been no other cells available after a busy night of corralling drunks. In a few hours, after they sobered up, there would be plenty of room. But there was nothing else at that particular, crucial, terrible moment that a co-worker locked her up while other co-workers watched, forced joviality slanting off the walls as they tried to make light of it. **You'll be out in no time, Laurie. We'll sneak you a knife in a cake.**

She'd had to sit on the same bed Kevin Leeds sat on. And even if Jojo was right, that he had nothing to do with this and was as caught in this terrible trap as the rest of them, it didn't help. She didn't want to share a jail cell with that memory.

And the joviality with which the jailers had placed her inside the cell had worn off. They knew now that it wasn't just Laurie flying off the handle and punching Yarwood. Now they knew that Laurie thought one of their own was holding a kidnapped teenage girl.

Which was, obviously, impossible.

Last week Laurie would have said the same thing.

"What if something had happened to Omid? What if he'd gotten worse while I was in there? Would you even have told me?" She was worried sick about Omid's health on top of everything else going on, and at the same time she was thinking about getting a divorce lawyer when this was all over.

When would it be over?

Sarah didn't answer; she just pushed the citation for Laurie to sign over the standing desk.

Laurie didn't reach for it. "**Now** you're finally citing me? Why couldn't they have done this at the beginning?" A citation was a promise that she would show up in front of a judge. The charges weren't being dropped; she just had to place her signature on the line and promise she wasn't going to run to Mexico. God knew she wasn't going anywhere. She could have signed it hours ago, but instead the fucking acting chief Brent Stanley had let her rot in the cell for hours while Laurie's daughter was alone and Harper was still missing.

"Wasn't up to me, Laurie. Stanley and Yarwood wanted to hold you, but now they say I can cite you out. I'm sorry."

That was the thing, though. Sarah didn't sound sorry. Sarah—Laurie's friend—sounded angry.

The department was highly dysfunctional, full of infighting and backbiting, but it was all the family some of them had in the world. Cops didn't usually stay married long. Most ended up sharing custody of kids, living alone in boxy duplexes that smelled of new paint and dryer sheets. The department was everything to a lot of people on the force, and that included dispatch, records, and the jail.

Laurie had just lobbed a bomb directly into the middle of it.

But she didn't have time to care too much about Sarah's feelings. "Did they check his house? Yarwood's?"

Sarah didn't look at her, just pushed the paperwork closer to Laurie.

Laurie scribbled her signature and pushed the citation back to Sarah. She leaned forward.

"I know you don't believe me, but something is going on, and one of **our** guys probably has Harper Cunningham. As his prisoner. I think it's Yarwood."

Sarah took a deep breath. "There was nothing there."

"In the garage, then."

"Nothing. Laurie . . ."

"Tell me." Maybe Sarah suspected someone else. Maybe she knew something.

"I think you have some kind of PTSD."

"What?"

"Jojo got attacked—"

"Raped." Now the word was a battle cry.

"And you found a dead body near her. The next day you witness a friend kill himself. That's got to fuck up anyone."

"So you just think I'm crazy."

"I didn't say crazy. I just think you're going to be really confused for a while, and that's normal. I **hate** it that you would suspect one of us, though. This isn't like you. It's so **not** like you that I can't stand it."

"It could be any one of them—"

"That's exactly what I don't want to hear." Sarah put a firm hand on Laurie's shoulder and steered her toward the door. "I don't want to hear your theories or your paranoia. I understand that you're going through a difficult time, and that's not made any easier by the fact that your boss and your husband is in the hospital. Your life is upside down right now." She yanked the door open and pushed Laurie into the hallway.

"I'm not paranoid. I have proof." But did she? As the thick metal door clanged shut, leaving Laurie alone in the hallway, she wondered if this was even true. She had a bunch of dick pics. She had a husband trying to help cover something up.

That was about all she had.

Heading downstairs to dispatch, she passed Frank Shepherd going up.

Laurie didn't open her mouth. There was nothing to say. Obviously he'd heard rumors. He looked at her like he'd just caught her stabbing a homeless person. And, surprisingly, it hurt. Shepherd was her friend, a man she'd trusted for years. Her stomach flipped, and she felt so dizzy she had to hold on to the stair rail until he was on the floor above, out of sight.

She could hear dispatch chattering from outside the locked door, but the sound ceased as soon as she pushed it open.

"Hi," she managed.

There was a chorus of low "Hey"s back, but none of them looked up from their screens. It was as if they had received a command to glue their gaze forward.

Dead silence. No one even squawked on the radio.

"Maury? Can I talk to you?"

Maury nodded and stood, heading automatically for the office. He closed the door behind them. Not that the conversation would remain private— Maury was as talkative as anyone else in dispatch, and Laurie knew that as soon as she left, the details of their conversation would be repeated and analyzed.

So she didn't waste time. "I need this next week off."

Maury nodded and looked at the open schedule book on the table. "We've been thinking you'd probably say that. We've got most of it covered, so don't worry about it. You have plenty of vacation time."

"Not vacation. FML." Seemed appropriate that "family medical leave" had the same initials as "fuck my life."

Maury finally looked into her face, but his eyes dropped quickly and he nodded again. "Sure."

"What are they saying?"

Through the glass window, Laurie saw Nate Steiner approach the door to dispatch. He looked in, saw her, and pressed his lips into a firm line. He turned around immediately, going back the same way he came.

Obviously the whole department hated her.

Well, fuck them. This was bigger than hurt feelings or a worry that she might say terrible things about some of their officers. This was literally life or death. Someone had Harper, and no one was helping.

"Never mind. Put me off for two weeks instead."

Maury didn't look up from the schedule book. "I'll cover you for three, just in case."

There was no one in the hallway as Laurie strode past Vice and then went up the stairs. She checked her mailbox out of habit and grabbed the few pieces of paper that were in it. One was an invite to a local crab feed benefiting Children's Hospital, another was a payroll form.

Underneath those was a photograph.

The eight-by-ten picture was of Laurie and Omid at the last Christmas party, the party that had been on the boat. Omid had been mildly seasick, even though the waves in the bay hadn't been bad, and Laurie had been equally mildly drunk. They'd had a good time, actually, not something that was guaranteed at a work party. The deejay was fantastic, and Laurie danced, something she hadn't done in a long time. In the photo she and Omid were standing near the prow of the boat, Omid's arm around Laurie's bare shoulders. She remembered how she'd shivered that night, though she hadn't actually felt cold, the alcohol warming her as much as the realization that they'd made it. Omid was chief of a tight-knit department, Laurie loved both him and her job, their daughter was healthy and happy. Behind them, in the distance, the lights of

San Francisco had glittered in that cold, crisp way that only happened in midwinter.

In the photograph she now held, Laurie's face had been shot off. A .45 round, judging by the size of the hole. She touched the shredded pieces of paper at the back. The hole was large enough so that she could stick her finger through.

Her forehead went slick with sweat.

Laurie left without seeing anyone else except a parking tech, who appeared to be cheerfully out of the loop and greeted her with a chipper hello.

She wanted to text Jojo, but her phone was dead. **She's home,** Laurie told herself. **It's six in the morning. Don't worry. She's sleeping.**

She made a quick stop at the hospital. Omid was completely out. The nurses said he was doing well but had been sleeping for hours. She paused and thought about kissing him. Why, though? She sure hadn't wanted to earlier. When the nurse wasn't looking, she shook his arm a little, hoping for him to wake.

He mumbled something unintelligible, and his face twisted in what looked like pain.

Guilt slipped through her veins again.

She inhaled sharply, letting the chemical scent of the hospital rush up her nose. She had to get home to Jojo. The sun would be up soon, and Laurie could make her oatmeal or take her out for Starbucks.

She drove home. Her body yearned for sleep.

As Laurie unlocked her front door, the sky just

beginning to lighten behind her, her toe nudged something soft. The weight moved easily.

She looked down.

A dead rat.

She swallowed the scream that was obviously the expected response. On the off chance someone was watching, she threw her head back and tried to laugh, but it didn't come out right. The sound from her throat was brittle.

She didn't bend to pick it up or even examine it—she just kicked it off the stoop as casually as she could. It was obvious that the rat had been shot. Most of the head was missing, but it wasn't a bloody wreck, so whoever'd placed it there hadn't **killed** it with a gunshot.

Keeping the false smile affixed to her face, Laurie stepped inside and closed the door behind her. She bent forward, propping her hands on her knees, taking a deep breath. Then she called, "Jojo, I'm home."

No answer.

"Jojo?"

Upstairs, Jojo wasn't in her room. Goddamn it, where was she?

Laurie went to the closet in her bedroom and knelt to unlock the safe.

The H&K conformed to her hand perfectly. It felt natural. Her shoulder holster still fit.

Next to her bed, she plugged in her phone with trembling fingers.

Laurie sat on the edge of the bed and checked to make sure there was a bullet chambered. Of course there was. In a cop's house, guns were always ready to shoot.

And so was Laurie.

FORTY-THREE

JOJO LOOKED AT the list she'd tried to write. She'd written down the names of the cops from Harper's social media. She'd also listed the names of the frequent fliers she knew from dinner table talk—the people who got arrested most often in town—and she'd Googled her father's name with the department's to see which cases had been most incendiary. Next to her, Kevin worked on the list for CapB. He was supposed to write down anyone he thought might be a mole in the organization, but he kept groaning that it was impossible. **Anita's too tight with our founder. Jerry is down to the bone a great guy.**

At the same time, he was supposed to list anyone against CapB, who might want to bring it down.

The people who hated CapB tended to be white and scared. Or they were cops, or families of cops.

"This isn't helping," said Jojo. "It's all too broad."

"We have to try, right?"

Jojo tried to think like a cop. "Okay, so forget for a minute about the mole idea. We have a list of people and groups who hate CapB. Cops, generically, aren't too fond of you guys."

"Us guys."

She nodded. "Yeah. Cops **have** to be the connection. We also have a list of actual police officers who all slept with a minor. Where's the overlap here?"

The pen looked tiny in Kevin's hand. "A cop who hates CapB and wanted to kill a member of it, who dumps two girls involved with the group into my unlocked house, where . . . No, it doesn't make sense. How would a cop even know you and Harper were involved with CapB? It's not like you two handed out flyers on campus, did you?"

Jojo shook her head. "We're still thinking too generally." She closed her eyes and rubbed the spot between her eyebrows, the way her father did at the dinner table when he was thinking about work. "Two groups are implicated right now. One group is CapB, from the signed text."

"But they didn't **do** anything."

Jojo didn't lift her eyelids. "That's what we think."

"That's what we **know.**"

Now she glared at him. "If you don't have an open mind about this, you can't help anyone."

Kevin's eyes narrowed, but he nodded.

Jojo continued, "The other group is a bunch of cops. Those are our two groups: CapB and a bunch of cops."

"Opposite lists. One a group of social-justice activists. The other group out to kill the black man."

"Quiet for a second." Sucking in a breath, Jojo felt the missing piece slip into place. That was it. "The overlap! It's just one person." She grabbed both pieces of paper and stared at them. "It's a setup. One person who wants to take down a whole police department. A **group** of people within the department wouldn't want to do that. Coups like that just don't happen—police officers have too much pride in their profession as a whole. But one cop on the force who's tired of the politics, who wants to get back at the department, who would **set up Harper** to sleep with all these guys so the whole PD will crumble? That makes a kind of sick sense."

"What about CapB, though? Why am **I** involved?" Kevin clicked the pen open and closed rapidly.

"What if you're just a bonus? Someone who wants to take down a department **and** someone who's not fond of CapB. Maybe you were just handy. A way to get attention. Grab us, put us in your house—"

"What about Zach?"

Jojo didn't know. She didn't know anything. "Collateral damage?"

"This is fucked."

She nodded. "Yeah."

Kevin scrubbed at his stubble. "Or it could be some wack job who hates everyone. Plenty of those in the world."

Jojo stabbed the paper in front of her with her pen. "It's more directed than that. Harper's messages to my dad say she knows that this kind of scandal will get everyone involved fired."

"That's just common sense."

"Sure, but she knows that at some point it will probably come out. She knows stuff like this doesn't stay buried. The scandal will hit the news. It seems like it must be about more than just money, doesn't it? It's personal. And if it's only one person behind this, whoever has her also hates CapB. So this person hates both the police and an anti-police-brutality group. So it has to be a disgruntled cop, or a scared one. It **has** to be one of the guys she was sleeping with." She circled Yarwood's name on her paper.

Kevin took her paper out of her hand and put it next to his. "Or an ex-cop. Someone used to hating CapB but someone who also has a major ax to grind with your dad's department in particular."

"Exactly." The link was there—she **almost** had it. "An ex-cop who hated our department in particular."

"You got something?" Kevin leaned forward.

It shifted into focus for Jojo, as if the page

had been slightly blurred until this second. "Oh, my God."

She pulled up Google on her phone again and scanned for an image. She'd almost forgotten about that whole thing. "Darren Dixon hates my father, a lot. Like, it's a racial thing combined with the fact that he didn't get the job he thought he was going to. He did this whole Facebook rant about Muslims taking over the department, and it was super ugly. He got fired over it, refused to back down. Do you know how impossible it is to get fired as a police officer? He really tried. Here he is." She showed Kevin the image—Dixon in a button-down blue shirt standing next to a white wall. In the photo he was smiling broadly, as if life were fantastic.

Kevin looked closer at the screen. "Wait, so this cop you're talking about is Harper's dad?"

"Huh?" Confusion frizzed through her brain. God, she was **tired.**

Kevin took the phone out of her hands and zoomed in on the picture. "I've seen this guy."

"What?"

"I've seen him at least twice. He's dropped Harper off at a couple of meetings. You've never seen him do that? I thought he was her father."

The truth was an electric jolt. "That's not Harper's father. Holy **shit**. That's her **boyfriend.** Oh, my God, Darren Dixon is Ray!"

Kevin nodded, but he didn't look convinced. "I don't get it. How would she even know him?"

Jojo was only stumped for a few seconds. "Jesus. He's the one who arrested us when we stole the rings."

"I'm lost."

"That was when he and my dad **really** started hating each other. Me and Harper were being stupid—it was supposed to be just a game. We didn't think we'd actually get away with stealing anything, and we didn't." Jojo didn't add that she actually **had** gotten away with it. Quickly, she touched the ring through her shirt. "He was the school resource officer, and I remember Harper trying to flirt with him to get out of it before my dad got there, asking for his number, being herself. That was one of the things I was super annoyed with her about, that she seemed to think it was such a trivial thing."

"How long ago was that?"

"Two years—I was fourteen and she was almost fifteen."

"You think she's been seeing him since then?"

"I don't know what to think. I'm beginning to think nothing Harper does will surprise me." Jojo stood, then sat back down.

"So wait, is she not being held captive, then? Is she **in** on it? Whatever it is?"

Jojo jerked her head back and forth. "They found her blood at your house, remember? Maybe they were together, but he went too far that night, or what-the-fuck-ever. He's holding her hostage now." **Please let her be a hostage. Please don't let her be dead.**

She went on, "We have to find out where he lives. My parents might know? But that might be doubtful, since he never got along with them, not even back in the day."

"Maybe his address is online," said Kevin.

Jojo shook her head. "No way. These guys value their privacy way too much to let that happen. If my mom wasn't in fucking **jail,** I could text her and ask." She checked her phone, "Or I could go by dispatch and ask them, but I have a feeling they're probably not in the mood to tell me anything, either."

"Can't hurt to try, though." Kevin typed on his laptop. "Okay, see, look. This site wants to charge me nineteen dollars to give me his background information." He removed a credit card from his wallet.

"I'm telling you, you won't get anything from that."

A minute later Kevin turned to her with a triumphant smile. "Check it out. Do you think he lives in Danville?"

"Oh, my God. You have an address?"

"House ownership is public record. You can't find me, because my house was bought through the corporation I set up for myself. But a regular person, unless he set it up in somebody else's name, like his wife's—"

"He's not married."

"That's why his information is there, then." He wrote the address down on the piece of paper in front of him. "What do we do now?"

This was madness. Whoever had Harper was undoubtedly armed. He was a murderer. And whoever he was, he would expect someone to come looking, eventually.

"We **go,**" Jojo said.

FORTY-FOUR

JOJO WAS GOING to scream if Kevin checked his watch again.

Of course, as soon as she had the thought, he checked his watch for what was probably the hundredth time. He thumped his leg so it juddered against his steering wheel. Outside the car windows, the neighborhood was coming alive—joggers ran past, people walked dogs, a newspaper delivery driver threw papers haphazardly out his window.

"Now?" Kevin asked again.

"Fine," Jojo said. It hadn't been quite thirty minutes yet, the amount of time she'd recommended they wait.

When they'd first arrived, twenty-seven minutes before, Jojo had gone into the backyard via the smooth-opening gate. It had been almost fully light then, though the morning was still chilly. She'd shoved up the bathroom window and crawled inside, her heart hammering. There was no car in the driveway, and the house was completely quiet. **Please, God, don't let him be home. Please let me find Harper.** She didn't dare think about what she'd do if he was inside the house—she'd scream and run and hopefully alert the cavalry. It was all she had.

She'd done a quick turn through the still-dim house, using her phone for light. She'd moved quickly through the rooms, almost expecting to feel a bullet slam into her back, to hear Dixon roar with rage at her for trespassing. As she ran out the front door, she knew without doubt that he wasn't home and that Harper wasn't in plain sight, but that hadn't stopped the terror. She and Kevin had sat in his car on the street as her shaking wore off, waiting to see if police cruisers pulled up. "If he has a silent alarm, dispatch won't hold that since it'll be registered to a cop. They'll send it out immediately. So if no one comes, no alarm."

They had waited. Kevin had grown antsier by the moment.

"This is crazy," he said now. "**You** could get into the backyard, but what's it going to look like for a huge black man to walk to the door? If there's any kind of neighborhood watch, we're fucked."

"I'm lighter than you, but I'm still too dark-skinned for this neighborhood. And I came out the front door and no one seemed to give a crap. I don't think anyone's watching."

"Don't you think we should go in through the back window again?"

"I think I was lucky to have gotten away with that the first time." Jojo took a deep breath. "Come on, I'll show you how it's done."

She held Kevin's hand as they walked up the front steps. She plastered on a bright smile. She looked up into his face as she pretended to ring the doorbell. "Okay, see how I'm doing it?" She laughed out loud. "We look like we're having fun, like we're just here visiting friends."

Kevin gave the fakest-sounding laugh Jojo'd ever heard. "This is a terrible idea!" His smile made it look like someone was torturing him.

Jojo leaned to the left and peered in the side window. She ostentatiously waved, as if someone inside were welcoming her. "Come in?" she said brightly and loudly. "Okay!" She opened the now-unlocked door, and they tumbled in.

Next to her, Kevin's smile fell off his face. He gasped a breath. "I think I'm having a heart attack."

"I looked in every room. He's not here."

He leaned forward and propped his hands on his knees. "I can barely stand up. I have no idea how you did that."

Jojo's pulse was racing even faster than it had been before. "I don't know either. We'll be okay."

"Do we need gloves?" Kevin asked.

Jojo had thought of that a little too late, after she'd come in through the window. Whatever happened, her prints were already here. If they found a crime scene and reported it, it wouldn't matter. If they **were** the crime scene—she tried not to think about getting arrested for burglary. "I don't have any. You can use a tissue or toilet paper or something if you want to touch anything. But I don't care very much."

"Right. Me, neither." Kevin looked like he felt a lot worse than she did.

Jojo gave him a quick side hug. "We can do this." She wasn't sure they could—oh, to have Mom there—but they had no choice.

Room by room, they explored. Darren Dixon was nowhere to be found, thank God.

But neither was Harper.

Two bedrooms and a bathroom showed no evidence of a woman ever staying there. The furnishings were dark leather, very male. No female clothing in the closets, no makeup in the bathroom cabinet.

Kevin whispered, "Where's the master bedroom?"

Jojo pointed at the room they'd just come out of.

He shook his head. "Too small for a house like this."

She hadn't even noticed the last door when she'd done her terrified rabbit run through the house earlier. Shit, shit, **shit.**

"I didn't see that door before." Her whisper was

so quiet she could almost not hear it herself. Jojo put her fingertips on the knob and looked at Kevin. He gave her a nod.

She slammed open the door, and Kevin rushed in, banging on the light switch.

No one.

It was a big room, with dark blue carpet and a huge wooden bed. The sheets were pulled back, so this was obviously where he slept. The en suite bathroom was empty.

Jojo dropped into a squat and panted, her heart thumping like a jackhammer. Holy shit, how could there be this much terror inside her chest?

In the middle of the room, Kevin turned in a circle, raising his arms. "Well, where the fuck **is** she?"

Automatically Jojo held out her hand palm-down to quiet him. Her whisper was harsh in her throat. "You think she's just going to be hanging out in his bedroom? He's obviously got her hidden somewhere."

Kevin shook his head and kept talking in a normal volume. "What if we have it all wrong? What if her boyfriend is just some dude who looks like this guy? I saw him in a car, twice. I can't be sure of anything."

"My dad always says there are no coincidences. Things look related for a reason. She has to be here."

"I think maybe we're going crazy."

Jojo ignored him and scanned the room. She looked under the bed, finding nothing, not even dust balls, and pulled open both walk-in closets. One held clothes, all male, and the other held sports equipment.

She moved around the space, pushing on the walls.

"You think you're going to find a hidden room or something?" His tone was sour.

"You never know." But yeah, she did feel stupid. She pulled open the bedside table's drawer, lifting it all the way out and up, to check for a secret bottom, not that she'd know what one would look like if she saw it. The drawer held nothing but a strip of condoms and an extra phone charger. Two photos were framed under the bedside lamp. One was an older black-and-white photo—his parents, maybe? The couple in the photo didn't smile, standing rigidly in front of what looked like a church door.

The other photo was the framed rear profile of a girl.

It was Harper.

"Kevin." It was the only word she could get out. The photo showed the back of Harper's hair, caught in a messy braid, the top of her shoulder, and just the side of her jaw. But Jojo knew that jaw. She'd laid kisses along it. She **knew** it.

"What?"

"This is Harper."

Kevin picked up the photo. "This looks like the generic white-girl picture that comes with the frame. This could be anybody."

Jojo stabbed at the jawline. The glass rattled. "That's Harper."

Kevin set the photo down. He moved to the other side of the bed and started to press on walls, the same way she had.

But what if she was wrong?

She looked again, and then for a tenth time.

The girl could really be anyone. Random girl in a frame. A million girls with that jaw. No other identifying features visible.

Screw that. She knew it was Harper—her very bones shook with the knowledge.

Jojo took out her phone and texted Mom again. **Don't freak. Inside Darren Dixon's house— he's not here—there's a pic of Harper. If u get this text, can u bring thermal camera?** It would take a miracle. She gave the address and sat on the edge of the bed to catch her breath, then jumped up immediately, disgusted that she let herself put her ass where Dixon rested.

"Let's get out of here."

Now Kevin looked at her incredulously. "But we know she's here. Or nearby."

"The longer we spend in here, the closer we are to getting caught."

"You're giving up?"

"Never." How dare he even suggest that?

A ping. **On my way.**

Jojo held up her phone triumphantly. "My mom's coming! I say we wait outside in the car for her to get here, and then we all come in together. If Dixon comes home now, we'll just get arrested or worse. If my mom is here, at least she knows him, and if she brings a thermal camera, then we can check the whole house, fast."

Kevin bobbed on his toes for a moment, thinking. "You go outside. I'll stay in here. I was lucky to get in once." Then he continued, his words slow and halting. "What if Harper's here? What if she's . . . dead?"

Jojo shrugged. "Then there's not much we can do, anyway." Such easy words for such an impossible thought.

Kevin's voice was cool. "Then we kill him."

Jojo paused. Then she said, "Okay."

FORTY-FIVE

KELLY, A CAPTAIN who worked at Fire Station Two, wasn't comfortable with any part of this, and Laurie knew it. Kelly kept looking at the door that led back into the fire station as if considering making a break for it.

As if Laurie were keeping her outside by force.

"Come on, Kelly. Please."

"You can't just borrow a thermal-imaging camera with no explanation, and expect me to just hand it over. You do realize that's a seven-thousand-dollar piece of equipment?"

"And you have one on every rig now, don't you?"

Kelly growled and stamped her foot. "Do you know how much trouble I'd be in if I roll up in the truck and we don't have that camera on board when we need it?"

"When was the last time you actually **used** one?"

Kelly answered immediately. "Last week, on Harrison, that fatal. There was a baby seat in the back, and we used it to check the bushes to make sure there wasn't a child lying there. You really want me to take a risk of not having that on my truck?"

Laurie and Kelly had been friends for at least seventeen years. It was anomalous in the city—firefighters and police personnel didn't usually get along, let alone hang out. But back when Laurie was on the street, she and Kelly had ended up working more than a few major incidents together, both of them wet behind the ears, both of them careful to get everything right. They'd hung out at the local brewpub more than they probably should have. Kelly had given her and Omid the biggest thing on their wedding registry—the KitchenAid stand mixer. For her fortieth birthday, Kelly and Sarah had taken her out dancing, and the resulting hangover had almost killed her, but it had been worth it.

Kelly hadn't understood when Laurie left the street. **Why are you abandoning me out here with all these dumb boys?**

Of course, Laurie had never told her the reason she'd gone into dispatch.

She needed that TIC. "A man was murdered, you know that."

"And what you're telling me is that you're going to catch the suspect?"

"Not at all. I just want to help find my daughter's best friend." Laurie made a conscious effort to uncross her arms, to keep her body facing Kelly's. "I have a couple of suspects in mind—"

"Do you hear how crazy you're sounding? You're not a cop."

"Omid is in the hospital," Laurie started. "And—"

"Jesus, Laurie, don't give me that shit. Of course I'm sorry, and my crew sent flowers. But you can't sob-story me into giving you this. And I gotta say, I'm getting really concerned. I know you've been through the shit this last week, and I think you're probably in shock."

"People who are in shock freeze. I'm not frozen. I'm just doing what no one else is willing to do."

Kelly folded her arms and leaned against the brick building. "There's a rumor you're accusing guys on the force of some crazy stuff."

"Man, word travels fast."

"I'm worried about you. You know how trauma can get its hooks in us, right?"

"I've been to all the same trainings as you have," snapped Laurie.

"You're displaying levels of paranoia that—"

"**You're** aware that paranoia isn't a PTSD symptom, right?" The only reason Laurie knew this was that she'd Googled it after Sarah had mentioned it in the jail. If she was going crazy, she wanted to know it, but she wasn't. "This whole thing sounds insane, but I promise you, Kelly, I'm not crazy. I have proof. I wish I could share it with you, I really do. You just have to trust me."

"But—"

Laurie went in for the kill. "What if it was Rebecca?"

"Don't do that."

"You know my daughter was **raped**, right?" Laurie leaned hard on the **r** and the hard **d** of the word. "She has internal traumatic injuries. Some monster raped my baby and killed a man inside the same house. That same person has Harper somewhere. What if it was Rebecca?"

Kelly's daughter Rebecca was fifteen and autistic, and she was the whole world to Kelly. It was the lowest blow Laurie could land, and she didn't regret it.

Kelly glared. "If you get caught with this, I'll tell everyone you stole it off the truck while I wasn't looking. I'll get in trouble for that, but at least I won't lose my job."

Laurie nodded. "And I will absolutely say that I stole it. Actually, I would've just done that if I knew where you kept it on the rig."

FORTY-SIX

LAURIE WANTED TO fly to Dixon's house, but she couldn't afford to get pulled over, so she kept the speedometer to ten miles over the speed limit. She could feel the bones in her body clacking against one another every time she hit a bump, as if she were suddenly ancient and brittle.

The GPS led her to the address Jojo had given her. Laurie had never been here before, of course. Even back in the day, Laurie and Omid hadn't gotten along with Dixon. He ran with a different group at the station, hanging out with the motorcycle guys, the ones who rented condos in Vegas for getaways and serially dated strippers.

It was a big house, but it was trim and tidy, the paint fresh, the yard neat. It was a wonder he could still afford it—this was too expensive a neighborhood for a liquor-store security guard. A trio of elderly women trot-walked down the sidewalk, their arms swinging industriously.

Laurie's heart rate accelerated. Jesus, if he weren't home now but pulled up? How could this possibly go well? What the hell was she thinking?

Ahead of her, Jojo got out of a black SUV. "Mom."

Laurie tugged Jojo roughly against her. "I love you." They felt like the most important words, the ones she wanted to say over and over again. What if she forced Jojo back into her car and they drove north? What if they crossed the Canadian border and never came back? Screw all of this. They could live in a cabin, and she could keep Jojo safe forever. If Omid recovered, he could come, too. Maybe.

"Love you back." Jojo pulled away. "We have to get inside. Kevin's in there—he didn't think it would be safe to have him come in and out."

So Laurie followed her up the walk and right in the front door, as if they had a right to be there. **We do. We have every right.**

In the entryway with the door closed firmly behind them, Laurie whispered, "Are you **sure** he's not here?" If a cop—any cop—heard noise in his house, he'd come out shooting more often than not.

"We're sure, Mom."

Kevin stood a few feet away, watching them with wary eyes. "Mrs. Ahmadi—"

Laurie rounded on him. "Jojo says you did

nothing wrong." And Jojo was growing up. She knew things the way an adult did. It was still a hugely difficult leap to make, to trust Jojo's intuition. "I'm trying to believe what Jojo's told me. Not going to lie, though, I'm having a really fucking hard time with you being here."

"He **drove** me here, Mom. **He's** the one who put it together. He saw Dixon drop Harper off at a couple of meetings."

"You did?" Laurie kept her eyes on him, willing him to stay still, to not move. The weight of the gun got heavier under her armpit. If he made one false step . . .

Kevin stayed completely still. "I just thought he was her dad. I didn't think much about it."

"Mom, are you okay? You actually went to jail?"

Laurie didn't want to talk about it. "It's fine. I'm out now. How was Colson?"

Jojo's eyes widened. "He was weird. Super weird."

Goddamn it. "Is he one of them?" Not Mark. Please, not him, too.

"I don't know."

"You okay?"

"I'm fine. Let's just do this." Jojo took several steps farther into the house. "He has a picture of her, framed. In his bedroom. Come look."

Jojo had said that in her text message, but the sheer gall of it hadn't registered until this moment. How had Dixon **ever** worked for the department?

Where was Harper? "Show me in a second." Carefully, she unboxed the camera and powered it on. "Where should we start?"

"Let's just go through every room, systematically, looking at every wall." Jojo pointed to the left.

The sheer horror of the fact that her daughter was saying these words—that she'd even thought to ask for a thermal camera—made Laurie want to cry. And perversely, she felt a certain pride that Jojo had been thinking so clearly. "Let's do it fast and then get out of here."

Jojo said, "What if we find her?"

"If she's here, we don't leave without her." **Or her body.** Though of course the thermal camera wouldn't show a cold, dead body, only a recently deceased one before it cooled. What if Harper were dead and cold inside these walls? Or out in the garage?

The living room was clear, as were the dining room walls. They found nothing in the kitchen.

Laurie pointed the camera at Jojo to make sure it was still working. It showed Jojo as a red-and-orange blur of motion. Laurie pointed it toward another wall that showed nothing. "What if the walls are just too thick?"

They all froze in place for a split second, and then Jojo said, "I'm going into the next bedroom. Check if you can see me."

And Laurie could. The heat register of her daughter's body was much smaller, as if Jojo had turned back into a child on the other side of the thick wall, but it was visible. "I've got you!" called Laurie, wishing she really did.

They cleared every other room, moving slowly through the master bedroom. Nothing.

"Look, Mom. It's her." Jojo pointed to the photograph. "I know it."

The picture of the girl on the nightstand **could** have been Harper.

It also—easily—could have been someone else.

Kevin was the one whose idea it was to go up into the crawl space, but it was empty of everything except cobwebs and two empty suitcases. (Laurie didn't ask Kevin to open them. He just did. They all had the same fear.)

The three of them were quiet as they walked back through the house.

A normal person would call the police, Laurie knew that.

But not now. This wasn't her jurisdiction, and she wouldn't know whoever answered the 911 call. She wouldn't be able to explain it shortly enough, clearly enough. The dispatcher wouldn't believe her, anyway. Dispatchers, as a matter of habit, believed very little.

"The garage?"

Kevin and Jojo were at her heels. All of them looked over their shoulders when they heard a car drive past the front of the house, but it didn't stop.

The garage was accessed by a shallow set of stairs

off the kitchen, and Laurie had to steel herself before pushing open the door.

But the garage was mostly empty. Two piles of boxes sat in one corner, and a large Ping-Pong table stood near the far wall. The washer and dryer looked clean, and there weren't even spiderwebs overhead.

Laurie used the TIC to check the walls, the ceiling, even the floor.

"Nothing." Jojo's voice held equal parts relief and disappointment. "This isn't right. He has her. Obviously. He's Ray. He's the boyfriend."

5211 LOG-ON—DARREN RAYMOND DIXON. Laurie could see his badge number and full name scrolling across the computer screen—she'd logged him in for so many years and had barely ever thought of his middle name.

Laurie reached a hand to touch Jojo's wrist, but Jojo jerked away.

"What do we do next, Mom?"

Laurie had no fucking idea. God, she wished Omid would wake up, and be healthy, and fix this. At the same time, she **hated** how much she wanted him to fix everything—he who had broken everything by keeping secrets. "Is there anything in his backyard?" She pulled open the back garage door. There was a small wooden patio and a large, unkempt lawn.

In the very back stood a small red shed, almost hidden behind an overgrown oak tree.

"Mama." Jojo's voice was just a whisper.

Laurie took a breath. "Stay behind me." She pointed the camera at the shed.

One red flare glowed.

A person.

They walked on the grass, avoiding the crushed-rock path, which would make noise. Laurie didn't realize she was holding her breath until she saw spots dance at the edges of her vision.

Somehow the camera was on the grass and her gun was in her hand. She didn't remember sliding it out of its holster.

Laurie pulled her jacket sleeve over her left hand and turned the knob of the shed.

She pushed.

And there he goddamn was.

FORTY-SEVEN

INSIDE THE SHED Darren Dixon snored.

He was laid out along an old brown sofa, one arm hanging off the edge, his mouth wide open, a dried slug trail of drool shining along his cheek. The room stank like cigarettes and old sweat and beer dregs and something harsher, vodka or rye. On the floor next to him were half-crushed beer cans and a full ashtray.

The room was lined with tools, the floor piled with magazines. One ratty brown armchair stood under the lamp. It was Darren Dixon's man cave, and he was the hibernating bear.

Behind her, Jojo pulled on Laurie's jacket as she whispered, "Mama, let's go."

Laurie shoved the gun back into her underarm holster. "Dixon!" she barked. "Wake up."

The man came to slowly, blinking in confusion. He rubbed his eyes as he sat up. "Who's here? Who's that?"

"It's Laurie Ahmadi." She made a shooing motion with her hands to try to get Jojo and Kevin out—they didn't need to be so close to him. Harper wasn't here. Laurie could handle a drunk Dixon. "Remember I saw you at the liquor store? I've got some questions for you."

"The fuck?" Dixon rose on unsteady legs. "What the **fuck**?"

"How do you know Harper Cunningham?"

"Get out of my house."

Laurie felt fear course through her blood, but although he was big, he was drunk as hell. His reflexes would be slow.

"She's missing. We know about her and you." It was a bluff—he wasn't on the list. That photo could easily be someone else. "Where is she?"

To Laurie's shock, tears rose in Dixon's eyes. "I don't know. I lost her. I think I lost her."

What did that mean? Laurie's breath caught in her throat, and she had to speak around a leaden lump. "How did you lose her?"

"She just stopped calling me. After that big black guy . . ." His eyes appeared to focus, and he craned his neck to look around Laurie. "Is that him? The one that raped your daughter, right? You fucking with me? Is that your daughter? Little Jojo? And you're out driving around with her rapist?" He fumbled with his zipper, as if his fly were down, which it wasn't. "You gonna stick it in her again, boy? Yeah?"

Laurie heard Jojo make a small whimper. "Shut the fuck up. Don't talk until I tell you to." She raised her chin and took a step closer to Dixon, keeping herself out of the danger zone of a sudden swing of his fists. "Where have you hidden her?"

But doubt filled her, cold and dank.

This guy could barely keep his pants up.

"I don't **know.** That's what I'm **saying.** I **love** her, and if that"—he jabbed a finger toward Kevin—"if he touched her sweet ass even once, I swear I'll kill you, boy."

Out of the corner of her eye, Laurie saw Kevin strain toward Dixon and then rein himself back in. A small, upsetting flash of disappointment rushed through her. She **wanted** to watch Kevin beat the shit out of this man. If she were honest with herself, she'd admit that Darren Dixon had always scared her. Something about how his look always slid to the side, something about how he never made real eye contact had always given her the heebie-jeebies.

"Just tell us where she is. I swear, I'll leave you out of it." Lies. And he'd know it. "We just want her back safe."

He laughed, a crackling, wet sound that made him seem twenty years older than he was. "Yeah, wouldn't you like that?"

She flushed with rage, feeling anger heat every inch of skin. "We saw her picture next to your bed."

"Oh, isn't she pretty?" he slurred, wobbling back and forth. "I don't know who that girl is, but she reminds me of somebody. Does she remind you of someone, too? Maybe someone's taking care of her someplace else. I bet she's fine. Like, you know, **really** fine." He cupped his crotch again.

Jojo leaped forward, but Laurie was just as fast, pushing her daughter backward. Kevin caught Jojo's other arm. Jojo shouted over Laurie's shoulder, "Did you kill her, you sick fuck?"

Dixon wiped his wet mouth with the back of his hand. "I'm not sure who you're talking about, baby girl, but I'm sure wherever your friend is, she's doing better than you are. I'd lay money on it. Of course, that's just my gut talking"—he patted his stomach contentedly—"and I've learned over the years to trust this belly of mine. And belly wants beer." He leaned down and picked up a beer can. He shook it, the contents sloshing around inside, then tipped the rest into his mouth.

Kevin continued to hold Jojo back. Laurie didn't know how he was managing it—what if this man **was** the person who'd killed Zachary? If she were Kevin, she'd have wanted to kill Dixon, just on the off chance that vengeance would be served.

But Dixon didn't have Harper. This guy was just broken.

Dixon tottered backward and collapsed onto the battered couch. "I should press charges. I should have you **arrested.**"

That would be the capper on this day. Getting arrested twice within twenty-four hours. She gestured for Jojo and Kevin to leave the shed first. "Let's go, we're done." She stepped backward, unwilling to turn her back on Dixon.

His head was tilted back, his eyes closed, but he raised a hand. "That girl's a good fuck, Jojo! You tell your friend she's a really good fuck! Tight little cunt. Are you like that, too? Not too stretched out? Not yet?"

Something snapped inside Laurie with an almost audible crack. "Outside," she said to Jojo and Kevin. "Shut the door."

Kevin shook his head. "Mrs. Ahmadi, we're not going to leave you in—"

"Do it."

Jojo tugged Kevin outside. Laurie jerked the door shut, her breathing fast and high in her chest.

She turned to face Dixon. "Tell me what you know."

He laughed again.

Motherfucker.

He reached for a cigarette and lit it with a snap. "I've always hated you, you know."

"Mutual."

"I hate your husband worse, though." The

slurring was less now. Was he putting the drunk thing on? "I hear he's dying. Or died? They got him back? Too bad." His eyes were closed as he inhaled deeply.

He'd only fucking know that if he still had connections. Not even Jojo knew that her dad had been technically dead for almost a minute.

As if Laurie had willed it out from the holster and into her grip, her right hand suddenly held the gun again. She could almost feel the chambered bullet burning in the barrel.

She leaned close—too close. If he wasn't really drunk, this would be too dangerous. He could snatch it away from her, turn it back on her.

For a brief second, she wished he'd try. Give her a reason to shoot.

"Open your eyes, you piece of shit."

Dixon did. "Ah, damn."

"Who has Harper?"

"You ain't gonna use that on me."

"Who has Harper?" The gun was steady, pointed directly at his head.

"**Fuuuuck** you, Laurie. You were a terrible cop, you're an awful dispatcher, your husband's a terrorist, and your daughter's a whore." He wasn't slurring at all.

With a twist of her wrist, she spun the gun so that she held it by the barrel. With a cold fury, she hit him across the face with the butt of the gun.

Her arm reverberated with pain, and Dixon flew sideways, the far side of his head hitting the metal edge of the table next to the couch.

He might not have been slurring anymore, but he bounced like a bobbleheaded drunk.

While he was still leaning against the table, she hit him again. Same side of his head. She heard something crunch.

Blood flowed in a stream from his eye down to his nose. He held up his hands. "Stop," he whispered.

"Who has Harper?"

"I'll tell on you. I'll report you to the department. You'll be fired so fast—" He slid farther into the couch, pulling up his legs.

The gun jumped in her hands as if it were coming to life. It would be so easy—so fucking **natural**—to turn it around and pull the trigger.

"Who has Harper?" Her voice broke.

"I'll report you. Please don't hit me again. Please."

He was in the fetal position now, and his whole body shook. She thought he might be crying, and she was glad.

And then she heard a gasp behind her.

The door to the shed was ajar.

Jojo had seen her.

FORTY-EIGHT

AFTER JOJO PEEKED into the shed, Mom had come out, shut the door, and steered them down the sidewalk to their cars. Mom had her by the wrist, but Jojo was numb, every nerve turned off.

"But my car is over th—" Kevin started to say.

"Just get in, come **on**." When they were both in Mom's car, Kevin in the backseat, Mom slammed it into reverse and backed up until they were out of sight of Dixon's house, blocked by the neighbor's hedge. "He's not in any shape to drive, but we'll be able to see if he tries to leave."

Jojo's breath wheezed high at the top of her lungs, her heart flapping so hard she thought it might rip. She was sweating out of every pore, but she was freezing and shivering, too. She'd seen Mom hit a person so hard it looked like she meant to kill him, and while Jojo wanted nothing more than to find Harper, she couldn't handle the fact that Mom could . . . that Mom had the ability to do . . .

"Joshi, breathe. It's okay."

She pulled in another breath as slowly as she could.

"Can I do anything?" Kevin reached forward to touch her shoulder.

"N-no." Jojo's heart still slammed in her ears, but the band of pain in her chest was releasing slowly. She yanked on the seat belt. "Can we go? Kevin, can you take me?"

"No." Mom hit the door locks, which **choonk**ed into place.

Jojo grabbed the handle, but Mom had the child-proof lock on. "What the fuck?" It sounded like a gasp instead of the shout she'd meant it to be.

"We have to talk."

It was probably true, but Jojo didn't want to. "You can't trap us here!"

"I wish you hadn't seen what you saw."

It wasn't the same thing as saying she wished she hadn't done it. "You **beat** him."

Mom looked down at her hands. In the sunlight that streamed through the glass, Jojo could see a streak of blood on her mother's wrist. Her own? Or his?

"Yeah."

"Mom?" Jojo hated the fear that lay below the word.

"He might know something about Harper."

"But he didn't tell you anything!"

Mom shrugged. "You're right."

"I can't believe—"

From the backseat Kevin said, "She was using what she had."

Jojo twisted to glare at him. "You're defending her?"

"Damn right."

"What is going **on**?" This wasn't how it worked. "Cops don't **do** that, Mom."

Kevin barked a laugh. "Sorry? What do you think you've been working to end? Why have you been marching, again?"

Mom's voice was small. "I'm not a cop."

Kevin pulled on the back of Jojo's seat. "If she'd wanted to kill that asshole, I'd have dug the hole to dump him in."

When Jojo tried the door again, the handle just moved ineffectively. "But Dixon doesn't **have** her. He fuc—He slept with her, yeah. But he's just a drunk. And he's going to report you, and you'll lose your **job.** You just beat up a pathetic drunk . . ." She trailed off—that hadn't been the mother she knew. Her mother got her father to carry spiders outside in cups. She cried at commercials sometimes. Mom said she quit being a cop to be a dispatcher because she was a mother. **Being a mother is more important than being a cop. I have to stay safe to keep you safe, Joshi. I don't trust myself on the streets.** "Shit."

Mom looked sideways at her, still not meeting her eyes. "What?"

"You didn't trust yourself on the streets."

Silently, Mom shook her head.

"What did you do?"

"Now's not the time."

"Mom, what did you **do**?"

FORTY-NINE

FOR SOME REASON Laurie had always thought Jojo would never have to know. It wasn't like it was the biggest deal, after all. No one died. Laurie had overreacted one day. That was all.

It happened to everyone.

It shouldn't have happened to her, though.

"I was working with your dad one day, and I kind of lost it on a suspect. That's all."

Jojo's voice was icy as she repeated, "What did you do?"

Laurie could feel the two pairs of eyes focused on her, Jojo from the side, Kevin from the back. "I tased a guy."

Omid had just been shot.

It was a cold January night. Both on dogwatch, Omid and she had pulled up next to each other facing opposite directions so they could talk window to open window. They were in the old library parking lot, back where the second streetlight had gone out. Omid had been trying to talk her into his car. "Just for a minute. You know you want what I got in here." He'd been so damn sexy, and the corny line actually made her want what he was offering. They'd fucked in the patrol cars a couple of times—both of them liked it, but both of them knew it was a matter of time before they got caught. If they were seen by a citizen, that would be embarrassing. But if they got caught by one of their own or turned in by that citizen, they'd face discipline.

She'd laughed. "Get out and kiss me instead." If she were lucky, he'd reach down inside her car, and maybe she could get off to his hand while he kept a lookout. . . .

They were parked so close that his car door bumped hers when he got out.

He'd stood above her, that smile that meant sexy trouble for her dancing across his mouth. "Kiss you where?"

Then there was a pop.

A firework—that's what she'd stupidly thought it was at first.

But Omid was already running toward the back of the library. Without thinking she was out and running behind him, her gun in one hand, her radio in the other. "Shots fired, in rear of Greene Library. Suspect on foot."

The man with the gun was fast, but Omid was faster. He tackled him and came up roaring, his arm pouring blood. It took a few seconds to realize that Omid had actually been **hit** by the bullet— he'd been **shot.**

Together they cuffed the guy. Pete Zimmer, white male, fifty-two, on a combination of meth and heroin. He was convinced that shooting a cop would get him some kind of bonus points for a role-playing game he was stuck playing inside his mind.

The dude was crazy. Someone to be pitied, someone to be hospitalized.

But as they shoved him into Laurie's patrol car, something snapped inside her. While they waited for the sirens to get closer, while Omid applied pressure to the wound that was only a superficial graze, instead of slamming the car door shut, she left it open.

With great care she unholstered her Taser. Time slowed to a crawl, and everything became clear. **Go slow to go fast.** They'd learned it in the academy— the slower and more relaxed you became, the more accurate your aim.

She turned it on. She spent a moment thinking about what she was about to do while she took a deep, cleansing breath.

Then she pulled the trigger.

The barbs dove into Pete Zimmer. The device itself was hard to hold—it bucked in her hand as time sped up again. His body went rigid, his head slamming back into the vinyl seat. His legs splayed, looking crooked and wrong. His face clenched, and his eyes rolled back so all she saw in the dim over-head light was the whites. His teeth clacked.

"Jesus! Laurie!" Omid scrambled to let himself out of the front seat. He was out and around to her side almost instantly, reaching for the Taser.

Laurie just said, "He shot you."

Her vision went dark, rage rising in her chest. The Taser had only one set of electrode wires and one gas cartridge, making it good for just one shot at a distance. But it still had ordinary stun-gun electrodes. Before Omid could grab it out of her hand, she leaned forward and pressed the gun to the man's arm. The car shook as his limbs slammed into the front seats, the windows, the floor.

Omid knocked the device out of her hand. He ripped off the barbs from the first shot. He gave her a look that acted as a mirror—she saw herself then, standing with legs braced, firing pain into a man who would have fewer working brain cells than he'd started with when she was done with him.

Omid was the one who handled it. **He came at us when we put him in the car. Superhuman strength, all jacked up. I couldn't help her—my arm, see? She had no choice. No, she only hit him once. Not sure why his heart is showing that rhythm. Freak thing, I guess. Or maybe the drugs.**

The suspect could have died. His heart flipped

around in his chest more than it should have, according to the EKG the medics ran. That was due to the two hits, of course. The two hits Omid lied about, the second hit that Laurie never confessed to.

Now, in the car with her daughter, she simply said, "I didn't need to tase him. Not even once. I did it twice."

"So you took yourself off the force. Like, some big atonement thing, is that right?"

Why was Jojo's voice so contemptuous? It **had** been atonement. "I also got pregnant with you." It could have happened that very night. She'd always suspected it had. She and Omid had gone to her place after he'd been released from the hospital with six stitches, and she'd been so panicked that she'd dragged him to the floor in the front hallway, ripping open his pants and riding him until she came. Then she'd cried like she never had before while he said words she couldn't understand into her hair.

"I loved being a cop, Jojo. It's all I'd ever wanted."

"You were a bad cop."

Her daughter's words were knives dipped in acid. And they were absolutely true. "I wish I hadn't done that, honey. Not then, I mean now. Today. Though I wish I hadn't done either of those—"

Jojo interrupted her. "Well, fucking shake it off."

Shocked, Laurie stared at her daughter.

Jojo pulled up her legs so that her feet were on the seat under her butt, something Laurie usually told her to knock off. "You did it. Whatever. Deal with it later. What do we do next? It's not him, is it?"

Laurie took a breath. "I don't know."

"He's too drunk. He looks like he's always like that. He's too **stupid** to have her."

Kevin said, "But . . . what if he knows who has her?"

It was confirmation of what Laurie was thinking. "Yeah. It almost sounded like that."

"Why?" demanded Jojo. "Why do you think that?"

Dixon had been just a touch too glib, the tears starting too quickly when he said he'd lost Harper, that he loved her, that she'd stopped calling him. It hadn't sounded real. "He said she wasn't in contact, that he'd lost her, but he knew she was okay. The two things together don't make sense. And even after . . . after I hit him"—she made herself say it out loud—"he still didn't answer me about whether he knew where she was or not."

"So he's lying." Jojo sounded furious.

"Yeah. But we don't know about which part."

"So he **could** have her." Kevin wrapped his hands around the headrest of Jojo's seat so tight that his knuckles clicked.

In the deepest part of her gut, Laurie didn't think Dixon had Harper. But he knew **something.**

"The picture in his house, Mom. That's her."

"Maybe. We don't know that."

"I know that."

"He has to go to jail." Kevin rubbed his palms against the thighs of his jeans. He rocked back and forth. "That motherfucker has to go to prison for whatever the fuck he did, or for whatever the fuck he knows."

Jojo said, "He has to go there **forever.** They'll get him. We'll find Harper, and he'll get what's coming to him, along with whoever else is involved."

They were so young.

"What now?" Jojo asked. She fiddled with the glove box, clicking it open and slamming it shut. Open, then shut again.

"Stop it." The words were snapped and automatic. Jojo rolled her eyes but didn't add anything else. "What now is we have to find Harper."

Jojo nodded. "So we follow him."

Laurie curled her fingers into her palms. "We can't just sit out here and wait for him to go to whoever has Harper. First, he's not going to sober up enough to even walk straight for hours. Second, he'll know we're following. He used to be a decent cop. He'll be able to shake us."

Kevin leaned forward. "How do you guys follow suspects at your work? Like, how do you attach those GPS things to their cars?"

Laurie laughed, but the sound hurt her throat. "We **don't.** Using something like that would be illegal. The feds could probably get away with it, but not us. And we'd need a warrant, anyway."

"Wait," Jojo said. Then somehow she was up and moving between the two front seats, wriggling her body into the backseat.

"What are you doing?"

Jojo practically sat in Kevin's lap and pulled the knob that sent half of the backseat flying forward. She clawed around in what was exposed of the trunk. "You've always got so much shit in here— last time I went in here for snack bars, I saw duct tape. You still have it?"

Laurie never cleaned her trunk. "If you saw it there, it's probably still there, but what—"

Jojo slammed the seat back up and held a ring of duct tape aloft, her face triumphant. "We'll tape my phone to his car."

FIFTY

IT WAS A great idea. Jojo couldn't understand why Mom didn't seem to think so. Yeah, it meant that Jojo wouldn't have her phone for a while, but since she didn't plan on leaving her mother's side until she was about forty years old, what was the big deal?

"I don't know, I just don't like it." Mom kept fiddling with the car key in a clicky way that was making Jojo crazy. "How do we know which car is his, anyhow? There's no car in the driveway."

Jojo pointed. "The black Range Rover."

"How do you know?"

"The 11-99 sticker." It profited a foundation for highway patrol officers and their families when they were hurt or killed—11-99 was the radio code for "officer down." Dad always said having one on your car was a good way to get out of a ticket, too.

"And his plate." **5211os.** Fifty-two was the start of all officers' badges in San Bernal. "Is that Dixon's old badge? 5211 On Scene?"

"Damn it. Yes." Mom jerked her head toward Jojo. "Did you see that before you and Kevin went in the house?"

Jojo shook her head. She hadn't. She **should** have, but where Kevin and she had parked, the sticker hadn't been visible.

Kevin's voice rumbled from the backseat. "It's a good idea."

"See? Kevin agrees."

"Yeah . . ." His voice trailed away. Poor Kevin. For as big as he was, he seemed to be crumbling, buckling like old concrete. That was understandable. He'd been in the same room with the man who might know something about how Zachary had died. The fact that he wasn't ripping Dixon's house down board by board was something he should be proud of.

Mom said, "What if they send something to your phone?"

"If I tape it to the undercarriage, he'll never hear it. I'll silence it, anyway."

Mom shook her head impatiently. "No, I mean what if whoever has her sends us more clues?"

As if on cue, Jojo's phone pinged in her hand.

Cordelia's getting desperate. It was from the same number that had claimed to be CapB.

"What?" said Mom. "What is it?"

Jojo held it out and then tried to catch her breath. She pushed the button to call it back.

"What are you doing?"

Jojo remained silent as she held the phone to her ear. Kevin gave her an alarmed look, and Mom reached to grab it from her, so she switched ears, huddling close to the window.

Someone answered the phone. She could hear breathing, then a rustling.

Then, "Jojo? Is that you?" Harper's voice was weak. Shaky.

"Harper! We're looking for you—where are you? Harper—"

"Help me—" There was a click.

Jojo held out the phone and looked at it. "She's gone." **Harper was alive.** Her blood sang with relief, with hope—

"**Fuck,** Jojo."

Mom was **mad** at her? "What? You think I shouldn't have called? It's **my** phone." She'd call again if she wanted to. Then, suddenly, she knew she wouldn't. Harper's voice had been terrified. What if by calling she was scaring Harper more? What if she'd made it worse for her? Jojo swallowed back the salt in her throat. "Can you trace that call?"

Mom shook her head. "You know we can't."

"I read that you can triangulate the cell towers. That's how they got that guy in Folsom—"

"It takes equipment and manpower and time.

We could probably get something in a day or two, but—"

"Then start."

Mom shook her head. "Jojo. They don't trust me now. I didn't tell you, but I got arrested. That's where I was."

Jojo's anger disappeared, leaving only a pathetic buzz of panic. "I **know,** Mom. I heard it on the radio."

"Oh, my God, of course you did." Mom's shoulders slumped.

They needed help. More help.

Jojo looked over her shoulder at Kevin, but his eyes were closed. He gave the impression that he couldn't hear them at all. "You okay?" She touched his knee.

Slowly, he shook his head. His eyes stayed closed.

Mom would know what to say. Jojo looked at her, waiting. . . .

But Mom just put her head on the steering wheel.

Daddy.

He'd know what to do. He'd take charge. He'd roll in, and he'd yell, and then he'd find Harper and swoop in, saving her, just like he'd saved Jojo. "Can we go ask Dad?" Even though he . . .

"Dad's too sick, baby."

"He's not. He's getting better."

Mom's voice was exhausted. "You know he's not strong enough. And he's . . ."

Jojo heard what her mother couldn't say—he

wasn't the man they'd thought he was. He wasn't going to come to the rescue. Not this time.

From behind her, Kevin finally spoke, his voice low and tight. "The police kill us on the streets. It's like hunting season for them, and they don't even know it. Probably every one of them who hasn't shot one of us would swear they never would. Then they get there, they see some big black man, and most of them get so scared they pull the trigger, again and again."

No one could argue with him.

It might not be Darren Dixon.

But it was probably some kind of cop.

"And then if they can't get us on the streets, they come into our homes and murder us. Picking us off, one by one. They come into **my** house. They kill in **my** home. And I can't do shit about it."

Mom just kept her head on the wheel. It looked like she was praying, but Mom wasn't religious. She finally muttered, "We're not all that way, Kevin. At least . . ."

They had to **act,** not sit around and talk. Every minute Harper might be slipping further away from being found. Jojo set her phone on the dashboard. "Okay, then can we do my duct tape idea?" She didn't want to look at the face of her phone anymore. She didn't want to see any more texts.

Mom straightened. "Honey, the duct tape thing is a great idea, but not with your phone."

"Why—"

"We'll use mine. We're connected in Location Services. You can follow me just as well as I can follow you. And we need whoever's texting you to be able to contact you."

"What if Dad needs you, though?"

She started to hand her phone to Jojo. "We tell him to text you instead. Wait, why am I giving this to you? I'll do it. Give me that tape." She tried to pull her phone back.

Jojo shook her head and held the phone firmly. "I want to do it."

"No way. Over my dead body." Mom looked as if she wanted to unsay the words.

Jojo yanked Mom's phone out of her hands. "I'll be right back," she hissed.

She left the car door ajar so that it didn't slam.

A mother pushing a stroller passed by on the sidewalk. Jojo pretended to look at the phone, keeping the duct tape roll behind her.

Then, as soon as the coast was clear, she squatted next to the driver's-side wheel well. She reached up, smelling oil and metal. Two quick straps of tape. One more for good measure.

Then she ran back. She tasted bile in her throat. She leaned inside Mom's car. "Let's go. Kevin, I'll ride with you."

Mom said, "I want you with me, Jojo. We'll go home and rest."

Kevin was out of the car, heading for his own.

"He needs me, though."

Mom blinked. Then she reached across the empty seat and patted Jojo's cheek. There was a beat of silence. "Okay. Have him follow me home, okay?"

"Yeah." Suddenly all Jojo wanted was to ride with her mother, to go home, to have hot cocoa, and to go to bed for three days. But she couldn't. "See you there."

FIFTY-ONE

WITHIN MINUTES OF getting home, Laurie watched Jojo and Kevin settle onto the living room couch together. Jojo got out the iPad and, instead of switching on the big TV, they sat side by side, hips and legs touching. Jojo kept her phone plugged in and in her hand, the screen constantly on. On the iPad they watched YouTube videos and spoke in low voices.

Their quiet talk was nice, a balm to the frayed edges of Laurie's mind. Maybe they'd actually sleep, even though it was barely nine in the morning. She hoped so. Suddenly there was nothing she wanted more than a couple of hours of rest.

And Omid. She wanted him. . . .

No, she **couldn't** want him. How could she be this angry at him—a volcano of rage slung inside her chest, charring her liver and lungs—when she missed him like she missed sleep?

And at the same time, she was just as furious at herself.

At the beginning of all this, she'd wanted to kill Kevin. She'd wanted to hurt him until he stopped breathing. She'd been completely convinced of his guilt, and she would have done anything to bring him to justice. An innocent man.

How many of them were like this?

Were all cops and dispatchers and ID techs and records clerks just brainwashed? Laurie didn't think so—she'd gotten into the industry in order to help.

They all had.

Hadn't they? The men on the list—they'd started the same way, too, right? With dreams and goals and the sincere wish to make the world a better, safer place? No matter what, they still made up less than ten percent of the force. . . .

She hung her bag on the hook in the kitchen and poured a glass of water. As she drank, she noticed her hand was shaking.

Her cell, before Jojo had taped it to Dixon's car, had been getting texts from Pamela and Andy on an almost hourly basis while she'd been in the jail cell. She'd only had time to send one back to them while she was driving to meet Kevin and Jojo: **We're doing everything we can. Will call you soon.**

She **was** doing everything she could. And it wasn't good enough.

Harper was somewhere, and every hour they wasted not finding her was making it less likely she'd get out alive. The department and the people inside it didn't matter at all, not when it came to finding Harper.

The department could go straight to hell.

We need to find her. Poor Harper—how would she recover from this? Laurie couldn't imagine how **Jojo** would start to heal, let alone a girl who'd been trapped for days after being used like a cat toy by a department full of predators.

But they all needed rest, too, though. The three of them were running on fumes.

Back in the living room, she said, "Jojo, can I have your phone?"

Jojo finished laughing at whatever they were watching on the iPad and then said, "No."

"Jojo."

Her daughter met her eyes, and for a fraction of a second Laurie saw the woman that she would be in ten years, thirty, fifty.

Jojo shook her head firmly. "We're both going to nap down here. We've already set an alarm, and every hour one of us'll look at the app. We'll get you if he moves."

"I can do that." That was her job. It wasn't her daughter's.

"Mama, you need to rest even more than we do.

We didn't go to jail last night. Go lie down." Jojo flashed her a quick but sweet smile. "Don't worry, we've got this."

Laurie swallowed the ball of emotion tangled in her throat. **She's right. My daughter is right.** She blew them each a stern kiss. "Sleep. I command you. It's going to be okay." The words were automatic.

Upstairs, Laurie pulled closed the blinds and then used the old landline phone to call Omid. She dialed the hospital room when he didn't answer his cell.

"I'm doing better," Omid said. "They say they'll let me out in a couple of days."

Laurie lay on the bed, his pillow tucked behind her head, her shoes still on. "Yeah? Because when I talked to the doctor, he said more like a week. How's your pain level?" What if he **had** slept with Harper? Would she ever know? Would she ever trust him again?

He made a dissatisfied sound, but it was his giving-up tone. He was even more tired than she'd thought. "It's fine. How's our girl?"

"She's doing okay." Downstairs, on the couch with a man who was a bailed-out suspect in her rape, a killing, and a kidnapping. Omid would have a third and probably final heart attack if she told him. "She's going to rest soon—we've been awake all night." She didn't tell him why. "You should rest, too."

"I love you."

No, no, no. They didn't say that to each other. That was for emergencies. Laurie's heart slammed in her chest. **Going to war. Apocalypse. The very last moment.** "I know," was all she could manage. "Me too."

FIFTY-TWO

JOJO HAD NEVER fallen asleep with anyone who wasn't her mom and dad or Harper, but being tangled with Kevin on the couch was nice. She could see what people got out of the whole thing. His body was big and warm, a long pillow with no give. As she'd drawn a blanket over them, he'd turned so that he was spooning her. Jojo held her breath—it was so intimate, this cradling. Her whole body was tense, and she didn't know how to arrange her limbs. But Kevin was good at it, and he slung an arm around her waist, pulling her against him. It felt safe. Good. Kevin rested the phone on the edge of the couch and kept one hand on it. "One hour," he mumbled into her ear.

Or less. The phone was plugged in, and Jojo

planned to look at the tracking more often if she could. How could she rest when Harper was out there? Hurting? Maybe dying?

But sleep dragged her down, and the first four times the alarm went off, they both jumped. All four times Jojo's phone hadn't moved, still sitting in front of Darren Dixon's house.

The fifth time, at almost 2:00 P.M., the phone was moving.

"Mom!" Jojo kicked her way out from under the blanket, ignoring the **ooof** that came from Kevin behind her. She raced through the living room and took the stairs two at a time. **"Mom!"**

When she reached her parents' bedroom, her mother was already standing. Okay, she was swaying, one hand out for balance, her face rumpled with sleep. "He's moving?"

"He's moving."

Kevin stomped up the stairs, too, and peered over Jojo's shoulder.

Mom grabbed the phone out of her hands. "Where?"

"Hey!"

But her mother held tight. She sat on the edge of the bed.

Jojo climbed up behind her and motioned for Kevin to do the same.

He hesitated.

"Hop up," Mom said. "We can all watch."

The image was small on the map, just a blue dot.

It moved slowly down the freeway, though it was probably going the speed limit or more.

"**Yes,**" said Mom.

Jojo felt a chill shoot up her arms. They would get him—and then what? "Do you have a plan?" Desperately, she needed her mother to say yes again.

Instead Mom just shook her head and said, "Shhh." As if she needed silence to watch a screen.

Kevin said, "He's going to San Bernal."

Mom nodded, and they watched the blue dot take the freeway exit that led to the Bernal Bridge. "Fuck."

Jojo's stomach clenched. "Why?"

"Why what?" Mom didn't look at her, just kept her eyes on the phone.

"Why 'fuck'?"

Mom just glanced at her, her gaze tight, as if Jojo had done something wrong.

But Jojo figured it out. "The police department. He's going to report you?"

"Probably. Although, jurisdiction-wise he should know enough to report it in the city it happened in—" Mom took a breath. "Or he's . . ."

Going to meet up with other cops. To talk about it. Together.

Mom finally continued, "Yeah, probably to report me."

"Will you lose your job?" It seemed like a funny thing to worry about right now, but Jojo still needed to ask.

"I might."

That wasn't the right answer. Mom was supposed to say, **It'll be okay. Don't worry about it. We'll fix this.**

"Will Dad?" Jojo hated that her voice squeaked.

"I don't know."

The dot on the screen took all the turns that led to the PD.

Jojo didn't realize she was stone-rigid until her mother said, "Hey. Breathe." Jojo panted, and, next to her, Kevin did the same. They all had morning breath even though it was afternoon, and while it should have been disgusting, Jojo realized that she almost liked it. They smelled like a den of animals.

She could be feral if she needed to be.

The dot reached the department.

It stopped at the corner, where the light was.

And then it kept moving.

"Holy shit," said Mom.

"Where's he going?" Jojo scooted closer to Mom, moving onto her knees. She leaned her body against her mother, and Mom leaned back. "I mean, I know we don't know. Where do you **think** he's going?"

Kevin's voice rumbled. "He's going to the Old Coast. My house."

But the dot kept moving, traveling down Smythe and taking a right on Fifteenth. Left on Rose. Right on Seventeenth.

At the corner of Hind and Seventeenth, the blue dot disappeared.

"Wait." Jojo reached out her hand, but her mother jerked the phone closer to her chest.

"Where did it go?" Mom refreshed the screen. Nothing. She looked at Jojo. "Where did it go?"

"Let me have it." Jojo didn't think her mother had done anything wrong, but who knew?

"Fine."

Jojo closed the app.

Reopened it.

Nothing.

"Your phone died."

"No." Mom's face was pale.

"He's moving too much—it's not like he could have found it while he was driving. And if it had just dropped off the car, it would still be transmitting. I think it just died."

"Fuck."

Jojo watched, horrified, as tears rose in Mom's eyes. "Oh, no." She lightly punched her mother on the shoulder. "Don't **cry.** If you go, I'll go."

Mom bit her bottom lip. "I'm sorry. I should have charged it longer, but I was in the jail without it and just plugged it in while I was driving to his house. . . . Oh, my God, we've lost him."

Kevin, silent till now, scooted forward and took the phone from Jojo's hand. "Nothing we can do about it. But what can we figure out from where he was going?"

Mom rubbed her face, hard. "Okay. Okay, yeah."

Their three heads converged again. Mom studied

the streets with new interest, zooming in and out while Kevin held the phone.

Jojo tried not to let the panic in her breastbone boil up and over.

"Okay," said Mom again. "He was a cop in this town for eighteen years. He knows the city as well as anyone. If he were going to the east end, he would have come off the Forsyth Street exit, not over the bridge. That means he wasn't going farther than Grand. And he avoided Bornemouth, which would have been faster for almost everything in that area, so that means he's close to where he means to go."

Kevin pointed at the screen, at the tangle of streets in the middle. "What's there?"

"Some older houses, a few Victorians, and a crap-ton of densely populated apartment buildings."

Jojo leaned closer. "Any other cops live there?"

"I don't think so. No, definitely not."

Jojo shook her head as she imagined the area. She'd flyered for the police Tip-a-Cop night in that area. "Too many doors. Even if we found his car, we wouldn't be able to knock at every single one. And it would take hours to drive all those tiny streets looking for his car."

"Even if we found the right door, he wouldn't answer it," said Mom. She pressed her palms together. "This is reminding me of something, though."

"What?"

"I don't know. Something about this street here—off of Hind—this feels familiar to me."

How did that help? Mom knew every street in San Bernal like the back of her hand, first from being on the street, then for dispatching for so many years. Everything probably felt familiar to her. "We'll never find him."

"No, there's something." Mom stood, bouncing the bed as she did so. "I've got to go to dispatch. I'll need to take your phone, but have Kevin text me if you need anything."

"But you said they don't trust you there—"

"I'll figure it out. My brain is trying to tell me something, and I'm too tired to work it out without CAD."

"What's CAD?" said Kevin.

"The computer system in dispatch," said Jojo. She stood. "I want to go with you."

"You stay here. This won't be a pleasure visit."

Like anything was right now. They were in hell, and Mom wanted to split up. "Mama. Please let me come with you."

But her mother was moving too fast. She tore off her shirt like she didn't even care that Kevin was sitting right there. Jojo's face flushed. At least Mom was wearing a bra, albeit an old gray one. She put on another shirt and darted into the bathroom to brush her teeth.

"You need to eat." The words came out of Jojo's mouth automatically—the words her mother had said to her a hundred-million times over the years.

Mom noticed it, too. Her hairbrush stopped

moving, and she looked out the open bathroom door. "You're right. I do. Can you do me a favor and get me one of those protein bars in the pantry?"

As if he'd been waiting for something—anything—to do, Kevin jumped up. "I'll get that for you. Be right back."

"Thanks."

Mom came out and pulled off her jeans then, and her underwear. She slid into a fresh pair and pulled on new jeans.

Jojo said, "Thank God you didn't do that while he was in here."

Mom smiled thinly. "I realized by your faces when I took my shirt off that taking off my pants might be a bit too much. Sorry that was embarrassing."

It wasn't true—it **would** have been any other day. But today Jojo wasn't embarrassed. Still, it was light talk—it felt like what she would say on a normal weekday. "Yeah, I would have died."

In midstep her mother paused. A quick freeze.

"Sorry," Jojo mumbled. "You know what I mean."

"Don't you dare."

"Don't **you** dare."

Mom nodded sharply. "Okay, then. We have a deal."

FIFTY-THREE

LAURIE STORMED THROUGH the back door of the police department, almost hopeful that the hallway would be full of guys at shift change. But the first floor was deserted—they must have been in lineup. No one to hurl her rage against.

In dispatch, Shonda and Charity looked startled to see her.

"Holy shit."

"How are you?"

"How's Jojo?"

"How's Omid?"

Their voices traded off, and Laurie ignored the questions. "Who's supe?"

"Rita. She's on a break." That meant she was upstairs in the lunchroom watching a soap on the DVR. Good.

Laurie sat at an open terminal. "I've got to dig through some records, okay?"

Shonda's voice was tentative, a rare thing for her. "Aren't you . . . aren't you on admin leave?"

That would be news to her, but it was probably true. "Am I? If I am, I haven't been told about it yet, nor have I signed anything. So I think that means I'm only on family medical leave, officially."

Shonda stood. "Maybe I should go get Rita. Just in case."

Laurie kept her hands moving over the keyboard. "Do what you need to do." Shonda owed her twelve hours, and Laurie hadn't been pushing to get it paid back, even though it had been more than a year. When she returned to work, she'd make Shonda work the time in the middle of her days off.

As Shonda left the room, Laurie started digging. Because she'd been trained to act as supervisor when needed, her log-ins still worked to get her into the back end of CAD. From here she could pull up almost anything from any of the mobile data computers in any of the cop cars. Dixon's MDC would show exactly where he'd been, at all times. And if he'd gone out at any particular location, it would have logged that, too. Even though he'd been off the force for two years now, the records came up as quickly as any other request.

Now to sort through all the data and search for that zone, that small segment of the map that included the area of Hind and Seventeenth.

The returns were massive. It would take days to go through the data. Laurie blew out a breath of frustration.

"Can I help?" Charity wasn't great at her job—too slow, too worried—but she was a sweet woman with good intentions.

"No thanks, hon. You probably don't want to, anyway." Who knew how far down this would take Laurie? She didn't need to drag anyone else with her.

Charity nodded and cracked open a bottle of nail polish.

Laurie narrowed the search down to the last two years that Dixon was employed.

Better. The data was still vast, but it was doable. Maybe.

As long as no one stopped her.

When 911 rang, Charity grabbed it. Laurie's nerves tensed. She was logged in, and there was a spare headset next to her. Rita was on break, and Shonda was somewhere chasing her down—that left just her and Charity in the room. Usually two dispatchers ran a call—one on the phone and the other on the radio, putting it out to the officers. Any other dispatcher would have answered the phone **and** put out on the air whatever kind of call it was, multitasking and using the mic pedal to switch back and forth between talking to the officers and the citizen on the phone, but Charity wasn't that dispatcher.

Shit.

Maybe it wouldn't be a big deal.

"He what? Where's the gun?"

Laurie could hear the screaming coming over Charity's headset. No way in hell would she be able to get info from the reporting party and talk to the units. Laurie pulled on the headset. The call landed on the screen in front of her. 2D71 and 3D42 were available. She attached them and the sergeant to it, then verbalized it on the radio.

Almost immediately Shonda was back in the room. She slid a seemingly grateful glance at Laurie and took over the dispatching while Charity continued to talk to the woman whose husband had just taken off with the gun and the dog, heading toward the freeway.

And almost as immediately, two people rushed into the room.

Rita moved quickly to stand next to her. "Can we talk in the supervisor's office?"

Laurie flapped her hand. "I wish I could. But I don't have time."

Behind Rita stood Mark Colson. "I knew that was your voice. What are you doing here?"

Laurie tried a grin. "Hey, I just got let out of the pokey, so I thought I'd come do a little pro bono work."

"Shit, Laurie. You shouldn't be here." Mark's voice was concerned.

"Why not?" Laurie kept her eyes on the screen

and the pages scrolling by. Every traffic stop, every lunch break, every hit-and-run, every cold burglary—every single thing Dixon had done on duty was logged. She could find it. She had to find it.

"You're on admin leave."

She made a come-on gesture with her left hand. "Bring it to me. I haven't signed anything yet. Haven't talked to my supervisor."

Rita said, "I'm trying to make that happen. Can you please stop what you're doing and come talk to me?"

"Respectfully, Maury is my supervisor."

Colson straddled a chair backward and scooted close to her. She minimized the search window.

Colson said, "That's beside the point. He's not here. Rita's in charge. And above her I'm in charge. You know that."

His voice was strained, and he wasn't the best under pressure. He had, though, always been a good man, as far as Laurie knew. He wasn't on Harper's list, but how could she trust any of them? How far did the rot go in the apple? "Please, Mark. I'm running one search."

"Okay, then, how about telling me what you're searching for?"

She folded her lips. "I don't want to tell you." Truth was best—he'd sniff out a lie, and she certainly didn't think she could come up with a good enough one, anyway.

"We'll be able to tell, you know. As soon as you stand up. We'll be able to look at what you searched."

She knew that. That was for later. "Please, Mark. I've got a hunch."

Colson gave a strained smile. "Let us help you, Laurie."

"Please. I'll ask for help as soon as I know what I'm looking for. I promise."

Colson folded his hands together, as if in prayer, and then shook them out. "Is this about Kevin Leeds?"

"No. This is about Jojo." Mostly.

"How is she?"

Laurie shook her head slowly. Maybe she could use this. "Not very good. Not good at all. I'm worried."

Colson had two teen daughters. "Laurie, I'm so sorry. Still . . ."

"Look. I've got this wild hunch. It isn't about a single person who works here, I promise you that I'm telling you the God's honest truth. I'm doing some digging. Please, Mark. It's for Jojo. For our little Car 143."

He shut his eyes. "If the chief finds out about this—"

For a moment Laurie was confused. Omid was—No, wait. He meant Brent Stanley. Omid wasn't the chief, not until he was better. And maybe not then, either. She wasn't a dispatcher, or at least she wouldn't be one after she got the admin leave papers. And who knew how long that would take to sort out? She might not have a job afterward. They'd change the outer door code—they always did whenever anyone went out on admin leave. Protocol. To keep them from doing exactly what she was doing—screwing around in the records database.

"He won't find out. We won't tell him, will we, guys?" Laurie looked at Rita, Shonda, and Charity, all of whom shook their heads.

"Other people heard you on the radio. They'll be coming in to find out why."

Shit, she hadn't thought of that. "Rita, can I use your office? I'll close the door and keep the light out. You can talk at me while I work."

"God, Laurie." Rita was already moving toward the office. **"God."**

A little more time, that's all Laurie needed. There was something in her brain, something about that part of town generally and Dixon specifically. She'd find it, and then she'd know where he was.

And then she'd do something about it.

FIFTY-FOUR

AFTER MOM LEFT, Jojo and Kevin had gone back to the couch, but it was different now. While they'd slept earlier, they'd cuddled. He'd felt so close. Once, after they'd checked the phone, before they'd drifted off again, Jojo had felt his chest shake and felt him cry. He'd been almost silent, except for softly sped-up breathing that sounded wet. Jojo had turned to face him and, without saying anything, put her arms around his neck and held him for a long time.

Now that Mom was gone, the house felt too big. As if reading her mind, Kevin said, "You want to get out of here?"

It should be fine, as long as she kept Mom in the loop. Mom had her phone—Kevin could text her and tell her where they were going. "Where do you want to go?"

Kevin spoke to his toes. "I want to go home."

Kevin's mother and the rest of his family were out of state. His church at home thought gays went to hell. Zach had been his person. Football had been his life. Zach was gone, and his career would be, too, she assumed. A player couldn't play while fighting felony charges, could he?

Of course he needed to go home. Jojo felt a surge of unearned luck run through her veins like gold. She still had Mom. And even if he'd lied, she still had Dad.

"Let's go," Jojo said.

KEVIN'S house was trashed.

"Fuck," he said as they entered each room. "Fuck **me.** Fuck."

Every piece of the living room furniture was broken, as if someone had taken a sledgehammer and beaten each one apart. The glass in the cabinets was shattered. It looked as if one chair had actually been sawed down the middle. Every wall was covered with swastikas and things Jojo didn't recognize but kind of understood: KKK, 14-88, GSS.

In the kitchen every dish was broken, every glass thrown against the wall. Each pantry item had been opened, and the floor was covered in a nightmarish goo of cornflakes and raisins and canned pineapple. Flour covered every surface, sticky and white.

"Oh, my God." Jojo covered her mouth with her hand. "What's that smell?"

Kevin crouched to look more closely at the filth covering the floor. "Yeah, that's shit. And piss."

Jojo gagged and sidestepped her way out to the hall, swallowing hard. "Should we be in here? Is it safe?"

Kevin slammed into a bathroom, kicking a path through broken porcelain. He raised his voice to a shout. "I hope it's **not** safe! I hope someone's here who I can tear into pieces!"

But it was too quiet. There was no one here but them, Jojo could feel it. "Why didn't the alarm go off?"

"I didn't bother to set it. I didn't think it could get any worse."

Each room was wrecked more than the last. Jojo tried to take Kevin's hand as they went into his bedroom, but he shook her off. His body radiated pure anger, and with every step he took, his breathing got heavier. A dark fug with a tang of uric acid hung in the air. The curtains were on the floor, and half the books on the shelves had been torn apart, page by page. Each wall was covered with something worse: KILLER, RAPIST, BURN AND DIE.

The only room left untouched was the spare bedroom, the one Jojo had woken up in. Kevin stuttered a breath as they entered, and Jojo stifled a scream. There, on the bed, was a single white rose.

Kevin yanked open the bathroom door.

"No. I can't . . ." He shut it again.

"What is it?"

"More roses," he said in a flat tone. "Right where his body was."

"What the **fuck**?"

Kevin sank to the floor. His legs splayed out before him, and he held on to his elbows. "This was all I had. **This was all I had.** I had my job, and I had Zach, and that's all I needed. It was everything. It's all I wanted." His voice was a bloody wound.

Jojo knelt beside him. "You still have your voice. CapB needs you." Stupid words. She knew that Kevin would throw all of CapB into the ocean if it would bring Zach back.

He hadn't seemed to hear her, anyway. "This is all because of what I did. This is all my fault. If I had just kept my mouth shut, never gotten political, never gotten involved . . . It's all my **fault.**"

It wasn't his fault—he was just the unlucky one who'd been targeted. Now he was broken. He didn't even look the same. His face had changed, as if it had been taken apart and put back together by someone who didn't understand what he was supposed to look like. The skin hung heavy under his eyes, and his cheeks were hollow.

It terrified Jojo even more than the rooms had.

"But we don't stop fighting." She'd heard it a million times in the meetings. **We don't ever stop fighting.**

Kevin flopped backward and stared at the ceiling. "Oh, yeah, we do. We stop. We always stop. They make us stop. They break us, and then we can't fight back. They force us to surrender. We never win. I can't believe I ever thought we could."

Jojo squatted to take his hand. "We have to get out of here."

"Never moving a muscle again."

"We should call the cops." The words sounded flimsier than the idea. Jojo wanted to shove them back into her mouth whole, but she'd choke on them, vomit them out again in pieces. **The cops were the good guys. They had to be the good guys.**

They weren't the good guys. Not now.

Kevin didn't bother responding.

Jojo's palms were sweating. "I'm going to get you a glass of water—" For a second she'd forgotten the damage in the kitchen. There was no glass for her to get. "Come on, Kevin, we have to go. There's no point in being here."

Movement in the backyard caught her eye through the window. Instinctively, she ducked. "There's someone out there." What if it was the people who had done all this?

Kevin didn't move.

"What if it's them?" she hissed.

Kevin kept his eyes closed. It was as if she weren't there, as if he couldn't hear her at all.

Jojo straightened so that she could just peek out the bottom of the window. She expected something terrible, a clown face at the window or a bonfire of nightmarish proportions.

But there, in the middle of the yard, wearing a yellow sundress and a gorgeous smile, Harper was flying, up and down, up and down.

Harper's ghost.

Obviously.

Harper was dead, and now she was there—flying up and down, her gorgeous tumble of long blond hair floating and falling like yellow mist. Jojo turned to ice and then to liquid heat—nothing made sense, but there Harper was. Even dead, she was beautiful. Jojo touched the ring at her throat and felt it hot against her skin. **Harper was dead.**

But—the ghost was jumping on the mattress she and Kevin had hauled outside last night.

And the apparition waved when she saw Jojo at the window. Through the glass, Jojo could hear a laugh. Did ghosts laugh out loud?

It **was** her. It had to be.

"Kevin! Shit, Kevin!"

She raced for the door. She heard Kevin get up and chase her. She slammed through the living room, dodging a broken chair and a balled-up rug, leaping over a shattered lamp. She threw open the door to the yard, and there:

Harper.

Smiling.

Reaching out to her.

But then Harper wavered in Jojo's sight, going blurry at the same time a great roar ripped through her brain, and that's when she knew for sure: Harper was dead, and this was her incorporeal form, come to tell Jojo she loved her for the last time.

Jojo tried to reach out a hand, but her own body was gone, she couldn't move, she had no thought except for a punch of stark fear—

And everything went dark.

FIFTY-FIVE

LAURIE CLUTCHED THE steering wheel. She sat in the department's parking lot and tried to breathe calmly, the way she'd been trying to learn in that damn yoga class, but what good was breathing when she was getting nothing **done**?

She looked at Jojo's phone. Almost 6:00 P.M. It would start getting dark in a couple of hours, and they were no closer to finding Harper now than they were three days ago.

About an hour earlier, Jojo had sent a text from Kevin's phone. Laurie had read it when it came in, but she read it again.

On our way to Kevin's, will keep you posted where we are.

When she'd texted back, asking Jojo to tell her when they got there, Jojo hadn't responded.

Stubborn. Just like her father. Laurie hadn't talked to Omid in hours. She should go to the hospital to check on him in person, but then she remembered.

She'd **finally** remembered what had been niggling at the back of her mind about Seventeenth and Hind—Darren Dixon's beat wife.

Lots of cops had beat wives—local resident women who liked men in uniform and gave them a place to "relax" between calls while still remaining on their beats. Some of them eventually became real wives, only to be left for a new beat wife a few years later.

Everyone at the department thought Darren had one. They'd never figured out who it was, but in dispatch they laughed about it. On his midshift break, no matter the time, day or night, his patrol unit often stopped in the same area.

They thought he'd been going there for sex.

But what if he hadn't? What if he owned another property?

A place to stash kidnapped girls? **It's not him,** her brain said. **He's a useless drunk. This is a rabbit trail. Leave it alone. Let the department find Harper—this isn't your job.**

Something tugged her, though. It kept pulling.

She'd combed through every record for the last two years of his career, hoping for the one time he put himself out verbally at a specific address on either Hind or Seventeenth, but he never had. Not once. She'd gone deeper into CAD and tracked his unit's motions, hoping he always parked in the same spot, but he never did. It made logical sense—the housing was too dense in that area to offer up easy, regular parking spaces.

She straightened her shoulders and swallowed, hard.

At least she could look for his Range Rover. She could do that much.

She drove Hind, and Seventeenth, and Brockley. She found two Range Rovers, neither of them with the 11-99 sticker and the 5211os plate. She combed side streets and went in circles, just in case she'd missed something. Her stomach hurt, sour and cramped.

Just as she was about to give up, she found it on Eighteenth wedged between a motorcycle and a dumpster in front of a broken-down apartment building.

No one was around the vehicle. No cars drove by. There were no pedestrians leading dogs, no mothers pushing strollers for an early-evening walk.

Laurie leaned down and grabbed her phone, ripping it out of the wheel well and shoving it into her pocket, duct tape and all. She stood straight again, her face hot, as if she'd done something wrong.

Which she hadn't. She **could** do something wrong, though.

What if she stood in the middle of the street? What if she screamed Harper's name until the neighbors called the cops?

That would be something. A rookie pulling up on a dispatcher losing her shit, the dispatcher who'd just been arrested for punching a police officer. Of course, they didn't even know about her second crime, pistol-whipping the ex-cop she was currently hunting.

Laurie rubbed her cheeks, hard. Her head ached. She looked up at the windows all around her. Too many. Too many old houses split into four or more units. Too many apartment buildings. The windows flashed the lowering sun back at her, glaring and painful.

He was up there somewhere, in one of them.

Fumbling with her keys in her pocket, she pressed the fob so hard she heard her car relock. It was lucky she hadn't hit the PANIC button.

She was losing it.

In just a block's radius from where his car was parked, there had to be more than eighty residences. Old Victorians stood skinny and tall, each broken into eight or more units. Next to them sprawled apartment buildings holding dozens more. She couldn't knock on every door.

She couldn't do **anything** except stand here, completely helpless.

Kevin's house was seven minutes away.

As she started the car again, heading for Kevin's house, Jojo's phone rang.

"Pamela, it's Laurie." She balanced the phone

between her shoulder and chin as she strapped in. "I've got Jojo's phone."

"Oh, thank God. I tried calling you first. Have you heard **anything**?"

"Not yet. I'm so sorry."

Pamela's voice sounded like it came over a string laced into a tin can. "She's gone. I can feel it."

"No, don't—"

"She's gone. That man—Kevin Leeds—is out, and he knows where she is, and it's not fair—none of this is fair. . . ."

"We'll find her."

Pamela said nothing. She just sobbed.

As she drove, Laurie set the phone on speaker and listened to Pamela cry. In the background she heard another snuffling noise. Andy. Both of them, sobbing on the open line.

"I'm here," Laurie said as she turned onto Ninth. "I'm here with you."

"You're not," Pamela finally managed to whisper as Laurie pulled up in front of Kevin's house. "No one is."

Laurie got out of the car and headed for the door, keeping the phone to her ear. "We're doing the best we can. I'm following a lead right now."

Kevin Leeds's front door stood open.

Something was wrong.

"I've got to call you back." She disconnected and stepped inside the house. "Hello?"

There was no answer. "Jojo? Kevin?"

She saw something glint on the hall runner—glass, shattered. Lots of it. "Shit." She should call for backup, but by the time they got here, she'd have found whoever might be here. And who would come, exactly? How could she trust whoever might show up?

Inside, the house was trashed. There was barely a solid thing left. Fear spiked in the back of her head, and she drew her gun. She yelled into each room before she cleared it. She kept her finger off the trigger, just barely—**what if she surprised Jojo? Or Kevin?** Laurie looked into every closet, under every bed. There was shit in the carpet and urine soaked a shredded couch. This wasn't the work of just one person. Two or more people had to have created this carnage.

But she found no Kevin.

Worse, no Jojo.

Desperately, she holstered her gun and punched Kevin's number on Jojo's phone. It rang with no answer. She sent a text. **Where are you both?**

Where are you?

Answer me, goddamn it!

Sweat slicked her skin. Her clammy hands shook badly. She dropped the phone into a mixture of something that looked like flour and smelled like cinnamon and shit. Not caring, she wiped it on her pants.

She went into the backyard, and her heart, already so wobbly, almost stopped.

The grass was ripped, the ground muddy. A mattress and box spring sat in the middle of the yard. Toward the gate, which still stood open, the earth was flattened and smoothed, as if something—or someone—had been dragged out and away. Dirt trailed down the concrete path that ran along the side of the house.

There'd been a struggle. If Jojo had been here with Kevin, one or both of them had been dragged away.

FIFTY-SIX

LAURIE RAN OUT Kevin's open gate and raced to the yellow house next door, tripping over a potted geranium, catching herself on the iron porch rail. She banged on the door and rang the bell and yelled, but the house was dark and closed.

The green house on the other side, then. She did the same, and this time the door was pulled back slowly. The resident left the iron screen door closed.

"My daughter! Did you hear anything next door? Did you see anything?"

But the older woman hadn't heard anything. She tugged on the single earring she wore. "I was watching the news. Hearing's not good. Volume up high. You know that guy next door? You know what he did?"

Laurie didn't bother answering.

It didn't matter how Omid felt, it didn't matter whether he was up to this or not. She needed him.

In her mind, as she sped through the darkening streets to the hospital, she could see only one image: Jojo's overalls. When she was five, she'd driven a nail through her thumb while helping Daddy with carpentry. It wasn't a big deal. The nail had jumped, and it had gone clean through the fleshy part. Jojo, of course, had pulled it out and bled all over her new overalls. They'd taken her to urgent care, and it had needed just cleaning and a bandage, not even stitches.

That night, though, Laurie had held up the overalls before dropping them into the washing machine, and she'd seen, for what felt like the first time, the sheer amount of blood that covered them. How could there possibly be so much blood—how was there any left in her tiny daughter?

In that moment at the washer, Laurie's mind had flashed to every single possibility of bodily trauma that could occur to Jojo in her life: a bicycle accident in which she was dragged under a car's wheels, an airplane crash in which no body was ever recovered, a house fire in which only charred, ashen bones were found. Laurie's entire job as a mother was to make sure that her daughter's blood and bones and guts and viscera stayed **inside** her skin, and she'd already failed.

Those overalls. Those tiny overalls were all she

saw until she was racing through the hospital cor-
ridors.

A nurse tried to slow her down, but Laurie shook
her off with a barked, **"No!"**

In his room Omid was asleep. Fury coursed
through her. "Wake up! Now!"

Omid jumped, and his eyes flickered open.
"Laurie? Wha'? Where's Jojo?"

It wasn't fair, to wake him like this and lay this on
him, and then Laurie remembered what he'd hidden from her about Harper and the men, and her
rage rose. "She's **gone.** Gone, you son of a bitch."

"What?" Omid's voice was a gasp, and his eyes
went black—darker than she'd ever seen them.
Terror filled his face. Laurie wanted to repent, but
she couldn't. This was on him, all of it. It had to be.
"What do you mean?"

"She was with Kevin. I think they were at his
house. The place's been torn apart. Signs of a struggle in the backyard. They're gone. I think whoever
has Harper has them."

Omid was already pulling at the lines hooked
to his arms and hands. Beeps rose around them, a
flood of screaming machines. "**Who?** Fucking hell,
Laurie, who?"

"I don't **know,** but I think Darren Dixon is
mixed up in it. I think it's been him all along."
She'd listened to her gut—the gut that said Dixon
was a drunk, that he could never pull off this kind
of thing.

But her gut had been wrong. For the umpteenth time. She'd been wrong, and now she'd be punished by losing her daughter.

"Then we go to him." He stood, his legs wobbling.

"Omid!" Laurie propped him up, and he gave her almost his whole weight. "Jesus, sit back down."

He yanked out another line of some sort, and blood flowed down his arm. "You think you can stop me? We go together. We get our daughter back."

Relief stabbed her lungs. **Yes,** she wanted him. She needed him. She couldn't do this herself.

Omid pressed the sheet against his arm and lunged with the other arm at the closet. He pulled out a plastic bag and dumped out the clothes and shoes he'd been wearing when he was admitted. "Where? Do you have any idea where she is?"

"In dispatch we always thought he had a beat wife in sector four—he would park at Hind and Seventeenth for his breaks. I went to the station to try to figure out the address, but—"

Omid's head jerked up. "I know it. I went there once. A long time ago. We were partners that day, and he had to take a shit and wouldn't do it at the station."

"Do you remember the address?"

He rolled his eyes and pulled out his phone. Only dispatchers remembered addresses. Cops remembered what properties looked like.

Omid stabbed at Google Maps. He zoomed in once, then again. "Street View, come on, slow-ass piece of **shit.**" He shook the phone as if that would make it work faster. "Here. This is it."

She recognized the house—she'd been right **there,** not even an hour ago, getting her phone from under Dixon's car. It was three doors up from the sketchy apartment, a run-down Victorian that she wouldn't have looked at twice. She pulled Jojo's phone out of her pocket—it was barely charged now, but it was better than her own dead phone, still wrapped in duct tape. "I'll call dispatch, get some cars to meet us there."

Omid put out a hand. "Wait." His face was drawn.

"Shit, Omid. No." It couldn't be this bad in the department.

"If Dixon **is** behind this whole thing with Harper—it's not good. He's still got a lot of friends. Obviously."

Friends who would fuck a teenager for money. "They might be shitheads, but they're probably not down with murder and kidnapping. They can't be." It **couldn't** be that bad—it was still San Bernal. It was still the department she'd loved for so long. Ben Bradcoe was on the list of men who'd slept with Harper, but he was the chairperson for the department's Toys for Tots drive. When Darren Dixon had written his Facebook rant, Dan Toomey—who was on the list—had defended Omid in the Internal Affairs investigation.

The IA.

The cops who rose to Omid's defense, publicly.

Ben Bradcoe. Dan Toomey. Will Yarwood. Sherm Naumann. Heinz Tollis. Names scrolled through her head.

"**Omid.** Every guy on Harper's list stood up for you at the IA."

"Oh." Omid's eyebrows shot together. "Damn, Laurie. That's **it.**"

Of course. Dixon was out to get every single person who'd been against him then. Get a girl to reach out to them, trap them, ensnare them. If Harper had feelings about Dixon, if he was the one who'd set up the plot, then all he'd had to do was feed her their personal contact details. If they fell for the bait, Dixon would be the winner.

"The list, though. Your list, the guys you were working with to get the money for her. Is that all of them?"

He shook his head. "I have no idea if that list is complete." Omid's voice was gruff, almost a cough. "We have to go get her. Now."

"**Them.**" There were two girls. Not just Jojo, though Jojo was the one who mattered most. Harper, though, mattered almost as much. Jesus, what was Darren doing to her? To them? And how the hell was Kevin involved in all this?

"Them," Omid agreed.

"He's insane." Laurie didn't have to say Dixon's name—he felt like the devil now. Say his name too many times and he'd appear.

"Clearly." Omid's gun was at the bottom of the plastic bag. He held it in his hand, still in his hospital gown, as if looking to see if it had a built-in holster. He looked pale except for two odd spots of bright color at the tops of his cheeks and red flushed along his forehead.

"Are you sure about this?"

"Never more sure about anything in my life. I'll kill the motherfucker."

Then Omid wobbled slowly and passed out, thunking his head on the metal rail of the bed as he went down.

Fuck, fuck, fuck. Fuck.

Laurie yelled into the hallway for help.

The nurses put him back in bed, reattached his lines, checked the lump on his head, and assured her that he would keep breathing. "Don't worry, sugar, he just got up too soon. Happens all the time. He'll sleep it off."

Laurie would have to do this on her own, then. She ran.

FIFTY-SEVEN

ONCE JOJO HAD had a dream in which a demon was sitting on her chest, paralyzing her. Maybe she was having the same dream now. It was okay, though—she could hear Bettina from dispatch talking about a yellow van parked in front of a fire hydrant. That meant she was home, that she could hear the police scanner—but she couldn't move, could barely breathe around the mouthful of . . . What the **fuck** was in her mouth?

Her eyes flew open.

She was in a dark, low-ceilinged cement room of some type—maybe a basement. She lay on her side on the cold floor, her hands tied behind her. Her legs felt tied together, too, and her body ached coldly. Her fingers were numb, and her wrists screamed in pain. Her mouth was full of cloth that seemed to be epoxied to her tongue. She spit, and coughed, and gagged, then stopped and tried to breathe through her nose, terrified that she was sucking the gag deeper. She couldn't see much—just a ladder propped against one wall and a set of dark stairs.

She coughed harder, trying to dislodge the gag. Her brain was sluggish, and she felt dizzy and nauseated.

A low light snapped on in the corner.

Harper said, "He taped it to your face. You can't spit it out."

Hysteria filled her blood—she'd die, she'd drown, if she didn't get it off. Her nose was running, and she was crying, and if she didn't get the gag out, she'd die right here. Panic rose, and her breathing got shallower. Her chest started to hurt.

Harper.

Still wearing the yellow dress she'd worn in the backyard, when Jojo had thought she was a ghost, Harper came nearer to Jojo. She knelt next to her and stroked her hair. "Shhhh. If I take it off, will you promise not to scream? You have to promise."

Screaming was so far past what Jojo wanted to do—all she wanted was air. Her lungs shrieked, and her chest heaved. She nodded as hard as she could.

Harper ripped off one side of the tape, and Jojo spit out the cloth. With it came a stream of bile.

She turned her head to the side and vomited onto the concrete. The gag hung next to her mouth from the flap of the other side of the tape, still attached to her cheek.

From somewhere behind Harper, Jojo heard Bettina's light voice on the scanner: "3V11, 933 audible, Safeway on Bryant. Unit to cover?"

Jojo panted as she hauled oxygen into her lungs. She spit out the remainder of vomit, and it dribbled down her cheek.

"Gross, dude." Harper slapped her lightly—friendly-like—on the biceps. "Suck it up."

It was so what Harper would say that it finally convinced Jojo—this was the real Harper. She was alive, and they were together.

"Come on, breathe."

She was **trying.** Couldn't Harper see she was trying? Air went into her lungs with a sick wheeze and left in a bubbling rush. She couldn't see, her vision blurring, clearing, and then going dark again. For a long moment, Harper sat and stared at her. Jojo managed to grab a whole lungful of stale air. Then another.

Slowly the blackness left her vision. Chills racked her body, even though she was still sweating from every pore.

Breathe.

They had to get out of here. Jojo had to save Harper.

Jojo glanced behind her, wincing at the way her shoulders ached. Around the panic in her throat, she whispered, "Untie me. We'll get away."

"I can't do that," said Harper.

From the far corner came a groan in the darkness.

"What? Who is that? Is that Kevin?" Terror rose higher in her chest. "Is that **Kevin**? What happened to us? Why are we here?"

Harper leaned forward, still on her knees, and pressed her hand against Jojo's lips. "Shhh. You have to be quiet. And if he comes in, you have to put the gag back in and pretend you're asleep."

Like hell she'd put the gag back in. She and Harper could get away, could run, could get help for Kevin. "Untie me and we'll go. Are we locked in?" Of course they were. "Or we can wait till Kevin wakes up, and then he can break the door down. One way or another, we're going to get you home."

Harper's eyes looked funny. Like she wasn't listening, or rather like she was listening for something else. "Shhhh," she said again. She made no move to touch the rope at Jojo's wrists.

"Harper, what's going on? What happened? Are you okay?" She wanted her hands free so she could touch Harper, so she could run her fingers over her best friend and make sure nothing was broken.

"Shhh!" Harper tilted her head. "He's coming. **Be asleep.**" With one swift motion that Jojo couldn't stop, Harper shoved the gag back into her mouth and slapped the tape in place again. Harper pushed Jojo's head down, and covered her eyes with her hand, as if to close her eyelids. Then she ran back to the chair she'd been sitting in when she'd turned on the lamp.

Harper was brainwashed. That must be it.

Jojo thumped her legs, once, twice. But then she saw Harper's face. She looked eerily calm. Confident. Almost . . . happy.

It terrified her.

So Jojo stilled. She forced her eyelids closed and tried to control her breathing so that it wasn't as ragged in her chest.

A heavy footfall came down the stairs. "They still out?"

"Yeah." Harper's voice was lazy and amused. "Are you sure you didn't give them too much? Because she was making noises like she was drunk."

"Just enough to keep them down a while."

It was Darren Dixon's voice.

They'd been **right.** He might be a drunk, but he was also a fucking maniacal kidnapper. Rapist. Murderer. Fear swarmed up Jojo's gullet, and she shivered uncontrollably. **Please don't see.**

"What are you going to do when they wake up?"

Jojo heard Dixon kick something, and she was pretty sure it was Kevin. "Have a little fun." She wanted desperately to slit her eyes, to peek through her lids, but when she used to do that at slumber parties, she was always caught. God help her—she couldn't get caught now.

"You said you wouldn't hurt **her,** though."

"Yeah, yeah." Dixon's voice was lower now, as if he were bending over Kevin. He didn't sound drunk in the slightest.

"You promised me, remember?" Harper was using her honeypot voice. "You said I could have anything I wanted, and that was the one thing."

"I won't hurt her. Much, anyway. I don't want to bang up the bait."

A noise came from above—a door being crashed through, or something else big and wooden being splintered.

Jojo's eyes opened. She couldn't help it.

Dixon raced for the stairs, and Harper's mouth rounded into a small, surprised O.

"Keep an eye on them!" he yelled.

On the scanner Bettina read a plate to someone—it was clear and current, registered out of San Francisco.

Another crash upstairs. Whatever was going on up there, it didn't matter. Dixon was away from them, and this might be their last chance.

Jojo scraped her cheek on the concrete floor to loosen the already torn-off duct tape and spit out the gag. "Come on, untie me."

Harper's eyes were still wide, and she looked up at the ceiling. More noises thumped above, as if someone were fighting. "I can't. I'm so sorry, but I just can't."

Jojo **had** to get through to her. "He'll kill us both. Come on, do it fast." She held out her hands.

"Don't be silly." Harper had a smile draped over her lips. "He acts big, but he's sweet. He wouldn't hurt a fly."

"How did we get here, then?"

Harper tilted her head as if considering. "He tased you both, but that doesn't hurt. He swears it doesn't. And the GHB he gave you is kind of nice. Like, for sex. Or sleep and stuff."

"He killed Zach."

Now the laugh came out, the light, peachy tone of it lilting from Harper's perfect lips. "Cut it out."

Jojo felt as if she were a feral cat caught in one of those humane traps. "He killed him. He kidnapped me somehow, raped me, put me on Kevin's spare bed, and killed Zach."

"But Zach's not dead." Her eyes looked strange, the green dimmed to a muddy amber. "He can't be dead."

Jojo had always gotten along with Kevin better, but Harper had adored Zach. Once Zach had brought her a bracelet he'd made at some craft fair—it was like a kid's project, but Harper had loved it, wearing it until it broke while she was playing basketball in PE. The beads had clattered all over the hardwood floor.

"Zach's dead. Your boyfriend **killed** him."

Jojo saw a flicker of confusion rise in Harper's

eyes, and then it disappeared, as fast as it had come. "He wouldn't. He's not like that. I told you, he wouldn't hurt anyone. He just has big ideas, and big ideas take big action."

"He hurt you."

From upstairs came a man's roar and another clatter, as if a whole cabinet of pots and pans had been upended onto a tiled floor.

Harper shook her head. "No way. He's never hurt me."

Jojo was losing patience, and judging from the sounds upstairs she was losing time, too. "Did you hear me, Harper? He raped me. Your boyfriend **raped** me."

"No he didn't." Harper's face brightened. "I did."

FIFTY-EIGHT

LAURIE HAD BROKEN down the door because fuck it. One kick and it crashed open. Adrenaline surged through her veins, and the gun was steady in her hand as she entered. Just like the old days on the street. And now everything hung on doing the one thing, the **right** thing.

And this time the wrong thing **was** the right thing. For once.

She'd kill him.

Then she'd save Jojo and Harper, and then she'd go to jail afterward, and it would be worth it.

The door opened into a small hallway that smelled of dust and spaghetti. A red floral rug on the floor ran to the back of the house. At the end of the hallway was a kitchen table with a bare bulb hanging overhead. It was getting dark outside, and her eyes had a hard time adjusting to the dimness. To the right a set of stairs went up to the next level. To her left another, narrower set of steps led down to a basement.

Darren Dixon barreled up those stairs, launching himself at her with a roar.

Laurie swung the gun and started to pull the trigger, but the son of a bitch moved too fast. He'd been five feet, then zero feet away in the time it took her finger to draw back. He knocked the gun from her hand. It clattered to the floor.

"No!" It was the only word she could think of to yell as he grabbed her arm. He tried to twist it behind her, but she knew all the moves, too, even though her body was rusty. She spun sideways and ducked down, trying to take him out at the knee with a kick.

But Dixon leaped, hitting the wall hard, using the motion to power himself back into the center of the hall.

He wasn't drunk. He didn't even smell like alcohol. His clothes were clean. His focus was sharp.

He'd sobered up. Showered.

He'd known exactly what he was doing. And she didn't, she didn't—

Dixon lunged for her with both arms like a vengeful bear, snatching a handful of hair as she tried to duck out of reach. He held tight, and Laurie heard the hair rip out of her head. It hurt, but the pain was nothing compared to the fear. **Jojo.** She was here somewhere, and Laurie would fight till she was dead if she had to, to give Jojo a chance to get away from this man.

He was behind her now, one hand gripping her hair, his other arm flailing, trying to land a punch. Laurie put her hand on top of his, locking it to her head so that her body knew exactly where he was behind her. She shifted her hips to the right and thumped her fist backward in an attempt to smash his balls into his pubic bone.

But he twisted at the last second, and her fist connected dully with his thigh. The gun was behind him. He'd let go of her hair, so she bent her knees and took off in a run down the hallway, toward the kitchen. **Weapon. Get a weapon.** A knife would do. Any knife.

He was right behind her, a thrashing, roiling mass of anger. She raced to the far side of the kitchen island, keeping it between them as if they were children playing tag. "I called 911. Cops are on the way," she gasped, scrabbling in a drawer for something—anything—she could use.

He panted, "Bullshit. You can't trust any of them. You didn't call."

The drawer she pulled open was the junk drawer—nothing but take-out menus and old rubber bands. He lunged to the right, and she went the same way. The island was big enough—as long as she could keep herself separated from him, she might find a weapon.

But he found one first. He opened a drawer on his side of the island and pulled out a carving knife. "This what you wanted?"

A person good with a knife could kill faster than a person with a gun, given a similar proximity. She hadn't believed it till she'd seen the study at work—and **shit,** he lunged toward her, coming at her **over** the island. He was fast as hell, but she was a mother lion, and she had to win. She ducked left and got to the same drawer, still hanging open. She grabbed a paring knife more suitable for slicing cheese than for self-defense, but it would have to do. Dixon was on the other side of the island again. This was a stalemate. They could do this all night, until one of them wore out.

Laurie didn't have all night.

She threw the knife at him.

The blade glanced off his brow in a lucky fucking throw, cutting downward across his right eye. Dixon gave a scream like a dog hit by a car and clawed at his face.

As he fell to his knees, blood trickling down his cheek, Laurie ran around the island and toward the basement stairs. Jojo had to be down there.

At the last moment, Dixon threw himself at her ankle like a soccer player preventing a goal, toppling her. Laurie's head smashed against tile, the wind leaving her lungs with a thump. She saw blackness lit with sparkles of stars. **No! Fight!**

She managed to scramble as far as the hallway. If she could just get her gun back—

Dixon threw himself across her, his weight holding her facedown. "I'll fuck you while she watches."

Laurie struggled to take a breath. **Coil your strength.**

"Then I'll fuck your baby girl while **you** watch."

Her hips bucked, trying to heave him off, but he was stronger and she was still seeing stars from the blow to her face.

"And then I'll kill you both."

Laurie stilled completely.

"I'll do whatever you want," she said.

She didn't have to fight this one clean. She'd go dirty. She just needed her moment.

FIFTY-NINE

JOJO BARELY REGISTERED the thudding overhead. Harper's words rang in her head. **I did.**
I did.

"I don't understand."

Harper scooted closer. "It wasn't like it was a real
rape. That's why I did it."

A vise closed around Jojo's chest, and her breathing got shallower. "I don't understand," she repeated.
They were the only words she had. Nothing—
nothing—made sense.

"Like, we'd already been together." Harper gave
the sweetest, prettiest smile, the one that made the
dimple appear in her cheek. "We knew it had to
look like you'd been raped, but I wouldn't let him
do it. So I just used my hand. You know?"

Jojo did **not** know. **"Why?"**

"To bring down Kevin."

In the corner Kevin gave a low moan, but he didn't wake up. His breathing rattled.

"Why?" Maybe if Jojo kept asking that one simple word, something would eventually make sense. Behind her, her bound hands burned.

"Because he's at the top of the chain. Everyone's eyes are on him, like the whole nation, you know? Half the men in America aren't even watching football, in protest of what he does, with his pin and his fist and his protests. He needed to be shut up. Like, in a way that no one would ever believe him or a man like him again. So we decided to do it this way."

That "we" was the scariest part. "But you loved Kevin. And Zach. And CapB. You weren't just acting." Yet even as she said it, Jojo felt it click into place. Harper had never been as into the politics as Jojo had. Harper had only gone to the street-medic trainings because Jojo wanted her to. Their friendship had rekindled at a banner-making meeting, but Harper had confessed that it'd been her first. She'd only gone back because of Jojo.

"You were at that first meeting because Ray— Dixon—sent you to it."

Harper nodded as if pleased. "Exactly."

"Why?"

"CapB hates cops, you know that. They **say** they don't, but you know they do—you've heard them talking. And that's not the American way. In this country we honor those who defend our streets, just like we honor our soldiers fighting for our soil."

They weren't Harper's words—Harper had never spoken like that in her life.

"Dixon isn't a cop anymore," Jojo said. "Why does he care? And what about the guys you slept with? Those are all cops, and you're blackmailing them. How does that go together—"

"Oh, no, those guys aren't real cops. They're the fake ones. They act like they're on the force, but really they're just friends of the chief. It's all, like, fake. We were just going after the bad cops, the ones who don't have the public's true interests at heart."

"Harper—what happened to you?" Dixon had done something to make Harper lose her mind. The thought made Jojo more desperate than she'd already been. "It's like you've gone insane."

Harper narrowed her eyes and drew backward. "He said you'd say that. He said anyone who knew about us would say that."

Another crash, and then a man's shout came from upstairs. The radio babbled on—Bettina saying something about a 415 female complaining about a neighbor's car blocking her driveway. But upstairs someone was fighting with Dixon, and that someone might not win.

If that happened, he'd come down and kill her and Kevin.

"He needs me!" Harper stood and looked up

at the ceiling. "I'm not supposed to go up there but . . ."

No, Jojo needed to get Harper back on her side, to break her out of whatever dream she was in. "Harper, listen. I'm sorry I said that. You're not crazy."

"Whatever." Harper put her foot on the first step. Her face was pale, and she paused.

Was Harper rethinking this? Could it be she didn't **want** to help him? The real Harper was still in there—she had to be. Maybe Jojo could reach her with words.

"Look," Jojo said. "Look at what I have around my neck."

"Huh?" Harper glanced at the ropes at Jojo's feet, as if she'd misheard.

"Come here." Jojo inclined her head. "Look at what's on my necklace."

Harper approached her slowly. "If this is some kind of trick . . ."

"It's not. Just look. Please."

Harper was close enough to push back Jojo's hair. She tugged the chain up and out of Jojo's T-shirt. The ring dangled. "Oh," Harper said quietly. "You're wearing it."

"Of course I am. You're my best friend." The words tasted like acid in her mouth. "I love you."

Harper kept the ring in her hand. She was so close that Jojo could smell her—a light scent of BO layered on top of Bombshell. "That was going to be the first thing I bought with the money, once I got it. A matching ring."

Jojo tried to smile. "We could go try to steal one for you. Maybe you'd get away with it this time."

"Like you did, you bitch." The words were warm, and Harper dropped a kiss on Jojo's cheek. "I've missed you, Cordelia."

"I missed you, too." It wasn't true—she'd missed the old Harper, the one that was now just a ghost, not this version of the girl she loved. "Please, **please** untie me. I'm begging you."

Harper stilled. They both listened to the upper floor shake. "Did he really kill Zach, do you think?"

"He really did." Jojo held her breath.

"He never told me that. I was in the car when we left you at Kevin's. He took a while to come out. He seemed kind of freaked out, but he didn't say anything. Nothing."

"I have a feeling there's a lot he's not telling you. Let me help."

Harper shook her head, as if trying to wake up. "I can't."

"Your mom is losing her mind, she's so worried."

Harper blinked.

"And Andy is, like, catatonic. They miss you so much. I saw his eyes all red and wet from crying."

It was the wrong thing to say—Harper gave a brittle laugh. "Crying 'cause he'll miss fucking me."

Jojo jerked. "Jesus."

"What? Like you didn't know."

"I **didn't** know. Are you serious? He did that? I **asked** you if he'd hurt you—remember?"

"And then you believed me when I said he hadn't."

"I believed you because that's what I do! I believe my friends! What happened?" They didn't have time—they had to get **out**—but this was key, getting Harper to trust her again. To break this spell she was under.

Harper shrugged. "Nah, it only happened a couple times, honestly, right around that time you asked me about it. I'd been drinking with him both times. I was stupid and let him do it."

Jojo gasped. "You did nothing wrong! You're the victim—he's a criminal."

"Eh, I get a lot out of guilting him into giving me whatever I want. I just threaten to tell Pamela. It's kind of great, actually."

"And your mom never noticed? Never asked?"

Harper tilted her head prettily. "You know her. She never notices a single thing about me."

"She loves you."

"I know **that.** She's just not like your mom, all concerned and careful and shit. Pamela trusts me. I guess she trusts Andy, too, which makes her pretty stupid, right? She never pays attention to what I'm doing. Ray, though. He does. He always pays attention to me."

Jojo's heart clattered in her chest painfully. "**I** always pay attention to you. **I love** you."

Harper's right eyebrow rose. "Do you, though?"

"I was **in love** with you!" Jojo couldn't breathe again—it felt like the gag was back in and she was choking around the words she hadn't even known were true till they hung in the air between them.

"Oh, Joshi, I know that. But you left me."

"What?"

"When my parents didn't want us to hang out after your dad got us arrested."

We got ourselves arrested by doing something stupid. The necklace hung heavy around her throat. "Harper. I'm so sorry. I missed you every day. I thought your parents were keeping you from me. And I thought you hated me. You wouldn't even **look** at me when you passed me."

"You didn't have to give **up.** You just gave up on me. You didn't fight for me. Nobody fights for me but Ray. He'll never leave me."

More frantic thumping came from upstairs.

Harper's eyes widened. "We should—"

A short, high scream, full of pain, came from upstairs. They were running out of time.

"I'm so sorry, Harper. I should have fought for you, for our friendship." Even knowing that something was so deeply broken in Harper that she could do **this,** Jojo still wanted to be near her. "I love you. I've always loved you."

Harper inhaled sharply. Jojo could **feel** her wobbling. "Look. Just untie me. At least then I can make my own choice to fight or not, okay? If he killed Zach, just think what he'll do to me. I'll tell him I got free on my own. You can do that, right?"

"I can't."

"He killed Zach."

Harper gave another rapid inhalation. "No, fuck that. Do you think—did Zach hurt? When it happened?"

What was the right answer? The truth would have to do. Jojo nodded. "I don't know. But I think so."

"Shit." Harper leaned forward and started working with the knots. "Ray did them tight. You have to tell him you got out of them. And I'm not helping you get past him."

"Hurry," breathed Jojo. The noise upstairs had quieted. Either Dixon was dead or he'd won, and she knew who she'd lay money on. "What's the address here?"

Harper frowned and tugged on the rope. "Why?"

"Just tell me."

"It's 11621 Hinds."

The second her hands were free, Jojo bent to undo the knots at her feet. Her muscles burned from being asleep so long. "Undo Kevin while I do this."

"No, just you."

Fine, Jojo would have to undo him later. Her leg rope was off. She pushed herself to standing. Then she lunged toward Bettina's voice. If it wasn't just a scanner, if Dixon had actually kept a department-issued radio at home, like so many of them did—

There it was. Tucked neatly into its base, fully charged, a Motorola just like the one her dad always carried. Just like the one she'd used in bed on birthday nights.

She lifted the radio to her mouth. She pushed the button and held it for the split second it took to open the channel.

Then, as Harper lunged at her, she said loudly and clearly, "Car 143, 11-99, 11621 Hinds."

Her old code, with "officer down." Jojo had never even heard 11-99 said on the air. It meant it was the direst of emergencies. She'd get in **so** much trouble later for saying it, with no actual officer down, but it had been the only thing she could think of to say. Even if half the cops at the department were corrupt, **surely** a few of them wouldn't be.

Harper was on her then with a shriek, punching and slapping. "You **bitch**!"

"Stop!" Jojo dropped the radio and tried to grab her wrists. "Get off!"

Harper connected with a fist to Jojo's jaw. Jojo's neck snapped backward with an audible crack. Harper jabbed at her again, but she dodged this time. Then Harper got her arms around Jojo's waist and heaved, trying to drag Jojo down with her.

Harper was serious.

She wanted to stop Jojo, maybe permanently.

Jojo lunged for the radio. She raised it, adrenaline pouring through her veins, acidic and hot. With a shout she brought it down hard on top of Harper's skull.

Harper dropped like a marionette with its strings cut, folding into a heap at Jojo's feet. Jojo's first impulse was to fall, too, to make sure Harper was okay, that she wasn't hurt too badly, but Kevin—she had to free him.

He was still out, but his eyelids were flickering quickly, as if he were dreaming. "Come on, Kevin, wake up. Can you wake up?" The knot of rope at his feet was easy, the one at his wrists more difficult. His hands were freezing to the touch. She ripped the duct tape from his face and pulled out the wet gag. "Kevin. I need you. **Please** wake up."

His leg kicked, and his mouth moved. He gasped a deep breath, but his eyelids remained closed. He gasped again.

So did she.

Harper was motionless, lying in a late beam of sunlight from a high, street-level window.

There was no air—**no air.** Jojo sucked in a breath and felt her vision narrow.

A female's scream filtered down from upstairs. **Mom.**

SIXTY

LAURIE WILLED HERSELF to be as still as possible underneath Dixon's weight. She stared at the tile in front of her. A thin tributary of blood ran toward the grout. His blood? Hers? Didn't matter. She'd fool him, trick him into thinking she would acquiesce because of the threat to her daughter. And then she'd do what it took.

She made the wrong decisions sometimes. She fucked up. She always needed backup.

But not today.

Today she'd finally do it right. By herself.

She struggled to draw breath underneath him.

I'll give you everything to leave her alone. Take me. Leave her. Let her go. For a second she thought of Harper. **Take Harper. Keep her.**

Dixon's voice was low in her ear. "I'm going to stand up. If you move at all, I'll kill you instantly. It'll be easier on you, but that'll be harder on your daughter when it's her turn."

GIVE ME MY DAUGHTER.

Laurie's blood was ice—terror shot through her exhausted limbs. "I won't move," she whispered.

"I'm going to have to tie you up. And you're going to let me, or it goes worse on Jojo."

She nodded. **A lie. It's a lie.** But she wasn't sure it was—would she be able to move at all? Her body was used up, depleted. If she had energy left, she didn't know where it was.

But she had to find it.

"I wouldn't have had to take Jojo if you hadn't come looking for me," Dixon said, as he scraped himself off her. "But when I saw you both together with Kevin, I realized I couldn't trust the legal system to punish him the way he deserves. Now he'll go down for her murder too—and you'll pay for hitting me with that fucking pistol." He slammed his elbow into her kidneys. She screamed. The pain was excruciating, like a hot knife to her guts, only that probably wouldn't have hurt as much. The stars came back with the darkness behind her eyes, and she longed for it to get darker, to be able to let go.

"Mama!"

She lifted her head.

Jojo was in one piece. One glorious, terrified piece.

"Get out! Run!" Laurie's voice was thick in her throat.

Her daughter stood at the top of the steps. "No!"

"Harper!" Dixon pushed himself to standing. He bellowed again, **"Harper!"**

It hit Laurie then—he expected Harper to come help him.

Both of them were in on this. All of this.

The three of them exploded into simultaneous motion at the same time. Jojo dove for the gun on the floor of the hallway. Dixon rushed at her, his hands aimed for her throat. Jojo twisted, falling onto her side, scrabbling at his hands to tear them off her neck. Laurie launched herself at them. **Get between them, get the gun.** Whatever it took, she was leaving here with her daughter.

A tangle then—a whirl of arms and blows and thuds and grunts. Dixon was strong, and the gun skidded into the middle of the tiled floor.

Go slow to go fast. Laurie felt the blur decelerate. Suddenly there was all the time in the world, and she saw their bodies in the terrible dance as if they were frozen—Dixon's arm was up, coming down slow as molasses to strike Jojo. Laurie slid sideways just enough to catch the blow with her shoulder. Jojo reached a long arm out—so slowly, so gorgeously—and caught the gun in her palm. Her daughter pushed against the wall and leisurely swam away from the snarl of Laurie's and Dixon's limbs.

Lying on her side, Jojo raised the gun. It didn't shake. Jojo was as methodical as Laurie was— Laurie could see it in the way her eyes moved. Carefully. Deliberately.

"Honey, **no.**"

Jojo looked at her.

Her daughter would pull the trigger, she knew she would.

And Jojo would never recover.

"Give it to me," said Laurie. She reached for the gun, but Jojo was too far—

A howl came from the stairs, and Kevin stumbled into the hallway. "You son of a bitch!" His roar blasted through time, setting the clock back into motion, and everything went fast again, faster than normal.

Laurie saw a look of fear smash across Dixon's face.

Kevin tackled him, clobbering Dixon and taking him back down to the floor. Sound was hollow and low, Dixon's scream ricocheting off the walls.

"Joshi." Laurie lurched toward her daughter.

With one move Jojo spun the gun around and handed it to her.

"Kevin! Hold him still!"

And I'll kill him. That was what Laurie meant. The gun was steady in her hands.

Kevin heard her say it. Their eyes met.

She would kill Dixon, and this would be over. Forever.

Kevin rolled, covering Dixon with his body.

He was motherfucking **shielding** him.

"Kevin! Get the fuck off him!"

Kevin shook his head. Dixon was quiet beneath him. "We don't kill him. We let him hang for it."

But he might get away with it. He might get off. Cops always do. Always.

Dixon's arm jerked underneath Kevin's body.

Kevin's face blanched. He rolled to the side, off Dixon, then scooted backward so he was resting against the wall.

A knife stuck out from the side of Kevin's ribs. Laurie heard the wet **shhhh** in his breath as his lungs lost pressure.

Dixon scrambled forward, his good eye wild, his other one solid red and leaking blood. He grabbed Laurie's leg, dragging her down, but she spun in the air a slow, balletic move. Jojo screamed.

Laurie had one long, slow second, equal to a year, to consider her action. **Investigation. Job loss. Shame. Guilt.**

Yep. Fine.

Laurie aimed at Dixon's chest, the gun a simple extension of her hand. Using her breath more than her finger, she pulled the trigger.

Dixon thumped backward, the blood from his chest mixing with the blood dripping from his eye. He landed hard, his torso propped up crooked against the wall.

He looked down at his chest, then back up.

"Fuck," he said questioningly.

The outer door was thrown open, and only after the uniforms raced in did Laurie hear the cacophony of sirens outside.

"Everyone, **FREEZE**!" Nate Steiner's voice was so loud it made Laurie's still-ringing ears ache. She dropped the gun and raised her hands automatically. Jojo was lying on her side, unmoving except for her heaving chest.

Behind Steiner came Omid.

He was halfway in his uniform, the shirt unbuttoned, no belt. He still had IV tubing connected to the arm that held his gun. He hurled himself into the hall, pushing Steiner out of the way.

"Medic!" Omid yelled over his shoulder. He moved toward their daughter, swaying slightly, as if a strong wind had blown him into the small space.

Laurie scooted through the blood, unable to stand.

They reached Jojo at the same time.

Then Jojo was in the circle of their arms. Laurie pulled them to the side, against the far wall, and blocked Jojo's line of sight with her body so she couldn't see the medics starting CPR on Dixon, so she couldn't see them putting Kevin on a stretcher and taking him out to the waiting ambulance.

Omid said things that didn't make any sense and kissed Jojo's hair a thousand times. Jojo was rigid but breathing evenly.

The medics stopped the CPR, calling it. Time of death 7:32 P.M.

"I'm glad, Mama," Jojo whispered in her ear.

Laurie kissed Jojo's temple. Feeling her daughter's rapid pulse under her lips, her own heart finally started beating again.

SIXTY-ONE

THEN, FOR A long time, chaos swirled. Laurie tried to pay attention to all the moving parts, but there was really just one moving thing that mattered: Jojo. Laurie's neck was killing her, and bruises were starting to rise in painful lumps all over her body. But she didn't let Jojo go.

Steiner moved them out to the front yard, where preliminary, abbreviated statements were taken as they sat in the back of his patrol car. Harper was brought to the backyard with Officer Connors, presumably to do the same.

Laurie answered automatically, her hand never releasing Jojo's. Omid sat on their daughter's other side. Everything would be explained at some point. Now was the time the officers would start scratching together the basic particulars, making sense of them to weave the story together.

That was Steiner's problem.

Not hers.

Steiner was staring at her, she noticed. She had no idea what he'd asked her, but she said, "Did **you** sleep with her?"

"What?" Steiner looked honestly perplexed, and he glanced at Jojo. "Who?"

"It'll all come out, you know." Laurie's voice sounded almost lazy, the way she felt. "All of them. All the men who slept with Harper, they'll lose their jobs."

"Maybe," said Omid. "You know what it takes to lose a job around here."

A sluggish rage rose in her, an anger that should twist and leap but instead just roiled slowly inside her chest. She didn't care that Jojo was between them. She stared at her husband, the man she thought she'd known. "And **you.** If you hadn't tried to hide it, to cover it up . . ."

She expected him to look away, but Omid's eyes met hers directly. "I'm to blame. I've never fucked up so bad in my life. I hope I never do again. I'm to blame for **all** of this."

"Daddy, no—"

Laurie broke her gaze.

Steiner had turned around, ostensibly working on the report. She wondered if he was taking notes on what they said.

She decided she didn't care. "Because of you, Harper and Dixon did all this. One girl raped, a man killed. Another one dead by suicide."

Omid's voice was strangled and his skin pale. "I know."

"Mommy." Jojo put a finger against Laurie's lips. "We all fuck up."

This wasn't a **fuckup.** This was a betrayal of everything important in life. "Honey, he—"

"No, wait! You think Daddy **planned** this? You think he did it on purpose? Don't you think that he was just trying to take care of us?"

Laurie's mouth went dry. Jojo's words were simple, but the truth in them was huge.

Omid had been doing his best.

His best had **sucked.** He'd gotten it wrong, so wrong, the worst kind of wrong.

But he'd been trying. The harder he'd tried, the more he'd stressed out. He'd literally killed himself trying to fix things.

Laurie took a breath and then met Omid's gaze again. His eyes were filled with tears. "You didn't mean for any of this to happen."

His face was miserable and pale. "I'd do anything to change it."

"You can't."

Jojo squirmed against her but stayed quiet.

"I can't," Omid said.

"You're going to lose your job."

"Probably, yes."

"You deserve to."

Omid nodded. "Without doubt. If they don't fire me, I'll resign."

"And those officers. Our **friends.**"

"I'll make sure in the investigation that they go down with me."

Laurie nodded, the knot in her belly uncoiling just a little. She let the silence sit for a moment as she stroked Jojo's hair.

Jojo said, "And Kevin? He'll be okay?"

"Yes," said Laurie. It had to be true. He had to be okay so Laurie and Jojo could thank him properly, hopefully in media view.

Then she said, "Poor Harper."

Jojo had told them in the broadest strokes what Harper had said about her stepfather, Andy, about her anger at Jojo for not staying friends with her, about why Harper had chosen Ray, and about how she'd defended him almost up to the last minute.

Jojo had said that Harper was the one who'd raped her.

Incomprehensible.

But you didn't blame an abused dog for its rage. You just kept yourself out of range of its teeth.

Harper was abused, broken. And she, Laurie, hadn't seen it. It hadn't started with the stolen ring and the girls' breakup—it had started before, of course. Harper had always been a little shattered, in such a charming way, like a music box whose song played too quickly, wound too tightly. Laurie had ignored the off-pitch jangle of it, enchanted by its prettiness.

Everyone had overlooked Harper while looking right at her. They'd **all** let her down. "We owed her better than that."

"What's going to happen to her?" Jojo's voice was stark with grief. "And what will happen with Pamela and Andy?"

Laurie had no idea. "I assume they'll all get counseling. If I were Pamela, I'd take Harper and leave Andy in the dust. But who knows?"

Jojo's expression was stiff. "Will Harper go to jail? She won't survive that."

Of all people who could, Harper would probably be able to—she obviously had the will to survive, no matter what. "I hope not, sweetie."

Omid spoke. "She'll probably get probation. She didn't know about Zach, and the only one who could testify against her is dead." His gaze darted toward Laurie, and she could see he regretted saying it.

She'd killed a man tonight.

She hadn't lost her temper—she hadn't done something she regretted. She'd protected her daughter.

The memory of the 911 call she'd gotten just days before flooded her—not Jojo's, the one right before it. The one in which the man had gone to sleep, forgetting that his daughter was safe with her mother. He'd called 911, thinking he'd lost her.

Laurie had lost her child for only a tiny amount of time and she'd almost gone crazy. Parents who lost their children permanently—it was unfathomable.

No matter what the story was, Pamela would soon be so, so happy to have her arms around Harper.

Zach's mother would never hold him again.

Laurie pressed a kiss against Jojo's hair and gloried in the fact that Jojo didn't pull away. "I love you," she said to Jojo while looking at Omid.

If she had to, she'd pull the trigger all over again.

JOJO could feel her brain start to sputter back to life. Something about the shock and the Taser and the fight and the gunshot—she'd barely been able to speak as Steiner took their preliminary statements in his car.

But now the three of them—her, Mom, and Dad—were in Mom's car, finally alone. Mom sat behind the wheel. Even though she'd started the car, she made no move to put it into reverse. Jojo sat beside her, Dad in the back.

He coughed, a raspy sound.

Jojo twisted in her seat. "Hey! Are you okay to be out of the hospital?"

Her father paused and looked down at himself. His shirt was buttoned crooked. He pulled the hem. "I feel pretty busted. But you're okay, and that's all that matters."

"But how did **you** know to come?"

"Steiner was visiting me. His radio was on. I heard your transmission." Dad stopped talking, his voice all weird and knotted.

"Are you hurt? Dad?" Had he been stabbed, too, like Kevin, and they didn't know it yet? **"Dad?"**

"I'm fine, Car 143." He cleared his throat. "I'm just fine."

Mom mumbled that she didn't get it, but for once she didn't demand an explanation.

Dad shook his head. "You're amazing. You're both amazing."

Jojo looked out the window as Mom finally started to back up.

There she was.

Harper was being walked out, Officer Connors at her side. Her hands were cuffed in front of her, but her face was bright, her head high. The streetlights had just gone on, and night had fallen, but Harper still glowed, all the light drawn to her. As always.

Mom said, "It's okay, Jojo. You're okay." But her voice wobbled.

Jojo's gaze didn't budge from Harper.

Harper's eyes met hers.

Then Harper smiled and blew her a kiss with both hands.

"No, no, no." Jojo had been so scared to love Harper, so frightened of what it meant. More than that—and worse than that—she realized now there'd always been a low-level thrum of fear that Harper would stop loving her.

Now it was broken.

Whatever it had been, whatever Jojo had prayed it would become—that was in the past. Gone.

Harper needed help.

And Jojo knew she wasn't the right kind of help. Maybe if she did it now, like ripping off a Band-Aid, Jojo could let go of her broken heart.

She grabbed the ring at her throat and tugged the chain. It came apart with a painful snap. The windows were down, and as Mom pulled away from the curb, she threw it into the street. Now neither she nor Harper had a ring.

She could—she had to—release Cordelia.

"What was that?" Mom twisted to see, gasping as she did so. She pressed a hand to her side.

"I stole a ring when Harper did. I never told you."

And instead of going off on her, Mom looked at Jojo.

And for once Mom seemed to really see her.

"You poor things," said Mom. Her voice made Jojo want to cry again.

The car moved through the night. Mom reached out and took her hand, and Jojo didn't pull away. Behind them Dad tapped his cell phone with one hand.

"Don't you need to go back to the hospital?" Jojo asked.

"I suppose so. Eventually. First the station, though. I have an investigation to open, and you both need to finish your full statements. Not that either of you needs my help with that."

"We don't." Mom paused, and Jojo heard her take a breath. "But, holy crap, I want you there."

Jojo swallowed hard and touched the place at her neck where the ring had been. "Me too, Daddy."

"My girls." He leaned forward and touched Mom's hair, then Jojo's. "My girls."

"Your women," Jojo said. "Get it straight."

AUTHOR'S NOTE

Dear Reader,

I'm a queer, white middle-class woman who lives in Oakland. While I did work 911 for seventeen years in the Bay Area before switching to writing full time, I had to use my imagination to dream up a police department as broken as the one in this book. There are bad actors in every department, and I believe policing in America is broken in deep, systemic ways; but I continue to have hope that most men and women in law enforcement want only the best for the nation and all its people. I also firmly believe that Black Lives Matter, and I stand as an ally, lifting my voice when I can from my particular place of privilege. CapB is not a pseudonym for BLM, and Kevin Leeds is drawn from no one in real life except a very nice baker I once knew. I had to imagine my way into Jojo's head, knowing nothing of what it's actually like to live in America as a person of color. The only part I really know is what it's like to "share" lip gloss with your best friend. Thank you to my sensitivity readers. Any mistakes I've made are purely my own.

ACKNOWLEDGMENTS

After I got my master's in writing, I took a 911 job because I thought it would be a good job to do while writing on the side. It was. (It also paid four times what teaching did, and I was deep in student-loan debt.) The job allowed me to hear and participate in the most emotional moments of many people's lives, an honor I never saw coming, an honor every writer could learn from. I learned from that job that fear sounds the same in all languages, but so does love. My deep thanks go to all three 911 ComCens I worked in over the years. Thank you, my old co-workers, you nutty kids! Whichever people you think I based these characters on, you're wrong, but I love you for thinking so stubbornly that you're right (a mark of a true dispatcher, a stubbornness I will myself continue to enjoy until my dying day).

Thanks, always, to the good men and women in police enforcement and the fire/medical profession, the ones actively working to make our world safer in all its glorious diversity. Thanks to my amazing agent, Susanna Einstein, without whom I would never have had the chance to tell this story (and thanks for her help in revision after revision after yet another revision. You knew what it needed to be). And to Stephanie Kelly, thank you with all my heart for understanding this story and bringing out the very best in it. You made these characters sing. To everyone at Dutton—thank you! What a team! I'm honored to work with every one of you. To Sharon Monroe and Jasmin Canty, thank you for amazing sensitivity reads. To my friends and family, thank you. You're my heart.

ABOUT THE AUTHOR

Stolen Things is the first suspense novel by R. H. Herron, the pseudonym of an author who lives and teaches writing in California. For seventeen years she worked as a 911 fire/medical dispatcher, and this book is inspired by actual events.